tc

IMPOSSIBLE CAUSES

JULIE MAYHEW

R A V E N 🐦 B O O K S

LONDON · OXFORD · NEW YORK · NEW DELHI · SYDNEY

RAVEN BOOKS
Bloomsbury Publishing Plc
50 Bedford Square, London, WC1B 3DP, UK

BLOOMSBURY, RAVEN BOOKS and the Raven Books logo are trademarks of
Bloomsbury Publishing Plc

First published in Great Britain 2019

A catalogue record for this book is available from the British Library

ISBN: HB: 978-1-4088-9700-3; TPB: 978-1-4088-9702-7; eBook: 978-1-4088-9698-3

2 4 6 8 10 9 7 5 3 1

Typeset by Integra Software Services Pvt. Ltd.
Printed and bound in Great Britain by CPI Group (UK) Ltd, Croydon CR0 4YY

To find out more about our authors and books visit www.bloomsbury.com
and sign up for our newsletters

For Dot

'In any case, a woman usually becomes a witch after the initial failure of her life as a woman'

– Julio Caro Baroja

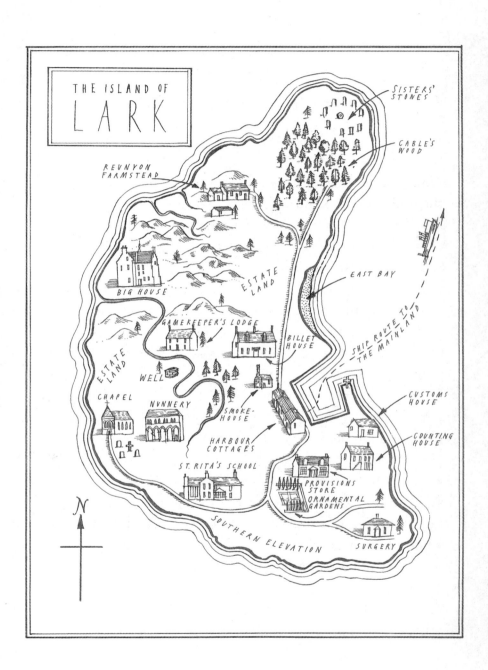

THE ISLAND OF
LARK

SISTERS'
STONES

CABLE'S
WOOD

REUNYON
FARMSTEAD

ESTATE
LAND

EAST BAY

BIG HOUSE

GAMEKEEPER'S LODGE

BILLET
HOUSE

ESTATE
LAND

WELL

SHIP ROUTE TO
THE MAINLAND

CUSTOMS
HOUSE

CHAPEL

NUNNERY

SMOKE-
HOUSE

COUNTING
HOUSE

HARBOUR
COTTAGES

ST. RITA'S SCHOOL

PROVISIONS
STORE
ORNAMENTAL
GARDENS

N

SOUTHERN ELEVATION

SURGERY

Nine granite megaliths set in a perfect circle. On one of them sits Viola Kendrick, teeth chattering, lips smudged red. The wet of the stone has leached through the quilting of her mother's long coat. The fleece of her pyjamas beneath is damp against her skin.

Below, in the jagged coves, the sea grumbles and it booms.

Through the morning fog strides a spirit, becoming more real with every step it takes towards her. It is dressed, improbably, in a police uniform – a yellow reflective jacket.

The spirit stops – in the centre of the circle next to the tenth stone. There is a hole carved in the heart of this stone and, for a moment, Viola believes her visitor will do it – get down on hands and knees in the soil and crawl through that ancient O. Performing this action cures you, no matter the ailment; that's what they say. But the spirit remains standing, surveying this undiscovered territory, claiming it with a nod of the head, then, with a shrug, giving it away again.

'You're not a real policeman,' Viola calls out.

This is her warning shot, but Dot is a traitor. She tugs on the red lead, eager to greet this visitor with her sandpaper tongue. The spirit steps closer, offering a hand.

Dot is assuaged; Viola won't allow herself to be.

'Not real, eh?' He stops his coddling of the dog to pat down the stiff, goose-filled fabric of his glowing jacket. 'I seem like the genuine article to me.'

'You shouldn't be here,' she tells him.

He steps closer still. 'You called me here.'

'I called you, but I thought… I thought you would send…' Who did she think he would send? 'Someone else.'

'What?' He grins. 'The local constabulary? The boys in blue?'

'You shouldn't be here.' On this, she is clear. 'Men aren't allowed in the circle. It brings on a terrible fury.'

The sea below obliges her with a thunderclap. The standing stones drift in and out of the mist like hallucinations. The imposter grins wider, baring a weaselly spread of small, sharp teeth. From his inside pocket he pulls a notepad and licks at the tip of a pencil, only because the act of doing so seems to entertain him.

'Come on then,' he prompts, 'I don't have time for your tricks. First ship of the year arrives at lunchtime. What's this all about?'

'I told you,' says Viola. 'And it's no trick.'

Still, he grins.

'What are you even doing here,' he asks, 'at this hour of the morning?' It is the tone her father once used – weary, amused. *What idea have you got into your head now, Vee-vee?*

'I'm walking my dog,' she tells him, indignant.

'Right.' He makes marks in the notepad, his eyes dancing from the page to Viola and back again. 'Out here last night with the Eldest Girls, were you?'

She shakes her head.

2

He snorts. 'Offering your naked selves to the gods?'

'No!'

'Begging for the devil to give you a good seeing-to?'

'No!'

Viola begins to tremble and a low, sonorous hum reverberates through the morning air; a sound only she can hear – and seemingly Dot, who begins to whine. Viola gathers the shivering dog onto her lap, not caring about dirty paws on her mother's coat.

'The girls won't let you join in, eh?' He sticks out his bottom lip, mocking her. 'Ah, what a shame.'

Viola squeezes her eyes shut, finds power in the thrum of the earth to bring them back to the meat of their conversation.

'I've found a body.'

'You said. Deer, is it? Badger? Big brown bear?'

She shakes her head, no acknowledgement of his joke, and watches as his smirk twitches, then falters. Panic strikes at the cords of his neck.

'It's not…'

Viola's turn to grin. 'No. It's not her. She doesn't come up here anymore.'

He licks his lips, the way an animal does after a fright, and returns to the distraction of his notepad. Viola knows his thoughts. *There is no body. Viola is playing her games again.* She experiences his process of judgement as if it is her own, feeling it absolutely. The weapon rests firmly in her hand – let's say it's a rock – and she holds onto it for a moment, considering its weight, the damage it could do. Then, she throws.

'It's one of your brothers,' she tells him, 'the body.'

The pencil freezes, suspended above paper. The notepad droops and Viola can see what is there on the page – not words. He has drawn an inelegant sketch. Of her.

She tips her head towards the beginnings of Cable's Wood, where, with closer attention, he will see the white snowdrops and yellow colt's foot wearing petals of uncharacteristic red.

'What happened?' he asks.

Viola shrugs. 'How would I know?' She waits for his gaze to return from the trees, adding: 'Maybe the devil gave *him* a good seeing-to.'

The sea growls; it gasps. The mist has thinned and Viola can see for certain that she is in the presence of no spirit, just a man. He can see what Viola is too – what she always has been – just a girl.

'I don't have any brothers,' is how he chooses to reply.

'No?' asks Viola. 'Are you sure about that?'

PART ONE

SOLAR PHASE

THE FOOL.

In the beginning, it was a heaven on earth.

The name of the island – *Lark* – had called out to them through the fog that embraced its shores, through the figurative fog that had descended on the mainland, shrouding Viola and her mother. The island was to be their salvation.

In the aftermath of the disaster back home, when fate had taken its violent strike, Viola's mother left the radio playing in the kitchen lest a silence should settle, the kind that invited in thoughts. A short feature had come on air – an inconsequential piece, a slice-of-life peppered with unusual accents and the cries of gulls. *Unspoilt*, said the presenter, in a voice that was too worldly and wry. *A place where children grow up at one with nature, in all ways safe.*

Viola's mother had looked up from her cold and forgotten tea and she had listened.

To journey to Lark, said the woman on the radio, *is to take a step back in time.*

At these words, Deborah Kendrick had risen, like a miracle, from the kitchen table, from the bleary depths of misery. She made immediate enquiries, ones that quickly transformed into plans and definite dates. She had told Viola in all certainty that their tragedy had been preordained, was unavoidable. That she was now willing to believe that fate could also be benevolent was a good thing. Wasn't it?

Forms were filled out, promises were made. All newcomers were assessed, medically, ethically, and asked to pledge how fruitful they would be, both in the practical sense and the biblical. Lark was a religious community: participation was expected, baptism a stipulation. Then, there was a house to pack up, a past life to give away, workaday tasks in which Viola's mother found a much-needed catharsis and impetus. Boat tickets were booked – the only way to reach this new existence, this forgotten British isle. They sold the car and boarded a train, out of the Home Counties to the coast.

That June they embarked on three sickly days at sea.

During the crossing, Viola found refuge in, if not a comfort from, her religious beliefs. She and her mother were the only passengers except for an anxious vet and a chain-smoking groom, who took it in turns to sit in a stall in the ship's bowels, calming a sweating horse, bound too for the island. A day in, when there was nothing to see but the roiling grey of the North Atlantic and the breathless emptiness of the skyline, an eerie gloom beset everyone on board, the crew not exempt. The ugly vessel gave off its industrial chug, the moody wind whip-snapped across the waters and a desperate Viola Kendrick searched the never-ending horizon for dry land. Ireland had long ago vanished in their wake. To the north, there were no glimpses of Iceland or Greenland, something the maps that they had studied before leaving suggested would appear. How could the real world be this much vaster in scale? On the second day, Viola convinced herself she had spied the ragged coast of Canada up ahead

but it was nothing but the reflection of a cloud – a hallucin-
ation. *Please let there be something out here*, she begged a
God she was unsure existed. *Please don't let us die too.*

And Viola's absent god responded.

Lark appeared.

They clung to the rail of the deck to watch the island's
evolution from a distant smudge to jutting cliffs. Drunk
on relief, Viola and her mother narrated each new detail
as it revealed itself – the high green broom of woodland,
the startling yellow tufts of wild grass on the rockface, the
hawk riding a thermal as it scanned the ground below for
mice. The ship rounded the northern headland and they
could see then, in all its strange glory, the hollowed-out curl
of the cape. In days of yore, when Lark lay much closer to
the main British Isles, a giant took a bite of the rockface
and didn't like the taste, so he pushed the island far, far out
to sea; that's what they say. Deborah Kendrick recounted
the fairy tale as the ship idled inelegantly into shore. Viola
had heard this story before, but it had meant nothing on
the mainland. Back there, it sounded slippery and fake –
a tale told to charm tourists. Yet in context, with the sun
glinting from the windows of the harbour cottages making
a constellation of daylight stars, with fishermen on the
decks of nearby tethered boats emptying buckets of fish in
great silvery spills, seagulls turning hopeful circles above
them, Viola heard it anew, and she *was* charmed. She was
enchanted.

Calls heralding the ship's arrival shrilled from the cobbled
harbourside, voices travelling up and along the ginnels
beyond. The sweating, uneasy horse was led off, legs quivering at the unfamiliar steadiness of terra firma, as Viola and

her mother were ushered into the stripped-wood interior of a Customs House, where more forms were to be completed. Deborah Kendrick shook away her traveller's daze to tick and sign under the officious gaze of a weaselly-looking man with epaulettes on his shoulders. The lengthier documents appertained to Dot, who was eyed cautiously, as if she were a dangerous breed, not a moustached Schnauzer of miniature size.

Viola sat on a wooden bench, Dot at her feet, their possessions spread about her in boxes and suitcases, sensing the effort of the journey alight suddenly, heavily, on her shoulders. She fought to keep her eyes open in the back seat of the battered Land Rover, no matter how bright the sun that day, how jerky the drive, so that she might take in the sight of a gathering of children standing on top of what looked like a set of wooden stocks, clambering over one another to get a better view of the newcomers as they drove past and away.

Steep fields opened out in an undiscovered shade of green, punctuated with cows and goats and sheep, a scene so idyllic it seemed set-dressed for their arrival. As they approached the farmstead, the unmade track gained in potholes and gradient. The weaselly man from the Customs House was their silent driver, playing brutally with the bite of the throttle, navigating the climb.

In the front passenger seat was their official welcomer, a Mr Jacob Crane, head of the Council, headmaster of the school, a large man with an imposing nose and a hard shell of a belly. He raised his voice above the crunching of gears to deliver his evangelism of the island, bellowing it over his shoulder to Viola and her mother, confirming all that they had been told before they came: *Everything on Lark is good. Everything. You need only look around you and see.* These affirmations somehow worked against the beauty playing out around them, not letting it speak for itself. Then came the old Reunyon Farmstead to disprove his theory after all.

Sitting on the blustery western elevation, it resembled a ranch house lifted from the Wild West proper and dropped on the island from a great height. It was in need of love and repair, something Deborah Kendrick said she understood very well when applying for tenancy of the vacant property. It wasn't a lie. She reiterated her suitability for the task as they pulled up, explaining how she wasn't afraid of hard work, that she had been a landscape gardener before having children. Viola watched her mother dip her chin after the casual usage of the plural – *children.* Mr Crane did not seem to notice.

They got out, Viola guiding Dot to a patch of rough grass to relieve herself. Her mother whisked a palm against the brittle paintwork of the veranda, bringing about a small storm of white flakes, already deciding what grade of sandpaper might do the job. Jacob Crane paced the dirt driveway as if it were a stage, regaling them with the origin of the farmstead's name. It was a dialect word for a seal, an animal that returned to the island in the winter, sheltering in the western coves to feed, ahead of the breeding season. The man then turned to survey the neglected land beyond the house, the lumpy soil, hands resting on the belt of his brown slacks, and began a list of what needed to be done. Weeds must be cleared. Seeds must be planted. Every tree was capable of bearing fruit if it was treated the right way. Viola seemed to be included in this last statement. Mr Crane fixed her with a benevolent blue-eyed gaze.

Viola's mother looked up from her assessment of the woodwork, alert, her pliant smile all of a sudden erased.

'You're the headmaster, you say?' she asked.

The man peeled his gaze from Viola to give the woman a firm, proud nod.

Then Dot barked, directing their attention to an animal meandering light-footed across the abandoned land, its fur as red as the hair on Viola's head – as the hair on her mother's head too.

Mr Crane's expression tightened.

'We shoot them, I assure you,' he said. 'We snare them. We don't let them get out of control.'

Viola crouched down low to loop a finger through Dot's collar, a question finding its way to her tongue. *How did the foxes get here?* The first farm animals, like the horses, came in the belly of ships, she presumed, their arrival as deliberate as her own. Rats and mice might become trapped accidentally within cargo, slip on and off a vessel unnoticed. But a fox...?

The animal paused to look back at them, reproachful, before disappearing into the tangle of a hedgerow, and in that moment it became clear to Viola that it was not her question to ask. The fox was demanding it of them. *How did you get to the shores of my beautiful island?* it wanted to know. *Who said it was a good idea for you to come?*

In the beginning came the end: the moment Jade-Marie Ahearn sang too loudly during morning assembly.

Father Daniel, gentle and grey, in appearance and in word, had introduced the liturgy without incident. Mentions were made of the day's saint – a man who had done the required amount of preaching, healing and converting of pagans, but little else to martyr him above all the others – then the eagle-head lectern was passed to Mr Crane.

'So, now we are alone,' said their Council leader, their headmaster, his smile inviting their complicity. The small congregation of St Rita's pupils, infants to seniors, along with their teaching staff, no more than fifty all told, laughed obligingly.

He was referring to the ships. The August one had been and gone, bringing the islanders the last batch of supplies from the mainland. The days were still bright, the sun making teasing promises to stay a while, but soon the fog would descend, making Lark unreachable. Unleavable. There would be no more ships until April.

'Closed-months Rationing' began at the Provisions Store at the weekend to ensure all 253 residents of the island remained well fed until spring. Now it was 1 September, time to knuckle down to a new school year, so Mr Crane's subsequent homily was on the importance of hard work. *Thessalonians* was used to strengthen his case. '*For we hear there are some which walk among you disorderly, working not at all, but are busybodies…*'

The Eldest Girls of St Rita's did not mutter at his speech, nor roll their eyes. Back then, at the start of September, Britta Sayers, Jade-Marie Ahearn and Anna Duchamp were still, for the most part, good girls, not worthy of attention. The teaching staff had given them each a brief up-and-down for uniform compliance. The younger senior girls, who were feeling mature having just risen a year, glanced the elder girls' way – a reminder that there was yet more growing up to do.

All three of the Eldest Girls had come of age, Jade-Marie being the last to turn sixteen in the middle of the holidays, and there had been a perceptible filling out of their bodies, new angles forming from the sharpening of their features. The boys who were old enough appraised these changes with furtive curiosity, as if peering through the glass of an oven door to judge the rising of a cake.

But none of this was done in chapel. The boys would have seen the girls in July and August, lying on their towels on the small beach offered up by the harbour at low tide, as exposed as they'd ever be, in rolled-up denim and coloured vests. They'd have watched the girls devour the summer's delivery of magazines from the mainland, sliding sunglasses down their noses to examine the few passing strangers, searching them for hints of what life was like in that distant outside world.

Three visitors came that summer: one couple (middle-aged walkers in audible, wet-wicking fabrics) and a solo traveller from the telephone company, trying yet again to convince the islanders of the benefit of installing a mast. The widow Esther Deezer put them up in her spare rooms, serving breakfasts and dinners sparse enough to encourage them never to come back, driving home the message that isolation was neither a tourist attraction nor a problem to be solved. The question of the mast was put to the men of the Council once again in July and as in previous years received a unanimous *no*.

Until Jade-Marie sang too loudly in chapel, the girls were a mere novelty, known by their collective moniker 'the Eldest Girls' – and long before their time. The font of St Rita's had sat dry and unused for four years now and there had been a similarly disconcerting absence of new babies on Lark between 1998 and 2000. This meant that the three girls, all born in 2001, became the most senior pupils at the end of Year Eleven. Or the 'Fifth Form' in old money, the kind of currency the school of St Rita's understood.

There was Britta Sayers, the true islander, a 'pure catch', distinguished by her long ropes of lucky black hair. There was Jade-Marie Ahearn, with her wild brown mane, a legacy of her missionary father, Neil, who'd arrived on Lark in the 1990s, departing it in the Great Drowning of 2002 while Jade was still a babe in her Larkian mother Mary's arms. Then there was Anna Duchamp, who would be forever marked out as a *coycrock* – an incomer – by her exotic blonde bob, scissored neatly to curl beneath the ears. Anna arrived on the island at the impressionable age of four, with her French father, her Scandinavian mother and her little brother, Julian.

And now there was another *coycrock* girl on Lark, arrived on the recent June ship. She too was born in 2001 and with her particular shade of hair, which was considered a bad omen by those who heeded the old ways, she might create a 'full set' with Britta, Anna and Jade- Marie. Black, blonde, brown, red. If three became four the inauspiciousness of the girl's coppery hair might be reversed. That's what was said; or rather what was not said.

Superstition singled out four as a powerful number – stable, real, encompassing north, south, east and west. A union would make the girls a formidable combination of earth, fire, air and water as they took their seats at the long desk in the north-facing classroom. Mr Crane taught the Sixth Form, alongside his running of the school. Those girls could become their own talisman.

But the small, pale *coycrock* with the red hair was not present at that first morning worship. She had not turned up for the first day of term.

During the second verse of that morning's hymn, the point in the song when the dancing spreads to the fisher-men, Jade-Marie raised her voice to match the registers of the younger children. By the third verse, when the dancer in all unreasonableness is strung up after curing the lame, Jade-Marie was no longer singing but bellowing the words, engulfing the operatic harmonies of Mr Crane's wife, Diana.

Britta and Anna, standing either side of Jade, lowered their hymn books, held only for appearance's sake as they knew the words off by heart, and they stared. It was Britta who laughed, just a small cough of embarrassment, though she soon turned serious and ashen like Anna. An understanding began to throb between the three girls as the fourth verse arrived, as Jade-Marie's voice grew yet wilder with pain:

I danced on a Friday
When the world turned black –
It's hard to dance
With the devil on your back.

A tear spilled down Anna's cheek. Britta's chest rose and fell in hitching gasps.

This was when Miss Cedars, the nice, polite teacher of the GCSE pupils, leapt from her pew and, with uncommon ferocity, yanked Jade-Marie from her place, the girl's hymn book hitting the stone floor with a slap. Teacher and pupil then wrestled their way down the aisle, Jade-Marie screaming the last lines of the fourth verse, as if issuing a final threat:

They buried my body
And they thought I'd gone,
But I am the Dance
And I still go on.

Then she was pushed out into daylight beyond the iron-work door.

Mrs Stanney at the organ continued to play at her usual sprightly pace, but the infant classes, who had never seen such behaviour in their entire lives, fell silent, their mouths forming little Os. Mr Crane slammed the spine of his hymn book against the lectern, issuing a clipped instruction to 'Sing!' The infants leapt in unison, then shrank small, searching for the words for verse five – words that would soon, like so many hymns and prayers and quotations, become second nature to them.

One of the boys who walked close to Britta and Anna along the cliffside path back to school after worship, said

17

that the girls had discussed, in whispers, not returning to their classroom. They would fall behind the last teacher, slip into the graveyard, make a hiding place of one of the tilting tombs, then skirt the edge of the nunnery to make their escape across estate land... but this plan was discarded as hastily as it was put together.

They had to go back. They had to be there for their friend. She was in the headmaster's office, with Miss Cedars her jailer. Mr Crane would return, Miss Cedars would be asked to leave, and then what?

And then what?

◉ THE BOOK OF LEAH

In the beginning, I considered peroxide.

The woman and her daughter who arrived on the June ship were my inspiration, the shock they sent through the congregation when they stood to receive the host for the first time. No one said anything aloud, of course. People would pat my head for luck in the Provisions Store and mutter blessings in my ear (a 'pure catch' they called me, even though there was a distinct lack of fishermen to be doing the netting), but voicing this kind of lore in chapel, admitting that you believed in a set of mysteries and superstitions beyond the bible – that was a step too far. Still, I knew their thoughts – this woman and her daughter were inviting catastrophe upon us with their flaming locks.

What a thrill.

I began to wonder if I, simply by altering the colour of my hair, could also bring about a change. If I went from black to white-blonde, transformed into my negative image, who would I be then? Would I also welcome in catastrophe?

Would catastrophe be preferable to nothing at all?

But let the record show, it was not Ben's arrival that caused Miss Cedars to disappear.

I had grown tired of playing her – because that is how it had come to feel, like a role upon the stage. Miss Cedars, the sweet, keen teacher of the senior years, the spinster nearing her ancient thirties, the one who had taken tenancy of the centre harbour cottage when everyone knew it was reserved for a young, married couple, people who could be trusted to go forth and multiply, earning themselves a property on the south elevation with extra bedrooms.

The loss of my first name had come to upset me. It had been deftly cut away as soon as I began teaching.

'No one will call you "Leah" anymore,' Ruth French had cautioned me. 'Not even the adults. It'll be, *Morning, Miss Cedars*, and, *Will we get a break in the clouds, d'ya think, Miss Cedars?*'

She had been three years above me at school, and was three years ahead of me in her teaching training. I assumed she was taking the opportunity to be superior – you never really leave the playground, after all – but she was right. I became Miss Cedars. Only Miss Cedars.

'Ah, you thought the likes of us would be exempt?' she said with a wink.

Ruth was a blackhead too, and while not a daughter of the Council, her colouring gave her some status. She was never bothered with ear-blessings and head-patting, though. She shared a house on the lower, less desirable stretch of the south elevation with Catherine 'Cat' Walton, the assistant curate with the spiky hair. Ruth wasn't a 'pure catch' like me. During her appraisals in Mr Crane's office, I wondered if he made her read the passage from *Leviticus* that warned of abomination.

I had become desperate for a shift in the way I was seen, to be known as Leah once more. Not compliant Leah from the good book, the one who raises children as a consolation when her husband takes her better-loved sister as another wife. Not that Leah. Not Leah the dope. I would be Leah with the tender eyes who goes to bed with Laban and deceives him into marrying her in the first place, convincing him in the dark, with her naked body, that she is as desirable as her too-perfect sister, Rachel.

True to form, I lost my nerve. I waited in line upstairs at the Counting House to use one of the computers (the school internet being strictly off limits for ordering goods from the mainland) and hovered the mouse over the 'buy' button beside a bottle of peroxide. Then I clicked away and bought myself a skirt instead. It was blue, with pleats and a mermaid shine. A daring choice, or perhaps a cowardly one.

Ben was merely a catalyst. Let's say that. He was a channel.

The Autumn term was rolling close – my favourite time of the year. Clean stationery, a fresh set of faces staring back from the front row of desks. In the replenishing sun of July and August, lying back on the harbour beach, I would reread the set texts – *Lord of the Flies*, *Gulliver's Travels*, *The Tempest* – stories we hoped might connect with the pupils. Then I would arrange an informal meeting about the year ahead over a glass of shandy at the Anchor. (A 'wam-bam' was what cute Miss Cedars called it.) Ruth French would be there to represent the juniors, her demeanour softened by two months of warm winds. Dellie Leven, the senior assistant, would bring a tin of something sweet from her stockpile of summer baking. My enthusiasm would spill across the table, enough for the three of us.

'We should hold some classes on the lawn overlooking the East Bay. It would really bring the subject alive!'

Every year I'd say it, always able to forget that the balminess and the clear skies were transient guests, small birds that would soon fly back to their real home. The fog crept up on you. Perhaps it is a measure of the human capacity for hope, or for self-deception, that I was able to believe the weather might, for once, that year, be different. By mid-September you could lose sight of your own feet on the coastal paths, and when the rains came, they did not mess around: they swung in hard. The idea of holding any kind of lesson outside was ridiculous. And that year I did not suggest it. I called no wam-bam. My copy of *Lord of the Flies* lay on the floorboards of my bedroom by my slippers, unread, its pages curling in the damp, gathering a musty smell like everything did if kept for more than a few days away from daylight. The island was a sponge, the sea seeping into the corners of every house.

I took my malaise to Margaritte next door; how could I ever have explained this strange wave of melancholy to Dr Bishy? Tuesdays were my evenings with Margaritte. I drew the curtains while she lit a stick of incense with shaking hands, the glow of the match revealing the thinness of her long white hair. We'd settle down opposite one another at the green-baize-topped table, as if we were going to do something as innocuous as play a hand of poker. We'd have a glass or two of Margaritte's home-brewed wine, swap the news that so often fell through the gaps between our generations, and then, almost as an afterthought, she would read my palm and deal out my future.

She knew what troubled me. Everyone was going. Everyone had gone. All four of my childhood friends and then, that year, my little brother, Paul. He didn't even wait for the return leg of the August ship, the last ship of the year, the one you were supposed to take for long-time leaving if you didn't want to tempt fate. So desperate was he for the possibilities of the mainland, that he took the first ship in April, the day after his twenty-first birthday. Mum and Dad, inexplicably, said nothing to make him stay.

This was the root cause of Miss Cedars' disappearance, of her slow evaporation. My elders had always told me that wanderlust was nothing but an unhealthy quirk of the genes – like original sin, it could be beaten back and conquered – but Paul was strong enough for the fight. He left, and my faith went with him. The colour of all my memories faded. Those days lost trekking across estate land for the best horse-chestnut trees, pockets full of shining conkers. See a black bird and you can't speak again until you see a white one. Forfeit is to throw three conkers at the high, mullioned windows of the Big House and risk waking up the Earl. Pink sunsets on the cobbles for the June cook-out. The lick-slap of the sea against the harbour wall. The smell of mackerel on the fire. Weeks spent in collusion on our effigy of St Jade, her construction never withstanding the door-to-door singing. One year her nose falls off; another, her arm. The next, more appropriately, her foot. Laughing until we couldn't breathe.

Miss Cedars was renowned on Lark for preaching the word of the island to anyone who even mooted the idea of leaving. She kept on preaching right up until they walked the gangplank.

'It's all right for you,' my friends would reply gnomically, and I thought I understood them. I *was* different – I had my teaching post, I enjoyed privileges as the daughter of the

23

gamekeeper, I was more at one with the land than them, but still I fought back.

'You won't find a place on earth as beautiful or as special as here.' My passion was hard to articulate; something always stoppered my throat. 'Lark is not the problem,' I told them, 'because we are Lark. We are its future. We are its blood.' I believed that.

Yet, when Paul said he was going, my mouth ran dry. He knew how wonderful the place was; he had lived it all alongside me.

'Maybe you should come too,' he said, and what on earth was I supposed to reply to that?

Margaritte turned over the card that signified my immediate future. The Knight of Cups. In the low, campfire voice she affected when doing her readings (not at all the voice she used when offering more wine), she told me, 'And here comes your love.'

I turned away, else I might cry.

Margaritte's shelves beside me were filled with books that she believed contained the true voice of the island, untainted by the prophets and evangelists who had washed up on our shores over the years. Titles such as *Past Lives: The Basics*, *Cosmic Ordering: A Higher Level*, *The Truth Within the Runes* – so much contraband in plain sight. She had created a circle of invisibility around her books and objects, she said. No one could see them unless she allowed it.

'You really believe that?' I'd scoffed.

'Do you believe that a man turned water into wine?' she replied. 'That he spat in the eyes of the blind to cure them? That he could walk on the surface of the sea?'

I paused. 'I don't know,' I said, which was a startling admission.

'I do,' Margaritte replied. 'I know it's possible.'

In the light of day, I believed that the creases on my palm signified nothing more than the way I clenched my fist. The outcome of the cards was as arbitrary as the roll of a dice. I was convinced by the messages only in the moment they were delivered, fleetingly. Once the reading was over, after Margaritte had knocked on the deck to rid it of me, walked three times round the room anti-clockwise and opened up the curtains, I returned to the idea that it was all silly, childish, harmless.

But, the Knight of Cups …

'Ha!' I managed in response to her prediction. I tried for lightness. 'Well, if the sky falls in!'

Margaritte tapped out a thoughtful rhythm on the shoulder of the Knight's horse with a crooked finger, her nail thick and painted. I didn't want to look at him, that warrior in his winged helmet, golden chalice in hand. He was false hope.

'What are you saying – that I'm about to fall in love with Saul Cooper?' I gave a short laugh. 'Because he's the only one left and he's old! Almost forty!'

Margaritte did not smile.

'He's come to us reversed,' she said, nodding sagely. This card was upside-down beside the others. 'He's a charming fraud sometimes, our Knight of Cups. A man who can't separate truth from the lies he tells himself.'

I waited for more.

She shook her head, shook away her doubt. 'But he's between two cards of good fortune so my instinct is to trust him.' At last, she smiled. 'Let's see who the August ship brings in, shall we?'

So, I became optimistic, buoyant, despite all efforts not to be. I thought idly of making a visit to the Customs House. Not to ask Saul Cooper for his hand in marriage – the mere idea of him, those small, ferrety features, his particular aroma of fishermen's mints and unwashed armpits – but I would go to him and request a look at August's incoming passenger list.

Again, my nerve deserted me. Or rather, rationality won out. Saul would take huge delight in my enquiry. He'd wear that thin-lipped smirk, the one that suggested he had material on you, pictures, things he would share on men's nights at the Anchor without hesitation – because it was said that he was the keeper of a stash of magazines, the odd VHS from the mainland, things that men liked to look at, boys, those who were willing to risk God's wrath.

'What do you want to know for?' Saul would have sing-songed at my asking, a hard brown sweet doing a dance across his gums. If I'd found a convincing response, his next question would be, 'And what do I get in return for showing you?'

So, I waited. News would reach me once the ship had docked. It had no distance to travel.

We were in the staff room on a prep day before the start of term when Miriam Calder announced it proudly, apropos of nothing: 'He has a specialism in science, you know.' Our school administrator was spooning sugar into a cup of tea she'd prepared for Mr Crane. 'A specialism,' she went on, 'that he will be sharing across the whole school.'

Ruth French and I were sitting on the low, soft chairs, piles of folders on the table in front of us. We snapped up our heads.

'Sorry, did you say "he"?'

It was Ruth who asked; my mouth was wide open in disbelief.

Never, in my living memory, had there been a male teacher at St Rita's. A male headteacher, yes. Before Mr Crane came Mr Bartle, who died just before I moved up to the senior classes. But a man serving as mere teacher alone... ? Mr Crane had been deputy to Mr Bartle in the years leading up to his death – he was preparing to take over, the outgoing head expected to retire, not die – but Mr Crane had done no time in front of the whiteboard then. I could only draw up memories of him speaking from the front in chapel, and of him standing at Mr Bartle's shoulder in his office. You needed to travel back fifty years, and several feet along the row of framed school photos in the main corridor, to find another male face looking out from that teachers' middle row.

'Oh, yes,' said Miriam, relishing this eking-out of information, 'our new staff member is most definitely a man. Did you not know?'

We didn't. She knew we didn't. We knew that Mr Crane had found no new likely candidate for teacher training on the island – an offer I had in my time seized on breathlessly, aged eighteen, ending the terrifying idea that I would need to go to the mainland to find a career. There is an invisible line on Lark dividing those who live by their intelligence and those who lean on physical abilities. I was able to rig up a snare and raise the game by beating, all useful to my gamekeeper father – everyone on Lark had a second skill – but my true strength was my brain.

'Will you actually be a real teacher?' Paul had asked. Eleven years old and he thought he knew it all. 'Don't you have to go away and do a degree for that?'

I had made sure, when it arrived, that Mum framed and mounted my curlicued certificate of qualification prominently in the living room.

In this instance, Mr Crane had placed an advertisement in a mainland newspaper, generating interest beyond the recruitment pages, as our sporadic call-outs always did. Miriam had pinned a resulting press article to our staff noticeboard:

A 1,500-mile commute, a class of four students, one pub and a single shop – could this be the remotest teaching job on the planet? Lying so far adrift in the North Atlantic, the island of Lark is unreachable by air or sea for five months of the year. Its temperamental climate is one of warm winds followed by dense, persistent fog, making it truly the ostracised cousin of the British Isles...

Miriam had crossed out 'five months' and corrected it to 'seven months' in the margin of the press clipping. A strange point of pride. There followed several paragraphs of inaccurate history and patronising anecdotes collected from tourists and expatriates – *traitors* – alongside some anodyne words from the teacher we'd recruited last summer – Amy Sparks. She didn't manage a year, exiting on the same April ship as my brother, staying just long enough to get over the failed relationship she'd crossed hundreds of miles of sea to escape. Long enough to think better of their split in light of the romantic prospects on Lark. Long enough for me to consider her a friend.

'But don't you miss all the shops, Leah?' That was her parting excuse. No mention of Lark's awe-inspiring landscape, the closeness of its community, the sunrises, only its lack of a high street.

'You can't miss something you've never experienced,' I said, the statement feeling immediately flawed, as wrong as a stone in the mouth.

A wedding invitation from her arrived on the August ship, which seemed like the cruellest of jokes.

'You're scared of the mainland!' she had said to me once, teasingly, thinking she had uncovered my naughtiest secret. 'You only talk about loving Lark so much because you're such a chicken!' Miles of sea between us and still she was taunting me.

The article in the mainland press was illustrated by our most recent end-of-year photo. Caption: *The entire pupil population – all 38 of them!* I look it up sometimes, that article, study the expressions of the three Eldest Girls on the back row – Britta, Anna, Jade-Marie. I search their faces for hints. Was it happening already? Was the idea in them then? But they seem as upright and guileless as the very small ones sitting cross-legged on the front row.

'Oh, yes, he's most definitely a man,' Miriam went on. 'Quite a dishy one at that.'

Ruth grunted at this turn in the conversation. 'Wow,' she muttered. 'A man. I never saw that coming, did you, Miss Cedars?'

My throat closed tight, sure that Ruth knew; had she spied on us through a gap in Margaritte's curtains, dabbling with the cards, predicting his arrival? Ruth went back to labelling folders, and I took her phrasing to be accidental, a coincidence.

'No,' I said. 'I really didn't.'

I tried to match her nonchalance, but my pulse was beating fast beneath my jaw, my blouse was sticking to my chest. Miriam Calder, who knew all and saw all, could surely hear my internal rapture. *The Knight of Cups! Here comes my Knight of Cups!* She stood over us at the table, steaming mug in hand.

'Well, Mr Crane usually prefers to hire women, as is clear to see.' She twisted her neck to assess our stickering system, pass her unspoken judgement. 'He knows that women will be far more... what's the word... ?'

'Malleable,' said Ruth bleakly.

'Reliable,' corrected Miriam.

Ruth looked up at her, with the silent instruction that she could piss off now, but the woman had more tattle to be free of.

'He arrived with just a single bag, according to Saul Cooper. Just one rucksack – and not a very big one either. What do you make of that?'

'That he's a light packer?' Ruth deadpanned. 'That he owns a flexible capsule wardrobe?'

'How old is he?' I blurted out.

Miriam grinned, validated. 'Young,' she replied, 'and pretty nifty with a Bunsen burner.'

Ruth sighed at my betrayal of our tacit agreement never to encourage Miriam and her chatter.

'Young?' I went on. 'Young, like… ?'

'Youngish,' Miriam clarified. 'Thirty.'

I stared at the folder in my hands, at a loss as to whether it should be labelled green or yellow. A domino run was toppling at speed across my mind: the Knight of Cups has arrived, and now I will fall in love, and now I will know what it feels like, and then I will be married, and then I will conceive at the cottage, and then we will fill a property on the south elevation with children, and…

'Green,' Ruth barked. 'Maths handouts we're labelling green.'

I pressed a large circular sticker onto the folder, let the action calm me. There was a system to everything, a right order.

'Oh, you won't be wanting to get mixed up with him, Miss Cedars,' Miriam said, turning away, gearing up for one of her enigmatic exits, while I flushed hot, so transparent in my desires. 'Just one rucksack,' she repeated ominously. 'He's running away from something. You mark my words.'

☙ FRIDAY THE 13TH – APRIL 2018

You do not accept lifts from strange men. Viola Kendrick knows the rules.

Say no to sweets. Refuse all invitations to see kittens. Tell a grown-up where you are at all times. Never walk home late and alone, but if you must, dress soberly, anonymously. Cross to the opposite pavement if you are followed and pretend to be on your phone. Take the sharp edge of your house key and brace it between your fingers as a makeshift weapon. Fill your lungs. Be ready to scream.

Viola was led to believe that these rules would not apply here, that they could be left behind on the mainland. But the rules cling like limpets to the bottom of the boat. Viola cannot unremember them. She cannot action them either. How can you cross to the opposite pavement in a place that has no pavements? What use is a phone at your ear with no signal to feed it? And who carries a house key when there isn't cause to lock your door in the first place? Still, it feels like a transgression to be bouncing down the East Road in the passenger seat of a 1980s Land Rover. The man behind the wheel in the black police uniform and yellow reflective jacket is not a stranger. But he is a strange man, certainly.

Viola scans the blur of pines through the window, searching for outlines, people, anyone who might see them hammering past, hear the noisy engine and smell the rotten exhaust. Anyone who might be willing to stand as a witness.

Her driver doesn't speak and hasn't since he instructed her brusquely at the Sisters' Stones to get in the cab. He rolls a hard mint from cheek to cheek, clicking it against his teeth, pausing every so often as if he might say something, but no words come. He offered Viola a mint before starting the engine, but she refused. Like a good girl.

As they leave the coverage of Cable's Wood, the sea spills out on their left, the surface of water still blanketed by fog. It is spring though, so this fog will lift when the sun rises, allow the first ship of the year to find its way. If she turned in her seat, Viola would see that giant's bite in the cliffside behind them, but she doesn't look back. They hurtle past the turning for her home – 'home' being not exactly the right word – to her mother, the old Reunyon Farmstead. That they have passed this exit is cause for relief but also sends a bitter wash of adrenalin to her mouth. She should speak, demand to be taken there, if only to show she is in charge. Instead, she pulls Dot, who sits damply on her lap, closer to her body for protection. The dog pants at the window, adding an extra layer of fog to the view. With every bump in the road, her wet nose draws ticks and swirls in the film on the glass.

Dot was acquired as a guard dog – Deborah Kendrick's first tentative step towards building a total defence against an unfair world, before the idea of Lark reached her consciousness. The error was clear as soon as the puppy arrived – tiny, incontinent, as fallible as a human baby. How would a miniature Schnauzer defeat all their unseen enemies – lick them into submission?

Dogs are not protectors on the island, they are not even considered companions – they have no soul. Viola disputes this absolutely. Dot has a soul, she can feel it now, emanating from the soft, warm creature on her lap, filling her with much-needed determination as they ride the rough track, seemingly harbour-bound, instilling her with the courage to speak.

Any resolve she has falls away as the road does, steeply, the East Bay revealing itself beneath them. The back end of the vehicle competes in the gravel to become the front, and Viola clamps Dot ever tighter, gripping the seat beneath her, fingers slipping into the foam insides where the leather has split. As her driver steadies the Land Rover in its skid, he is the one who finds the wherewithal to say something.

'How come you knew where to find him?'

'Huh?' Viola is unprepared, still gulping away fear from their slide down the hillside. 'Who?'

The driver snorts, abusing the gears. He wants to appear scornful, all-knowing, but Viola can see how his hands tremble on the wheel.

'Oh, the body,' she says. 'I didn't. I didn't know.'

A new set of mainland rules bobs obligingly to the surface. The rules for how bad things happen, how they come to be known.

'It's always the dog walker who finds the body,' she tells him, because this is a truth.

The dog walker is the first voice in the story. They stare, pale-eyed, down the journalist's camera lens, describing how their usual morning became exceptional. Then, the revelations begin.

Her driver won't know this. He won't have spent weeks, months, away from school, ostensibly to mourn, had mainland television deliver the news with each mealtime, had Radio 4 fill a kitchen with tragedy every hour on the hour. Here on the island there is only static, a foreign voice if you're lucky, calling through the storm as you gently turn the dial. You might hear a snatch of a song you thought you once knew.

He also won't know that a third of accidents happen within a mile of your home, that relatives asked to make public pleas for the return of their missing loved ones are often the prime suspect and, for all the advice about strange men and cars, that most perpetrators are well known to their victims.

'I think you went looking for him,' says her driver. A challenge.

The sight of the blood spatters, the boots, the coat submerged in ferns… it rises up into Viola's vision, bringing the heart-flutter of panic, a spike of guilt. She won't have it. She pushes it back.

'I was just walking my dog,' she says, as breezily as she is able. 'I didn't expect to find anything.' A lie. The dog walker is always primed for discovery. Sometimes, darkly, they wish for it, for their usual morning to become exceptional, for something to flip the day's routine. An escape – from the silence of a dilapidated farmhouse perhaps, from two-step linear equations and exponential functions that must be learnt alone, without the help of a teacher and the camaraderie of fellow classmates. From the miserable sight of an expanse of abandoned soil, a flaking veranda, still waiting for love and repair.

'I think you went looking for him,' the driver persists.

Viola shakes her head.

The mist has lifted on a sea that has calmed at the arrival of the sun, a rebellious child who quietens when the adults show up. At the limit of the dogleg stone jetty, the large metal cross stands dull and grey, reflecting back none of the trifling light. Today, it suggests, God is out-of-office.

'You knew they'd done this.' He spits when he talks. 'Maybe you even put them up to it.'

The Land Rover swings, too fast, past the harbour loading bay and the smokehouse. The herring gulls gather on the railings, barbing, jostling – half a dozen or so, not enough to signal the imminent return of the three-day trawler. The driver brakes to a halt outside the Customs House.

She must speak, take control, decide how this will play out. The revelations must dance to a tune of her picking. Otherwise what was the point of such an early start? Why be the only dog walker on the island?

He kills the engine. They sit quietly for a moment, listening to the gulls' disputes.

'Well, if you think that I'm in on it –' these are the words she eventually chooses '– what does that say about you?'

She reaches for something inside her mother's long, quilted coat, exciting interest from Dot who knows that treats live in that pocket too. Saul looks down at the object she places onto the scuffed and empty seat between them. She keeps her hand tight upon it.

'You can give me that back,' he says.

She shakes her head, tightens her grip. He is the one to peer out of the window now, checking for people, early workers on the harbourside, anyone who might witness this scene: Viola Kendrick, the red-haired *coycrock* girl, and Saul Cooper, Lark's almost-forty-year-old Customs Officer and sometime policeman, sitting together in a stand-off in a steamed-up Land Rover just after 7 a.m.

There is no one there.

Saul's eyes return worriedly to the object. It is one half of a set of walkie-talkies.

THE MAGICIAN.

◉ THE BOOK OF LEAH

Spend too long admiring someone from a distance and you convince yourself that you know them, but it's an ambush. So it was with Ben.

We were formally introduced on the first day of school, Miriam Calder drawing us into a circle in the staff room. She took hold of him by his upper arms and manoeuvred him forward, as if he were a small boy who might need some cajoling to join in with the silly girls. He smiled awkwardly at us, at this unnecessary, quite literal, manhandling.

Miriam's voice came like syrup: 'Now then, ladies, I'm sure you'd like to welcome the lovely Mr Hailey to St Rita's School.'

'Ben,' he corrected as he began his round of greetings – the primary teachers first, then an unimpressed Ruth French, followed by Barbara Stanney, who grasped his hand and shook it with the same manic passion she applied to the keys of the chapel organ.

'Yes, *Benjamin* Hailey,' said Miriam, as if his first name, the full version of it, belonged to her.

I could feel the heat rising up my neck as he worked towards me, greeting our part-time assistants next, reaching down for the hand of Faith Moran, who was matched

39

in height by some of the juniors she helped to teach, then Dellie Leven, who gave a quiet 'hello'.

My turn.

'Hi, Ben,' I said in a voice as cool and dry as the hand he placed in mine. Then I spoilt it by gushing, 'It's so good to have a man on the team at last!'

My cheeks stung with the too-muchness of myself.

A man – he was certainly that. Tall, clean, vital, yet vulnerable-looking, boyish. He was an exotic blond, his gaze narrow and green. *Ask, and it shall be given you*, says the *Gospel of St Matthew, seek and ye shall find; knock, and it shall be opened unto you.* I believed in the notion, but this was an extravagance, obscene. Ben was a white rabbit being pulled from a hat, a coin appearing from behind an ear. I wanted to laugh at the outrageousness of it all, which would have been preferable to my actual response – withdrawal. Our greatest fear is not that we'll never receive the thing we long for, but that we will, and then what?

I ignored him, stretching only to pleasantries in the corridor, and, like the other women, I helped to nudge him through the timetable of the day. He fell easily into the role of the hopeless boy, not knowing where anything was, how anything worked. Merrily, we played the eye-rolling matri-archs, smug in the solving of his problems. It was a smart initiation. Mr Crane rarely breached the threshold of our staff room, unless announcing something important or call-ing us to prayer. We weren't used to a man in our small, private space. Ben made himself as unthreatening as possible.

Yet still I hung back. I watched Barbara Stanney giggle with him at the kitchenette, transformed into a young woman again in the flow of his jokes and patter. She would bump her hip against his impishly, put a hand to his back – 'Oh, stop it, Mr Hailey, what are you like!' Even Ruth French dropped her defences early, delivering cutting assessments of Ben's shirts and ties, snorting at the way he'd styled his hair. From her, this was acceptance, even affection. Each of my female colleagues was gifted their own individual way to be comfortable in his presence; I remained empty-handed.

One lunchtime in the staff room, he shared his desire to move on from his boarding situation with the widow Esther Deezer. The others cooed their dismay at Esther's treatment of him – the meagre meals, the strict curfews. ('Have you told her you're not one of those fellas from the telephone company?') I, meanwhile, affected a lack of interest. I slipped off my heels, hooked my feet beneath me on one of the low, soft chairs, as if I was at home, as if I was alone. I chewed on an apple and looked down into a book.

I kept an ear out for what was going on, of course. It was Faith Moran who proposed the Billet House on the edge of estate land where the harbour master, Abe Powell, lived with Saul Cooper, our Customs Officer, and Reuben Springer, a boatman and occasional barman for his brother Jed who ran the Anchor. The young Cater brothers lived there too, Mark and Andy, both farm labourers, along with Luke Signal, a wiry lad always in an oversized wax jacket, recently apprenticed under my father, the gamekeeper. This was much to the annoyance of Mary Ahearn, Jade-Marie's mother, a rugged woman, capable, strong. She had been my father's deputy for the last fourteen years and had long thought the senior post would go to her as my father prepared to hang up his boots. Then along came Luke, a male heir, and we all knew how that was likely to work itself out.

It was a bad idea for Ben to go and live in the Billet House, though it was hard to express why. The lodgings were basic, a little harsh, suited to a certain kind of man. They were built in 2002 not long after the Great Drowning, when ten new workers were hired from the mainland to replace the lost and needed to be housed all at once. It had been a necessary move – the recruitment, the swift construction – but was considered clumsy, as if the Council believed the only problem to solve in the wake of the accident was one of economics, of hands on deck. A couple of those drafted-in men married into the community, but most of them left.

Every one of the Billet House's current residents was, in himself, a respected islander, but all of them there together, in that place… it gave me a creeping, anxious feeling. If I could have found the words to explain my misgivings, still I'd have kept them to myself. Around Ben, I was bound tight. I was gagged by my knowledge that he was the Knight of Cups. That he was meant for me.

I believed that unequivocally. His arrival was no coincidence, not a hopeful connection between a random card and an existing passenger list. He was a supernatural gift – and this terrified me, rendered me mute, taciturn at best. It was a disaster. Ben was building an idea of me from a distance, as I was of him, but all he could see was someone serious, difficult, prissy. If only I'd behaved like the old me – sweet, eager Miss Cedars – she was so much easier to love.

Then the rains came.

I told Margaritte of my predicament with Ben one Tuesday evening and my need for some kind of intervention. She had picked the heads of the clover that lived in the cracks in the path leading up to her door. To these, she added some leaves from the climbing ivy at the front of her cottage and pressed them with a stem from a potted jasmine. She wrapped them in paper, muttering as she folded, and told me she would drop them on Ben's doorstep at midnight. To her, it was a cure as straightforward as a painkiller for a headache.

Margaritte said the subsequent downpour was an answer to my wish; the universe listening and responding. I said that the September rains always found a way in, it just happened to be my classroom's turn to be flooded.

Michael Signal, my eldest Fifth Year, received the first torrent. The storm growled its approach and when the clouds gave way, so did the ceiling tile above his head. He leapt from his seat, yelping. My pair of Fourth Year girls, Eve Grogan and Abigail Pass, squealed with delight – 'Michael's wet himself! Michael's wet himself!' – until the ceiling tile above their heads gave into the second spill, destroying their felt-tip diagrams of erosional landforms. That second deluge, the one that fell on the girls, I am willing to believe was divine interference – or divine punishment. *Against whom do ye sport yourselves?* says the *Book of Isaiah*. *Against whom make ye a wide mouth, and draw out the tongue?* No one but yourselves, that's who.

'All of you, up!' I yelled. 'Into Mr Hailey's class! Off you go!' They made swift armfuls of their bags and books, bumping one another out of the room, exhilarated by disaster.

'Michael!' I called. The boy turned to me, bedraggled. 'You're already wet, so you might as well be the one to fetch Mr Huxley from the harbourside.'

Our caretaker spent his mornings by the water once he had opened up the school, boat maintenance and net mending being his second skills.

But Ben was all of a sudden there, in my classroom, throwing down a heavy cloth bag, clattering tin buckets beneath the ceiling's streams.

'It's alright, Michael,' he said. 'No need for Huxley. You get dry in my classroom. Mrs Leven can find you a towel. I've got this.'

The boy left and Ben dragged a ladder in from the corridor, grinning, as thrilled by this crisis as the children were.

'I'll go and assist Mrs Leven,' I said, feeling surplus to requirements and doubting Dellie's ability to handle all sixteen of our students at once.

'No,' said Ben, 'I'll need you.' He gave me an even bigger grin, a disarming one. 'I'll need someone to pass me tools.'

My eyes went to the heavy cloth bag he'd thrown down at safe distance from the pooling water. His initials and surname were etched onto the fabric in marker pen. *B. E. Hailey.*

Elijah? I wondered. *Ezekiel?*

He set up the ladder near the source of the first torrent.

'You brought tools?' I said.

Miriam's story about the single rucksack – I had believed it. He'd left everything behind, I'd decided, physical and metaphorical. But the tool bag couldn't be the single bag, else how did he get all those shirts and ties here, and the tacky product he was putting in his hair, and the something he wore on his skin that smelt of coconut?

'Yeah. I brought tools. That's okay, isn't it?'

'Of course!' I said. 'Of course! Sorry!'

There it was – a glimpse of the old Miss Cedars. Sugary, apologetic.

He crouched at my feet and opened the bag. The buckets, half full, chimed tunelessly, the first streams settling to heavy drips. Ben stood up, a torch in hand, and caught me staring, solemnly reappraising him.

'What?' he asked with a cautious smile.

I shook my head. 'Nothing. Sorry. Hadn't we better crack on?'

He climbed the ladder, and I passed him a large screwdriver, then a knife, as he prised out the dampened tiles above us. While he worked, he explained that he had brought a large crate of equipment from the mainland too, along with his tools. Saul Cooper had hoodwinked Miriam Calder with that just-one-bag story no doubt, knowing she would spread word fast and wide, bedding in suspicion about our newcomer right from the start.

Inside this crate were science-lab essentials – microscopes and Petri dishes, three-way switches and soldering irons, boiling flasks and Bunsen burners. Ben said he'd got a sense from his telephone interviews with Mr Crane that there would be very little apparatus to play with at the school. He'd even made an advance order of chemicals to arrive with him on the August ship. Everything was stacked up in Esther Deezer's front room and would need fetching across to the school soon, since Esther didn't believe in using her front room for anything, not even for tea with Father Daniel when he did his rounds.

'So, all I need now,' said Ben, as he passed down the sodden tiles, 'is for someone to help me steal a gas canister from the kitchen?'

'What for?' I asked.

'To make fire!' he pronounced in a conjuror's voice.

He hauled himself up into the crawl space above the classroom to find the source of the leak. It took us about an hour to fix it, me making trips up and down the ladder, holding torches, passing pliers, finding cloths and nails. At one point, Ben requested a fifty-pence piece, as if I would have one on my person. I laughed, thinking it a joke, but he genuinely needed it.

'You settle everything at the end of the month,' I found myself explaining, 'at the Anchor and at the Provisions Store. There's little reason to carry cash.' It was not the first everyday and obvious thing that he had needed spelling out to him. His delight at these details, his amazement even – it could make you feel weird and backward, but also exceptional, glamorous.

I went into the other classroom to retrieve some change from Ben's jacket and, after returning and handing over the coin, I offered: 'The black thing in your pocket with the money...' I'd pulled out a smooth, almost-alien object to get to the coins below. 'Sorry, that was rude,' I countered swiftly, speaking only to the movement of him above me in the darkness. 'You don't have to say, it's just that...'

'The iPhone?' he called down.

'I thought so!'

'It's the SE. I left too early to get the Eight.'

I had seen them before, in pictures, online – Smartphones – seen older versions in the hands of tourists. I had never touched one.

'I can't get used to not carrying it with me,' he yelled.

'Of course,' I said. 'Of course.'

I had read an unfathomable article about phone addiction in a mainland magazine. It was illustrated with an image of a couple sitting together but alone in bed, their faces illuminated by the blue light of their handsets. After holding the delicious weight of Ben's phone in my palm, I thought I might begin to understand the attraction.

'I have music on there, you see.' I could hear him grunting with effort, had no idea what trick he was pulling off with that fifty-pence piece. 'I take pictures with it too, so it's not completely useless. Same with my iPad, I brought that as well.'

When he descended, his shirt was smutted, his knees damp. There were cobwebs in his hair. Our students next door had been let go for lunch, making the dash across the playground from main house to canteen in the still sluicing-down rain. We had missed out on teachers' first dibs at the hot plates, so stayed behind to clear up the damage.

I took down the classroom portrait of St Rita, her eyes rolled back, the beam of light striking her forehead. Ben watched me wipe dry her face and the frame, as he worked the mop across the floor.

'That St Rita,' he said, 'she's a Catholic saint?'

'Well... yes and no,' I replied. 'Augustinian, certainly. She's the patron saint of impossible causes.'

'And abused wives,' he added, 'and heartbroken women.' A man who did his research.

'Heartbroken and abused are the same thing,' I said, returning St Rita to her nail on the wall, 'wouldn't you say?'

He gave me a sideways look.

I faltered, 'Y– You wouldn't?'

He pressed his lips together as if shaping an answer but returned to his initial point. 'What I mean is, you're not Catholic, here on Lark?'

'Oh, it's a leftover,' I told him, 'that's all. A Catholic missionary came here in the… gosh, I don't know, centuries ago, and he named the chapel, and the school was named for the chapel, and sometimes history wins over religion. Plus, we like the saints.' I nudged St Rita, making her level. 'So, we're not Catholic, but we're not Protestant either really. We're not anything. We're just… our own thing.'

'You can say that again!' He laughed, mopping a figure of eight with a flourish.

I couldn't help but smile wide. My Knight of Cups was coming alive right before me, now that our talk had evolved beyond timetables and the right cupboard in which to find teabags. He was not what I had observed from a distance, was more than a man-shaped wish fulfilled. He was real, completely real, and I could not entrust him to Miss Cedars only to watch her lose her nerve again. So, I spoke in a new tongue.

'*You can say that again!*' I said, imitating him, coyly. Then, bolder, I added, 'What is that supposed to mean?' I adopted the same mischievous tone he'd used when talking of stealing gas canisters, of making fire, this Prometheus in our midst.

He stopped and considered me. I didn't flinch from his gaze.

'Your hair really is black, isn't it?' My hand went to my crown. Years of unwanted patting had created a reflex. 'I'd read that black hair was a thing here, but…' He paused. 'It's almost, sort of navy in the light, isn't it? No, not navy, but…'

'What?'

'I don't know,' he said. 'That girl in Year Twelve has it too.'

'Britta Sayers. One of the Eldest Girls.'

'Yes. She and her –'

I cut him short. I didn't care that he had brought up the Eldest Girls in conversation, not then. I cared that we were straying from what was supposed to happen next.

'It's lucky,' I told him. 'My hair.'

'Is it?' He smiled, waiting for the punchline.

I nodded, let my hand fall away from my head, and in my newly found voice, the voice of Leah, I asked him: 'Would you like to touch it?'

They walked differently.

They didn't trip and scurry anymore, powered by laughter and chatter; didn't curl over and into one another, tugging down sections of hair to cover their faces. They unfolded their arms away from the former embarrassment of their blooming chests.

Overnight, they became tall.

Promenading side-by-side, their strides long and certain, linked elbows were their only concession to past girlishness. From main building to canteen, from chapel to school, they took their time as they went, letting you look, wishing to be acknowledged. This desire to be noticed was nothing new – they were sixteen-year-old girls – but no more did they seek attention by pretending they didn't want it.

'They glide now,' said a boy from the First Year seniors, 'they float.'

'Like ghosts?' said his mate with a snigger, to which the first boy replied, dead straight, 'No, like… Queens.'

They took on a different scent.

A Second Year senior girl spotted three pairs of feet beneath the door of one cubicle in the toilets at lunch-time, mid-September, two weeks after the singing incident in chapel – Anna's buckled T-bars, Jade-Marie's brown brogues, Britta's laced-up black boots with the heavy soles. They were sobbing in there, said the Second Year, or at least one of them was, while the others issued calming whispers and spluttered curses. This wouldn't have been thought of as unusual – teenage girls were supposed to hide away in bathroom stalls if they needed to cry – but the aroma of them made it strange.

The signature scent of September was a sweet fizziness. The school toilets and changing rooms were a haze of cheap body spray, supplies still plentiful from the summer shipments. But the girls' bathroom that day smelled earthy, meaty, feral. Laced across it was the churchiness of incense.

It was a smell that was disconcerting in its familiarity.

There were no more grand scenes of rebellion during worship. The girls' protests in chapel became silent. They stood for each hymn, books open at the correct page, but their mouths remained flat lines. It was assumed amongst the teachers (and those pupils concerned with the fair meting out of justice) that Mr Crane was overlooking their behaviour as some kind of strategy – like a mother quashing a toddler's public tantrum by deliberately ignoring it. He did not slam his hymn book against the oak lectern, issued no instructions to sing, just lifted his gaze to check on his charges at the end of each verse. The girls paid him no notice; they took their lead from the women in the biblical scenes in the chapel's windows and on its walls, casting their eyes reverentially downwards or up high, as if in holy awe.

And this was what chafed against the community the most – the way the Eldest Girls became stingy with their attentions and their courtesies. They had been nice young women who looked their elders in the eye and replied *yes, sir* and *no, miss* without a trace of contempt. They'd started mannerly conversations made up of polite enquiries, pleasing a speaker by giggling at their jokes, whether funny or not. But now? In the words of a Third Year senior, the Eldest Girls had become, 'up themselves'.

In the Provisions Store one Saturday, the usual conversation around the fresh produce shelves was reduced to dust by a sudden, blasphemous shriek.

This toddler tantrum could in no way be ignored.

If it had been Britta Sayers, named for St Brigid and her constant fire, behind the outburst, there would still have been shock, though less surprise. Britta's mother, Rhoda, who worked at the Provisions Store counter, could be as rough as a bear paw in arguments over rations. Even clumsy Jade-Marie was a more likely candidate for this public, sacrilegious display, considering her past record in chapel.

But Anna Duchamp … She was an angel, couldn't have looked more like one if she'd grown six wings and cried *holy holy holy*. Her mother, Ingrid, cut her daughter's blonde bob into an immaculate copy of her own, and spent her days, when not tending to a horse she stabled with the hunt animals, making demure pastel dresses for Anna in dainty flower prints. If Britta and Jade-Marie were ever colluding on some ill-considered plan, it was Anna who would preach prudence, 'Oh, but do you think we should?'

Yet, that day in the Provisions Store…

'God damn you!' she yelled into her mother's face, her cheeks as pink as if they'd just been slapped, before striking out at a display of Egremont Russets, sending the crate to the floor, reducing them to a crop good only for cider, making all of the collected shoppers gasp.

The following Monday, Adrien Duchamp was seen at St Rita's School, waiting in the corridor outside Mr Crane's office. His daughter's insolence had spread to the classroom, it was said – backchat to the teachers, laziness with her homework (the detail of the crimes depended on to whom you spoke). Her punishment: Anna was banned by her father from spending time with Britta and Jade-Marie outside of school. Yet the very next day the three of them were seen together on the harbour cobbles, making their way towards the track past the East Bay, coats zipped to the chin, arms linked, wearing shoes unsuitable for the terrain that lay ahead.

The other version of events was that Adrien Duchamp was visiting Mr Crane merely to discuss an insurance claim, and not his daughter at all. Anna's father, with the assistance of accountant Robert Signal, managed the finances of almost everyone on the island. Everyone, that is, who had finances beyond the stash in their biscuit tin.

'Because didn't you hear, the school roof fell in!'

This was the talking point at Hope Ainsley's monthly pop-up hairdressing salon in the scullery of the Counting House.

'It collapsed on the head of that handsome new teacher,' continued Elizabeth Bishy, the doctor's wife. Her audience was the line of women who waited their turn. 'A whole classroom utterly destroyed!' she proclaimed.

Hope Ainsley worked pin waves into Mrs Bishy's peppery black hair and nodded her agreement, while Martha Signal, beneath the heat lamp, put in: 'He was almost killed, you know, that new teacher, so says Huxley's wife.'

And this was not the only well-travelled story involving the handsome Mr Hailey.

The Eldest Girls had been seen communing in the senior corridor one breaktime, voices too hushed to be overheard. Britta Sayers was doing most of the jawing, confidently flipping those ropes of black hair over her shoulders as she spoke. The other two made noises of encouragement, geeing her up for the task ahead, then they scattered as if choreographed – Jade-Marie outside to the playground, Anna towards the infant and juniors' block, Britta into Mr Hailey's classroom.

'Ah, Miss Sayers!' was the greeting that was reported, its warmth suggesting Mr Hailey knew Britta well. Which he shouldn't have – since the Eldest Girls had no teaching contact with him yet. Mr Hailey was still involved in the business of setting-up his science lab, rigging up gas canisters ('*Stolen* gas canisters,' said some), decanting and storing chemicals. There was much to be done before he was ready to branch out from his day-to-day teaching of the younger seniors and share his specialism across the whole school – and with the Eldest Girls.

Perhaps he had sought them out. Perhaps the girls had been drawn to him, this Pied Piper from the mainland, with his shiny gadgets and fancy shirts and waxy way of styling his hair.

No one could say what went on in that classroom that breaktime with Britta Sayers – the door was closed – but a certain spy, who had been better placed on a separate occasion, said Mr Hailey liked to use coin tricks as a seduction technique, had said the black hair of Lark women aroused him and – whisper it – had been seen trying to stick his tongue down the throat of that lovely Miss Cedars.

Britta Sayers was alone with him for a good twenty minutes. A low mumble of voices came from behind the door but with ominous gaps. Britta emerged flushed with colour, all the breath in the top of her chest.

'Thank you,' she said meekly, her voice an uncharacteristic squeak. That she had been heard to address him as 'Ben' alongside her thanks, was likely an embellishment added to the story later.

Sympathies regarding the situation were proffered over drinks at the bar of the Anchor. A young man in the classroom was certain to confuse the feelings of such impressionable girls. He was nothing but a cat among the pigeons, they said, or should that be, a pigeon among the cats?

'That poor, new teacher,' ran the popular line, 'arriving on the island just when those Eldest Girls were ready to pounce.'

◈ Friday the 13th – April 2018

Viola Kendrick sits in the Customs House and waits, a musty blue blanket draped across her shoulders. In her grip is the walkie-talkie, at her feet lies Dot – curled up, chin on paws, making a damp print of herself on the sanded boards.

From the back office drifts Saul Cooper's voice. Viola cannot make out the sentences he's using, just the music of them. First, the staccato codes of communication – letters, digits, short forms – then, longer phrases, affirmations, contradictions. He will be using the satellite phone, she presumes – the Atlantic line can be unreliable. The Marine VHF is of no use here, unless there was to be the most fortuitous alignment of boats and masts. Saul has explained all of this to Viola, an age ago it feels, back when he was happy to humour her.

They had stepped free of the Land Rover and Viola dictated the next move: 'Now we call the *real* police.'

As she spoke, she held the walkie-talkie in clear sight, as a reminder, as collateral. *Do what I say, and no one gets hurt.* The phrase was on the tip of her tongue; Saul wouldn't have recognised the cliché. There were monthly cinema screenings in the Counting House, a carefully curated selection of the obscure and the inoffensive, with regular popular repeats. No one on Lark was fluent in film speak.

We can do this the easy way or the hard way.

I could tell you what I know, but then I'd have to kill you.

You just don't get it, do you?

Viola has these phrases rehearsed and ready, should she be stuck for something to say.

They had gone inside – Saul first, Viola behind, resisting the urge to push the walkie-talkie into the small of his back like a weapon. The bald wooden floor of the Customs House had echoed their arrival, magnifying their footfalls and the rustling of their coats. Viola had started to follow Saul into the back office, like always, but he'd stopped her, put up the palm of his hand – 'No, you wait here' – before gesturing to the bench below a browning pastel map of the island. This had thrown her off-guard. She'd given him a look that asked, *Really?* He'd nodded, waiting for her to move away and sit. That was when he'd taken one of the blue blankets from the wire basket by the door, provisions for occasional overboard fishermen, and arranged it across her shoulders, paternally, almost. She was dealing with official Saul, Saul-at-work.

He'd raised the hinged front desk, the section bearing a taped-on laminated timetable for this year's mainland ships, closing it behind him, and then disappeared into the office beyond.

On the opposite wall to the bench there is a series of framed black-and-white images of the estate – the Big House in some long-gone heyday, the seat of the reclusive Earl. Viola has heard so much about this invisible sovereign, this silent ruler of the island (or rather she has heard the same small slices of information on repeat), that the man has morphed, in her mind, into the fickle, fairy-tale giant who bit a chunk out of Lark and pushed it out to sea. At his whim, might the Earl push the island right back again – if he were ever to show his face?

Viola looks down. The toe of her boot skims the coast-line of an old stain on the otherwise pristine blond-wood floor, a stain that wasn't there last time she rested on this bench, limp and ocean-tired, the day she arrived on Lark. It would be easy for her to think that she is different now, that these ten months on the island have transformed her – once bewildered and full of sorrow, she is now upright, focused, and in possession of the ball – but it would be a lie.

The two-way radio is growing sweaty in her grip. Her back is slowly slumping. Dot has given up all hope of break-fast and fallen sleep.

Viola isn't in charge. She called one shot and then landed herself on the wrong side of the counter, away from the action.

Get up, instructs a voice inside. *Go into that back office!*

But here comes another voice, slicker, more practised, telling her that she hasn't been blindly obedient to Saul, rather she's chosen to put her faith in his clear authority. She must not fall into the trap of assuming that every man is up to no good.

But he IS up to no good! screams the first voice. *We know this!*

Do we? asks the second voice in all reasonableness. *Can we really trust your opinion on that?*

Viola stays put, desperate to know how the morning's discovery is being retold, desperate to hear snatches of the mainland coming down the line, even though those sounds of home might derail her, bring on a dreadful, gasping claus-trophobia of the kind she experiences sometimes when the fog closes in and she allows herself to think how very far away everything is.

Before Lark, before the terrible incident back on the mainland, Viola used to cocoon herself in the darkness beneath her duvet, pretending that she was in a stricken submarine, miles below the water's surface, or in a small pocket of air beneath a fallen building. A test. Could she breathe deep and not panic should the very worst thing happen to her? Her method for counting seconds was robust – *one-elephant, two-elephant, three-elephant...* But she could get no further than twenty before throwing off the duvet and gulping for oxygen. The very fact that Viola is able to draw breath every day on the island feels like a pure miracle.

She sits back against the damp-encrusted wall, fragments of the plaster attaching themselves to the roughness of the blanket, making her think of the peeling balusters of the farmstead veranda. She must plan, formulate her next move. She returns to the language of film. She could mimic the suspects she has seen on screen who grab power by demanding a phone call – to their family, to a lawyer. But she is not a suspect, Viola reminds herself, a little belatedly.

And there is no one she can call.

The farmstead is out. Her mother would likely collapse on the other end of the line, shifting the locus of the tragedy to herself.

The Eldest Girls cannot be contacted. To bring them into this now would result in a fait accompli, confirming suspicions too easily, too quickly. The girls must be kept at arm's length for as long as possible.

There is only one person left, someone Viola half-expected to be pressing his nose against the window of the Customs House right now.

She could call Michael.

Their new start was going so well.

Viola and her mother walked to chapel every Sunday, and sometimes on Saturday too for Evening Mass. The services seemed to gratify her mother, lift her up. They stood in line to receive the host, Deborah Kendrick meeting every wary glance from the congregation with her warmest smile, her intention behind this clear – she would settle for nothing less than complete acceptance, for herself and her daughter.

After service, Viola's mother joined in with the preparation of teas and coffees in the nave, didn't wait for an invitation. She fussed, she bustled, she made herself useful. Viola would sit in a pew, at a distance, cup, with a saucer and biscuit on her lap, banging her heels against the wood until it was time to go, an audience to her mother's convincing performance of eagerness. It was hard to believe this was the same stricken woman whose head had rested in the cradle of her hands for days on end at the kitchen table back home.

Then one Sunday morning in July, there was a shift. Viola watched as a small, busy-looking woman pulled Deborah Kendrick aside for a quiet word. The woman started speaking and her mother's enthusiastic smile twitched, then tilted, before righting itself into something not even passably genuine. Viola understood straight away that she was the subject of this exchange; her mother's eyes skittered towards her in the pew, then back to the woman. It was a nervous action, one of someone who was all of a sudden on guard. It was a chink through which Viola glimpsed once again the broken, tormented woman her mother had been on the mainland.

Later that same week, the busy woman had landed on the doorstep of the farmstead. Out of the kitchen window, Viola saw the Customs Officer leaning against the bonnet of his Land Rover – acting as taxi driver again. His head was down, which she translated as embarrassment at being there.

The woman announced herself formally to Viola's mother – 'Miriam Calder, *the* school administrator', her emphasis hitting the definite article – and Viola's mother had responded with a sweet but terse reminder that they had met several times before and this introduction was unnecessary.

'You need to enrol your daughter in school,' Miriam said, in lieu of any pleasantries.

'More forms!' came Deborah Kendrick's reply, the humour forced. 'Goodness me! When does the paperwork stop?'

Viola had slid into the hallway then, had seen how Miriam took in the yellowing wallpaper and the trail of dry leaves blown in from outside. Her mother attempted to close the front door, keeping her voice bright as if this might soften the rudeness of her actions. 'I'll be sure to pop up to the school soon and get that done!'

'I have the forms here,' said Miriam, her hand meeting the wood of the door, its peeling paintwork. 'We can fill them out now.'

Her mother had reluctantly let Miriam in, but not offered her tea. She filled out the lines and boxes of the forms briskly, belligerently, her pen piercing the paper every time it encountered a deep groove in the battered kitchen table. Miriam stood over her, casting an eye about the room, collecting its details – the bread left out on the board, the sleeping dog, the dripping tap.

Viola had wanted to stand over her mother too, find out which class she was being enrolled in. She had failed her GCSEs on the mainland, missed too much school in the wake of the incident and fallen behind. She had come to think of herself as a dunce, a div.

As it was, whatever Deborah Kendrick put on those forms was of no consequence at all.

On their trip to the Provisions Store that weekend, Viola's mother had enquired of one of the aproned women behind the counter how she might go about ordering something to arrive on the last August ship. The aproned woman had pointed them towards the Counting House, where upstairs they had waited in line to use a computer. Deborah Kendrick had clicked, scrolled, bought.

A chill lifted the hairs on Viola's skin, despite the clement weather that final summer month, when she watched her mother unpack the box that arrived. Teaching materials for Maths, English, Geography and French were arranged neatly in their corresponding piles on the kitchen table.

'I'm really going to enjoy this,' her mother had trilled, breaking the spine on a *Tricolore* textbook. '*Et toi?*'

There they were, on the remotest property on the remotest island, and now Viola was to be home-schooled. Yet, she said nothing – could find no way to protest. Just as she was careful not to wake Dot as she dozed in the radiating warmth of the kitchen Rayburn, Viola could not risk disturbing her mother from this lightness, this reverse of sleep. She had seen how delicate Deborah Kendrick's mindset was in that brief moment with Miriam in chapel. She was under a precarious spell, one that could be easily broken.

So, the battered kitchen table became Viola's school, her pencil now piercing the paper whenever a sentence crossed a groove in the wood.

'Do you think they used to butcher animals on here?' she asked her mother. 'Slaughter them, even?'

'It's a timed test, you know,' was Deborah Kendrick's reply, 'you shouldn't be even thinking about chatting.'

Viola only spoke to break the silence, make the situation feel normal and not a step too far, an isolation within an isolation.

In the timed tests her mother set, Viola felt no urgency. The pink grains of the hourglass flowed slower on Lark. *One – eeeeeeellllllleeeephant. Two – eeeeeeellllllleeeephant....* With no distractions – no texts from friends, no radio, music or television – the silence stretched. It made Viola restless.

In the afternoons, lessons done, she clipped on Dot's red lead and headed out, south, down the main track from the farmstead. Her mother had been uneasy the first time she had pulled on her boots in the hallway.

'But this is why we're here, isn't it?' Viola had argued, as steadily as she could, not wanting to give away how desperate she was to escape the confines of the farmstead and her mother's company. 'It's safe here, we know that. I can wander where I want.'

Deborah Kendrick had given a reluctant nod – heading out herself to turn the lumpy soil and mark out vegetable beds, cursing at the midges and the slugs as she went.

At the end of the farmstead's dirt track, Viola turned right and headed towards the East Bay. She had entertained thoughts of paddling along the shore, combing the line of seaweed for interesting shells. That was before she'd discovered the true close-up violence of the waves; the bay could only be enjoyed as a view, from the raised lawn above.

Sometimes she trekked across the green estate land that spilled down from the Big House upon its rocky promontory, the acreage sectioned by woodland, given over in part to allotments. There she came upon a small cluster of stables and two enclosures for dogs, Dot greeting her fellow animals with sharp, delighted barks. There were half a dozen muscular beagles in one pen, and in the other, two grey-faced whippets with hostage eyes. Viola had reached over to caress the long, smooth nose of one of the whippets, while its companion leant against the fencing, trying to access the warmth of her thigh.

'What are you doing?' a man had bellowed at her, striding across the stable yard, making Viola's hand fly guiltily away. He was a thin, stooped shape beneath his waxed jacket and khaki trousers. Old – though not quite granddad age, with a wiry beard, almost white.

'I'm just stroking them,' she'd said, and though he had made it perfectly clear that she wasn't welcome, Viola tried to keep the conversation going, realising only then how hungry she was for talk. She asked if the dogs were working animals? (Yes, the beagles for the hunt, the whippets for catching rats) and if they had to stay in their pens at all other times (they did).

'Isn't that a bit cruel?' she went on, gently, politely. 'I mean, doesn't it make them sad?'

The man snorted. 'You talk like they have souls.' He leant over the pen, as if checking what damage she might have caused.

'Souls?' Viola was taken aback at the swift philosophical turn of their conversation but pressed on. 'And don't they?' she asked. 'Have souls?'

He laughed at the question. He hadn't been speaking philosophically at all, it seemed, only stating the facts as he saw them, but Viola's sincere response had a sobering effect. He went from delivering a firm stare to looking anywhere but at her face.

'I should get going, if I were you. You don't want any trouble.'

'Trouble from who?' she wondered aloud.

'The gamekeeper.'

'Who's that then?'

'That then,' he replied gruffly, 'is me.'

Other days, she ventured as far as the cobbles of the harbourside, considering it a search for the island's potential, the secret it had yet to offer up. She gripped tightly to the doomed hope of discovering a coffee shop, somewhere to sit and have a milkshake, but found only a smokehouse with herring and mackerel turning gold on their racks, a tiny, hardly ever open library in one of the lanes, and a pub that was more of a men's social club, since it didn't admit women until the weekends, and under-eighteens, never.

There was the Counting House, with its upstairs computers, the sort of building that would have been populated by lithe women with yoga mats on the mainland, but on Lark was the venue for (according to a poster in the marbled lobby) 'fascinating and informative' sessions with Dr Tobiah Bishy, MBBS, MRCGP, including 'Correct Usage of the Island's Defibrillator', 'Know Your Blood Pressure' and 'A Walk-in Skin Clinic (Lancing of Boils, etc.)'.

The island's only shop, the Provisions Store, had been charming in its strangeness to begin with, but soon fulfilled its destiny to disappoint – nothing but a warehouse piled with stock, smelling of ripe cheese and even riper fish, lorded over by a brace of fierce, middle-aged women. Viola ached for the shiny persuasions of a Tesco Extra.

On one visit an argument broke out in the fresh produce section, providing a brief glimmer of interest. A pretty blonde girl around Viola's age was standing with her mother behind a pyramid of plums. They were debating urgently in a language that sounded like Swedish, or Danish maybe. Viola feigned interest in a tray of walnuts, so she might edge closer, hear more.

The girl, at the height of her exasperation, switched the quarrel to English. 'You're not listening to me!' she hissed. 'That's not what I'm saying, Mum, I'm not saying that at all.'

The woman, her hair cut into the same neat bobbed style as her daughter's, snatched the girl's wrist, looking worriedly about them for eavesdroppers. 'Then why say it?'

The girl drew breath to speak again and the woman, frantic to make her quiet, drove her nails into her daughter's skin.

'Ow!' She wrenched her wrist away, catching the corner of a crate of apples as she did, sending the fruit to the floor, bringing one of the fierce women running from her position behind the counter.

Viola craned to watch the girl flee the scene, her flat, buckled T-bars slip-slapping against the concrete.

'And you can get rid of that filthy animal, 'n' all,' said the attending fierce woman, turning on Viola in the chaos. 'What on earth do you think you're doing, bringing that thing in here?'

That Viola had a dog – as a companion, as a familiar – was very strange to the residents of Lark, she quickly realised. The cats were feral, not pets, kept fat on the island's plentiful supply of mice – creatures Viola and her mother did daily battle with, forced to place a rock on top of the bread bin at night to stop them breaching the lid. The stares Viola endured on the cobbles were never greater than when she crouched to scoop up Dot's poo. They were the same looks you received on the mainland when you did the opposite – walked away and left it, indifferent.

So, Viola took the left-hand path at the bottom of the farmstead track for a while, heading away from the harbour, to walk Dot in the anonymity of the woods.

As they progressed uphill, the scrubland was taken over by great swathes of ferns, the distance between the pines growing smaller. The world turned denser, browner, the trees enclosing them, making the clatter of a bird's wing come blanketed and soft. Viola's boots crunched against the needled path, a satisfying soundtrack, convincing her it wasn't voices she craved so much, just a different kind of quiet.

The peace, though, was short-lived.

He came jogging up behind her one afternoon, arrived seemingly from nowhere, his breathing laboured when he reached her side. Viola recognised the St Rita's uniform from her excursions to the harbour – knitted navy jumper, red-and-black striped tie – and the boy wore his with a grey wool duffel coat, toggles bobbing.

'You're the redhead!' he gasped, matching her pace. 'I've been *dying* to meet you!'

His hair was liquorice black above a high forehead, above a large jaw – a face best suited to gloom. When he smiled therefore – this being so unexpected – it was difficult to resist smiling back. But Viola did resist.

'Is it like birdwatching?' she enquired tartly. 'Do you need to tick "redhead" off your list?'

He looked confused. 'Birdwatching?'

'My name,' she said, 'is not "the redhead". It's Viola.'

'Oh!' he said, catching on – perhaps – and they did not speak for a while. Viola waited for him to get bored, to trail away, but he stayed beside her, leather satchel banging against his hip. They paused in unison when a small herd of deer tripped anxiously across their path, and once they had resumed their walk, the boy said: 'Do you know, I hate Violas!'

Now Viola was confused. She had never met anyone who shared her name. There had been a Violet in the year below at her mainland school, and a precocious Violetta at a drama club she tried once and immediately hated. How had this boy encountered enough Violas on an island of 253 souls to form such a strong opinion?

'I mean the flowers,' he said.

'Oh!'

'They look like they have faces.'

'Yes.'

'Weird eyes that creep you out.'

He was younger than her, Viola deduced, fourteen, fifteen maybe, though it was hard to say for sure. The kids at the harbour who looked to be her age physically, seemed young in their behaviour, childish – except perhaps for that blonde girl at the store. The island did it to them, Viola presumed, built them heartier, kept them innocent. You could only blame the lack of internet.

'I'm named after a character in a play,' she told him, trying to impress.

'Oh, yeah. Which one?'

He was definitely younger. Either that, or more of a dunce than her.

'The Shakespeare one,' she enunciated.

'Well, he wrote a ton of plays, didn't he?' the boy countered. 'You're going to have to narrow it down.'

'The one with Viola in it,' she said, toying with him.

She didn't fancy him; she wasn't flirting. There was just an easy familiarity between them – big sister, little brother – and she liked being teasingly superior, used as she was to being the younger one, if only by a few minutes.

'Has it got sex in it?' the boy asked. 'The Viola play?'

She wondered if he had misunderstood their rapport, if he was flirting with her, but his enquiry seemed genuine.

'Not really. Just a bit of cross-dressing.'

'That'll be why then,' he said.

Why what? she would have asked if he hadn't leapt in and flipped the subject.

'So, are you heading for the Sisters' Stones too?' he asked. This was followed by a monologue about the perfect circle of nine Neolithic stones that lay beyond the wood, and a deconstruction of all the hypotheses for why it had been built in the first place – time-telling, worship, the strange proclivities of ancient druids. The tenth stone in the centre of the circle – a hollow stone – had healing properties, he said, if you crawled through its middle.

'Have you tried it?' Viola asked, triggering another lengthy speech from the boy, this one on local legends, including the giant's bite story. He told a tale of how the sea surrounding Lark claims a child every seven years, then something about black-haired virgins – the word 'virgin' making him blush profusely – before he arrived at his point.

The Sisters' Stones, as their name suggested, belonged to the women of the island. Everything else on Lark belonged to the men, which they could share with the women, if they chose to, but the stones … The boy couldn't go near that hollow rock, even by invitation.

'It's bad luck for a man to enter the circle,' he said gravely. 'It invites a terrible fury.'

Dot strained impatiently at her lead. Viola hadn't gained enough knowledge of the landscape yet to let her run free. Everywhere was the risk of an unexpected cliff edge, a drop into the sea.

'Where does the fury come from?' Viola asked. 'From God?'

'No!' The boy looked shocked. 'Oh, no!' He crossed himself. 'Not Him! Not Him!'

'Then who?'

'I don't want to say it aloud,' he replied. 'I'm a good Christian and that's pagan nonsense.'

'But you said –'

He interjected, diverting her with another soliloquy. This time: about how he was going to be an archaeologist when he was older, discover more about Lark's ancient cultures. He scooped up a fir cone and methodically stripped it of its scales. There was no precedent for this kind of career on the island, he told her, but that was no obstacle; the lack only indicated a demand. Once the island got a telephone mast and everyone had wi-fi (Did Viola know what wi-fi was? Had she heard of it?), he would be able to study an online course very easily.

Then he flipped the subject again, onto his older brother, Luke, who had just moved out of the family home and into the Billet House. He had begun an apprenticeship to the gamekeeper, which the boy explained was a 'really very powerful role on the island'.

Viola thought of the stooped, white-bearded man who had yelled at her for bothering his dogs. He had been grumpy certainly, but powerful … ?

'His daughter's been given one of the cottages on the harbourside all to herself!' the boy exclaimed. 'And she doesn't even have a husband!'

A rare pause opened up into which Viola thought she should offer some information of her own, a juicy detail of life on the mainland, quid pro quo, but he steamrollered her again with talk of fishermen and a tragedy at sea that had killed a load of them, way back when.

For someone '*dying*' to catch a glimpse of the new redhead, he had no interest whatsoever in anything that redhead might have to say.

'And you'll have to take your dog back to your house, now,' he said, as if this was a logical continuation of the story. 'He'll get in the way of the spying.'

'She,' corrected Viola. The woods were thinning now. There was the close-by sound of the sea. 'And who are you to be telling me what to do?'

'Oh, I'm Michael,' he said, apparently immune to her resentment. He thrust forward his hand for her to shake, a gesture too late and too grown-up. It was oddly endearing. The boy meant well, Viola guessed. His rudeness, his social hopelessness, could only be born of interacting with the same handful of people every day. She shook that hand.

'I'm named for Michael who leads the armies against Satan,' he told her.

Viola grinned. 'Oh, yeah, which play is that in?'

'Oh, it's not in a play,' he said.

'I know.'

'Then why did you –'

'Spying!' she threw in, employing the boy's own tactics on himself. 'You said spying. Who are we spying on?'

'The Eldest Girls, of course.' He pointed to the needled ground beneath them. 'Look, they've left a trail to lure us.'

There were rose petals there, red and bruised, a scattering leading away from the wood.

'Well, me,' Michael clarified. 'It's men those girls are after.'

So, what were the Eldest Girls doing at the Sisters' Stones? This.

Britta held the book and called out the orders; she always liked to take the lead. Picture her: shoulders back, chin raised, thrusting the manual forward in one hand, looping the other arm casually across her waist. This was the stance she adopted when reading poetry aloud in class, as if she thought herself a holy orator, a female pope.

Or it was Anna who bent over the pages of that book, instilling the words with her trademark authority and reason, golden hair falling forward, shadows playing across her face. It wasn't hard, since her tantrum in the Provisions Store, to imagine her in that dimmer light.

Or it was Jade-Marie. She could have been the one to read aloud, to call the shots, a bitten nail working its way along the words, her delivery stumbling, doused in amazement.

Whoever it was, they were in it together. One was as bad as the other.

They were united in their task, despite their disagreements about the right way to do things.

Should they loop around the Sisters' Stones three times *deosil* or *widdershins*? they asked one another. Jade-Marie thought it unlucky to go against the way. Anna argued: how could it be? The world turns anti-clockwise and God created that.

His name came into their discussions often, never with a hint of shame.

'It won't matter,' said Britta firmly. 'It will work which-ever way around, if our intentions are right.'

There was no shame in the saying of this either – the suggestion, the conviction, that what they were doing was right and good.

The circling done, they laid down knives, purposely crossed. They placed a stoppered bottle of water on the most westerly stone.

Another argument.

'The wood is to the east, so that stone is the west.'

'Wrong! The wood is south-west of here.'

'No wonder you're always getting us lost on the way back, Jade-Marie Ahearn. Do you even know your backside from your elbow?'

Nervous laughter, quickly fading out.

Tealights were lit in strict contradiction of the Closed-months Rationing rules regarding candles. If it was dry enough, they collected scrub and made a small fire, in strict contradiction of Article 5 of Lark Council's Woodland and Pasture directive. They could not claim ignorance as their defence. The TV and VHS were rolled out of the school cupboard on their trolley at regular intervals to play the safety video. Its message was clear: messing around with fire was no joke. One spark and the whole of Cable's Wood could go up. One fire with the right wind and the whole island would roar alight. Jade-Marie, more than anyone, should have known better; her mother was in the volunteer fire force.

They dressed in white, pulling old nightdresses from the bottom of their satchels and tugging them on over their uniforms. There were visible mends on the garments, suggesting age, but that hardly narrowed down who had given the girls their ghostly robes. Everyone on the island knew to make good and pass on. The dresses were large, drowning them, and from that detail, perhaps, the culprit might be found. Someone had to be helping, putting ideas in their heads. This wasn't purely the stuff of instinct, their lying in the grass, star-shaped, hair spilling, black, brown, blonde.

Palms to the sky, they offered themselves, brazenly.

'Visualise yourself becoming one with the earth,' a voice intoned. (It was hard to see whose mouth was moving when they were lying down like that. From a distance, all three voices sounded alike.)

'Let this terrible foulness seep into the soil.'

(They knew that's what they were – foul.)

'It's not ours to carry, we can let it go.'

(Wishful thinking.)

'And now we sing!'

They sat up.

Another argument.

'I don't want to do any of the songs we know.'

'Why not? We can take them back. We can make them our own.'

Anna began a teasing verse of 'Lord of the Dance'.

Jade yelped and covered her ears.

Britta lifted her mouth to the sky and began to howl, coiling vowels, the sound startling the others into silence.

'Ooooooaaaahhhhhhhheeeeeeeeeeeaaaaaaaahhhhh!'

'What on earth is that supposed to be?'

'I'm making it up, aren't I? Our new kind of singing.'

The other two shrugged – why not? – and joined in. They added their own discordant harmonies to this hymn sent upwards to a tracing-paper moon.

On other occasions they kept their silence and knelt, eyes closed, writing on pieces of paper resting on their laps. Blinking awake from this trance, the girls read aloud their scribbles, sounding astonished at what was there, believing they'd played no part in the composition.

They joined hands. They made up chants

Clean we are, pure we be
Our minds fall open and we can see
Take the dark, turn it to light
Wash this away before the night.

They summoned the dead, wearing headdresses made from the fat spiked leaves of the hawthorn tree.

A prayer was said for Bethany Reid, the girl who was swept away from the dogleg jetty to a watery grave in 2011. The sea surrounding Lark claims a child every seven years, so in the coming year, they all knew – time's up. There had been doubts that Bethany's death counted; she had turned sixteen the summer before, so was a woman, not a child. Would the sea be a stickler for its conditions? No one was sure. Mothers held children's hands very tightly until the calendar turned to 1 January with no other soul lost. Rejoicing went on behind closed doors. *Bethany was the sacrifice after all! God save the rest of us!*

The Eldest Girls asked Bethany to speak to them via a swinging pendant – a small chunk of green stone strung on a silver chain. Britta held the piece of jade aloft; Anna asked the questions.

'Will you help us? Circle for "yes", go back and forth for "no".'

Did Bethany respond? This is not a question you can ask if the truth and the light is genuinely in your heart.

They moved on to someone else. The girls asked 'him' to come to them, to speak, to enter them.

The young man with the gun eagerly reported this part.

He was out for the foxes, keeping down their numbers, when he was distracted by female voices, drawing him from the wood to the brink of the stones. This 'him' they were trying to summon came with no capital H; the young man was sure of it. No one asked for the Lord to come unto them like that, barefoot in the open air, arms aloft. They weren't pulling themselves, hand-over-hand, closer to heaven; rather they were reaching high as they sank down to where Old Harry lives.

The story travelled through the Billet House, the Customs House, the Anchor. The Eldest Girls were an abomination, they said, for raising up heathen persuasions that Lark had long ago put to bed. But in the silence that followed these rough and noisy judgements, as the men sipped their beer in small groups of trusted fellows, sure that the girls' fathers – the two who were still living – weren't within earshot, they raised a tentative question: *What kind of spell, do you think, those girls are casting?*

Little debate was needed to arrive at a consensus. They were girls – what else could it be? It was a spell for love, for a certain kind of communion. The three had recently come of age, and that did something funny to a woman. They'd be thinking of nothing but marriage now, babies – common-sense flown from the window. Sense enough would remain for them to see the bleeding obvious, though: the number of eligible men on Lark was diminishing. Too many traitors were leaving for the mainland. The girls were calling on every bit of help they could get – from up above and down below – to snare themselves a mate.

Eyes went to the young man with the gun when this was said, and he began to see how they saw him. As something special.

Those girls could not rely on their soft looks. Even Britta Sayers, the one with the blackest hair … she had flaws in her genes. Take one look at the mother, Rhoda, on her shift at the Provisions Store – that jutting tooth, the heaviness of her brow, her body gone to fat. Britta might be bonny now, if you liked them feisty, but the men knew their proverbs. *As is the mother, so is her daughter.* Who wanted to go to bed with a vixen one day and wake up beside a toad?

Jade-Marie's mother, Mary, was no guarantor for her offspring either. There she was, working at the foot of the gamekeeper, trying to claim a job that rightly belonged to a man – to a young man with a gun, to be precise. It was unnatural. Mary Ahearn had been forgiven for a while, with a dead husband and all that, but kindness had its limits.

As for Anna, she was angelic-seeming now, but she had French blood, Scandi blood, who knew how that might turn out?

Yet, you still would.

That's what the men said, leaning in, smirking. Now that those girls were full-grown, you absolutely would. And despite all the attention given to their differences, there was no sense in picking a stand-out beauty. Each girl had an allure that was intensified, multiplied, by them being one of three. Their number made the men greedy. The appeal was to own the full set.

They had pricked one another's fingers, said the young man with the gun, warming to his role as storyteller, and red had dripped onto the white of their nightdresses. They offered their fingers to each other to be kissed and sucked, whispering promises.

They knew they were being watched then, the older men told the young one, why else would they have smeared their lips with the stuff, if not for show? The young man went on to tell them of the rose petals, the trail of them leading from wood to circle.

The men sat back in their chairs, arms folded, case closed.

They were possessed with it, the Eldest Girls, possessed by him, that young man with the gun, and they were issuing a twisted invitation. The only question left was, how he would go about doing it – claiming his rightful prize?

◉ The Book of Leah

And then I understood Leah, in a way I never had before.

The good book has Laban, her father, putting her up to it; saying she should offer herself to Jacob in the dark, pretend to be her sister, Rachel, secure a husband by deception.

That used to make sense to me.

Daughters do as their fathers tell them. Eldest daughters should be married first, no matter how beautiful the younger. There is a system to everything – an order. The moral of the story was distinct, familiar – winning at all costs is a man's prerogative. If Laban wanted Jacob in his family, if Laban needed a husband for his least-favoured daughter, he had the right to kill two birds with one stone. Leah's feelings were not important. We could sympathise, but we would also understand – she did it for the good of her family.

Anyway, it all concluded well. Jacob took two wives, both sisters, so he got his beloved Rachel in the end. Leah lacked Jacob's love but was rewarded by God, made fertile, while the younger sister stayed barren (so she wouldn't get too big for those pretty boots). Justice played out. Of a kind.

But what if Leah was no unwilling pawn?

She wanted to go unto Jacob in the dark, that's what I believe. She'd already had a taste, a small savour of someone, somehow – fingers reaching forward tentatively for a strand of her astounding hair, the sudden crush of lips upon hers, unexpected but wanted, a warm tongue, a hand slipping to the base of her spine, pulling her body closer.

She desperately wanted to feel that again.

So, Leah suggested the double-cross, pretending to her father that it was a sacrifice, if only to ensure history recorded her as a martyr, not a whore. Women are the true masters of deception, have always had to be. They don't get to decide which of their behaviours are virtues.

'What happens now?' I said as we broke apart.

I moved straight to the classroom window, flattening my hair, checking who had seen. Everyone was still in the canteen.

He picked up the mop again. I watched his hands upon it.

'Do I take you out for dinner?' he said.

I laughed, and he caught up quickly. 'Oh, yeah! Stupid me.'

Unless you have a boat, I thought. *A boat that could take us to the mainland. I would get on a boat like that with you. With you, I would.*

I didn't know where it was coming from, this desperate rush.

'There's always the Anchor,' I said. 'On weekends, Jed lets women in.'

So, we made a plan. A double-cross of our own.

I luxuriated in the painful wait for Saturday, everything speaking to me of what had happened in the wake of that flood. Eve Grogan, one of my Fourth Years, intoned the lines of Elizabeth Barrett Browning's 'I think of thee!' to the class and the words lifted from the page. Seven pairs of eyes pierced me as I sighed at the idea of a tree trunk set all bare. In chapel, I sang 'Make Me a Channel of Your Peace' with a sinful fervour. Prints made by the lower school went up on the corridor walls – tomatoes and pomegranates, split in half, spilling their seeds, obscene in their pinks and reds. I blushed and looked away. Whenever he was near, I ached for his touch, to be there again, beneath the white-hot gaze of St Rita.

'Shall we go to the Anchor tomorrow night?' I proposed to my colleagues in the staff room on Friday.

They looked up and around, certain that someone else must have spoken, not sullen Miss Cedars who had taken to sitting alone on the low, soft chairs in breaktimes, chewing on an apple.

'It's been a difficult week, hasn't it?' I went on. 'Doing that walk to chapel every day in the rain.'

'*We glory in our tribulations!*' shrilled Miriam from the kitchenette, not turning from the sink. '*Knowing that tribulation worketh patience!*'

Ben's gaze flickered across to meet mine and away again – our plan thwarted at the first move – but Ruth was wise to our silent exchange. She grinned at me wryly, one sinner to another, said: 'But a beer will help though, Miriam, don't you think?'

I prepared for that evening by working on my verses, scripture being the most effective retaliation to gossip. I did not want this to play out on Lark's stage, for my precious Knight of Cups to be dissuaded by too-hasty rumour. Welcoming strangers so easily wasn't our usual way – though it should have been. I cautioned my own reflection in the window as I did the washing-up, arming myself, rehearsing, justifying my friendliness to Ben, negating it. '*Be not forgetful to entertain strangers,*' I told that echo of me in the glass. '*For thereby some have entertained angels unawares.*'

Upstairs, I tried on the mermaid skirt, turning my hips to make the pleats fly.

'*For I was an hungred,*' *and ye gave me meat*: I told Leah in the mirror. '*I was thirsty, and ye gave me drink: I was a stranger, and ye took me in.*'

I put the skirt away. If I wore it, everyone would know, immediately.

The Anchor was full, as was typical for a Saturday; it took just thirty bodies to bring the place elbow-to-elbow, the last lifeboat in a storm. Jed Springer had rolled up his sleeves and broken into a sweat getting everyone served. He called terse instructions to his brother, Reuben, his slender double, a boatman usually – and a wet blanket, a loser, according to most on the island you spoke to, him being so different from garrulous Jed. Eleanor, Jed's skittish, wide-eyed wife, completed the trio behind the bar, unsmiling in her bartender's waistcoat.

The clan from school were in their usual factions – Dellie Leven and Faith Moran stuck close to their boatmen husbands; Ruth French, with housemate Cat Walton, jostled at the bar. Beneath a cluster of painted buoys hanging from the ceiling at the end of the room, sat Miriam Calder and her whiskered husband, Frank, his crutch propped at his side. They were embedded at the headmaster's table, Miriam force-feeding Diana Crane all the latest buzz. Frank was known for repeating the last few words of each phrase that tumbled from his wife's mouth, as if providing assurance that all she said was true.

I arrived alone, the Anchor lying just a few yards from my front door; the roars of male laughter travelled into my bedroom on still weekday nights. Ben arrived last, on the arm of a beaming Barbara Stanney. Heads turned when he entered – of course they did, he was our stranger – and Barbara played up to the stares with a teenage relish. She pulled Ben towards her, snuggling into his chest, raising laughter with this charade, making him blush with embarrassment. I could feel Ruth's gaze on me, expecting me to be annoyed, but I laughed along. The distraction was good. Let everyone talk about Barbara's ignominious display with the *coycrock* teacher young enough to be her son; let the wagging tongues stay well away from me.

Three drinks in, we took possession of a table, Ruth, Cat, Ben and I; Barbara had relinquished her toyboy early on for the lure of the dominoes. We huddled close on our stools, standing drinkers jostling at our backs. Ben's presence continued to work its strange magic on Ruth. With him there, she no longer spoke to me like we were in the schoolyard. Cat spoke easily too.

'I notice we haven't seen you in chapel yet, Mr Hailey,' she challenged. She wasn't serious in this reprimand, but also she was; maintaining attendance was one of her clerical duties.

'I'm there every day of the week,' he shot back, understanding the game. 'What on earth are you accusing me of?'

'A violation!' Cat slammed a palm to the table, making husbands and wives, fishermen and labourers, look down on us for a moment. Ben turned in his seat to give them a genial nod. Ruth sniggered into her glass.

'Weekdays are for work, Mr Hailey,' Cat persisted. 'Saturdays and Sundays are for true devotion.'

'I couldn't agree more,' he said with a wink, taking an exaggerated gulp of his drink and loading his top lip with foam. 'But seriously,' he said, 'what do you all do on the weekends for fun?'

'This,' said Ruth, gesturing about her, eyebrows raised imperiously as if to ask, *is this not enough?* She lifted her gin and tonic. 'And also, this.'

We launched into another round of 'Cheers!' and Ben pulled his phone from his pocket to take a picture of us, drinks raised, stretching an arm so he could be in the frame too.

'I'll just post this to Instagram,' he pantomimed, prodding exaggeratedly at the screen. Then, 'Oh, wait...' He tossed the phone to the table and pretended to sulk. We eye-rolled at his joke.

'Come on, guys!' It was Ben's turn to slap the table. 'Let's get that petition going for a telephone mast. Let's drag Lark kicking and screaming towards the shores of the twenty-first century! The revolution starts here!'

We shook our heads slowly.

'Why come to Lark,' asked Ruth, skewering him with logic, 'if you only want what you left behind?'

He shrugged.

'I mean, what did you leave behind?' she continued, not letting him answer. 'Something messy, no doubt, or painful or boring or difficult.' With each adjective her voice became more impassioned and Ben's smile became weaker. I could have pointed out that she was using Miriam Calder's line of reasoning to drive home her point, but Ruth would likely have poured gin over my head. 'Everyone comes here to escape something,' she said. In the silence that followed, we awkwardly sipped our drinks. 'Am I right?' she asked.

Again, Ben shrugged.

'Listen,' said Cat, shooting Ruth a withering look, 'I grew up on the mainland and I got my degree there. I know it can't compare. I'm telling you, I've never felt closer to God than when I'm on Lark.'

'Oh!' Ruth swallowed her mouthful of drink quickly, eager to join in the fervour. 'Have you seen a sunset from the west coast, yet?'

Ben shook his head. Ruth slammed down her glass in disbelief.

'No? You have to! You must! Climb up to the Big House, head into the gardens round the back, don't let the Earl see you and...' Ruth's eyes slid to me. She grinned. 'Leah will show you.'

'I'll tell you what, *coycrock*,' said Cat, rescuing us both from Ruth's clutches. 'I'll cook for us next weekend, how's that for something to do?'

Ben leapt on this. 'Yes! Then you can do the weekend after, Leah, and I'll do the weekend after that and we'll all score one another!'

'What?' Ruth spoke our confusion.

'Like on the TV show,' he said to our blank expressions, adding limply, 'the one none of you have ever seen.'

The reason I said very little during these exchanges was because, beneath the table, Ben was slowly working his hand under my skirt. I wasn't wearing the alluring mermaid pleats, just a simple, denim A-line, a style most of the women on the island owned, but still it enticed his touch. His fingertips massaged the soft flesh at the top of my thigh. The sensation required all of my concentration, all of my breath. Only when a hand, someone else's entirely, landed heavy on my shoulder, making me start, did I burst into gabbling speech.

'Mary!'

'You're not getting drunk are you, Miss Cedars?'

It was Mary Ahearn, Jade-Marie's mother, still in her greens after a day on the land, her cheeks red from the wind. She was smiling, not really appalled, but her grip stayed firmly on my shoulder. I snipped my knees together to stall the progress of Ben's hand.

'Oh, no! Just a little tipsy!'

I hadn't seen Mary since I'd dragged her daughter down the aisle and away that first morning at chapel. She was a good friend of my parents; I didn't want her upset. I supposed that she had been called in to see Mr Crane about Jade-Marie's misdemeanour, yet I had no memory of her waiting there on the chairs outside his office. Did she even know what her daughter had done? Nausea flickered at my throat.

'You won't go telling the girls you've seen us like this, now, will you?' I laughed too brightly, and Mary narrowed her eyes as if considering her options.

'I reckon your secret's safe with me, Miss Cedars,' she said, patting me gently and moving away.

My jumper clung hot and sweaty at my shoulder where her hand had rested.

We left as planned; me first, feigning tiredness, Ruth creasing her brow suspiciously at this early retreat. I went home, drew the curtains and waited in the kitchen with the lights off. The moon was new; I was guided only by what I could hear. The gate latch clicked, footsteps sounded in the small concrete yard. I opened the back door.

'I can't see you,' he said.

'Don't worry. Your eyes will adjust.'

He reached for me. You are Hades, I thought, the unseen one. I am Persephone, soon to be lost to the underworld. His lips found mine, and I became instantly liquid, alive, though still laced with doubt.

'I don't know what I'm doing,' I said, surfacing for air.

The sabbath would roll around in minutes. Engaging in works of the flesh is to deny yourself a place in the kingdom of God. And then what? What would be the price?

'Of course you know what you're doing,' he said. His voice was as soft as warm sand upon the skin. 'You know, you know...'

FRIDAY THE 13TH – APRIL 2018

There is a bang – plastic hitting wood, a phone being thrown down with some force.

Viola stands swiftly, yanked from her deliberations. Dot stands to attention too, skittering sideways to avoid the blanket that falls from Viola's shoulders.

Saul curses in the back office and kicks out at something. A table leg? Silence.

Viola barely has time to share a questioning glance with Dot before Saul is there, wresting up the hinged counter and slamming it down in his wake, muttering curses into the stiff collar of his reflective jacket as he zips it up and makes a grab for the door handle.

'Wait, where are you going?' Viola chases him, out into the cold air, Dot following, the end of her red lead carried hopefully in her mouth.

Saul stops abruptly on the cobbles and Viola almost crashes into the back of him. She retreats as he turns, his grey face orange in the early light. The sun has pulled itself free of the sea and burned the worst of the fog away. The boatmen will be there soon, retrieving their pots set the night before.

'They want to know who it is,' he tells her. He grinds his teeth against his lips, flexes and clenches his papery hands.

'But that's their job, isn't it?' She trips over her sentences. 'To find out who it is. Once they get here, start a proper investigation, then we'll know who –'

'The body, stupid!'

She feels the spittle of his exclamation land on her face. 'Oh.'

'They need positive ID of the body. From me.'

He makes a break for the Land Rover. Viola goes too.

'But I told you who it is!'

'And we're to trust the word of a ginger fucking *coycrock*, are we?' He means to hurt her and he does. Viola takes a moment to rebound. Saul gets behind the wheel.

'But you looked at it yourself,' she implores.

'Not the face, I didn't,' says Saul. His tone is sarcastic, self-punishing, and now she understands where this fury has come from – he's messed up. The people on the other end of the line have pointed it out. *You're not a real policeman.*

He slams the door.

'Wait!'

She runs around to the passenger side. She must go with him. He could do anything – move the body, hide it, make it look different. Saul could change the story. Viola scoops up Dot and tries the door. Locked. He starts reversing.

'Wait!'

She bangs on the window, bringing him to a halt. He leans over and slides the glass across, just enough for them to speak.

'You stay here,' he tells her.

'I need to come too.'

'Why?'

'Because…'

92

He revs the engine.

'Because…'

'You don't need to come.' His foot itches at the clutch. 'You've already seen who it is.'

It strikes her again, that blood-spattered image. The feet. She's seen the feet. The boots, the legs, the coat – the right coat – but if she had trampled into the ferns to see anything more, she'd have spoiled the scene. And anyway, she didn't need to. Because she knows who it is. She knows.

'I know who it is,' she says meekly, to avoid telling a lie.

'Well, there you go.'

He goes to slide the window back across, but she thrusts in a fist, a last gasp.

He sighs. 'You just need to wait here, cherub.' His voice is coaxing, parental, tired. The *cherub* soothes Viola. He doesn't hate her, not really. She removes her hand.

'I've told them you'll be waiting in the Customs House,' he says.

'But…'

Too late; she is behind glass.

'Told who?' she yells, banging at the window once more. 'Told who?!'

No one will be arriving in the short while Saul Cooper is at Cable's Wood. The ship doesn't arrive until lunchtime, and Viola has seen the way the islanders cluster on the cobbles waiting for their deliveries; the ship is always late.

The Land Rover reverses, swings to point north.

Unless, Viola reasons, there is a quicker way to get to Lark, and always has been, some covert system of speed-boats and helicopters impervious to the conditions out there, some method not available to mere mortals.

She steps out of the path of the Land Rover and drops Dot back onto the cobbles, retrieving the lead from her mouth.

Of course not. It takes days to reach Lark.

Then it dawns on her, seizes her like a hand to her throat. She has messed up too. Failed in Geography and Mathematics all over again. She really is a dunce.

This whole thing has been orchestrated to coincide with the arrival of the April ship, but that's no use. It needed to be timed to coincide with its *departure* from port, three days before, so the mainland police would know to board the ship in the first place and be on their way now. Viola's stomach lurches; she is sickened by her own stupidity.

'They won't keep you hanging around for too long,' Saul calls before driving away. 'They'll be here any minute.'

The Land Rover kicks up dust on the road above the East Bay.

Viola snatches her head around towards the Counting House, then the other way, up towards the estate, the chapel, the school.

Then, knowing what she knows, Viola runs.

◉ The Book of Leah

The game continued into October.

By day, I walked the earth in all obedience – teacher, daughter and pure-born catch. In the queue for the online computers one Saturday, Sarah Devoner told me how she hoped for a grant from the Council to order more books for the library, and she reached up to pet my head for the luck she needed, thinking she was touching the black hair of a virgin. I did not flinch; I only smiled. Sarah didn't know who I was now; I was Leah with the tender eyes.

I had knelt in front of him in my bedroom, watched him shake his head and grin, say, 'ladies first' as if this was a joke we shared. I followed his lead, let him edge me back onto the bed and ease apart my thighs. He worked his fingers there until something began to reverberate through me. He placed the coldness of his tongue between my legs, making the release sweeter yet.

'Touch yourself,' he liked to say as we moved together, which felt like permission or a gift, one that I understood was mine to use when I had only thoughts of him, and not him in the flesh.

Afterwards, we lay there in almost perfect blackness. Other times, when the moon was waxing gibbous, our limbs were picked out, iridescent. I felt none of the shame I had anticipated, no gravitational shift, no fiery judgement. The same ceiling hung above me. The rigging sang against the masts in the harbour as it always had. I felt whole, intact, though I was supposed to feel the opposite.

I understood what my body was capable of now. I had experienced joys it had thus far kept hidden – that I had kept hidden from myself.

Listening to Ben's breathing as it slowed into sleep gave me something to savour, a sensation to recall, when we were in the staff room together in plain sight, discussing something necessary and mundane. I would think of it in chapel and when negotiating my weekly shopping with the gatekeepers at the Provisions Store. When I looked out to sea and thought of those who had left, I no longer experienced that sharp stab of rejection. Knowing I had lain beside Ben made everything that was painful, boring and difficult on the island – all that I wished to escape – feel entirely bearable.

Sharing a pillow in the early hours, we compared our lives. I'd grown up with a younger brother, he an older sister. His dad had left his mother and married someone else when Ben was a teenager. A man deserting his family like that shocked no one on the mainland anymore. I told him about my father, the gamekeeper, and his decision a few months before to step down from the early work to set a path for retirement, and how he now resisted those plans as if they had been made by a rival, one plotting his downfall. My mother was losing her patience.

'We often run away from the very thing we know will make us happy,' Ben said and we smiled at this, at his efforts at playing the sage, but also because we thought ourselves victorious. *Look at us*, we were saying with those smiles, *we're not like everybody else.* We had grabbed what we wanted. I reached out across the island of my bed to feel the warmth of his skin: proof.

We could have built our relationship gradually, I knew that – done things properly, in the right order, not leapt immediately into the delight of our bodies, yet how easily we could have slipped through each other's fingers. He was my Knight of Cups and I was proud of myself for snatching hold of him, without question.

In the early hours, one chilly October morning, he said: 'You need to help me out with something…'

He was twisting a strand of my hair between his fingers, weaving a black line of it up and over his knuckles. I thought he was going to ask me to steal something else for that lab of his, the one burgeoning in the corner of the lower seniors classroom.

'What's the deal with the Eldest Girls?' he asked.

I rolled onto an elbow to face him, my hair pulling free of his grasp.

'That is what you call them, isn't it?' he went on. 'I've heard people say it, like it's a band name or –'

'It's just what they are. They're the eldest.'

'– like they're some kind of legend.'

I paused. His expression was strange in the moonlight, oddly transfixed. Dreamy.

Familiar.

I knew how the girls were talked about now. They'd come of age, they were women, beautiful, soon ripe for the picking. The idea of it withered me instantly, aged me a thousand years. Ben was not supposed to see them like that.

He was supposed to see them as I did – as pupils, girls. Just young girls.

'What do you mean, "the deal"?' I said, sitting up, wrapping a blanket tightly around myself. This wasn't a conversation to have naked.

'Well, you hauled one of them out of chapel on the first day of school,' he said. His speech was tentative now; he'd noticed the way I had stiffened.

'An isolated incident.' This was my teacher's voice. I didn't want to be using it, not there, in my bed. 'Jade-Marie is usually very well-behaved.'

'And the dark-haired one?'

'Britta?' I offered.

'Yes, Britta. I know her name. I just didn't know if you did.'

'Of course I know her name!' I was irritated at this too-swift ownership of St Rita's pupils, this unearned authority. They had been *my girls* the previous year – a pleasure to teach. The three of them were bright, without being exceptional – Anna the most academic, Britta the strident debater, Jade-Marie surpassing the others in creative tasks. I knew them far better than he ever could.

'What of Britta?' I asked.

'Well…' He pulled the sheet free of the end of the bed and covered himself too. 'Well, she… she…' He took a levelling breath. 'Look, I've become friendly with all three girls. They sought me out early on. They wanted to know what music I had on my laptop, what films I'd seen, mainland stuff. But this one time…'

I swallowed hard. Was I frightened of what he was about to say? Jealous? I was both.

'This one time she came to me alone.'

'Right,' I said. 'And?'

'Well, it began with our usual chitchat, music, fashion, that kind of thing... but then... then she put me in a really difficult position.'

The word 'position' conjured images I did not want to see. Lips pressed together under the gaze of St Rita. Bodies wrapped around one another, contorting, defiling a bed.

There had been a shift in the girls recently, since they had moved up to do their A Levels. I had witnessed it – their harder edge, their strange confidence. Still, I had no time for the rumours about them reclaiming the Sisters' Stones and meddling in Lark's pagan past – it meant nothing. I too had been intrigued by that part of our island's history when I was young. Girls can be silly. They push the boundaries of what is acceptable, then they snap right back. They grow up.

I was happy with my good memories of them, how they used to be. I was happy to look away.

I laughed anxiously. 'Is this the right time to be talking about them?' I said. 'I mean, am I the one you should be talking to? Don't you think you should take this to Mr Crane if it's a matter of –'

What was it a matter of? I was desperate to know and not know.

'You're right. You're right.' He swung his legs from the bed and started retrieving his clothes. There was a change in the breeze and the powdery tang of the smokehouse drifted in through the gaps in the window frame. It was a smell I had learnt not to notice until Ben brought it to my attention one night, shocked that I had managed to tune it out.

'What kind of difficult position?' I said. The dread was there now, the doubt; like the September rains, it had found its way in, there was no way of ignoring it.

He carried on dressing – jeans, t-shirt – his back to me. He had various combinations of casual clothes – a wardrobe like no other person on the island. He wore soft jogging trousers and sweaters with capacious hoods as he ran lengths of the harbour wall, falling to the grass above the East Bay to perform endless repetitions of soldierly exercises. Recently, the Cater brothers had joined him in this routine, disciples in a strange cult.

He stood, ready to go. We were still keeping our secret. Ben hadn't managed to extricate himself from the widow's lodgings yet; he had to be back before day broke, so she did not know his curfew had been broken.

'I'm sorry,' he said. 'I regret mentioning it. It was all very innocent, I'm sure.' This was *his* teacher's voice, the one used on parents – impassive, controlled, fake. He dragged a palm down his face to wipe this persona away. Then, he sat on the edge of the bed, placing a hand very deliberately on my arm. 'It's just that, when you said, that first time when we… Downstairs. When you let me into the kitchen, and we…' He forced out a sigh. 'You told me that… You said that you didn't know what you were doing, and I thought you meant… I thought you meant it metaphorically but… you literally didn't know what you were doing.'

The way he was looking at me, I wanted to die.

I knew from magazines what the mainland thought of purity; it had no value over there. Or rather it did, but bewilderingly, at the same time, it was something to be frightened of, considered weird. I had convinced myself that my innocence would pass beneath Ben's radar, but he'd found me out. I was a black-haired virgin when he met me, an aged, unwanted virgin. I was so embarrassed that I found myself biting back tears.

'Oh, god, no, Leah, don't!' He lifted a consoling hand. I snatched my face away. 'It wasn't a criticism, Leah. I wasn't saying that. It was great! You were great! I think this is all... great!'

I tried to move away, distance myself from his unbearable sympathy, from the awful juxtaposition he'd made between what we did in the moonlight and those girls, those young and beautiful girls. He gripped my arm.

'Listen to me,' he said. 'I only mentioned it because I wanted to know... I wanted to understand how on Lark, as girls, as women, you are taught about... Oh, god, I don't know how to say this...' He stopped, inhaled deeply. 'Look, when Britta came to see me alone, she wanted to talk about Eve.'

I looked up, confused.

'Eve Grogan? In my class?'

'No, Eve-Eve! The Eve! She wanted to talk to me about the part in the bible where God catches her naked with Adam and asks... Sorry, I'm not very good on the wording of –'

'*What is this* that *thou hast done?*'

'Yes, that! And Eve replies something about how –'

'*The serpent beguiled me, and I did eat.*'

'Exactly!'

This was fiery judgement in another form, God demonstrating precisely what he thought of my Knight of Cups, forcing me, sullied and naked, to deliver aloud verses that should have been closer to my heart. Ben smiled; my offering of these lines, my cooperation, was somehow reassuring to him. Embarrassment sank away, replaced by a resurfacing terror. Was I to brace myself for a terrible confession? Was the double-cross finally complete, never mine to engineer? I thought that I had climbed into bed with Ben, just Ben, but it seemed that the Eldest Girls been lying there all along.

He continued: 'Britta wanted to know, "with my mainland view of things"…' He mocked this appraisal of him, the idea that he should have some influence over us, but he knew that he had. It had been there in his playful talk at the Anchor. *Let's drag Lark kicking and screaming towards the shores of the twenty-first century!* Britta was no fool.

'She wanted to know if… And I just assumed this was some kind of trick, a test to make the new teacher uncomfortable, but if it was, she's a good actress, because…'

I didn't want to hear it, but I asked. 'And what was it? Her question?'

He looked down, a silent apology. He removed his hand from my arm.

'She wanted to know if… That's how it really happens?'

'How what happens?'

He spoke gently, his gaze on the mess we'd made of the sheets.

'How sex happens.'

Viola became a spy too, crouching low in the ferns, fronds spearing her cheeks.

They kept their distance, so as not to be seen, and so Michael would not be considered to be trespassing and invite down that terrible fury.

The mist obscured their view at times, drifting towards the cliff edge, but when the vapours parted, when the curtains opened, the scene took Viola's breath away. Those fat grey stones rising up from the meadow grass gave her a sense of dread – of the past, of the huge unfathomable distance of it stretching out behind them, of the people who had placed the stones there in the first place, using just their bare hands and rudimentary tools. It was as if these forebears had understood this future would exist – this exact one, with Michael and Viola in it – so had left them a monument as a message, as a warning.

Balancing on his haunches, grinning proudly, Michael had played the role of the smug tourist guide as he introduced Viola to the sight of the Eldest Girls and their ceremonials. Viola had been careful to keep her amazement to herself, lest Michael should think he held all the power.

'I *do* know one of them,' she'd whispered to him, lying nonchalantly. 'I got talking to the blonde one in the Provisions Store once.' The truth was, of course, that Michael had brought to her attention something wonderful, something life-changing.

Everything about the girls, ethereal in their white nightdresses, particular in their rituals, mesmerised Viola – confounded her too. When they lit matches, she presumed they would smoke a joint, cigarettes at least. That's what rebellious girls did on the mainland – they inhaled substances or swallowed them, numbed themselves, then loaned out their bodies to boys, piecemeal, in return for status. Instead these girls burned herbs, wafting the air with their scent. They lit candles in jamjars as they muttered indecipherable prayers. It was weird – the weirdest! – but could Viola say it was any stranger than drinking and smoking your way towards an unwanted fumble?

When the girls formed a circle, holding hands and speaking low, the real magic happened. They tipped back their heads, eyes closed to the last meagre helpings of sun, and the earth began to hum.

'Oh my god, can you hear that?' Viola gasped the first time it happened.

'Hear what?' said Michael.

'Doesn't matter,' she'd replied.

If he had to ask, he couldn't hear.

The ground pulsated, singing with something, speaking to Viola in the purest way. This was the true reason she was here on Lark, the vibrations said, so she could make friends with the Eldest Girls.

Such conviction was out of character for Viola; it had to be caused by a spell. When it came to friends, she never did the picking, was rarely first-picked. She was not distinct enough to be popular – or to be bullied, aside from the inevitable comments about her ginger hair. She occupied the social middle ground back home, forming alliances with those who trod the same path. The idea that this group of magical, disobedient creatures would welcome Viola Kendrick, an average human being, was implausible, yet still Viola knew it was her unavoidable fate.

She needed to start going to school, to St Rita's, be close to the girls. This became her goal. She would tell her mother that it was the best course of action for both of them; Deborah Kendrick's interest in teaching had already begun to slide away.

It had been a rule that Viola must complete all her school-work before walking Dot, but that boundary had shifted.

Viola's refrain every morning went: 'Do I have to do *all* of this?'

No longer was it met with a firm, routine, 'Yes!'

'I suppose we could finish up a little early,' her mother had taken to saying. Or, 'Maybe just one chapter is enough.'

With November approaching, Deborah Kendrick's replies had grown thorns. 'You're a big girl, Viola, you can work out for yourself what needs to be done!' She had started wearing a thick, home-knitted cardigan, with holes in sleeves and a missing middle button, every day and even to bed. She sat out on one of the broken wicker chairs on the veranda, surveying the land – 'Just plotting what to do next, Vee-Vee.' The tools leant against an outhouse, turning orange with rust. The cup of tea in her mother's hand went

106

cold before she remembered to drink it. Deborah Kendrick's only excursions were to chapel on Sunday – but straight home, no shift at the tea urn – and to the Provisions Store. And really, where else might she go?

It was Viola who was the wanderer.

She walked Dot whenever she wanted to now, the dog being hardy enough to stand it. Viola learnt when to trek across estate land and avoid the routines of the gamekeeper, how to hit the cobbles at an hour when a fishing boat came in so there was something to see. At the end of the afternoons, when the bell at St Rita's sounded, the echo of it reaching across the fields, she made for Cable's Wood to meet Michael, onwards through the pines to the irresistible Sisters' Stones.

Those hours she spent walking, Viola considered how to get what she wanted – to go to school – how to position it to her mother without sinking her any further. Deborah Kendrick was gradually slipping, slipping, going under once again.

Then, the island intervened.

Viola returned from a spying trip one afternoon to see the Land Rover parked in front of the farmstead, the Customs Officer leaning against the bonnet. He nodded at her as she passed with Dot, a hello that also felt like an apology. On the veranda, a man had pulled up one of the wicker chairs so he could sit close to her mother, who looked fixedly out at the horizon of trees, not at their visitor. Viola came slowly up the wooden steps, the guest turning in his seat, smiling, standing.

Mr Crane.

'Ah, here she is!' he said, as if talking to a much younger child. 'Viola Kendrick! We were just talking about you!'

Viola stalled on the top step. She felt Dot stall too, sensed the dog looking up at her, enquiringly, asking, *What now?*

'I wonder if you could tell me how you are doing with your home-schooling, Viola?' The man strode towards her, hitching up the belt of his trousers. When he reached her, he placed a hand on her shoulder, too gently. 'Do you think that you are getting all that you need from it?'

He leant in, bringing them eye to eye, this huge man and she a slight girl, a gesture that told Viola she could tell him the truth, that it would be all right; he would rescue her. And she needed rescuing, she wanted out. This was her way to win. But Viola could see her mother leaning forward in her chair, making herself seen behind the bulk of the man. She was giving Viola a slow, warning shake of her head, her mouth making an exaggerated shape – 'no'.

The vibrations at the Sisters' Stones had been strong, this message was stronger.

'It's going really well. Thank you,' Viola said, returning Mr Crane's gaze. Her lungs felt tight, squeezed empty of breath.

Mr Crane straightened up abruptly, his smile gone. He stared at her for a moment, the acknowledgement of the lie passing between them.

Above, a red kite squealed plaintively in its search for prey.

'That so,' he said, not kindly, but not unkindly either, and there were few pleasantries exchanged after that, before the man tendered his final goodbye.

He made his way down the stairs towards the Land Rover, and as he went, he ever so quickly and hardly at all pinched Viola on the cheek.

† Ordinary Time: Autumn 2017

The letter was sent home with the children.

It could also be found, folded in three, inside every hymn book at Saturday Mass. It took up the whole of pages four and five of the *Lark Chronicle*, a quarterly, stapled pamphlet, typeset by Miriam Calder. The *Chronicle*'s pastel-coloured pages rotated with the seasons, pink, green, blue, yellow, but the front cover illustration remained unchanged – a pen drawing of the harbour by a long-dead resident. The notices inside were unchanging too, only the dates shifted. So, this letter was something else.

```
Residents of Lark,
    Let it be clear: that our beloved island
was built upon superstition and mystique
is no excuse for a pursuit of the dark
arts. For those were shaky foundations
and dark times, before the light of Jesus
had touched us, bringing word that God
created all. He shaped Lark, let it yield
grass, herb and fruit, siting it in a
location that provides us, the fortunate
and chosen few, with splendid isolation.
```

We have maintained it well, upholding His word, keeping this island a place of beauty, free from so many of the sinful temptations that are permitted to flourish upon the mainland.

But we are not without struggle. Daily, we must battle with the devil, dousing his desires to engage us in conversation, enticing us as he does with his mystic cards, his vices and his rituals.

Be convinced: a dialogue with Satan is never entertainment and must not be justified as distraction or play. His symbols and his polished stones, his rhymes and his actions, will never bring protection, only harm.

Uncertainty about the future is understandable as we continue to welcome strangers to our beloved isle (just as the righteous welcomed Jesus, not knowing that He was the Son of God). The strangers come in person but also in words and images, in publications and in films, and in the shape of their physical items. The foundations of our principles will be tested by these strangers and their objects, but we must not hide from this challenge. We shall not shirk our responsibilities. We will face them and be strong.

If you require answers, turn only to Him, keeping with you the understanding that some things are not for us to know. He is your one true God, your one true guide in this life and the next.

Do not be swayed towards forgiveness or complicity, dear elders of the island. The burden is on you to reject this voodoo and necromancy, or else the sins of the fathers will be visited upon the generations that follow. Steer our young towards good. As Jesus tells us in the *Book of St Matthew*: Any person allowing a child to slip from the path of right-eousness may as well have a millstone hanged about their neck and be drowned in the depth of the sea.

I leave this to your morals.

Mr J. R. K. CRANE

The congregation extracted the letter from their hymn books and grew pale. The parents who had pulled the missive from their children's satchels the previous day, nodded at the familiar words, grim-lipped. Not a one of them was without sin. They had all told tales of giants, feared seven-yearly sacrifices to the sea or petted the black hair of a virgin for luck. Each person assumed the letter was meant for them alone and, at the same time, knew absolutely it was written about everybody else. Guilt was strong in this congregation, but indignation at the misdeeds of others was stronger.

111

Surely, the letter had the Eldest Girls in its crosshairs, designed to reprimand them in the most public way for their behaviour at the Sisters' Stones. Though, if this was so, it didn't seem to be having the intended effect. Britta, Anna and Jade-Marie sat together at mass, dressed demurely in chapel best, displaying no outward signs of mortification. Their mothers carried no extra visible burdens either. Did these women not know that the image of the millstone had been included for them, a reminder of the consequences of not keeping their offspring in check?

Perhaps not. Gossip on Lark spread rapidly but strategic-ally, and never near the subjects or their kin. It was quite possible that these women were ignorant of what their daughters were getting up to, and saw no reason to feel any disgrace.

Theories shifted.

Those with children in the senior classes reported how the hand of the lovely Miss Cedars had shook as she distributed the letters at the end of school. Some embellished this account to give her reddened eyes and a particular catch of the breath. It made sense. The word 'strangers' was mentioned no less than three times in the letter, and Leah Cedars had been seen entertaining that new teacher more frequently than was necessary. An excursion, just the two of them, to view the sunset from the west coast was extending hospitality too far. The woman's easy trust of the man was folly.

'Plus, she spends every Tuesday evening with Margaritte Carruthers.'

This became the main topic for discussion at October's pop-up hairdressing salon, Elizabeth Bishy, the doctor's wife, as usual, cutting the first turf.

'And when she's at Margaritte's house,' she went on, 'they close the curtains, so we don't see what *that* kind of woman gets up to.'

Hope Ainsley paused in her application of perming solution to the rows of tightly wound curlers on Elizabeth Bishy's head. Martha Signal, who was rereading the letter in the *Chronicle*, her hair an armadillo of highlighter foils, looked up aghast.

'Are you saying that... ?'

Elizabeth nodded firmly and mouthed the word, so she might not be blamed for raising something from the island's history considered long dead – *witchcraft*.

Quietly, knots made from rowan twigs went up in the corner of doorframes. Old odd shoes poked out of spare gaps in rafters. Front paths were sprinkled with salt, ostensibly for the prevention of slugs, an explanation that did not account for the collection of stones placed there too, ones selected from the accessible edges of the East Bay specifically for the holes in their middle – hag stones, whittled by the action of the sea.

'They're pretty and unusual,' said the women who threaded them onto ribbon and scraps or garden string and hung them from fence posts and railings. 'We just like the way they look.'

These same women fell in love again with their arrowhead brooches, wearing them prominently on sweaters and jacket lapels. They told young children, more forcefully than before, to smash a hole in the bottom of the shell when they'd finished their boiled eggs: 'So that the remains can't be used as a boat.'

The children were bemused. Who could make themselves small enough to make a vessel of an eggshell? The women would not say. If you were to talk of who, that was an admission that they existed, that your own trust was being placed in talismans and rituals and that you, in your bid to ward it off, were engaging in black magic yourself.

Theories shifted once more.

The gunsight moved gently across, onto the stranger himself. How had they not let themselves see it, that the new teacher's mastery of science was a cover for darker arts? In his crate of equipment from the mainland, Benjamin Hailey had brought pestle and mortar, glass globes, a cauldron, ingredients for potions. The man had stolen a canister of gas and showed no aversion to making fire. These were the 'objects' spoken of in Jacob Crane's letter, objects to be feared and refused.

Talk turned quickly to the stranger's likely dismissal. Though he could be released from his teaching post, there would be no means of ejecting him from the island until the boats restarted in April. Did that prison room still exist up at the Big House? some enquired. It was time, they agreed, the situation grave enough, that someone alerted the Earl. Yet Mr Crane, keeper of the children's morals, keeper of the principles of the whole population, seemed intent on rehabilitation, not punishment. His letter in their hymn books had been nothing but a shrewd method of recruiting an island of watchful eyes, a righteous army to show their wayward newcomer the right path.

Mr Crane had not admitted this in so many words, of course; he had kept his counsel on who was the true target of his explosive epistle. He would only say that 'a soul knows its own stain', and that those who have transgressed should 'bring forth their offering of turtledoves'. But it could be made to add up. The lovely Miss Cedars and the impression-able Eldest Girls were not perpetrators; they were victims. This was not the island's occult history repeating itself; this was a virus from the mainland.

Britta, Anna and Jade-Marie had recently been taken under the new teacher's wing. The girls had been convinced – by Miss French, it was said – to choose a science as one of their A-Level options, to make the most of Mr Hailey's arrival at the school. On Fridays from October, Dellie Leven taught the younger seniors while Mr Hailey gave the girls some 'practical scientific experience' – the phrasing of the gossipers (suggestive emphasis placed on the word *practical*).

Wary of the mathematical demands of chemistry and physics, the girls had opted for biology, the study of nature, life and human beings. In that classroom, that laboratory, under the tutelage of Mr Hailey, the girls wore white jackets and plastic goggles as they ground down gritty substances in the aforementioned mortar, the smell of rotting fruit – or nail varnish, perhaps – drifting into the corridor. Other times they spilled India ink onto thin slivers of glass, cooing as they peered at them through the lens of a microscope.

Their stories matched up when asked what they were doing –

'We're marking out the boundaries of cells,' they said.

Or 'We're using chromatography to distinguish the pigments within leaves.'

– but when their experiments took them to the grave-yard, the outcomes were clearly less scientific.

They squatted amongst the tombs in the drizzle, the teacher and the girls, conferring in the long grass, attracting

115

the attention of the trio of nuns who lived in the stone enclave beyond. In a break from prayer and from the tending of the island's green vegetables in their convent plots, the sisters watched these goings-on, initially from the shelter of the cloisters, one hand to their white headdresses so they might not lose them to the wind.

According to the sisters, Mr Hailey and the Eldest Girls were 'searching for Chuggy Pigs' or should they say 'Monkey Peas', for that was what the stranger had named them, making the girls whoop with laughter. For the purposes of the lesson, they were to write down *woodlice*, followed by the creature's taxonomy – *Oniscidea* of the order *Isopods* within the class *Malacostraca*. The nuns admitted to joining in with the hunt for these little armoured beasts, lifting rocks and splitting tufts of grass, Mr Hailey adept at creating enthusiasm for the task.

It wasn't insects they were searching for, he explained, but crustacea, woodlice belonging to the same taxon as lobsters or crabs. An old butter tub was populated with the animals, then the girls set about marking each one of them with a dot of paint, before releasing them again among the tombstones.

They came back a week later, Mr Hailey and the Eldest Girls, their conversation flowing effortlessly, more intimate now, something that could be deduced very easily, even from a distance, by the movement of their bodies and the gestures of their hands. They repeated the exercise – searching for woodlice and placing them in the butter tub – and were then given an equation to work out. (They hadn't managed to escape mathematics entirely.) Take the number of animals from the first search, multiply it by the number of animals found during the second search, and then divide by the number of animals in the second sample that were marked by a dot of paint. This, the stranger explained, was the Lincoln Index.

But something had gone wrong. None of the second sample of woodlice bore the white spot, and the teacher was foxed. Had the paint he'd provided – non-toxic so as not to cause harm – washed off in the island's insistent rains? One of the nuns, Sister Sarah, suggested that woodlice on Lark might be, unexpectedly, more nomadic than mainland woodlice and didn't like to stay in one place for as long as a week. No one was convinced and the discussions continued. Britta Sayers, usually the most determined contributor in these kinds of situations, remained silent to the last. Only when all other possibilities were exhausted, did she offer up her conclusion, as if it had been *the* conclusion all along, no further argument required.

'The marks protect them,' she said.

The teacher urged Britta to go on.

'By marking them like we did, we stopped them from being captured again.' Britta's face took on a beatific glaze.

'I don't see how that would ever work,' said Sister Clare, folding her arms.

'Well, it's like the runes, isn't it, Sister?'

'I beg your pardon!' exclaimed Sister Agnes, stepping forward.

But Britta was not to be squashed. 'It's like the mark of Algiz for healing, Eihwaz for protection, Teiwaz for strength.'

Sister Agnes' face went as purple as the aubergines she cultivated in the convent greenhouses.

Still, Britta persisted. 'It's like the cross that stands at the end of the jetty, to stop our fishermen from dying.'

The holy sister clutched the small wooden crucifix, strung with beads around her neck, Britta seizing upon the action:

'Like what you're wearing now!'

This conversation might have been lost and forgotten, dismissed as a young girl sent giddy by the novelty of a lesson outdoors, if the three Eldest Girls hadn't come to school the following week with matching bandages on their left wrists. There was the smell of rubbing alcohol about them.

Mr Crane had not been in school that morning to demand they remove these non-regulation affectations, and Mrs Leven who stood in his place, was always one to avoid confrontation. It was the lovely Miss Cedars who challenged the girls in the canteen, instructing them to remove the bandages at once. Jaws that had been working away at beef patties and cabbage, slowed and stilled. Every pupil's gaze settled on the girls lined up before the hot plate.

The handsome *coycrock* teacher, his back to the scene, was one of the last to notice the stand-off. He rose abruptly, chair legs squealing, his mouth open, ready to protest, but Miss Cedars stopped him with an icy stare.

She turned her attention back to the girls.

'Come on!' said the once nice, polite teacher, who had grown stricter of late, shorter in wick. 'Take the bandages off! Unless you've really hurt yourselves. You've not really hurt yourselves, have you?'

The Eldest Girls shrugged, unsure, and unravelled the white gauze, revealing the skin beneath, pinpricked and bloodied.

'What is this?' asked Miss Cedars, appalled.

On Jade-Marie's inside wrist was a crude etching of a tree; on Anna's skin, a skewed *Z*; and on Britta's, an upward arrow.

India-ink tattoos.

'Algiz for healing,' said Britta, 'Eihwaz for protection and Teiwaz for the strength of a warrior.'

All went quiet. Miss Cedars was lost for a response. She had not absorbed Britta's explanation, this elucidation on the runes. Instead she had watched how the girl held Mr Hailey's gaze as she answered; how the new teacher dropped his chin guiltily to his chest.

◉ The Book of Leah

I drew the curtains and turned off the lights. When I heard the click of the rear gate, I hurried upstairs and hid beneath the blankets.

I can't see you, I told myself. Or rather, I do see you. I see you so much better than before.

'Leah! Leah!'

He wouldn't stop calling; he was going to wake the neighbours. I had to go downstairs and open the door – just a crack, let in a small breath of cold air.

'You locked it!' he said, smiling, thinking it a silly mistake.

'Go away,' I replied.

'Are you okay?'

'Just go away.'

These were the only words I could manage.

'Is this about … Is this about today, with the girls?'

I said nothing.

'Because I can explain what that was. It isn't what you –'

I shut the door, latched it again and stood with my back against it.

'Leah!' he called gently. 'Leah?'

I could hear him sigh and shuffle, lingering, trying to work out the right tenor of comeback. Then the rear gate clicked, marking his retreat.

I stayed behind the door for a long time – the crown of my head against the glass, my palms against the painted wood. How inevitable this had all been. From the moment he mentioned Britta Sayers' difficult question, my doubt had grown stronger and stronger, until it was bigger than the joy of his presence, more persuasive than any prospect of true love.

I told myself I was lucky. He was Hades and I was Persephone; it was a mercy to be free from the underworld before any real damage was done.

I returned to my Demeter, to the bosom of my family.

All Hallows' Eve, I walked up through the estate to the gamekeeper's lodge where my parents lived, past the furthest reaching walls of the Big House, along the winding path there, the bricks beneath my soles slimy with moss. The light hadn't fallen completely and labouring continued in the fields; a trio of figures moving across the land. The fog had been thin that day; they had to make the most of the conditions. October 31st was supposed to mark the end of harvest, but there was still work to be done. The date didn't mark the end of summer either. That had vanished long ago.

I carried a bottle of wine, gripped tightly by the neck – an expensive purchase, in payment and in effort. I'd dropped the name of both my father and the Father in the Provisions Store to secure it. Wasn't I duty-bound to honour them both with a good bottle on this most holy of nights? Wouldn't it be unchristian to refuse me?

Rhoda Sayers, cow-eyed and heavy-jowled, was unimpressed. The good stuff was to be held over for Christmas rations, she said, no exceptions, no matter who you were. I knew these rules, but winning against the woman suddenly became important.

'I think you owe me this,' I said quietly, in all reasonableness.

She folded her arms. 'How's that?'

'Sparing your Britta punishment for those pagan tattoos.'

We locked eyes.

'That's not what she said,' said the woman.

I floundered. 'Huh?'

I had let the girls' actions go, not followed them up. I was too engrossed in my own error of judgement, my own heartache. Mr Crane would have seen what they'd done, those scars scabbing at their wrists. Perhaps he meted out a penalty later.

'So, they were punished?'

It wasn't enough of a question to prompt Rhoda to respond.

'What did Britta say?' I stumbled on.

Rhoda shook her head, disapproving of my fragile grasp of the situation, but she slid the bottle of wine across the counter towards me.

'Take it,' she said, claiming victory in this surrender. Then she turned away, sighing as she wrote my purchase in her ledger.

I didn't want it anymore, the wine, my thirty pieces of silver. I could see what I was doing – challenging the mother in lieu of the daughter, a girl who had been through enough already, manipulated and led astray by our charming newcomer, just as I had.

Sister Agnes' account of Ben's graveyard lessons had spread; we all knew where the idea for the tattoos had come from. We all knew that he was the only person on the island with stashes of India ink. I should have been comforting Rhoda in the Provisions Store that evening, assuring her that no one was acting friendly with Mr Hailey in the staff room anymore. I should have apologised for the polite smiles that we hid behind, the way we awkwardly circled questions, not daring to ask. Why was Benjamin Hailey still teaching? Why did Mr Crane still pat him on the back when they passed each other in the corridor?

Instead, I left the store with a muttered thank-you, a gutless one.

I passed the estate's stone well on the walk uphill to my parents' place, a familiar structure, but that evening it delivered me a lost memory. Not one I'd forgotten as such, rather a memory I had set aside – an object placed on a high shelf to be brought down when its usefulness was realised.

There were stories attached to the well. My father delighted in telling me that gold lay in its dark, unfathomable depths, along with diamond rings, priceless art and, most hauntingly to the younger me, sacrificial teddy bears. The well would grant you absolute truth on a matter of your asking in return for something you held dear. When my brother, Paul, took over these stories (the gift of the gab bypassing me, the older child, and travelling down the male line), they became more sinister. There were ancient bones down there, he told me, and some not so ancient as you'd expect. There were the remains of prized cattle too, beloved wives and – he knew when to hold a pause – the bodies of favourite children.

I understood his inference, the moral of this parable.

'I'm not the favourite,' I snapped back.

'Yes, you are,' he replied levelly, no invitation to argue; he was stating a fact. 'Mum and Dad are making sure everything works out all right for you.'

He was ten then. I'd have been sixteen.

I leaned over the well's edge and peered down into the dripping dark. With my adult eyes, I still expected to see the flash of gold or a white splinter of bone. I wondered what I could throw into the depths so that I might know the absolute truth about Ben, about his relationship with the Eldest Girls. Had I been right, I would ask, to cut him off, not to let him explain? But that would mean admitting that I still held him dear, despite all efforts not to. Would I have to throw Ben to his death, only to discover his innocence?

The last stretch of the journey to my parents' house was a steep incline, scented by the zest of pine needles, sycamore keys pirouetting around me. In books, adults returning to a childhood home after many years become overwhelmed by great Proustian rushes of emotion at the things they see and smell and hear, faded memories leaping vividly alive. It occurred to me then, as if I had just thrown something precious into the well to receive this realisation, that I would never really know how that felt. Not the true extent. I would never experience the way a long absence can remould a place, make it warmer, kinder, more palatable.

I passed through the front gate and walked down the side of the lodge to my parents' back door, bracing myself for my mother's greeting.

The tone of it came as expected: 'Oh, here she is, gracing us with her presence! I swear, Leah Cedars, that you are worse than a flea to catch.'

I stepped across the threshold, offering up my excuses – the latest rules from the mainland on testing, along with the implementation of the new GCSE grading system meant my workload was immense, the paperwork never-ending. I kept talking in this way until the perverse urge to confess deserted me. *I have been spending almost every evening with the stranger, Mum. I thought that I loved him but it seems he's not the sort of person I should love, a man who leads young girls to the devil.*

Then I might have spoken more truths. *Since Paul went, since you made no effort to stop him, this feels like no home at all.*

I divulged nothing, having no wish to burden her or compromise her position in Lark's hierarchy. I perched on one of the stools at the kitchen island – a kitchen that was the envy of all the women for its shiny white cupboards and flecked marble surfaces – and I watched her chop vegetables and baste a chicken too big for the three of us, especially on this evening that was supposed to involve a fast.

In front of me, she placed a bowl of olives, something she had taken to ordering in large jars when the ships were running, and I picked at them as she embarked on an anec- dote about the Earl.

'They thought that he'd died at the weekend,' she said, eliciting the gasp from me that she so clearly wanted. He may have been an invisible ruler, the Earl, a disenfranchised one, at his own discretion, leaving Lark's deciding to the Council, but the idea of him dead was terrifying. The island would be a ship without a captain, without a figurehead, without a rudder.

The climax of my mother's story had Hannah Pass, leader of the Earl's diminishing housekeeping team and mother of Abigail, one of my Fourth Years, breaking into his locked bedroom to see if he was still breathing. The anti-climax: he was – still breathing, that is. He had merely taken to his bed for a few days, as was his way. The worst of it was that the 'gazunder' – the chamber pot – was full to overflowing.

My mother moved on to updates of the latest movements of Elizabeth Bishy and Diana Crane, Martha Signal and Eleanor Springer. Her sweetly worded aspersions on these women, her friends, were not dissimilar to those made about her in return – conversations that I was not supposed to overhear.

'I wouldn't trade my kitchen for Susannah Cedars' "spaceship" for all the riches of Abraham.'

'And isn't that exactly what it cost her to have it sent over?'

'Imagine how it shows up the muck!'

That was how I knew for sure my mother was envied.

'You'll be going to the Anchor later for the celebrations, will you?' Mum asked, lifting the cork out the bottle, not waiting for Dad. There was a directness to her speech that I had not inherited, nor learnt through imitation. We looked alike; I could see my future in the way her lips had thinned and how the skin between her eyes furrowed. I knew my black hair would give way to strands of silver. But I doubted I would ever own that voice.

'I won't be, no.' I pushed another pitted olive into my cheek, enjoying the sensation of its flesh giving way between my teeth.

'It's open to women tonight,' she went on, telling me what I already knew, 'even though it's a weeknight.' She poured two very generous glasses of wine. 'I think you should go and find out where that handsome teacher is hiding himself.'

I stopped chewing and stared at her.

What handsome teacher? was the reply that rose childishly to my lips. What smashed window? What muddy footprints in the living room?

I took a large mouthful of wine and washed down the olive. I still wasn't sure if they were truly pleasant things to eat.

'I see him every day of the week at school,' I said with a tight smile. 'I think that's quite enough, considering the current situation.'

'Such a shame,' she said.

'Yes,' I replied cautiously; her inflection was not that of a woman appalled at a stranger's behaviour. Quite the opposite.

'He seemed so perfect,' she added wistfully, grasping my hand on the cool of the countertop. I flushed hot and gulped more wine. 'A fella from the mainland,' she went on, squeezing my hand tighter, beseeching me with shining eyes. 'He might have broadened your horizons a little.'

I had no idea how to respond.

The island was against Ben, thought him in conversation with the devil – so my mother must think this also. For all her gentle slanders of Diana Crane, she and her husband were important allies of my parents; together they sat on the Council. Or rather, my father and Jacob did; Diana and my mother brewed the tea and made the sandwiches.

127

The letter Mr Crane had written was aimed at Ben and the girls, wasn't it?

Wasn't it?

Yet Ben was still teaching. Mr Crane still patted him on the back when they passed in the corridor. I should have found the courage to ask my mother what was going on, but my father opened the back door at that moment, making her hand fly from mine, sending her back towards the hob. I was startled at the sight of Dad; the whiteness of his beard and his stoop that had become, all of a sudden, more pronounced.

'Will you come in for some dinner, Luke?' called my mother to my dad's young apprentice. Luke Signal loitered outside on the hard-standing, waiting for the formality of an invitation. He nodded at me, sheepish, as he stepped inside. I'd taught Luke for his GCSEs just three years earlier, my first official class when newly qualified, aged twenty-four. I had reprimanded him for the way he tied his tie, the grubbiness of his homework, his difficulty with spelling. His younger brother, Michael, almost sixteen, was in my current class, and always raised his hand, an answer ready. He was a real show-off. It seemed impossible that the two boys were related.

'You should fill your belly, Luke,' muttered my father as they wrestled free of their boots and shook off their wax jackets, Luke's two sizes too large for his wiry frame. 'You'll need it for our night ahead on the lamp.'

'Ah, Peter, no!' My mother threw down her tea towel and was off. Did my father not remember that he was supposed to be retiring? What on earth was he doing still volunteering for evening work? She would brook no argument about the severity of the fox infestation, because there was Mary, there was Luke now, both trained up to take over the night-time lamping.

At the end of her speech, my mother's voice became tender. 'I just want to spend more time with you, Peter,' she said.

When only family were present, she would go on to suggest a holiday, a cruise or a visit to Paul on the main-land. When she'd first proposed these things, I'd assumed them a provocation. *Look how angry I am, Peter! Listen to what blasphemous things you have me suggesting!* But I began to wonder, after the way she'd grasped my hand that evening, if she truly meant to go.

Four places were laid at the table. As was the custom on All Hallows' Eve, one setting was for the most recently departed family member – in this case, my paternal grand-father, John, whose heart had given up on him four years previously. This was precisely the phrase my mother used – 'his heart gave up on him' – and I was beginning to understand the expression viscerally. I couldn't shake the sensation that our extra setting was not for Grandpa John, but for my brother, Paul, or for a handsome teacher maybe – two people who had not died but, in their different ways, had slipped through my fingers.

An extra place was found for Luke, so the untouched knife and fork could remain, and my father asked him to say grace. I watched Luke's Adam's apple ride his throat at the prospect. He was neither a master of words nor memory in my class-room, though I'd heard he'd developed a particular swagger lately, holding court at the Anchor if he had a story to tell. His name was used as a reliable witness in gossip about the

Eldest Girls and I imagined that he had an eye on one of them. His classmates Bernadette Dean and Tom Ainsley had left the island as soon as their exams were done and married on the mainland. Luke would need to look to the younger girls, to Britta, Anna or Jade-Marie. Perhaps they thought him appealing in return. He was nineteen, aspirational, had the same black hair as his fifteen-year-old brother. Both brothers were tall, the height difference barely noticeable, despite their age gap, though Michael carried more meat on his bones. Luke was the one with the sculpted cheekbones and jaw. There was a not-unattractive dirtiness to his skin that I imagined would remain no matter how hot the bath.

Luke launched into a stuttering, 'Be present at our table, Lord …' and we all closed our eyes and clasped our hands. Amens done, enquiries were made as to the health of Luke's mother and father. Dad carved the chicken and Mum piled Luke's plate too high with vegetables. This would be discussed in the Provisions Store the following day: how Susannah Cedars served up food like it was going out of fashion, as if rationing didn't apply to her; how my father probably pinched what he fancied straight from the allotments.

'Hold the wine for me and the boy,' said Dad, putting a hand over Luke's glass as my mother wielded the bottle. 'We need a steady hand for the rifle.'

In defiance, she filled my glass to the rim, hers too. I watched Luke take this in, saw its onward prattling journey. *The Cedars women are true sots. You wouldn't think it, but they are.*

'And what's new with you, Master Luke?' asked my mother, spreading a napkin over her lap. 'Is the boarding house still suiting you? Not missing your mother's cooking? I bet she's disappointed you're not with her tonight.'

My mother was seeking ammunition of her own – *Martha Signal's dinners are so bad, even her own son left home to escape them!* – but the boy came back with: 'That stranger's moved in.'

There was the shortest, loudest silence. Luke continued to fork food into his mouth. My mother's eyes flitted to me, then quickly away again.

I told him not to, I might have said to her if the circumstances had been different. I told him to stick with his lodgings with the widow, wait it out, see what else might come up.

'Oh, that's no good.' My mother's voice was too unctuous to be sincere, and my father could hear it. He looked to his wife, then to me.

I took a large gulp of wine.

'Esther Deezer threw him out,' Luke went on, oblivious to the tension, his focus on the heaping of his next forkful. 'Abe Powell said someone ought take him in.'

'Well, you boys are bound to set him on the right track, aren't you?' said my mother gaily.

My father grunted and turned to me. 'You're to steer clear of him, Leah, you hear me? He's worked his way into Jacob Crane's pocket and...' He took a mouthful of food as if plugging the barrel of a gun.

Luke stopped shovelling, understanding well the pattern of Peter Cedars' moods – how to recognise the signs of a coming storm.

My father swallowed. 'He's just not to be trusted, all right?'

We ate without talking, my mother and I taking great slugs of wine, until, fortified by alcohol, my mother decided to return to the subject.

'The man made a momentary stumble,' she said. 'That's all it'll be, I'm sure.'

'"Momentary stumble"?' My father threw down his cutlery. Luke visibly jumped.

'Well, we must have hope in him changing his ways, mustn't we, Peter?' my mother persisted. 'Because... Because...' Her eyes went upwards in search of scripture.

My mind worked faster.

If we confess our sins, He is faithful and just to forgive us our sins, and to cleanse us from all unrighteousness.

My father was silenced by the quotation, but not satisfied.

'Aren't you hungry, Leah?' he said.

I had pulled apart a potato and eaten just a small morsel of chicken.

'I had too many olives,' I said. 'Before. And –' The words left my mouth before I knew what I was doing '– now I have to go.' I drained my glass and stood.

'Where?' demanded my father.

'The Anchor. I promised Ruth and Cat I would see them there.'

My mother twitched at the lie but tamped down her impulse to call it out.

'Sit down,' said my father.

'I can't, Dad. Sorry.'

'Your mother has cooked. You will stay and eat,'

Luke's eyes went wide at this spectacle, his former teacher being scolded like a child.

'Let her go, Peter,' said my mum, forcing a laugh for Luke's sake. 'She's a grown woman; she can do what she likes.'

My father looked up at me, as if what my mother had said was news to him, as if the last twelve years had passed him by and he still expected to see a fifteen-year-old girl standing there. I couldn't bear it, that feeling of being small under his gaze, so vulnerable. I left the table and put on my coat.

'You have a lovely time!' my mother called after me, a cue for those who remained to be cheerful now. 'You young ones,' I heard her say to Luke, as I opened the door, 'you have so much energy, you make me green for it!'

I stumbled back down through the estate, past the syca-more and the pine, sliding on catkins, tripping on the brick path. The Cedars women are not sots at all. They practise too little with the stuff; it knocks them unsteady.

I went to the Anchor because I'd told my parents that was where I was going, because it's wrong to tell a lie. I met Ruth and Cat; I was true to my word. They expressed surprise to see me there. Was I really up for such silliness when we all had to be bright-eyed for school the next day? I shrugged away their assumptions, feigned offence at the idea that I would not be in the market for fun.

I was wary though, of being in that bar room. If Ben showed up, I would be forced to have the conversation that I had closed my kitchen door upon – explain why I believed, without question, he was doing something terrible with those girls. He wasn't there, of course. He was supposed to be doing penance and drinking in public would never do.

133

I felt no such restrictions on my own behaviour. The wine had relaxed me. Standing up to my father had filled me with a strange sense of rebellion. I tipped back every glass of rum that was brought to the table, and time slipped. I found myself joining in with the dooking for apples hanging from the beams. Ruth laughed uproariously as I stumbled towards her, a mangled fruit gripped in my teeth.

'You look like a suckling pig,' someone was saying, and I looked down to see that apple juice stained the front of my blouse, turning it transparent.

Then, Saul Cooper's whiskery face was close to mine, yet there was none of the revulsion I usually felt when in proximity to the man. I was mesmerised by the way the hair on his head had prematurely greyed, the centre of his beard too, but not his eyebrows, nor the remainder of his facial hair; that was all still darkest Larkian black. I think I might have licked a thumb and stroked one of his eyebrows into place, then joked about how his appearance seemed different while I was under the influence of rum.

'Hallelujah, it's a miracle on earth!' I cried at this discovery and Saul was not offended, nor rude in return. He laughed and pulled me close in a friendly way, urging me to shush so I didn't get into trouble for using the Lord's words in vain. The rest of our exchange is hazy, but I was definitely the one who suggested we go outside because the bar was too full, too hot. Then, when the cold wind hit the dampness of my blouse, I suggested we go inside the Customs House for blankets.

The record skips again, and the next thing I know we are on the floor of the front office of the Customs House. I am naked, on top of Saul; he is hard inside of me. I am reaching down and fingering myself, bucking towards a shuddering climax, and he looks afraid, says, 'What are you doing?'

Another skip. He is reaching up for me, sucking on one of my breasts. The blankets we've laid on the floor are bunched together, not enough to stop our backs and knees from skinning as we grind against one another. I kiss him as violently as I'd seized that apple, biting at his lip and drawing blood. He pushes me over, flips himself on top of me, finishes what we've started, pulling free with a groan and spilling himself across the wooden floorboards.

'That will leave a stain,' I have the wherewithal to say.

Then, I am on my sofa, dressed, and I have woken breathlessly, my head hammering. I was dreaming of dragonflies, iridescent and beautiful, but trapped, banging themselves hopelessly against the glass of my kitchen window. A hopeful thought arrives: all that went before was just part of this same nightmare. Then I feel the stickiness between my thighs, the pain pulsing from the raw skin on my knees.

I did all that I did.

I realise I could have left this out, not mentioned what happened that night. But if we confess our sins, *He is faithful and just to forgive us our sins, and to cleanse us from all unrighteousness.*

FRIDAY THE 13TH – APRIL 2018

Viola Kendrick does not run very far. How can she? In every direction, there is nothing but sea.

Hiding is the only option, so she slots herself into the stone arch in the Ornamental Gardens, pulling up her feet – and Dot – onto the recessed bench. She rests her back against the nubby surface, catching her breath. Shells – common cockles, blunt gapers, periwinkles – have been pressed into the render of the arch in patterns. Small red spiders run dizzy paths across these undulations.

She cannot be entirely certain who is coming for her, or from which direction they will arrive, but Viola knows that when they reach her, it will not be good. She strokes Dot, almost violently, for reassurance, the dog's eyes stretching wide with this backward force. Then she decides to pray – proper hands-together, eyes-closed, chin-to-the-sky praying.

Dear God, if you haven't given up on me completely, please make Michael Signal come around that corner and...

She needs a friend. Desperately. She needs Michael's intrusive, encyclopaedic knowledge. She needs his help to find a way out.

She squeezes her eyes tighter still, imagining the boy into being, scuffing along the smooth path of the gardens in his heavy grey duffel coat, satchel banging against his hip.

She pictures herself making room for him on the bench, their fingernails digging around a shell each as they talk, believing they can pop one of those stuck-fast periwinkles free.

Who is coming to question Viola about the body at the stones?

What should Viola say when they find her?

Michael always has an answer, to everything.

'So, if we're expecting the boss of the island,' Viola would say, kicking things off, 'that'll be Mr Crane, right? It's a no-brainer.'

'Officially, that would be the Earl,' Michael would reply, not able to resist an opportunity to contradict her. 'The Earl is the official "boss of the island" as you like to put it.'

'So, the Earl's coming?'

'Goodness, no! The Earl's a recluse. What kind of recluse nips out of the house to handle a murder enquiry?'

She would be the grown-up, not retaliate.

'Then, who's next?'

'In line for the Earldom? His young wife, the Countess, but she left Lark years ago and took their kids with her so –'

'I mean, who's next in charge!'

That she cannot even have a make-believe conversation with Michael without squabbling comes as no surprise.

'Then you're back to Mr Crane.'

'But it won't be him, will it? Saul wouldn't do that, would he?'

'He'll have to. He'll have to inform the Council. All of them.' Michael would count them off, teacher-like, on his fingers. 'Dr Bishy, Father Daniel, Abe Powell, Jed Springer, Robert Signal and... I was going to say Peter Cedars.'

They would both wince. Poor Peter Cedars.

'What do I say to them, Michael?' she'd ask, in all earnestness, in true anguish, once their bickering and one-upmanship was done. 'What on earth do I say?'

Viola keeps her eyes tight shut for a last burst of prayer, as the island wakes up around her, a sluggish beast rearing its head. From the harbour below there is the crank and clatter of hands on deck, the gentle putter of an outboard motor.

Please God, make him appear... Now!

She opens her eyes, expecting magic, believing she is capable of it.

But Michael is not there.

🌿 NOVEMBER 2017

Once again, Viola returned from her walk to find a Land Rover parked in front of the farmstead – a different one, even more ancient than the vehicle driven by the Customs Officer. It had a dirty tarpaulin hood stretched across its open back.

Viola's mother was not in her usual chair on the veranda, the sliding temperatures no bar to her habit of sitting outside. She had found a moth-eaten sheepskin coat, left behind in one of the bedroom wardrobes, and wrapped herself in that. A scarf twisted around her unwashed hair completed the look: a grandmother from a fairy tale.

The vacant veranda and the unfamiliar truck forced a sour uneasiness into Viola's throat. She picked up her step towards the house.

'Don't you be going in there!'

The gruff voice made her jump, skid to a stop.

The Land Rover, parked in the shadows of the trees, had appeared empty, but as Viola wheeled around, twisting herself in Dot's lead, she saw the gamekeeper, his white beard framed by the window of the cab. Last time they'd met, he had threatened trouble. Viola's disquiet began to rise.

'Why not?' she said. 'Why shouldn't I?'

'Because the doctor's in there looking after her, isn't he?'

His words tipped her into panic. Viola sprinted for the wooden steps, taking them two at a time, exploding through the front door, preparing herself for how her mother might have tried to do it. Their stash of paracetamol? Surely not a knife?

But in the kitchen, her mother was sitting upright, intact, rebuttoning her blouse, with no sign of disaster. At least, not the disaster Viola had anticipated. A barrel of a man in a formal navy suit tossed his stethoscope to the table, letting it snake across the top of Viola's school books, then he leant in to finger the glands at Deborah Kendrick's neck.

'What's going on? Are you sick?' Viola demanded from the doorway, the adrenalin making her splutter.

Dot, picking up on the mood, gave a sharp, strangled yip.

The doctor turned, assessing Viola from behind his circular spectacles, a brief judgement, before going back to Deborah to boom out his conclusion.

'There's absolutely nothing wrong with you.'

'But –'

Her mother was cut off by a short jeer of objection from the doctor. He retreated into the cushions of his chin, raising a solid finger. 'There is absolutely no reason, Mrs Kendrick, why you shouldn't be out there. In fact, some fresh air and hard work might do you good.'

'But on my GP records,' Deborah continued meekly, 'you'll see that I've been prone to iron deficiencies and –'

'I doubt it!' The man laughed. He faced Viola now to deliver his final dismissal of her mother. 'The greatest lesson I learnt from my training on the mainland was that doctors there go looking for problems where there are none. Live your life, Mrs Kendrick, that's my advice. First, because worry is the biggest killer, and secondly, because Lark does not suffer malingerers. Now!' He angled a single eye to pin down Viola. 'Word has reached me, Miss Kendrick, that you are also claiming a sickness that is keeping you from your island duties?'

Viola's mouth fell open.

'One that is,' the man continued, 'keeping you from school?'

'She *is* at school.' Deborah Kendrick spoke more forcefully for Viola than she had for herself. '*This* is her school.' They all looked to the papers and clutter spread across the battered kitchen table. The doctor extracted his stethoscope from the chaotic scene, winding up its tail and posting it into the stretched-wide jaws of his leather bag.

'Your mother has been given a clean bill of health.' He spoke as if Deborah Kendrick were no longer there; his business now only with Viola. 'But you, young lady, have a consultation outstanding.'

'What for?' Her mother rose from her seat, inserting herself into the exchange, her voice combative, frightening to Viola.

The man turned to face his challenger, retaliating with condescension. 'All young girls on the island are given a routine check-up when they come of age, Mrs Kendrick. It is our civil duty to them.'

'Oh, yeah?' she replied. Viola watched her mother grip the thick edge of the kitchen table to still her shaking hands. 'And what about the boys, then?'

The doctor held Deborah's gaze. Viola was sure she saw her mother's mouth twitch into the beginnings of a triumphant smile, and willed for it not to come, in case it should provoke a violence.

'The boys too,' the doctor said flatly, eventually.

Deborah's face fell. The tension was released – though no one was satisfied. He made for the door.

'My surgery is on the south elevation,' he told Viola coolly, on his way out. 'You'll come and see me there, tomorrow, in the afternoon, four-thirty.'

Viola automatically nodded.

'You will not,' her mother instructed, once the Land Rover had swung across the yard and growled away down the track.

'Why not?'

Her mother ascended the stairs for a nap, one that would likely extend late into the evening, merging with bedtime.

'Because that doctor…' said Deborah Kendrick, leaning over the bannister, releasing her hair from its scarf as she chose her words carefully, '… is not a nice man.'

She disappeared into the black of the upstairs landing. There was the sound of her heavy bedroom door clunking shut. Viola would be lonely without her in the dark of the house, her senses on edge, Dot barking at every sound, sure that foxes were trespassing on the veranda. Yet she had to find some comfort in the way her mother had spoken. These were strong words, seditious even, but they were not the words of surrender.

Viola would not go to that appointment – if only because the late afternoons were reserved for spying. If she couldn't get close to the Eldest Girls at school, she would have to keep her vigil at the stones, slowly building the courage to step inside the circle.

But, before that, she'd need to get rid of Michael.

His company had been valuable to her; his knowledge of the island exhaustive, his discretion completely lacking. ('Huxley fell and snagged his bean-bags on some rigging once and they say Dr Bishy had to amputate one of them.') Every anecdote was delivered with the self-regard of a precocious child at a spelling bee, his embellishments sign-posted by the rising of his voice.

'Britta Sayers is always stopping me in the school corri-dors to ruffle my hair or straighten my collar, that kind of thing. She's very... tactile.'

He was so obviously pleased with the word 'tactile' that Viola had snorted with laughter.

Michael defined each girl as a clear archetype – Britta was the gobby one; Anna, the angel; Jade-Marie, the friendly klutz. It made Viola wonder what easy classifica-tion he applied to her when she wasn't there, because surely he did talk about her. This was currency – first-hand contact with the redheaded newcomer, the one with the obstructive mother who was growing as reclusive as the Earl.

Could Viola describe Michael with a cute little phrase in return? He was such a keeno, such a neek, king of all the boffins... No, nothing was quite right. Archetypes were what boys used to label girls – so they could get past the tedious business of empathy and nuance, and focus on the gawping, deciding if the art deserved a place on their wall.

When repetitions started to appear in Michael's stories, signalling that he had little else to reveal to her, Viola made her move. She needed to break free from the way he watched her as she watched the girls, making comments on her every reaction. She wanted to enjoy the vibrations, tip her head back as the girls did, allow the sensations to shiver gratifyingly through her body.

He was her friend and she liked him, but Michael had to go.

She put it to him straight. 'You need to leave this to me.'

They were walking back through Cable's Wood, Dot making reckless zigzags in pursuit of rabbits, pine needles pluming in her wake. Viola had found the confidence to release her from the lead now, letting her snuffle beneath logs and mark territory as her own.

'You have to let me watch the girls by myself.'

The boy looked at her, wounded; she'd known that he would.

'I'd love to keep you with me, Michael, truly I would, but with the terrible fury and everything ...' He gave the faint beginnings of a nod. 'If I'm alone, I can approach them, be part of what they're doing, experience it. With you there, that can never happen, because we'll always be hiding and straining to listen.'

'But you can't join in,' he replied, appalled, his face pale. 'You mustn't participate in...' he whispered it, '... witchcraft!'

Viola laughed too loudly; Michael's wounded expression returned.

'Look, I don't think it's witchcraft,' she told him. 'I think it's...'

She stopped and called for Dot, rewarding her return with a scrap of cold sausage. She refastened the lead, buying herself a moment to think. Michael stood, fists in pockets, pulsing with hurt.

'I think it's just girls' stuff,' she said, a lie and also not a lie. 'But we'll never know for sure unless you let me get closer.'

They continued their walk, Michael still brooding. Viola didn't want this to be a trade-off – her only friend on the island in exchange for the possibility of three new ones. She wanted to have them all.

'But we should meet somewhere else,' she said, 'to compare notes.'

He lifted his head at this olive branch.

'I think you could start an investigation of your own.' She spoke the idea as it formed. 'You could go and watch, I dunno ...' She sifted through the things she'd seen on her wanderings, the people she'd observed. 'What about that guy who works in the Customs House?'

'Saul Cooper?'

'Weaselly-looking, white shirt with embroidered thingies on his shoulders, drives a Jeep –'

'A Land Rover actually.' Michael gave a little skip – another point scored. Viola was winning him back.

'I go up to the harbour in the mornings sometimes,' she told him. *When I can't sleep*, she didn't say, *when the silence at the farmstead is suffocating and I need to see some people, some movement, anything.* 'And that guy will leave the Customs House, take the alley between the Counting House and the Provisions Store, and wait until this woman comes up the hill –'

'What woman?'

'I dunno. Black hair like yours, lives by the harbour, always got an armful of folders.'

'Miss Cedars?'

146

'Like I say, I dunno. Anyway, this guy, he waits in the passageway and then he steps out as if it's a complete coincidence that he's bumped into her – really weird it is, sort of funny – but she never stops. She does this big loop away from him, even if he calls after her.'

'If it is Miss Cedars, she's a teacher, you know!' Michael was a little breathless at this news, this possible scandal. 'She's *my* teacher!'

'Lisa, I want to say...' Viola replayed the moment, the Customs Officer shouting her name. 'No... Leah.'

Michael sounded it out, reverentially almost – 'Leah' – turning over the knowledge of his teacher's first name like a shiny new coin.

'We thought she was dead,' he said, 'and we thought they daredn't break it to us, because she disappeared after All Hallows' Eve, was gone for nearly a fortnight. Then she came back, different.'

Viola nodded, as if this was interesting, as if it meant something to her.

They continued on their way, lost in their own meditations – Viola thinking about the Eldest Girls and what she might do, Michael repeating, like an incantation, the names of his new quarry.

'Leah Cedars and Saul Cooper. Leah Cedars and Saul Cooper...'

◉ THE BOOK OF LEAH

The cottage had no phoneline; I couldn't let them know. So, they came to me.

Miriam Calder was the first ministering spirit. How could she resist? The story of too-many glasses of rum drunk on All Hallows' Eve, combined with my absence from the All Saints' Day service the next morning at school, would have had her salivating.

'You don't *look* very well,' Miriam said, appraising me on the doorstep. I pulled my long dressing gown tight around me, so the wind wouldn't lift it and reveal my bloodied knees. Miriam narrated the reshuffling of teachers that had been necessary to compensate for my not being there, the immense effort it had required, claiming credit for this orchestration. I denied her my thank-yous and well-dones.

'Anyway, I can't stand here talking all day,' she said, her monologue done. 'I expect you'll be better tomorrow though, eh?' She gave me a knowing smile and an almost wink.

Rage swelled up inside of me at this priggishness, at her undeserved pride. It was an emotion so pure, so full, it thrilled and terrified me in equal measure. I could have lifted the woman by her prim, flowery collar and thrown her over the harbour wall.

'I'll see how I go,' I said.

I didn't return to school the next day.

The skirts I owned would cover the mess of my knees when I was standing, but not when I was sitting, and Jacob Crane had made clear his views on female teachers wearing trousers.

Also, I was truly sick.

The body knows when an illness might come as a kindness, I think, when the psyche needs to retreat. Everything I ate, I threw up, forcing me into a fast that could only be good for my murky soul. Let me vomit up this sin, I told myself, or starve the devil within.

On the second day, Ruth French was my ministering spirit.

She came with arms laden – milk, apples, a loaf. She delivered her compassion with characteristic brusqueness.

'Take them, then,' she said. 'Take them off me!' I didn't want them. Even simple foods made my stomach roll. These items would sit in my kitchen, curdling, rotting, the sight of the apples reminding me of my transgression, of the juice that had soaked my blouse. 'It took three forms and a promise of some private tutoring to get the crones at the Provisions Store to let me buy something under your ration,' Ruth went on.

I could not refuse.

'Do you need anything else?' she asked.

I shook my head. 'I just drank too much, that's all.' Now it was a lie, it seemed easier to admit.

'Are you sure about that?'

'Yes!' I said. 'All I need is sleep.' I thanked her and closed the door with a slippered foot.

150

But I could not sleep. My mind galloped, trying to piece together my actions, not just the physical movements that night from pub to harbour to Customs House and home, but what drove me to behave that way. *You enjoyed it*, said a voice within, replaying the memory of my legs twined around Saul's body, the cry I'd given out at the point of release. *You'd had a taste with Ben and you wanted more. That is who Leah is.*

I was the favoured child, lying at the bottom of the estate well, sprawled on top of an embarrassment of gold, no conceivable way to climb out.

The night after that, as I lay awake, there came a click – the rear gate – followed by a gentle rap against my kitchen door. Not all ministering spirits are angels, I knew; this was the devil come to tempt me from my fast. I held strong. I didn't answer, even when his voice lifted gently, so compellingly, into the night air. 'Please, Leah, I just want to know that you're okay.'

At the weekend, Margaritte let herself in by a door I was certain I had latched. She found me dozing on the sofa. I swung myself quickly to sitting, the swiftness of the move-ment making my sight go black.

'Put your head between your knees,' I heard her say. I felt the weight of her dropping onto the sofa beside me, her powdery smell close. She stroked the curl of my spine and my vision returned like vibrations settling on the surface of a pool. In front of me, on the coffee table, was a small, stout bottle of cloudy liquid.

'It's a tonic I made from bistort root.'

'I don't want it,' I told her.

'I heard you being sick, through the wall. This is good for that.'

151

'I said –'

'It's good for wounds on the outside too.' She was looking at my knees, covered by a pair of marl pyjamas.

'Did you see?' The thought that anyone had witnessed me leaving the Customs House, dishevelled and bleeding, brought on a fresh and brutal wave of nausea.

Margaritte shrugged evasively.

I got up, staggering to the opposite side of the room. I needed there to be space between us; I had to see her for what she was – a deluded woman too attached to the old ways.

'You take that stuff away,' I told her.

'But it's just herbs, Leah.'

'You know it isn't. I should never have been sucked in. What you do is against God.'

She laughed loudly. 'You tell that to Father Daniel!' she replied. 'After he fell out with Dr Bishy and couldn't be going to his surgery anymore, I cured his pink-eye with a clary water, just like that.' She clicked her fingers.

I did not know what to question first – the reverend's engagement in the dark arts, or his falling out with the doctor. Both were irrelevant.

'Jacob Crane has his sights on you,' I warned. 'On me too.'

She sighed and looked down for a moment, blinking upwards again to ask: 'Are you frightened of him?'

'Yes!' came an unbidden voice. To my surprise, it was my own. Was this true? Was I scared of Jacob Crane? And if I was, couldn't it be justified, wasn't it to be expected? I had known him only as my headmaster, then straight away as my superior at work. Didn't everyone on the island hold him in some kind of fearful reverence?

'Aren't you?' I returned. 'Frightened of him?'

'Actually,' she said, easing herself up from the sofa, placing a hand gently on my arm as she left, 'I think it's time that he was frightened of us.'

On the Monday, when I still hadn't returned to St Rita's, Cat Walton knocked on my door, the tails of her curate's gown flapping beneath her short, bulbous Puffa jacket.

'I'm here in my professional capacity,' she said, 'responsible as I am for all the souls of this parish.'

She made us both tea and, as we sat at my kitchen table, told a story from the Classical Greek – of Metanoia who walked in the wake of the god of opportunity, cloaked and tearful, urging those around her to be sorry for all the moments that they had missed. Cat was at liberty to do this – apply the lives of the pagan gods to ours – even in chapel. She had a degree in theology, obtained on the mainland, making her – academically, at least – closer to God than Father Daniel was, since he had trained at the feet of our previous reverend.

Cat lifted a tin of biscuits from her bag and insisted I take one. I waited for the story's moral.

'Maybe you just seized the moment,' she said. 'Perhaps Metanoia would be proud.'

I had to believe she was talking about Ben – only Ben.

'I seized the wrong moments,' I said, the sweetness of the biscuit making my stomach clench. 'And now I need to repent.'

'Well, that's something,' said Cat with a kind smile. 'Let's work with that.'

I let her visit me each day and talk me into leaving the cottage. We would go and sit in the still midday air of the chapel, sometimes just enjoying the silence; other times, Cat would read to me from the books of *Jeremiah*, *Ezekiel* and *Revelation* – words of contrition are not enough, a person must act, carry out the 'first works', or else God cannot support them in their transformation. Sometimes we bowed our heads and prayed: '*Almighty God, Father of our Lord Jesus Christ, maker of all things, judge of all men: we acknowledge and bewail our manifold sins and wickedness…*'

'And they are manifold,' I told her in the quiet that followed, 'my sins.'

Cat took my hand. I admitted my greatest fear: 'Underneath all of this… niceness, I think that I am wicked.' I began to cry. 'Jacob Crane's letter was for the Eldest Girls and for their mothers and for Margaritte and for Ben, but most of all, it was for me, because … I am the witch.'

I was breathless at the relief of saying it aloud – it was an exorcism. I readied myself for my penance. Cat trembled in the pew beside me, her large chest shaking, then she let go of the sound – laughter, bouncing startlingly from the stone walls. She pulled me in to her, hugged me, the vibrations travelling from her warm body into mine. I didn't submit, though; I couldn't, I was rigid.

'Oh, Leah!' she sighed. 'Come with me.'

She took my hand, guiding me towards the chancel, to the recess that held the relic of St Jade – her mummified foot, beneath a dirty wrapping of linen, in a box of smoked glass. In the fourteenth century, Jade had quite literally stamped out evil on Lark. Impervious to venom, she used her bare feet to destroy the poisonous snakes that once picked off

154

our children, driving her heel into the serpents' throats. A painting above the case depicted her in action, mouth wide in ecstasy, black hair and green robes flowing, knee raised in preparation, a startled creature on the ground beneath her.

'Are we to pray to St Jade?' I asked.

'If you like,' Cat said, meaning 'no'.

She reached up for the wooden voting box that rested beside the glass case. Here was another relic of our past, seventeenth century probably. It was a means for islanders anonymously to report anyone they suspected of witchcraft. At school, we were taught that it was a symbolic object and never used. It merely acted as a physical reminder not to meddle with black magic, lest your neighbour be watching. It was easy to imagine our barbaric forebears using that box though, to settle grudges or to seek vengeance. Even as a child, I knew my young ears were being given a softened version of history.

Cat handled the voting box with a roughness unsympathetic to its age, popping the hinged door underneath and shaking free the dead insects and bat droppings within.

'Nope,' she said, 'no one has put your name in here.'

'Don't joke,' I told her. 'I'm serious.'

'So am I. Take this.'

From her pocket she retrieved her Agnus Dei, placing it in my hand – the remainder of an Easter candle crushed and imprinted with the image of a lamb. I had one of my own on the mantelpiece at home.

'So, is it working?' she asked. 'Are you melting? Do you feel your insides burning up?'

'No.'

'Of course not.' She reclaimed the wax block. 'Witchcraft isn't practised by accident.'

'But I did.' I lowered my voice. 'I did practise it. On purpose.'

Cat set the box back and folded her arms, unconvinced. 'How?'

'With cards.'

She shrugged. 'So have I.'

'You!'

'You need to know your enemy, don't you? And, well, I can see how it might be done for fun. Did you do it for fun?'

'I suppose.'

'Then I forgive you.' She grinned; it was that easy for her. I had to wonder if this was something a mainland upbringing gave you. Ben had it too – the ability to shake things off, not to worry. 'You didn't do it because you are wicked or possessed. I think God can forgive you too.'

'And Jacob Crane?'

Her smile faltered, his name echoed about us – an anomaly, an intrusion.

'I don't speak for him,' she said.

I kept my chin to my chest. We weren't done; I had to find the courage to be free from it all. 'And what about sexual deviancy?'

She stayed quiet.

I pushed on: 'Do you do *that* because you are wicked and possessed?'

I looked up. She narrowed her eyes. 'Which "you" are we talking about here?'

'Me,' I said. 'Who did you think?'

She had been holding her breath and now let it go.

'Oh, I didn't mean… I wasn't talking about you and Ruth if that's what –'

'No, I didn't suppose that you were.'

The silence was drawn out and awkward.

'There was love in your heart,' Cat said eventually. 'I saw it. Ruth saw it. We both know love when it comes along.'

She *was* only talking about Ben.

She had misunderstood me all along. I had been talking about sex, which was my sin alone, something selfish you can do with someone else. Cat had confounded sex with love, a united act, and in doing that perhaps she saved me. Her mention of the word came like a rope knotted at intervals and thrown over the side of a well. *Let love be without dissimulation. Abhor that which is evil; cleave to that which is good.* If Metanoia was not to wail her remorse at my missed opportunity, it was time to pull myself free.

We continued to meet daily for a week or so, until I felt strong enough to return to my job. Though she did not speak *for* Jacob Crane, Cat said she would speak *to* him, smooth the path for my return. I had sought out time and space to commune with the Lord, was what she told him, how could our headmaster argue with that?

As I hugged her in thanks, there was a click – the latch lifting on the door.

'My next parishioner in need,' Cat said, breaking our embrace. 'Unless you would like to stand in for me on this occasion?'

This was her final attempt at ministering to my soul. She was Cupid disobeying the orders of Venus. I turned to see Ben – walking down the aisle.

157

The path was clear, no Michael in her way, but Viola's conviction dimmed.

Her mind was two wild horses – one galloping remorse-lessly forward in pursuit of friendship; the other fleeing, certain of rejection. She had heard the Eldest Girls call out for a sun god, for mother moon, for the ghosts of Lark's past. How disappointed they would be when Viola, a mere mortal, rose from the ferns.

She decided to prepare an offering. A task that would take her away from the stones for a while, from the anxiety they now caused her. A simple procrastination.

She sifted through books at the farmstead, still sitting in boxes, awaiting shelves and her mother's enthusiasm. Viola had been momentarily buoyed by the sight of green shoots in the tilled plots outside, until she realised it was November, not the time of year for that kind of thing, and these were nothing but hardy weeds. If this continued, there would be more visits. First the headmaster, then the doctor – who would come next?

'What are you looking for?' her mother called distract-edly from the veranda, disturbed by the sound.

Viola sat amongst piles of mildewed Penguin editions and dictionaries in various languages.

'Do we have any books on, like, magic and spells and stuff?'

No answer drifted back.

Viola considered handing the girls the Kendricks' copy of *Macbeth*. Maybe it was one of the Shakespeare texts that Michael had hinted were forbidden. There was no cross-dressing in the play and only a suggestion of sex, as far as Viola could remember, but there was plenty of *double, double toil and trouble.*

Viola had seen how the congregation quivered over that letter about 'mystic cards' and 'polished stones'. A similar letter (minus the fire and brimstone) had gone out to parents at Viola's old school when an obsession for Ouija boards swept through Year Eight, but the parents back home had scoffed at it – necromancy and fortune-telling were bunkum, and the girls having nightmares needed to snap out of it, quit attention-seeking.

What exactly would Viola be saying by giving the girls a copy of *Macbeth*? That there was a parallel? Three Eldest Girls, three weird sisters. She threw the play text back into its box.

She trawled the estate land next, hoping to find a stone in the shape of a heart or a lucky clover with an extra leaf. She could press the sprig between the pages of the heavy atlas, then affix it to a neat piece of card, explaining its auspiciousness when handing it over (just in case four-leafers didn't have the same meaning on Lark). She would be like one of those colonial explorers ingratiating themselves with an isolated tribe before engaging in their local rituals.

But she found nothing, only attracted, once again, the attention of the stooped and bearded gamekeeper. He pulled up alongside her in his tarped-over Land Rover, asking her why she was out on the hills alone.

'You reckon it's a good idea, do you, wandering about like this?'

His questions confused her, containing as they did echoes of the mainland rules, the ones that made it Viola's responsibility not to put herself in a vulnerable position, not to make herself easy prey – the ones that weren't supposed to apply here.

'I'm just walking my dog,' she told him.

'Well, keep it away from the cattle,' he replied.

'Oh, she doesn't chase anything that big, only rabbits.'

'I'm thinking of the diseases she'll have from that mainland of yours.'

There was a rugged-looking woman in the passenger seat beside him, about the same age as Viola's mother. She wore a thick green jumper, her black hair scraped back into a perfunctory bun.

'Leave her alone, Peter.' The woman tutted, nudging him in the ribs.

He gave a grunt in response before pulling away, his eyes on Viola as he went, not on the landscape ahead.

His phrase – 'that mainland of yours' – had struck Viola. Like a priest was God's representative on earth, the Kendricks were the mainland's representative on Lark, defender of its principles, accountable for its actions, unless of course they chose whole-heartedly to convert. Would Viola be up for that? Could she ever be convinced to call Lark her true home?

She made the Provisions Store her next stop, thinking an offering of chocolate or cake – a literal sweetener – might charm the girls, if there was an allocation in the Kendricks' ration for that kind of treat. Remembering how the bullish women behind the counter felt about Dot, Viola tied her dog to the wooden stocks before going inside and walking among the flat pallets of tins and packets, peering into the fluorescent insides of the refrigerated cabinets. Nothing appealed. She picked up a pomegranate and squeezed it thoughtfully – wondering where on the island it could possibly have grown. There was a myth Viola had heard once, or a ritual, involving the fruit, the dropping of it maybe and the spilling of its seeds, but she couldn't recall it exactly. Anyway, she swiftly put it down when a snaggle-toothed woman wearing a shop apron bellowed that there was to be no 'looking with your fingers'. Viola left, shame-faced, empty-handed.

Outside, Michael was on the cobbles, petting Dot. Passers-by stared at his roughhousing of the dog's ears, and the way Dot spilled onto her back, spreading her paws and baring her gums, submissively offering up her pink-grey belly.

Viola's heart sank lower. Michael would ask her how she was getting on with the Eldest Girls, expose her for her dithering.

She leapt in first. 'So, what's the word on thingumebob and whatshername?'

'Leah Cedars and Saul Cooper?' he whispered.

'Yeah, Leah and Saul.' She said it at full volume, making him hiss at her to shush as he checked over his shoulder to see who might have heard.

Viola untied Dot's lead from the wooden stocks, thinking how, in any market town on the mainland, they might have served as a bike stand, but the inclines on Lark made cycling an impossibility.

'I've found an intriguing pattern,' Michael said, as they made their way towards the white sculpted chimneys of the smokehouse. 'One that tells me they're definitely doing it.'

He reached into his satchel for a notepad, flicking to a neatly drawn table of dates and times, filled out comprehensively with light pencil dashes and hard Xs.

'I've been tracking her every move.'

He thrust the notepad into Viola's face as proof.

'Great,' she said, pushing it away. 'But you're not being weird about it, are you?'

'What do you mean?'

'You're not, like, stalking her?'

'But that's what you told me to do.'

'No, I said...'

What had she said? Viola did not want to spar with Michael, have him demand, *if you're such an expert on all this, better show me what info* you've *collected so far.*

'It's fine,' she said. 'You're doing great.'

'You told me I should follow Leah so that you could speak to the girls alone.'

'Yeah, I know.' Viola began to walk faster.

'So, you could get in on whatever they were doing and –'

'Yes!' she said. 'I know!'

Then, the skies opened, instantaneously, as they were wont to do, and Viola had never been more pleased. Mother Nature was playing for her team. She would get soaked right through to her underwear before she reached the cover of home, but it would stop Michael following her there.

She started to jog. Michael, madly, joined in.

'So, how's it all going?' he said. 'What have you found?'

There was a great flash of lightning and that, at last, brought him to a halt.

Everyone on the island was scared of the electrical storms, the swift, metallic ferociousness of them. Viola had witnessed a strike at sea not long after they'd arrived – a pink zag of light across the water – but it was land these firebolts were really after, or people, a means to earth themselves.

Was this support from Mother Nature, she asked herself, or a scolding for her inaction? *Stop hiding in the ferns and do what you must, or else I will take aim!*

'I'm really hitting it off with them!' Viola called back to Michael as the thunder sounded. 'I have so much to tell you.'

She began to run, full pelt for home, because there was another reason lightning came, and that was to strike down liars.

And so, it came to pass – three became four. The red-haired girl joined the Eldest Girls' number.

The women of the community had wished for it; they couldn't say that they hadn't.

Four corners, they'd talked of, four pillars, a wholesome union of love, faith, hope and luck – the allusions were endless. This would make the girls a balanced group, strong, with no need for their illicit rituals. Though what these women failed to see was that their belief in numerology was an illicit ritual in itself. It could not be trusted, and sure enough, as soon as three became four, doubt made its way in, as slippery as the eel.

The *coycrock* girl was not the right person to steer those girls back towards the light. The evidence had been there all along; they should have taken note. She loitered in fields, in alleyways and at the harbour. She had been caught meddling with Peter Cedars' dogs and kept an animal of her own as a familiar, watching it defecate on the cobbles, tying up what it produced in little bags that she carried home for some mysterious purpose. She had been observed in the Provisions Store damaging the fruit. Clearly, the girl was in excellent health with all the wandering that she did, yet still she did not attend school.

The mother was also skiving, from the land and, more recently, from chapel. So many families over the years had applied for a place on the island and been rejected, including one with a trio of hardy-looking sons. What error of judgement had led the Council to choose the Kendricks?

The sympathetic proposed that Deborah Kendrick, an upright, practical and pious candidate, had simply fallen ill and was now struggling to cope. This hypothesis gave rise to panic. Was she battling a mainland disease, one that Lark immune systems might not have the armoury to survive? In the Provisions Store, whenever the woman showed her pale face – what you could see of it beneath those wild curls – she was given a wide berth. Hands went to mouths to avoid the inhalation of germs.

Dr Bishy was forced to schedule a talk at the Counting House to allay the islanders' fears. It was held in place of the planned session for the public removal of the plaster cast from Andy Cater's broken wrist, an event the young of the island had been ghoulishly looking forward to.

What Deborah Kendrick was suffering from, the doctor reassured those who sat forward on their chairs in the meeting room to hear, was not a deadly flu strain, or Typhoid. It was certainly not Ebola. The woman had a sickness of the mind, something common on the mainland, something not unexpected at her time of life, with no husband to care for, her childbearing done.

Women of a similar age in the audience shared wary glances.

'But, be confident,' the doctor continued, leaning against the raised stage at the head of the room to convey how relaxed he was about the situation, 'these sicknesses are not sicknesses at all if left well alone, if they are not pandered to or the patient mollycoddled.' Then he repeated the prescription he had given the woman herself. 'The only cure is fresh air and hard work – which Lark, I'm pleased to say, is able to provide in bucketfuls.'

Meanwhile, the daughter's influence on the Eldest Girls was starting to display its symptoms.

'We refuse to do *A Midsummer Night's Dream* as our A-Level text,' Britta Sayers had announced in class one morning, with a flick of her long ropes of hair.

Dellie Leven was teaching them that afternoon, Mr Crane being indisposed.

A slim volume was pushed across the desk for Mrs Leven's attention. It had a black shiny cover with a photograph of a white-shirted actor playing the titular role.

'*Doctor Faustus*,' Dellie read aloud, picking up the book.

Anna Duchamp quickly corrected her pronunciation – 'It's *Fow*-stus, miss, I believe, not *For*-stus' – then she delivered a short summary of the play. 'It's about a man who sells his soul to the devil in return for knowledge and power.' She said it so demurely, tucking her hair behind her ears.

The teacher immediately dropped the book at the mention of Old Nick, realising she'd grasped the wrong end of the poker. Dellie inwardly cursed herself. She always let the girls do this – bait her – whenever Mr Crane was away. She could never see these challenges coming or head them off at the pass. ('Was it very painful when you first had sex?' Jade-Marie had asked her during one lesson, apropos of nothing.)

It was Jade-Marie who spoke now, making a declaration of their intent. 'We want to study it,' she said, 'and we also want to do it for the Easter show.'

It was traditional that the outgoing Sixth Formers gave a performance of their set text, a theatrical swansong before exam season began, and that set text was always *A Midsummer Night's Dream*. With no students in the school year above them, the girls would, come Easter, have to don the fluted-sleeved dresses, the wire wings and the papier-mâché ass' head to give the island its annual show. Come the Easter after that, they would have to perform it all over again.

'No,' Dellie Leven replied. She may have avoided confrontation with the girls in the past, turned a blind eye to their wrist bandages, for example, leaving it to poor Miss Cedars to uncover their tattoos, but on this, she claims, she was firm. 'We will not be using that blasphemous book. Absolutely not. And think how disappointed the little ones will be, come Easter, if they don't get to see The Mechanicals.'

Dellie's only error, perhaps, was not to confiscate the offending book, not to notice when Britta Sayers slid it back into her bag. She might have demanded it from them later, if the girls hadn't returned so diligently to their discussions of meddling fairies, debating the rights and wrongs of making Titania fall in love with a donkey, and more earnestly, the reasons why the young people in the play decided that what happened to them should be considered a dream.

It was Saul Cooper who was challenged on the matter of the intruding play text. His log of the Kendricks' incoming property had them arriving with an embarrassment of books. Had the Customs Officer checked every title? Could he swear on his ageing mother's life that not a wrong one had made it through?

Yes, he said, yes, he could.

A likely story. Those who had, in the past, accused Saul of petty bureaucracy as they supped their beers in the Anchor, bemoaning his absence of light and shade in the upholding of the law, how he never let a damn thing past if there was a box that needed ticking, now called him a clock-watcher and a shirker, someone guaranteed to do the bare minimum, and decidedly less if no one kept an eye.

But all this was a wasted discussion, if you considered that the *coycrock* girl might not have given them the book at all.

She had held out an apple, cupped in the palm of her hand, as a welcoming gift when she stepped into that stone circle – not a play text – according to reports. Others had it as a pomegranate, for hadn't the girl been seen trying to shoplift one from the Provisions Store? Wasn't she often roaming through the nunnery gardens uninvited, sneaking into hothouses? The educated curate had once told the congregation the story of a goddess who ate six seeds from that fatal fruit, then found herself bound to the underworld. It wasn't hard to see what the *coycrock* girl intended.

The other version of events was that she took them no gift all – gave them only the charm of her tongue.

The Eldest Girls cried out in surprise when the girl emerged from the undergrowth. The mists were known to thin a little in November, before the climate doubled-down, sending temperatures plummeting. The *coycrock* looked like an apparition in the drifting haze. Here was that minion of Beelzebub they'd been calling out for. Here was Bethany

169

Reid risen from the dead, albeit with the wrong-coloured hair.

'Who sent you?' Britta Sayers demanded, for the girl did have the air of a reluctant messenger, pushed forward to speak.

The Eldest Girls could look majestic in their white night-gowns as they danced and called, but they cut ridiculous figures standing stock-still, caught out, their muddied hems dragging, their cuffs hanging lower than their hands.

'I'm Viola,' said the girl as she moved closer, across the peaty ground. 'Hello.'

'We know who you are,' Anna had replied cautiously, 'we've seen you in chapel.'

There was a pause, as the *coycrock* girl searched for a way to break the tension, deciding in the end to thrust forward a hand for the girls to shake – a gesture that could be seen as too late and too grown-up, but one that could also be oddly endearing. It softened Jade-Marie. She stepped towards the *coycrock* girl, catching her toe in the hem of her nightdress, falling forward with a 'Sorry, sorry.'

Britta Sayers slapped their two hands apart.

'Who sent you?' she demanded again.

'No one,' replied the *coycrock*. 'I've just been watching you and...'

'Spying!'

'No! No, not –'

'She's the one!' Britta Sayers swung herself towards each of her friends in turn, hair whipping. 'I told you someone was reporting back.'

'It's not me!' The *coycrock* girl's voice grew desperate. 'It's not me! I would never!'

170

Anna came closer, her tone cool, analytical. 'Why should we believe you?'

'Because...' The *coycrock* girl was trembling, close to tears. 'Because who would trust me?' The Eldest Girls fell quiet at this. 'They doubt me,' she added, 'more than they could ever doubt you.'

Jade-Marie spoke gently, wary of another of Britta's slaps. 'She's from the mainland.'

'We know!' Anna sighed. 'We get it! We understand what she's trying to say!'

'No, I mean...' Jade-Marie adjusted her nightgown where it pulled at her throat. 'I mean, she will know. She will know things. Just like we thought Mr Hailey would. We can ask her if he's telling the truth.'

Anna and Britta looked to Jade-Marie, then slowly back at the girl. They bit their lips.

'Who is Mr Hailey?' asked the *coycrock*, nervous under their stare.

And this is where the tone changes, as if a new roll is loaded in the projector, belonging to a different film. The same actresses perform, in wholly different roles.

Accounts have the girls going limp at the knees as they describe the new teacher; they giggle, groan, their language a little oily, maybe hysterical. *Oh, his eyes!* they say. *Oh, his golden hair! Have you seen the muscles in his stomach, and the size of his* ... Their tongues go sibilant. They are in a trance with their thoughts, reaching for the mounds of their own private parts through the cloth of their gowns.

They start talking of other men in a similar fashion. They grasp at the swell of their breasts, and even though they are wearing layers of school uniform beneath those night-dresses, the detail of their hardening nipples finds its way into the story as it is passed around.

I wonder, says one girl – Britta in some accounts, Anna in others – *if that boy with the gun has something else as long and powerful as his rifle.*

The girls scream at the idea, urging the *coycrock* girl to come nearer, to join them in their quivering huddle.

Have you ever done it? they want to know of her. *Have you? Have you?*

They reach out to touch the strange redness of her hair and stroke the freckles of her cheeks. At this juncture, some listeners want to know if the girls kissed.

'No,' says the teller, 'because they didn't know they were being watched. Girls only do that when they're being watched.'

The *coycrock* girl was pulled into the Eldest Girls' circle, subsumed by them.

This part of the story seems to hold up, even among its participants.

She had started speaking low and fast, the *coycrock* girl – like wizards do when communing with the dead, if the *Book of Isaiah* is to be believed. She told them all the things that she'd seen, all the things that she'd heard, all the things that she absolutely knew. Britta put an arm around her, Jade-Marie too, the sides of their oversized nightdresses becoming wings. They gathered her up, these seeming angels, and whether they laughed there in that close embrace, or sighed, or wept for one another, for all that they had endured, one thing was true, no matter the interpretation – three were now four.

Four became one.

☙ Friday the 13th – April 2018

Viola is running again, bones juddering as her boots strike the hard earth. The two-way radio in her pocket bangs against her thigh. One foot lands in a grassy pothole and she bites her tongue at the jolt of it. There is blood in her mouth. She doesn't stop.

Sitting still was no longer an option. The women were arriving for their early shifts at the Provisions Store. Tobacco smoke coiled its way into her shell hideout – the men making for the harbour, lighting their first roll-ups of the day.

The island was closing in on her and she was flooded with memory.

Hide and seek, played with her brother in the generous spaces of their 1930s house on the outer reaches of the M25; making herself small behind the vacuum cleaner in the cupboard under the stairs, breathing in the dry fug of its dust bag; Seb's voice calling out, 'Coming! Ready or not!'; his footsteps immediately there, the door swinging open to let in a brutal light. 'Found you,' he'd say with a sigh, expecting better sport.

This glimpse of the past was a warning, a premonition. She had to find a better place to hide, not make it so easy for them.

At full tilt, Viola drops into the channel that runs between the netted allotments at the nunnery. The narrowness of the passage makes her speed feel wild, her breath loud. Dot does her best to keep up, mouth open with the joy of it – a joy that is spiked each time she falls out of step and the lead snags her neck. Viola prays that the holy sisters are too busy with their kneeling and contemplating to see the flash of maroon coat and grey dog streaking across their land. Even if they were to report her, they'd say she is heading where she isn't.

This is a roundabout route. This is a ruse.

They reach a fence dividing the allotments from the sloping land of the estate and Viola throws Dot over, then climbs the wooden rails herself, landing with a thump on the other side. They sprint across open ground, making for a stripe of trees. Once concealed by hawthorn and hornbeam, they turn nonsensically downhill, back in the direction of the east coast and the harbour, almost towards where they started. This convoluted route will take them away from the usual paths, the ones the rest of the island use to deliver children to school and themselves to work.

It means she will not bump into Michael, but she doesn't need him now. She has a plan of her own – one of distraction, of delay. Her only regret is that she won't catch sight of the Eldest Girls heading up the hill to St Rita's as she instructed, acting as if this is just another day.

Though it is Viola who has given the girls their orders, she is not in charge. She is equal to them; that's what she likes to tell herself, though she understands deep down how separate she will always be. Viola is a mainlander; the Eldest Girls belong to Lark. They know the island right down its blackest core; it has shaped them. And more than that, the girls are magical, heaven-sent. Viola cannot shake this belief, no matter how much she has seen behind the curtain.

Her complicated route reaches its conclusion: Viola and Dot dart along the ginnel behind the houses. They go through a gate, in through a door.

'Hello!'

Viola's hair is squally from the run, strands of it sticking to the sweat of her brow.

'Hello!'

There are footsteps on the stairs. Dot whines in anticipation of who will arrive in the small hallway beyond the kitchen. When she appears, dressed formally, as if for work, a hairbrush in her hand, Dot tugs forward, eager to offer a greeting.

'What are you doing here?' the woman demands.

'It wasn't locked,' says Viola, still breathless from the sprint. 'I let myself in.'

'I can see that. Don't they teach you to knock first on the mainland?'

'It's important!' Viola gasps.

'Why?' The hairbrush hangs limp in the woman's grasp. 'Has something happened?'

'It's Saul Cooper.'

'And?' says the woman, trying for nonchalance.

'He's at the stones.'

'Why would Saul Cooper be –'

'He's with... a body.'

The woman's eyes go large. 'What body?' The hairbrush drops. 'Where's Ben?'

'You didn't find him last night, did you?' Viola keeps her grip steady on the reins, holding the woman's gaze, waiting for the mask to fall.

'No, no, I didn't but... Are you saying that... What are you saying?'

Viola says nothing, she lets the woman fill in the gaps. The colour drains entirely from her skin.

'No,' she whimpers, sinking to the floor. 'No, no, no, no!' She clutches the end of the bannister to stay afloat.

'Get up,' says Viola sharply, playing the adult. 'You need to get up.'

The woman does not. She mutters her denials.

'It looks really bad,' says Viola, raising her voice. 'For you, I mean, this all looks really bad – with the ship arriving today...' She gambles on the next part. 'Your name in the ledger...'

The woman does not object. She quietens, still clinging to the bannister.

'You need to go up to the stones.' Viola's breath is her own once more. 'Get a story straight. But you need to go now, before it's too late.'

The woman stands, her face wholly changed. A switch has been flicked. Here is what Viola always knew was behind that mask: someone selfish. The woman gives a nod of resolve and pulls on a coat, thrusts her stockinged feet into sturdy boots. Then she is off, pushing past the intruder in her kitchen.

The baton has been passed.

Viola depresses the button on the two-way radio and she speaks. 'You need to stay where you are,' she tells Saul, buying herself some much-needed time. 'Leah Cedars is coming to find you. Over and Out.'

Tuesday night, I knocked on her door.

'I've brought a bottle,' I said, holding out the small, stout vessel – empty now.

'Did it work?' she asked. She knew the answer. The skin on my knees was as perfect as it had ever been; old netball injuries from the schoolyard left more lasting marks. Margaritte had allowed me to emerge unblemished from what I'd done. I might even pretend it had never happened.

'So,' she said, taking the bottle from me, 'are you coming in?'

We drew the curtains, lit incense and settled down opposite one another across the green baize. Margaritte leaned heavily on the table as she lowered herself into her seat, wincing at the movement, cursing the cold of December. I looked up unthinkingly for a clock, as if the face of one might tell me where the year had gone.

We worked through our experiences of the recent storms, giving an inventory of the plants in our window boxes that had survived the onslaught, and then, these topics exhausted, she asked, 'What brings you to me, then?'

'Tuesday nights are our night,' I replied.

I smiled, thinking this was enough, that we would not speak of it anymore, that line we crossed when we were last together in my front room, how she had reached within me – seen me. This was the Larkian way. We avoided difficult subjects, lifted the carpet, swept them beneath, carried on.

Margaritte took up the cards from their wooden box, freeing them from their scrap of coloured silk. She shook her head.

'It was difficult for you to come here.' She looked up from her unwrapping to see my smile falter. 'Let's not pretend it wasn't.'

With one deft movement of the wrist, she fanned the cards across the table.

'I had a crisis of the soul,' I told her, 'that's all. But I have decided now that I am going to believe.'

She nodded – a sign that I was to go on.

It should be an effortless task, I explained – to believe – I was merely out of practice. I needed only to remind myself of the good book and how straightforward it was to put one's faith in that. This skill was surely transferable. Universal, even. I could apply it to every story I was told. For example, if a man came and sat next to me in the midday quiet of the chapel and said that he knew nothing of the girls' tattoos until I had asked for those bandages to be removed, or if he swore that he had been teaching them science – only science! – then wasn't I at liberty to believe him? If the story seemed like a noble one, with love and truth at its heart, I was surely duty-bound to put my trust in it. One decision, no going back, no questions.

Margaritte drew the cards into a pile and signalled for me to cut. She wanted more.

I told her that my love for Ben was stronger than my suspicion; that my lack of confidence in him – in myself – seemed unfathomable now.

'How could I think that he was capable of such terrible things, think that all of this...' I gestured to the burning incense and the cards in her hand – here was the apology that was most overdue. 'That this constituted witchcraft!' I gave an embarrassed laugh. 'I was thinking like a child!'

Margaritte shrugged. 'But we are all still children, deep down,' she said.

I ploughed on, a preacher of wild conviction, telling her how I was back in my stride in the classroom, feeling stronger than ever. When Miriam Calder had launched into a scissoring attack on Dellie Leven in the staff room, questioning Dellie's judgement during one of Mr Crane's absences, I had stepped in.

'That is none of your business, Miriam,' I'd told her crisply. 'You are the school administrator and you work for us, not vice versa.'

Miriam stole away to her office and Ruth French started a round of applause – one that Miriam must have heard.

Margaritte nodded in acknowledgement of my account, a basic receipt in return in for its telling.

'And did your Knight of Cups applaud too?' she asked.

'Sorry?' I took a large of gulp of wine and let my breath catch up with me. The certainty and the triumph I had talked of were all of a sudden gone, scared away by the passion that I'd used to describe them.

'Ben Hailey – your Knight of Cups,' she asked again, 'did he applaud?'

'He wasn't there,' I told her. 'He was out on a field trip with the Eldest Girls.' I resisted the urge to ask what she was implying; I shied from it.

Margaritte dealt a small cross of cards onto the green.

'I like those girls very much,' she said.

'So do I,' I replied – a lie, and not the first time I'd told it, if only by omission.

When Ben and I had sat alone in the chapel, reunited in that pew, he'd expressed worry for the Eldest Girls. They seem fearful of what life will be like for them now that they are almost grown-up, he'd explained to me.

'I am just as protective of them as you are,' he'd said, squeezing my hand, and I didn't correct him, didn't admit that I had, in recent weeks, wished those girls away. This would have been too terrible a thing to say out loud and too easily misunderstood. It wasn't that I hated them or wanted any misfortune to befall them, only that I could hardly bear the way they made me feel – like I did not understand my own mind, not just about Ben, but about Lark, about life. It was as if these girls, who should know nothing compared to me, knew everything.

'They're our future, the Eldest Girls,' Margaritte went on, as if she could see my thoughts and was nudging them into line. She tapped each of the cards in my spread, neatening the cross. 'They'll be the ones to save us, you mark me.'

I snorted. *Save us from what?* was the question that rose within but I pushed it down; I hid from it.

'So...' she looked down at the spread '...you have decided to put your unquestioning faith in Ben.'

'Yes,' I replied.

'Yet here you are with questions nonetheless.'

I opened my mouth to object, closed it.

When I eventually spoke, I did so quietly. 'It will be the last time,' I said. 'I promise.' I didn't know who I was promising this to – myself, Margaritte, the forces that made the cards land the way they did. 'Just let me know that I am right to trust him.'

She gave me a sympathetic glance, said, '*He that wavereth is like a wave of the sea driven with the wind and tossed*' – quoting from the *Epistle of James*. Then she started turning those cards face-up.

First came the Eight of Cups, telling me what I already knew: that I must turn my back on a way of being, a way of feeling, liberate myself but not lose hope.

Next, the Lovers, marking the challenge that would cross my path: a choice between the holy and the temporal, the teachings of my youth or the possibilities of the future.

The Tower followed this: a symbol of ruin. A structure I had come to rely on would be razed to the ground.

And my guide through the aftermath? The Two of Swords: a blindfolded woman sitting at the water's edge, her weapons crossed protectively at her chest, unwilling to see, unwilling to know – for now. A difficult balancing act lay ahead, before I could be gifted a final truth.

The last card – more swords, three of them piercing a heart.

Margaritte sat back and sighed. 'Our deepest fears,' she said. Then, 'Death, more death.'

I had been a guest at that table enough times to know that hanged men and punctured hearts were not to be read literally. Even the death card itself, with its skeleton riding a horse into town, didn't necessarily mean a life would be lost. These cards indicated an end, one that might involve pain and struggle, but one that also offered the possibility of a brilliant, new beginning.

Margaritte's eyes were red. A tear slipped down the creases of her cheek.

'We lost ten men fifteen summers ago,' she said.

I pushed away from the table, confused, perhaps a little scared.

'I know,' I replied, 'but what's that got to do with –'

'I think we might lose more.'

'Right.' I had no idea why this should show itself in my cards; there were no fishermen in our family. 'And you think another boat will go down?'

Margaritte shook her head. 'You weren't there.'

'I *was* there,' I replied. 'I *do* remember.'

I had seen the reverberations at least. I was twelve years old. I understood what the small boats were searching for – wreckage. The wives stood at a safe distance on the East Bay, praying for the tide to be charitable and return the bodies. One of the women started up a call-and-return folk song about hearts dissolved by salt – *Come back, my bonny boy, turn back*. A ceremony on the cobbles followed in the weeks afterwards, my father part of a choir of men singing 'Eternal Father, Strong to Save', those voices so deep they vibrated within me, as if I was singing too.

Paul had brought up the accident at the breakfast table some time later and Dad had rapped him hard across the knuckles with a spoon, told him: 'We don't speak of men who are taken by the sea.'

Then Mary Ahearn was at our door, come the summer's end, uncharacteristically thin from her grief, a summer dress hanging loose across her collarbones, Jade-Marie in her arms, a baby with springy curls and fat wrists. Mary begged my father for work and when he said that he had nothing, that what she was asking for was unreasonable, impossible, she grew hysterical, threatening. My mother lifted Jade-Marie from her arms and placed the soft animal weight of her in my lap at the kitchen table, before leading Mary into the back garden to talk more privately. Jade-Marie had snuffled and blown bubbles, staring up at me expectantly with her green-brown gaze. So, I had sung to her, because that seemed to be the answer to everything then: 'Lord of the Dance' – we had just learnt the harmonies in Sunday School.

Here, my mind stalled. It couldn't have been that song, the same one that Jade-Marie had, all grown-up, bellowed in chapel at the beginning of term. My mind was playing tricks.

I searched my memory for details that were definitely true.

The huge metal cross at the end of the harbour – that was real. It was still there, erected after a campaign by Jacob and Diana Crane, in memory of the drowned men, to protect the island from another fishing disaster. Single lives had been lost before but never ten men all in one go. Trawlers were usually crewed by four, maybe five. That there had been so many aboard one boat was unnecessary, maybe even dangerous. It must have been a time when we were more desperate for fish.

That harbour cross always nagged at me; I didn't like it. It was ugly and ostentatious. A contradiction.

'Not a man has died on the boats since that cross went up,' Diana Crane liked to boast to whoever would listen, which meant that it was nothing but a charm to appease a magpie god, no different from a rabbit's foot, or a hag stone, or the stroke of the mane of a black-haired virgin.

I don't know how long I was lost to these reflections, but when Margaritte spoke, it felt as though I had been in a deep sleep and she was pulling me to its surface.

'The cross wasn't put there to stop bad things happening,' she told me.

I leapt up from the table, red wine splashing across the cards. How did she know what I'd been thinking? My hands went to my scalp, as if I might stop her reaching in and seeing more.

'The cross was put there to keep a story straight,' she said. No more tears. She was dry-eyed and deadly serious. 'You know that, don't you?'

I shook my head.

'Trust your instincts,' she instructed.

'Okay,' I said, 'okay.' I backed towards the door, smiling because I wanted everything to seem fine, normal. I was lifting the carpet, sweeping it all underneath. 'I'll see you next week,' I told her, leaving as calmly as I could.

That was the first Tuesday of Advent.

The goat was found on Saturday.

They were sitting cross-legged in the middle of the stone circle, despondent.

Anna, Britta and Jade-Marie wore their white night-dresses over their school uniforms, coats on top. Viola was zipped up in a long, maroon padded jacket that belonged to her mother – Deborah Kendrick preferring the moth-eaten sheepskin for her vigils on the veranda. All of Viola's main-land coats were too thin for the dropping temperatures, no matter how many jumpers she layered underneath.

The girls had offered to get Viola a nightdress too, which had thrilled her initially as a sign of acceptance, but she had politely declined. Viola's confession, the afternoon of their first meeting – the whole truth of it spilling out of her, the reason why she and her mother had left their old life to be here on Lark – had allowed the girls to confess in return. They were the keeper of each other's worst experi-ences now – but this had reduced some of the trappings of their magic. Once Viola understood why the Eldest Girls gathered at the stones, what they were trying to achieve, she couldn't see how a nightdress would help.

Nothing was working. Terrible things continued to happen. The sky was darkening, the ground was cold and hard. They rested their chins on their hands, their elbows on their knees.

Viola could feel it festering within them all – the notion of futility.

She had to do something, say something, lift them from this abyss.

'There is a reason,' she said, 'why none of this is working.'

Viola poked a finger at the pebbles that they had carved into runes. Beside them was a bowl of water in which they hoped to catch the reflection of the waxing fingernail moon.

Britta sat up, always primed to challenge. 'Oh, yeah. And what reason's that?'

Viola met her gaze squarely. 'It's because none of us believe it will work.'

They were all quiet in response; no quick rebuttals. She was right, their faith had wavered.

A tealight candle flickered out in the twitching of the winds.

'So,' shrugged Britta, 'what are we supposed to do?'

'Stop dabbling at the edges,' came Viola's definite response.

'Meaning?'

'I say we do something big.' Viola could feel it, the sensation growing inside her – rebellion, recklessness, an appetite for fire. 'I say we do something that will actually make a fucking difference.'

She had never heard the girls swear and hoped that her use of the word would demonstrate her seriousness, shock them into action.

'But, what is there left?' Jade-Marie asked. 'What haven't we tried?'

'Plenty!' Viola recruited each one of them in turn with a fervent stare.

She was not as steeped in all this as they were, but she had read books that they hadn't, seen films, visited museums. She knew the extremes – where they needed to tread. An image came to her of a glass cabinet in a gallery seen on a school trip, way back. Within that cabinet a grisly offering, the bloody object of a curse, with a handwritten card explaining how it had been used.

She relayed it to the girls, Anna looking sick at the suggestion.

'But that's a bad spell,' said Jade-Marie. 'We don't do bad spells, only good.'

'Says who?' Britta replied quickly.

Jade-Marie was emphatic. 'No, Brit, that's not right. We turn our cheeks, like my dad did. We respond in the right way, we don't stoop to their –'

'And how did that work out for your dad, then?' Britta was enraged. Jade-Marie's eyes welled. 'Turn the other cheek?' Britta spat. 'Turn the other cheek! You know how the rest of that passage goes, don't you? It says that, if they've taken our shirts, we should hand them our coats too. You want to do that, do you?'

Jade-Marie hung her head.

Britta bellowed out a great cry of frustration. Anna put a hand on her friend's shoulder, pulling her back from the edge, before carefully manoeuvring herself towards it.

'But if we were to do this,' she said, 'and we were acting against evil, then it *would* be a good thing.' They all looked at her – cool, calm Anna, the voice of reason. 'We would be doing God's work even,' she went on, 'because, well, that man would deserve everything he –' She paused here to glance at Viola, '– everything he fucking gets!'

They allowed themselves to laugh at that. Viola thought of *Macbeth*, the play text she had almost given the girls, and a school production she'd seen back home where the Weird Sisters had cackled manically at the end of every scene. How she'd rolled her eyes at their performances, but just look at her now.

'We have to believe, though,' Viola put in, returning them to the seriousness of their cause. 'It will never work, if we don't truly believe.'

'I believe,' said Britta defiantly, as if swearing an oath.

'I believe,' said Anna.

'I believe,' said Jade-Marie.

Viola echoed them – 'I believe' – because in that moment she did, or she truly wanted to, or she understood that this was all that was available to them. These girls were her family, her sisters, and there had to be a way to stop terrible things happening to the ones you loved.

They went sky-clad that afternoon as the light faded. Viola couldn't remember who suggested it. Perhaps it was a collective, organic impulse, that sloughing off of their clothing, bringing themselves forward naked, ready for the next phase. No longer were they children flirting with symbols and chants; they were women with a power that no longer frightened them.

Viola had always shielded her body in the school changing rooms but this situation did not compare. She felt free, unleashed from judgment. Of course, she noticed their individual differences as they undressed – the flatness or not of their stomachs, the shape of their thighs, the spread of their pubic hair – but she felt no embarrassment, no sense of competition, not even the fleeting, confusing sensation of desire. The girls' bodies, she had thought, would look like they belonged on Lark. They would be country bodies, feral and tight and brown, their heels blackened from contact with the earth, but this wasn't the case. The Eldest Girls were as inconvenient and as pale as Viola, because Lark's landscape wasn't one you romped across or lounged upon. You battled with it. You wore clothing like armour.

The four girls lifted their arms to the darkening sky, shivering. It was so very cold.

'We are here for you, Bethany Reid!' said Britta. 'You are not forgotten.'

'And to the ten men gone,' called Anna.

'We defend the ones we love from evil,' said Viola, her voice strong and loud.

'No matter what!' affirmed Jade-Marie.

And then there was a flash.

The girls gasped and wrapped their arms around themselves. There had been no rain, no thickening of the air to suggest a storm was upon them. Had they brought this burst of light into being with their naked conviction? Was this a sign that those on the other side could hear their pleas, that they were there now, with them in spirit?

Then came laughter. Male laughter.

Anna realised first; screaming, crouching low, snatching at one of the oversized nightdresses to cover herself. Another flash, and Jade-Marie, Britta and Viola were grasping for clothing too. Not fast enough. Another flash. The girls bundled together – one cold, pale animal with many naked limbs.

The figure was indistinct, dancing within the shivering circle of light printed on their retinas, becoming clearer with every blink.

'Go away!' shrieked Jade-Marie. 'Go away!'

'Why is he here?' cried Britta. 'Oh, god, I can't believe he's seen us like this!'

'He has a torch,' said Anna. 'Why's he flashing us with a torch?'

'No,' said Viola. 'It's not a torch.' She was the only one who recognised that smooth rectangular object in his hands. 'It's not a torch,' she said, the words seeming to soothe them, though they should have done the opposite. 'It's not a torch, it's not a torch.'

✿ FRIDAY THE 13TH – APRIL 2018

Viola fills a glass, the squealing of the tap so loud in the silence of the cottage. She pours half of the water into a cereal bowl and places it on the floor for Dot, who is panting expectantly at her feet, then walks through to the tiny living room, eyeing the fine fissures in the walls, the quality of the carpet, the small pieces of furniture, as if she were a prospective tenant.

Through the oatmeal glow of the closed curtains, Viola can clearly make out the large paint splat coating much of the front window, the shadow of it like an oversized hand. She turns her attention to the charred stillness of the fireplace next, to the shelf above, where there is a framed family portrait. Peter Cedars, the gamekeeper, stands at the back. He is upright, smiling, would be almost unrecognisable if it weren't for the distinctive crinkle of his eyes. Viola feels a tightening of her throat at the sight of him, at this strange, lighter version. He is holding hands with a woman – Susannah Cedars it must be, though she too is hard to recognise. Her hair is long in this picture, and Viola has only ever seen the woman from a distance, her face raw from crying.

Leah Cedars poses stiffly, soldierly, at the front, looking around thirteen or fourteen years of age. Her dress with its velvet yoke and ribbon at the neck belongs to a much younger girl. Her smile is wide but rigid, and she has a very late gap in her teeth at the side of her mouth. The boy beside her is eight or thereabouts, wearing tailored shorts, cut high on his skinny legs. He doesn't fit in; he isn't even trying to smile.

Viola finds herself staring at this boy, who is real and not real, wondering why she hasn't met him yet, if she has failed to recognise his corresponding adult walking past her on the cobbles. But it is not just the anonymous boy that makes this picture feel off-kilter. It takes Viola a moment to realise what unsettles her: no one takes photos on Lark. On the mainland, every moment is captured, a phone is pulled from the pocket, and *snap* – happiness recorded, memories logged, shame inescapable forever.

People back home complained that photos never got printed anymore, that they sat idle and unlooked-at on hard drives, but that wasn't true. Cabinet tops were clustered with framed holiday pictures, and school portraits trailed up stair walls. Bleached-out studio sessions looked down upon kitchen tables. Viola's mother had gone around their house after the tragedy and taken down every single picture, not able to cope with the way a gaze might catch your eye and seem so alive. She'd put them all in a box, shoved behind the vacuum cleaner in the understairs cupboard, perhaps so Viola would not find them and be tempted to put them back. Her mother did not realise that that cupboard was the first place anyone would look.

Viola had found them, of course, taking one framed photo for her suitcase – all four of them in an open canoe, oars aloft, victorious. It was taken the summer before; the family at its zenith, joy unsullied, because no one in that picture knew that it would soon end.

The only other photos Viola has seen on the island, apart from this staged mantelpiece portrait, are on the wall of the Customs House – historic pictures of the estate.

And, of course, there are the pictures that Mr Hailey took.

It occurs to Viola that Mr Hailey might have taken pictures of Leah too. It feels good to think of the teacher by just her first name. The Eldest Girls still called her Miss Cedars out of habit; Viola always hit the *L* hard, demeaning her, making her small.

She heads upstairs, cautiously, as if someone might be sleeping there. The stairs are steep and the landing is but a metre squared. To the left, there is a step that leads down into a bathroom with a pastel blue curtain around the tub. Viola enters, feeling the air still misted from an early-morning shower. She opens the cabinet above the sink, finds very little, just moisturiser, aspirin, an almost empty tube of steroid cream. She presses a muddy boot to the pedal of the small bin by the toilet and is hit by the stale smell of blood. Inside are sanitary towels soaked through, bright red – too red, almost. She exclaims and backs away.

Across the landing is the bedroom; the curtains are open here, the window framing the tallest bobbing masts of the harbour. On the outside of the glass, there is a small spray of red paint spots from the main splash of it below. A crudely carved wooden heart hangs on a length of brown cord wound around the window catch. The object is almost as lumpy and malformed as an anatomical heart, rather than smooth and symmetrical, like the symbolic one it is supposed to resemble. That Leah Cedars would display this in her home and not be reminded of all that has happened only deepens Viola's mistrust of the woman.

To the right of the window is a door that she pushes open, expecting to find a cupboard within, or a walk-in wardrobe. It is larger than that, though not much. There is a paper frieze of illustrated ducks dancing around the centre of the lemon-painted walls. There is space enough for a cot, but the room is bare. The emptiness of it makes Viola shudder and she shuts the door again, eager to be rid of the sight, of the feeling too.

Leah's bed is made just so, with cushions on top of pillows, a counterpane folded back from the duvet – Viola expected as much. She also knew she would find the full suitcase on the bed, ready to close, but still she tuts and shakes her head – disappointed. There is a glimpse of petrol-blue fabric beneath the piles of neatly folded items in neutral colours. Viola tugs the blue thing free – a gaudy pleated skirt – and holds it up before tossing it, watching it slide from the bed into a clump on the floor.

She sees now the track of muddy footprints she's made across the cream rug. The damage is done, so she lies down, right in the middle of the bed, letting her feet mess the counterpane too. She is Goldilocks with the wrong-coloured hair. *Who's been eating my porridge? Who's been sleeping in my bed?*

Mr Hailey has slept in this bed, has done things with Leah in it. Viola closes her eyes and imagines him crawling across the blankets until he is there, above her, his mouth close, the scar fresh on his chin.

She could never admit it to the Eldest Girls, but she understood his charm after seeing him that night at the stones – a man who feels like a boy, a boy who is so obviously a man.

196

She pictures herself succumbing, having him press down on top of her, slide his warm hands under the layers of her clothing. Viola slips her own hands between her legs, pulling upwards against the fabric of her pyjamas, and feels the beginnings of a shiver of pleasure.

Then Dot leaps onto her, red lead dragging, licking Viola's face.

'Get off!' she squawks, shoving the dog onto the floor. 'Get off me!'

She growls at the ceiling to keep Dot at bay, to be free of the moment. She sighs. What is she doing anyway, messing around like this? Viola swings her legs to sit on the bed's edge and picks up a tall stoppered bottle from Leah's night table. *Mercury's Lavender* reads the handwritten label. The purple liquid inside is half-drunk. Viola opens it, sniffs its pungent floweriness, puts the bottle back.

She is wasting time, she knows it.

The quiet of the cottage is a gift to exploit. This is her chance to hide away, to breathe, to work out every possibility that could come from Leah meeting Saul in the woods, of her seeing that body.

That body.

Viola doesn't want to think of it as a real person with a name. It is easier that way. Anyone could be lying dead in the ferns. *Don't take it personally* – that was the phrase the boys at her mainland school used if a girl was ever upset by an insult. *Why do you have to take everything so personally?* Calling a girl a *sket* or a *ho* was no excuse for that girl to think she was something special. All girls are skets and hos, if boys decide they are. The insult is universal, and so, in that case, is the body in the woods.

Viola lets Dot leap onto the bed this time and nestle beside her thigh. She pets the animal's head as an apology for shouting.

Beside the bottle on the bedside table there is a wooden jewellery box. Viola lifts the lid, fingering through the few silver pieces there, plucking out a brooch shaped like an arrowhead, set with green stones.

She puts it in her pocket. It feels like a fair exchange. Or rather, it's not quite enough. For now, Viola will take it as part payment.

◉ The Book of Leah

It was my birthday and my mother had invited me to lunch.
I had to go, if only to lay foundations. News of Ben and me
would reach them soon, and though my mother might be
pleased, my father would not. I was challenging his authority, being the rebellious teenager at last, but I couldn't
stand the thought of rejection, that he might cut me adrift.
Somehow, that felt like a possibility.

Ben and I agreed to take things slowly this time –
'rewind', as Ben put it. He came for dinner at my house
and I saved my meat rations to make something special. I
lit candles. We stretched out on the living-room floor – just
like teenagers – and worked through my small collection of
records and CDs. Ben said that he would bring a cable and
his phone next time, link it to my hi-fi system, so he could
play the music that he liked – all the bands and songs that
hadn't reached us yet.

He didn't stay the night; we kissed on the doorstep. This
felt more momentous than what we had done by moonlight
in my bed. We were working towards a commingling of
minds, a more intimate endeavour. The uniting of bodies
was something, I had ably proved, that could be done with
anyone. The flesh was easily pleased, easily fooled.

Saul Cooper had certainly been misled. He had taken to leaving the Customs House for a walk at the same time as I left the cottage to go to school – an accident he repeated every morning. I was civil, I said, 'Hello', but he wanted more.

'Leah,' he called after me. 'Leah, Leah, Leah', as I walked on and ignored him.

His bitter edge had gone, pared away by what we'd done. He smiled, and not sardonically. I'd achieved an uneasy peace with the events of that night, but it had been hard won. I could not let in fresh guilt, let myself believe that I owed him.

I set him straight.

'It's Miss Cedars,' I shot back one morning, swivelling on my heels. The rain was heavy, water gushing down the hill and swilling around our feet. Michael Signal was there, out early as seemed to be his way, too fascinated by our exchange.

'My name – Mr Cooper – is Miss Cedars,' I said, making clear to all present the nature of our relationship, then I continued up that path that flowed like a river.

Ben and I took lunch together in the school canteen, although not too often. When a piece of your personal information becomes pupil currency, there is a power shift in the classroom; you lose control. The Eldest Girls noticed these lunch dates, of course; they obsessively tracked Ben's movements. He had generously given them his ear and now they seemed to think they owned him. When we sat together to eat, the girls positioned themselves at a table in my eyeline and regarded me solemnly, picking at their food, rubbing at the indelible tattoos now healed at their wrists.

'They're watching us,' I whispered across the table.

200

'Who?' he asked. 'The Russians?'

I didn't understand that this was a joke.

'The Eldest Girls,' I said, a hand across my mouth so they couldn't read my lips.

'You're imagining it,' he replied.

But I wasn't. I wasn't imagining it.

He changed the subject, by asking me to go to the Billet House for our next date.

I refused. 'No, that will be far too weird, being in that house full of men, having them all laugh, Reuben Springer and –'

'Reuben's not like that,' Ben cut in.

'– and Abe Powell and Saul Cooper and –'

I tried to make it sound casual, but he grabbed at the name: 'Saul Cooper?'

There was an awful pause.

'Yes,' I said, wondering how I might confess, how it could ever be made to sound acceptable. *We had broken up, and I was drunk, and you have slept with other people before me so...*

'There's no Saul Cooper living with us,' he said.

'Yes, there is!' My voice had risen. It came in a series of squawks. 'I mean, where else would he be living?'

'How should I know?' Ben protested. 'And who's Saul Cooper anyway? Have I met him yet?'

I fished for an answer, my mouth opening and closing.

'Oh, he's, he's, no one very interesting,' I said eventually.

I agreed to the date at the Billet House and began mentally preparing myself. I pictured a crude dwelling, lacking the basics of table and chairs. There would be a dirt floor, a fire and the straw beds of a lions' den. Luke Signal would circle me with the rest of the pride, ready to report back to my father. *She's not steering clear of that* coycrock t*eacher like you told her to, you know.*

I had never not followed my father's advice.

'Keep your head down, do as I say, and you'll be fine.' This was the refrain of my teenage years and I didn't question it. I was starting to realise what Paul had meant when he said Dad was making sure everything worked out all right for me and not for him. There had been no corresponding mantra guaranteeing Paul's safety in return for obedience.

On the day of the lunch with my parents, I helped Dad check the snares. Mum was fretful that he would otherwise miss this meal and not see his own daughter on her birthday, so preoccupied was he with his war against the ever-burgeoning fox population. Mary and Luke had worked too many weekends lately. Dad couldn't ask them again without having to explain himself to the estate for the extra overtime expenditure.

With my help, the job would be done faster and I could – as per Mum's instructions – stop him from getting engrossed in the fixing of something else, steering him home by 1 p.m. I could also stop him wandering into the workers' shed by the dog runs for a tea break that would lapse into a quick nap. Mary had let slip to Mum that Dad had been caught regularly sleeping on the job.

We parked up on land beyond the old Reunyon Farmstead, where the red-haired newcomers had moved in. There had been complaints that the woman and her daughter had not done any of the work they had promised, but even from this distance, progress was clear. Beds of soil had been shaped and turned, wild hedgerows tamed. Wood cladding still hung loose from the face of the building and the balusters of the veranda remained broken and splintered, but that was a huge task to undertake – too much for just one woman and a child. I wondered why the Council hadn't offered to send over Mark and Andy Cater to help. The brothers could have lodged in one of the many spare bedrooms, given the women some feeling of security out there on the isolated west coast, then maybe she'd have felt happier letting her girl go off to school.

My father and I zipped up our jackets against the piercing cold and got out of the cab, heading for a patch of overgrown land that abutted the once beautiful tiered gardens of the estate. Seals sometimes basked in the cove below, but there was no sightline to their colony from the land, the cliff was too sheer. You had to rely on the reassurances of the fishermen that the animals had returned each year.

I carried the lump hammer in one hand, enjoying the weight and swing of it, and in the other I brought the tool bag, should any snares need resetting. I followed Dad's wax-jacketed back down the funnel-through, his breath making clouds as he called over his shoulder – 'Careful not to make any fresh paths, Leah!' He spoke as if I hadn't done this a hundred times before.

The two snares we'd already checked had been still standing erect, unbothered, and I prayed, if only for Dad's mood, that this next one would have something in its loop, so he could make use of his rifle. When I heard him curse ahead of me, the kind of language he never used when Mum was around, I knew he was to be denied. This snare was empty too, but worse – the loop was flat to the ground. It had dropped or been knocked over – or, in all likelihood, not been set correctly in the first place.

'That stupid bloody boy!' My father kicked up a divot of soil in frustration. 'I swear, if he fell from a great height he couldn't be trusted to hit the ground.'

'Let me, Dad.' I pushed past him and knelt, spreading out the tools. I urged him to return to the cab, to wait there – he was so furious he was wheezing – but he wouldn't go. He watched over my shoulder as I worked, my fingers numbing quickly in the cold, and he chipped in instructions that I didn't need.

'Put your pliers down by the ground anchor, Leah. They're brightly coloured and they'll make sure you don't lose your spot.'

I bit my tongue.

We got back in the cab in time to hit Mum's lunchtime deadline, but Dad said, 'We need to pop in at the farm-stead, let them know about the snare, so they don't catch a foot.'

'They won't wander there, Dad,' I assured him, 'it's too wild.'

'That girl gets everywhere,' he replied, taking the decision from my hands, turning up the track that led to the Reunyon Farmstead.

The mother was sitting outside on that splintered veranda when we arrived, even though the temperature was dipping near zero. At the sound of our engine, the girl came out too, crashing the door back on its hinges, running down the veranda steps as if she might launch herself at my father when he stepped from the cab, for an embrace perhaps, or to bundle him aggressively to the ground. I stepped out too, driven by a protective impulse. Was this why I wasn't so sure about listening to his advice anymore, because our roles were reversing? Was it my turn to look after him?

'I haven't been anywhere near your dogs!' the girl yelled. 'And Dot hasn't been anywhere near the sheep!'

This was the first time I'd got close to her, heard her speak. Her accent was similar to Ben's but not quite the same; the vowels rang flat. Her face was startlingly pale, the freckles picked out, like they are on the cheeks of Lark girls at the end of summer.

'I came to warn you of a snare,' said my father.

'Oh.'

She was extinguished just as swiftly as she had caught fire, my father's words the wet thumb against the flame. She pulled the too-long sleeves of her sweater over her hands and glanced at her mother who was pushing herself to standing, angling for a better view. The girl gave her a neat shake of the head that translated quickly – *no need to worry* – and the woman sat down again.

'What's a snare?' asked the girl, returning her attention to us.

'It's for catching foxes.'

Her eyes widened at this.

'Don't you or your dog be getting caught up in it.' Dad pointed towards the west cliffs. 'It's set in the thick of the brush, that way.'

I knew that voice – the extra gruffness put there to hide a tenderness beneath. It was unnerving to hear it being used on someone who wasn't me. Would he tell the girl to keep her head down next, to do as he said so everything would be all right?

She nodded her understanding. We climbed back in the cab and drove away.

The clock slipped past one as we bounced down the steep hill towards the lodge, to Mum and to lunch, to the small parcel I'd seen wrapped on the kitchen sideboard that would be a piece of jewellery made by Charity Ainsley, Hope's sister – an arrowhead of silver, decorated with some foraged jade. We would not be on time, but we would be close.

Then we came upon the goat, lying in a pool of its own blood, its body ripped in two.

Dad stopped the Land Rover and we got out to examine the carcass, its gaping chest and ravaged head, the congregation of flies.

'Foxes, do you think? The girl's dog?'

Dad was ashen. 'A goat this big? This amount of damage? No way. And look – the tear down the middle is clean.'

The edges of its slitted pelt were straight, knife-cut. The lungs had been pulled free of the ribs, along with a spill of its other organs.

'Not the girl herself?'

'No! No!' he said, and I bristled at his swift shielding of her from blame. How did he know what she was capable of?

'Well, she was pretty defensive from the moment we pulled up,' I suggested.

'No,' he said again, certain.

'Why would she say all of that stuff then, just out of nowhere, if she wasn't guilty of something?'

'It wasn't out of nowhere.'

'What do you mean?'

He dipped his head and sighed. 'She isn't a bother, really,' he said, no straight answer at all. 'It's just she's on her own and she can be … She just needs …'

'Needs what?'

Fear rose within me – had something terrible happened between them?

'She needs someone looking after her,' he said, avoiding my eye. 'You saw the state of the mother. She's poorly, no matter how Bishy puts it.'

I laughed sharply, anything to avoid my real emotion. I knew absolutely how Paul had felt now – his envy, the injustice.

'But she's a *coycrock*,' I spat. The bigotry I'd been brought up with swelled easily to the surface. 'And you know she's been seen up at the stones with the Eldest Girls too, getting mixed up in their nonsense. The kids in my class have been talking about it.'

My father stared at me levelly. I felt ugly under this scrutiny, exposed.

'Same might be said for your *coycrock* teacher,' he replied, returning fire. 'Hasn't he been getting mixed up with those girls 'n' all?'

I was breathless. He already knew, understood that I had taken his advice and discarded it. I wanted to say sorry, to beg his forgiveness, and at the same time I wanted to defend Ben – *He teaches them science, only science!* – but we were stood either side of a bloody carcass, the grassy stench of it rising up, so I said nothing. The situation felt messy enough.

'Let's get some tarp from the back,' said my dad, 'get this thing into the truck.'

We worked quietly, carefully testing that the animal's limbs could take its own weight before we grabbed a pair of hooves each and lifted.

'Can you see its missing horns?' asked my dad. 'Or any of his insides? I don't want any remains being found.' We poked around at the edges of a nearby copse but there was no trail of sinew, nothing to suggest an animal had dragged part of the goat away to chew on later. We gave up, Dad latching the end of the vehicle's load bed.

'You'll be telling no one about this,' he said as we got back in the cab. His tone was fierce. 'Or else I'll have Elizabeth Bishy working everyone into a frenzy, saying there's a wolf on the estate, or a big cat, or some such. I've got no time to be patrolling for mythical beasts, not with real bloody foxes to contend with.'

We stayed silent all the way to the incinerator behind the Big House. We both knew it wouldn't be 'wolf' that Elizabeth Bishy cried if she got word of this. She'd say it was a ritual slaughter, part of some ceremony or spell, proof that supernatural practices were alive again on the island. From what we had seen – the goat's belly neatly sliced, the removal of its organs, the torn-off horns – would we be in any position to deny it?

My mother reprimanded us for arriving late, for the smears of blood on our clothes and the bacon-like smell of the incinerator in our hair.

'Got one that put up a fight, did you?' she asked, after delivering orders to change our clothes quickly so that lunch didn't spoil.

'One daft bastard, yeah,' said my father, loosening his boots. 'They're clever beggars, foxes, but you'd think they'd work out that keeping still in them snares was the best way not to get hurt.'

It was smooth, his lie, astonishingly so.

The Billet House was as minimal and characterless as I had been led to believe. The walls and floor were panelled with strips of treated pine, giving the place a temporary, unfinished air, a nod to its rapid construction all those years ago. Still, it was neater than I had anticipated. A log burner beamed warmth from the corner and on the dining table, alongside a vase of clumsily arranged anemones, music played from a small speaker connected to the thinnest, sleekest computer I had ever seen.

'It's... nice,' I said, unable to keep the surprise from my voice. 'Tidy.'

'I've been cleaning all day,' Ben replied. 'Don't look under anything, will you? Don't open any cupboards or you'll be killed in the avalanche.'

I listened for the other residents as he took my coat, could smell the musky recent presence of them under the high notes of furniture polish.

'They're at the Anchor,' Ben said, seeing my gaze twitch towards the open-tread staircase that presumably led to the bedrooms. 'I bribed them.'

He had only just showered, I noticed – I could see the afterglow of it on his skin – and it made me ache for the intimacy of his body again. Would it be so bad, I asked myself, just to give in?

'Wine?' he asked.

'Please! And who did you bribe to get a bottle outside of Christmas week?'

'It's stolen,' he replied, enjoying my shocked expression. 'Reuben helps himself to a few bottles at the Anchor when he's helping out.' He leaned close. 'Just don't tell his brother.'

We sat together at one end of the glass-topped dining table, eating an adequate spaghetti Bolognese that Ben proudly called his 'signature dish'. As the songs coming through the speakers changed, he announced the names of the artists and gave a short summary of their backlist, their origins, and so on.

'Is there going to be an exam at the end of all this?' I teased, and he winced.

'I'm trying too hard, aren't I?'

'It's okay,' I said. 'It's nice. It's great.'

I thought of him comforting me in bed after our conversation about the Eldest Girls, when he'd told me he knew that I was a virgin. *It was great! You were great! I think this is all great!*

I put down my knife and fork.

'Maybe we should just go upstairs,' I said. 'Break the tension.'

He looked at me for a long moment, unsure that I was serious, then grinned, made an elaborate display of dropping his cutlery and throwing back his chair. We left our half-full plates and took the music and the wine upstairs.

We did it on the floor. A thick, embroidered rug covered the boards of his small single room, and he pulled down blankets and pillows to keep us warm. His bed creaked and moved with him in the night, he said, and wouldn't withstand any kind of – he chose the word carefully – any kind of 'action'.

I thought that it would spook me, being on the ground like that, a reminder of how I'd behaved at the Customs House. Would Ben's face become Saul's in the midst of it? Would the spirit of that night come back to haunt me? The opposite. The similarity of our positions, the situation, the comparable fear of being heard or discovered, made the exorcism complete. This was who I wanted to be with.

It was only as we lay back afterwards, our skin sticky with sweat, my head falling to one side, that I took notice of the things he had stuffed beneath his bed in the rush to make the place tidy. Ben had not expected us to come up here, to lie like this – he couldn't have done. There were carrier bags under there, boxes, a crate of dusty measuring beakers, an empty rucksack. And something else, resting just beyond Ben's head.

I had decided to ask no more questions though; I had promised that I wouldn't. Doubt only brought me uneasiness and misery. So, I chose not to see those two great curling lengths like dinosaur's teeth, their ends tufted with hide and stained with the freshness of blood.

I did not see the horns of a goat.

The setting of a curfew in the midst of Advent was no way to prepare for a cheerful Christmas.

All had been well on the last Sunday. Three candles were lit on the wreath by a youngster of the congregation, Victoria Totten from the juniors being chosen for the task. Everyone in the congregation congratulated the girl on how confidently she had held the taper – less a compliment and more a reference to the previous year when Sapphira Dean had fallen to weeping, spooked by the way the flame crept closer to her hand and the wax dripped hot down her wrist.

Father Daniel wore brand-new vestments, beetroot-dyed and French-seamed by Martha Signal, with holly and ivy embroidery added afterwards by the handful of older ladies of the nursing home. The robes were a deep pink for the bringing in of joy, and Father Daniel's reading spoke of a radiance in the dark, of how John had borne witness to the light so all men, through him, might come to believe.

'*John was not that light,*' Father Daniel told the gathered, the words accorded the emphasis of a tiny printed clause in an otherwise straightforward contract, '*but* was sent *to bear witness of that Light.*'

This talk of 'witnesses' should have resonated with the Eldest Girls as they sat together in a pew, their white Sunday-best crisply ironed beneath their coats.

They themselves had been witnessed.

They had been seen moving away from the light and closer to the dark. They had been observed going naked in this descent. Photographic proof existed, according to whispers. Pictures had been taken for the purposes of confirmation and the administration of justice. (For what other purposes could there be?) Though it was not known who had pointed the camera, and who now held the images; these were details only the prurient would request.

The girls kept any shame they felt well concealed. They lifted their voices uncharacteristically high for the hymn 'Come, Thou Long Expected Jesus', and during the second verse, as if taking their lead from Barbara Stanney's organ flourishes, they slipped spontaneously into beautiful counter-melodies, smothering Diana Crane's routine efforts to mark herself out.

'A perfect three-part harmony, it was,' Hope Ainsley remarked at the post-service gathering in the nave.

'It was, in fact, a four-part harmony,' Miriam Calder cut in, sipping delicately at her tea. 'Rather like it is with the four gospels.' There was a glance here to Father Daniel for his approval of the analogy. 'The gospels are like harmonies colliding to provide us with one complete and uninterrupted meaning.'

Hope's voice came back sharply. 'How it can it have been a four-part harmony, Miriam, when there's only three of them?'

'Oh, did you not realise?' Miriam smiled sympathetically at the Lark hairdresser. 'The red-haired girl was joining in at the back. I could make her out clearly, but perhaps I just have an ear for these things.'

The red-haired girl, seated alone yet again, might have been the next item for discussion that morning, if not for the recent actions of the lovely Miss Cedars.

Over the previous weeks, with the assistance of the curate, Leah Cedars had made sure Benjamin Hailey attended chapel at the weekend, as well as on school days, and this had gone some considerable distance to allaying suspicions about the handsome *coycrock* teacher. If Mr Hailey was guilty of holding any questionable beliefs, about faith and science and phone masts, they were merely a hangover from his mainland upbringing. With regular chapel attendance, he could so easily be cured.

Then, that very morning, the lovely Miss Cedars had walked into service hand-in-hand with Mr Hailey and all residual doubt concerning the new teacher's soul was instantly washed away. Because – hallelujah! – after a dearth of several years there was going to be a wedding on Lark!

One had looked likely the summer just gone, anticipation at full sail as Tom Ainsley and Bernadette Dean prepared to leave school; the pair had made no secret of their plans to marry. Hope Ainsley staged public bridal hair-styling sessions in the Counting House, her future daughter-in-law the model, and every woman had an opinion on how the chapel should be decked out in flowers for the forthcoming ceremony. Then Tom and Bernadette had eloped, on the June ship, for a new life on the mainland. Hope had cancelled her salons for July and August, so she could hide away and nurse her disappointment. Everyone was let down twice-fold: there were no nuptials and, for the summer months, no shampoos-and-sets either.

Martha Signal had since taken on the mantle of expectation. Her son, Luke, had grown into a dashing potential groom, in a smouldering sort of fashion, and was certain to give the Cater brothers a run for their money once those Eldest Girls left school.

All rested on when the Eldest Girls left school.

But now there was Leah Cedars and Benjamin Hailey – a union that would surely lead to an imminent baby. Leah Cedars was nearing thirty, she couldn't be messing around. Pining eyes fixed on the long-dry font as the congregation in the nave discussed this exciting new romantic development, and when Susannah Cedars eventually spoke up, she did not chide the women present, though she would have been well within her rights to do so. *You were falling over each other to condemn my daughter and that teacher a few weeks ago, and now here you are wanting to place a sixpence in her shoe! You fickle furies!*

Instead, Susannah said: 'Let's slow down, shall we!' This mild attempt at firmness was spoiled by a creeping smile. She was excited too; she couldn't not be. 'You've got to give young love room to blossom.'

For all the delight that Sunday had brought, for all the pink embroidered robes and beautiful harmonies and hopes of a new baby, something else was brewing on the island, something less joyous. The moon was waxing towards a full flowering. There was a pervasive tension, felt as a tightness in the breastbone, one that could only be ignored for so long.

Mary Ahearn, Rhoda Sayers and Ingrid Duchamp did not remain at chapel to chatter, and were not usually inclined to do so. Mary and Rhoda understood themselves well enough to know that they would not be warmly welcomed. They each held authority, at the Provisions Store and on estate land, but did not have the status of those women who supped tea with Father Daniel. Ingrid, being married to the island's financial adviser, might easily have participated, though she preferred to keep herself to herself – an aloofness that the other islanders excused on account of her foreignness.

The three women left together and made the journey side-by-side towards the Duchamp residence, one of the larger constructions on the south elevation, designed with plentiful windows to drink up the meagre sunlight. These women were not friends, nor enemies, merely an unlikely gang – one woman was soft and practical, one angled and neat, the last fierce and hardy. They were connected only by the accident of their daughters' similar ages.

And by the pressing question of what on earth they were going to do.

There was a meeting scheduled the following day at the school; the women had insisted upon it, or Mr Crane had demanded it, depending on who you spoke to. Either way the three mothers were seen waiting in the corridor outside his office on Monday, having agreed, it seemed, during their Sunday morning assignation to make a distinct effort with their appearance. Even Mary Ahearn, who never wore anything but her worker's greens, or a simple blouse and trousers for chapel, had taken greater pains.

'Mary Ahearn is wearing a dress!' Miriam Calder was heard exclaiming in the staff room, prompting everyone to take their turn at the glass panel of the door to behold this spectacle. The situation had to be serious, it was decided, though the three women did not seem intimidated by what lay ahead, rather determined, warlike, in their prettiest outfits. The only thing out of place in this display was the small, rough bag Mary Ahearn carried with her, of the kind usually employed for the carrying of fresh-shot game.

Inside, was something crucial to their testimony.

A heart.

It was not completely hardened, though its outer layer had dried and cracked. It was a heart about the size of your fist. A heart deliberately punctured through with nails.

The morning after his meeting with the mothers, Mr Crane entered the staff room to address his team.

'*Except the Lord build the house: their labour is but lost that build it...*' These were his words as he came in; he had skipped all pleasantries to launch into a prayer of sorts.

A circle formed automatically; heads bowed.

This was the psalm about children being a gift, how they are like arrows in the hands of giants; a man should make sure he had a quiver full of them. The Lord had not blessed Jacob and Diana Crane with their own children; the pupils were his young. He was father to the whole island.

Mr Crane gave a *glory-be*. The staff gave their amen. Then he delivered his pronouncement: 'Jade-Marie Ahearn, Anna Duchamp and Britta Sayers –' he had never been one to use their collective moniker '– are subject to a strict curfew from this moment onwards. They are to go straight back to their individual homes after school each day. If they are seen idling, congregating or taking any kind of circuitous route, they are to be challenged immediately and the matter is to be reported directly to me. Is that understood?'

'Yes,' murmured the staff. Another *amen*.

'I consider it part of your duties to enforce this matter even after the last bell has rung.'

'Yes,' they murmured again.

Amen, amen.

Were any glances exchanged – between the *coycrock* teacher and his sweetheart, perhaps? If so, it was done with great stealth.

It was the three mothers who had demanded action, it was said. They had implored Mr Crane to intervene. The heart was proof that someone was harassing their daughters at the stones, leading them to darker places. None of the girls, not even the red-haired newcomer, possessed the strength or wherewithal to kill a goat and extract its heart – Mr Crane had to concede that. Then, he must correspondingly see that the Eldest Girls were not the perpetrators. They were victims. Though a curfew was likely not what the mothers had in mind when they went to the headmaster for his help. Wasn't it protection for their daughters that they sought, not punishment?

The opinion in the Anchor that evening – men only, it being a Tuesday – was that this was an inevitable conclusion to a saga that had been allowed to go on for far too long. It was unsavoury timing though, to be confronting this ungodly business, with Christmas just days away. As soon as Jacob Crane joined the gathering in the bar, however, judgement shifted – the timing was spot on. There were so many jolly distractions to come – carol-singing in chapel, the lighting of a tree on the cobbles, the last day of term, the baking of cakes, the lifting of wine rationing – who would find themselves dwelling upon the matter at all?

Still, there was one nagging detail that could not be made to hang straight, no matter how you nudged it. The girls had likely not procured the heart, a female being too weak for the task, but shouldn't they still be held, in some way, responsible for what happened to it?

That is to say, the nails.

Everyone on the island knew what an object like that was supposed to represent. It was the same as a poppet skewered through with a long, sharp pin, or a wax effigy tossed into a ceremonial fire. That goat's heart was a curse upon one of their number.

All in the bar that evening fell silent and looked around for a likely target for this hex, settling on no one in particular, though in the process it was noticed how Peter Cedars' face had grown pale, then turned a strange shade of red. He had been quiet during all of their discussions, giving only grunts that could not be construed as disagreement or assent. Now, he was breathing heavily. Now, he was sweating. It was as if the mention of the goat's heart and its true intent had unstoppered the bottle, unleashed the spell.

The gamekeeper's glass of beer slipped from his grasp and shattered on the ground. His other hand, the one that was still working, went to his shoulder and squeezed. His face pinched in pain.

It was only when Peter Cedars fell to the floor that everyone remembered Dr Bishy's recent talk at the Counting House, the one about the correct usage of the island's defibrillator, and there was a common understanding of what exactly was happening.

Reuben Springer ran for the machine. One Cater brother raced for the doctor, the other for the gamekeeper's wife, as Saul Cooper fell to his knees on the beer-swilled floor and pumped out a rhythm on the old man's chest.

219

The heart full of nails was indeed a crucial piece of testimony.

It was a sign perhaps that someone had led those girls to darker places, but was now undeniable proof that the Eldest Girls were witches.

PART TWO

LUNAR PHASE

◉ The Book of Leah

I had seen the card – the three swords piercing a heart. I had known it was coming and done nothing to stop it.

Still, I asked him: 'What have they done to you?'

Shocked back to life, he'd been brought to a bed in the nursing home. A drip fed a bloated vein in his thin, grey arm. It was a charade of care. He needed a mainland hospital. He needed a boat.

'They've done nothing,' he told me. 'Don't you go accusing them.'

We both knew who we were speaking of.

I shook my head. 'I will kill them,' I said. Did I mean it? Did I really believe in such voodoo? Could a nail driven into the bloodied organ of a goat be enough to bring about this? It didn't matter. I needed someone to blame. 'I will kill those girls for what they have done to you.'

'My heart was weak all along,' he replied.

I could hear my mother's words: *His father's heart gave up on him, and his father's before that, and his father's before that …*

My father could hear her too. He told me: 'You be the one to break the cycle, Leah.' Then he said: 'I can't protect you anymore.'

'Yes, you can,' I insisted. I ignored the tears that spilled silently down his cheeks. 'When you get better, you'll be there for me.'

He shook his head, as much as he was able. 'A wise man knows when his fortune has run out.' His voice was like paper. 'And now I need to confess.'

I didn't want to hear it; I wasn't ready. Would I ever be ready?

'A boat will come,' I assured him, 'and then you'll be –'

'There is no boat. I need to confess.'

'I'll fetch Father Daniel,' I offered, but he would not let go of my hand.

'I want to confess to you, Leah.'

If I could have run from that room, I would have done, burst out into the cold air, into a winter's day too bright for the season, too bright for what was happening to our family in the sickly yellowness of that room. I would have shielded myself from what was to come, had my father die a good man, complete, intact – the man I had always known. But I knew that these were our last moments together, that there would be no more, that I could do nothing but stay, listen.

He swallowed hard. 'I let the rot set in. I let a boat go down. I have watched those girls –'

'Stop!' I called out.

'I have watched those girls and I know what they're doing. We've turned our backs on them so they've turned to the devil. We cannot call ourselves Christians.' His gaze was fervent; this passion was the only strength he had left. 'Forgive me,' he said.

'That's not up to me, that's –'

'Forgive me!'

His breath came as a desperate rattle. My tears joined his.

'I have looked my enemy in the eye,' he went on, 'and shown him love, because I was afraid he'd punish you, my daughter. Forgive me, forgive me.'

I nodded, because that was what he needed. I should have gone to the door, summoned my mother into the room, not let her miss this moment, but I could not let go of his hand; it was all that tethered him to the earth.

'You need to leave, Leah,' he said. 'You need to go to Paul and talk to him about what is happening here, make a plan, help those girls.'

'Nothing is happening here,' I said, words spoken automatically as my mind ran the truth on a loop – a truth I had always held within me. *Paul left because he knows. Paul left because he knows. Paul left because he knows.*

'Remove the beam from your eye, Leah,' my father said. 'Don't be afraid to see.'

'All will be well,' I persisted, 'a boat will come.'

'It is too late for me, but not for you.'

'All will be well.' It was a prayer now, a mantra. 'All will be well. All will be well.'

'*Be not deceived,*' he told me, a last clutch at scripture. '*God is not mocked: for whatsoever a man soweth, that shall he also reap.*'

And then he fell silent.

And then he was gone – my father, dead; the Lark I knew dead with him.

✽ FRIDAY THE 13TH – APRIL 2018

Viola is downstairs again in the quiet of the cottage, standing in front of Leah's mantelpiece. She is ready to move on.

When Leah and Saul return, Leah will be a mess and Viola doesn't want to be here for that. Never return to a firework once it's lit.

Before she goes, she turns the Cedars family portrait face down. Peter Cedars' gaze is what she cannot bear. He would be furious at what she is doing, dragging his daughter into all of this, but Viola refuses to shoulder any guilt. She turns away from the mantelpiece.

Leah Cedars was not dragged into anything. Leah Cedars inserted herself, made promises she had no intention of keeping. She had told Viola and the Eldest Girls that she was named for a woman in the bible who was skilled at deception; that meant, by implication, so was she. It should have come as no surprise that Leah was leading them on, using them to get exactly what she wanted.

'She deserves everything she gets,' Viola tells Dot, snatching up the dog's lead.

They head through the kitchen, out the back door, the rhythm of Dot's claws against the hard-standing familiar and comforting.

Viola knows where she must go next – to the very seat of justice – because it is time for the island to wake up. To really wake up.

Out the back gate they go, into the ginnel that runs between the two lines of cottages. They must sprint again; St Rita's bell will ring soon.

But a hand is there, on Viola's shoulder, before she can pick up any pace. It is a powerful grip, one that spins her around.

'Where are they?' is the demand hissed into Viola's face. 'Where are the Eldest Girls?'

Christmas came and went at the Reunyon Farmstead without mention.

Viola and her mother had not celebrated the previous Christmas either, back on the mainland, because the incident had happened just weeks before. Cards landed on their Surrey doormat, some expressing sympathy, some offering good wishes for the season – probably. All were carried at arm's length straight to the dustbin and deposited, unopened. The television and radio remained off, so there would be no ambush of cheer. Viola spent Christmas morning praying that her mother would not give her a present. In her grief, Viola had not thought to buy her one in return. How was Viola supposed to react to a gift anyway? There were no reserves of joy or gratefulness to call upon. No presents were exchanged. For lunch they had eaten something on toast, and then spent the rest of the day in bed, because every corner of that house held a reminder of merrier holidays past.

In many ways, a Lark Christmas was easier. On the island, there was no precedent for happiness.

Come Boxing Day, Viola took Dot to the Sisters' Stones at their usual time, in the slim hope that the Eldest Girls would show up. They hadn't been to the circle for over a week now and, though Viola was growing uneasy at this, she reminded herself that the run-up to the 25th, for normal families, could be filled with any number of time-consuming celebrations.

Viola had considered wandering down to the harbour to see if she might find the girls there, engaged in some activity around that decorated tree by the stocks – an impromptu bout of carolling perhaps – but she had stayed away. Festive music was a guaranteed trigger for sadness, and for this same reason, she had thought she would avoid chapel on the last Sunday of Advent. The girls had convinced her to go. This was the last time she had seen them.

'The Christmas hymns make me cry,' she'd confessed, 'they remind me of Dad and of Seb. I can't be there.'

She felt weak making this admission. Britta, Anna and Jade-Marie went every week, and to school every day, regardless; they faced down their fears while Viola and her mother had run as far as they could from their tragedy.

Still, the girls had been kind, talking her through every detail of the upcoming service, it being the same every year, and these details, in their unfamiliarity, had convinced Viola to go.

'We couldn't do the four-part harmonies without you,' Anna said – a final persuasion.

Viola leant against the middle stone of the circle that Boxing Day for almost an hour. She scanned the ferns for their recent guest, worried that she would be responsible for entertaining him alone, and what 'entertaining him' might necessitate, but anxiety soon dissolved into boredom.

She threw things for Dot to fetch, who would make the initial dash, then pull up, as if remembering belatedly that she wasn't like other dogs and didn't get excited by stupid sticks.

Restless, Viola had crawled through the hollow centre of that middle stone, Dot liking this game at least and joining in. Viola wasn't sure that sorrow was an ailment that could be cured by the stone gods but she hoped they might give it a try.

'That's your worms and fleas sorted, too,' she informed Dot as they headed back through the wood for home.

The day after Boxing Day, a large dappled horse sauntered into the farmstead yard. Riding it, dressed head to toe in worker's greens, was the woman Viola had seen with the gamekeeper, the one the same age as her mother. The woman hefted herself off the horse with a grunt and an awkward swing of the leg, gravel crunching as she hit the ground. She introduced herself as Mary, before telling Viola that she would like her to sit down for what she was about to say next.

Viola had sunk down instantly, thudding onto one of the peeling wooden steps of the veranda. Mary, who had clearly expected to be invited inside on that bitter December day, was taken aback for a moment. She stood unfastening her riding helmet while Viola inhaled deeply, then held her breath as if she was about to be submerged by water.

Viola understood this moment – knew it viscerally. Someone says they have something to tell you and that you need to sit down.

Then they say it.

Then your whole life changes.

Mary perched beside Viola, the weight of her making the step bow and creak.

'It's Peter,' she said, her eyes glistening at the mention of his name.

Viola let go of the air in her lungs. 'Who?' she asked.

'Peter Cedars,' said the woman, her voice sharpening, irritated by the need to clarify.

Viola shook her head, slowly, apologetically.

'The gamekeeper?' Mary offered.

'Oh, yes, him.' Viola relaxed a little; they were back on track.

'Well …' Mary eyed her cautiously, 'he had a serious heart attack.' She paused, as if checking that it was all right to go on. Viola nodded. 'And though Saul Cooper managed to keep him alive while Reuben Springer ran for the defibrillator, we have only limited resources here on Lark, and what with it being winter and no boats passing near, well …' She took a great shivery breath. 'I'm afraid he didn't make it.'

'Okay,' said Viola, because it was obvious she must respond. 'That's –' what would be the right word? '– sad.'

'It's a lot to take in, isn't it?' said Mary, a tear travelling down her pink and doughy cheek. She grabbed Viola's hand and squeezed it firmly, and they stayed like that for a while, quiet, listening to the rapid, expressive undulations of a robin's song. It was comforting, somehow, to be held so tightly, her own mother not in the market for physical affection right now, but still, Viola could feel dishonesty swelling inside of her.

Eventually, she said it: 'I didn't really know him.' She gave Mary a quick, tight smile. 'Sorry.'

Mary dropped Viola's hand and tipped away from the girl, her whole body asking the question: *What do you mean?*

'I talked to him a few times,' explained Viola, keen to draw the woman back. 'Usually because he was cross with me for trespassing.'

Mary stared. Viola felt herself being reassessed, reclassified.

'But,' Mary narrowed her eyes, 'he said… Peter said that he was looking out for you, because your mother was…' She glanced back at the house and lowered her voice. 'Because she's not so well at the moment and that I was to do the same. I was to make sure you were okay if I ever came across you, because you were often out alone and Peter was worried that…'

Viola stared back at the woman and did some reassessing of her own.

'He was worried that something might happen to you, that someone might…'

Now Viola did feel sad; she felt awful. *You reckon it's a good idea, do you, wandering about like this?* It had been concern, not a telling-off. Viola felt a bubble of something rising in her throat – grief, terrible grief – though not necessarily, not completely, for the man they were speaking of.

'You came on a horse,' she said quickly, diverting that bubble, making it pop.

'I'm finding it hard to get back in the Land Rover.' Mary sighed and looked off into the middle distance so she might not cry, a technique Viola recognised, had used many times herself. 'It used to send me mad, all those balls of string and wire in the cab, the slips of paper and his empty Thermos flask, but now, that mess of his…' She stopped, sniffed, licked her lips: more techniques Viola had in her own arsenal. 'Anyway!' Mary slapped her green thighs and forced her voice towards brighter tones. 'Ingrid Duchamp has been helping me get better control of Dandy here, and I, in return, have tempted that Swedish ice queen out of her big glass box for a change.' She said all this with a wry smile, as if Viola should understand what was funny.

'I don't know who Ingrid is either,' Viola confessed.

Mary laughed, seemingly grateful for the opportunity to do so. 'What are we like, eh? Princesses in our towers, the lot of us. You should start introducing yourself a bit. It's much harder for folk to be rude about you when you've made the effort to say "hello", take my word on that.'

Viola nodded that she would.

She also agreed to go to the funeral – it was what Peter Cedars would have wanted.

Deborah Kendrick had been more than ruffled at the sight of her daughter in the kitchen, later that week, dressed in smart black trousers and a roll-neck.

'Why are you wearing that?' she demanded. 'Where are you going? Not the school, not that doctor...'

The presence of her mother in the kitchen, out of her bedroom, not lost-eyed on the veranda, might otherwise have been the right moment to broach what was going unsaid – *What are you so scared of, Mum? Tell me, and I'll tell you what I'm scared of too* – but for the moment Viola was only concerned with quelling her mother's rising panic.

'Peter Cedars, the gamekeeper, has died and I'm going to his funeral,' she explained, in her haste not realising what she had done. If festivities reminded Deborah Kendrick of lost Christmases, the mention of a funeral would send her right back there, to the aftermath.

'Oh, Viola!' Her mother dropped her head. 'You don't have to. We came here to escape all of that.'

'I don't think you can,' Viola replied very softly, heading into the hallway to put on her coat – a thin, inadequate black one, suited to the occasion if not the weather – before embarking on the long, cold walk to the chapel.

On the coast path, ahead of the service, Viola encountered Michael Signal. He bounded up to her, gasping in her ear, equal parts appalled and thrilled: 'What are *you* doing here?'

He pulled her behind the shelter of a wind-scooped hedge, out of hearing of the line of mourners, and proceeded to tell the story of the goat's heart driven through with nails, how it had been delivered by Mary Ahearn to Mr Crane's desk in a game sack, and how the girls were now under curfew.

'Then,' said Michael with unsavoury delight, 'Peter Cedars fell down dead – of a *heart attack*! – cursed by the Eldest Girls! And from what I've heard, by you too!'

He folded his arms over his suit and tie. He nodded resolutely.

Viola's mouth was empty of an immediate response. She felt dizzy, sick, horrified by the connection. The heart wasn't meant to harm Peter Cedars. This wasn't their fault.

But then came another realisation, sly, fierce, rising fast – the heart had worked. Incorrectly and indirectly, it had worked! The power that Viola and the Eldest Girls had tried to harness within themselves existed; it was real, and this fact, separate from any affection she now felt for the late gamekeeper, gave Viola a sudden sense of boldness, of invincibility.

'You should keep your trap shut,' she shot back.

Michael's eyes widened. 'Why should I?'

Viola smiled darkly. 'In case they find out who it was who fetched that heart for us, that's why.' Then she shoved him hard, so that he fell backwards ingloriously, into the hedge. She rejoined the queue of mourners and the boy chased behind her, dishevelled, heckling weakly in her wake, 'What's that supposed to mean? What's that supposed to mean?'

This boldness carried her through the service, forming a dam against the memories she did not want flooding back.

Mary stood beside Jade-Marie in chapel, her arm around her, as Father Daniel led the coffin's procession up the aisle, declaiming, '*I am the resurrection and the life!*' and only then did Viola join up the dots – Mary was Jade-Marie's mother. Why had she not worked this out before? Probably because Jade-Marie talked mostly about her father (Neil, dead at sea) and because the girls stuck close to one another for mass at the weekends, giving few hints as to who in the congregation were their parents.

Here, at the funeral, the girls were hand-in-hand with their respective mothers, the family resemblances startlingly obvious. Anna's blonde, bobbed hair was the image of her mother's, and the discovery that Viola's Provisions Store nemesis was Britta Sayers' mother was perhaps no surprise at all.

The girls were being held close that day because they were not welcome. Yet, they had to be there; absence would have been an admission of guilt. Mary's failure to mention this to Viola seemed an enormous oversight. Did she not know of the *coycrock*'s friendship with her daughter, of her involvement in all of this? Or was it like Jade-Marie not speaking of her mother, was Viola no topic of conversation away from the stones?

Viola decided the omission was a kindness, so that she had not been afraid to come, and also a denial by Mary that the girls could ever have hurt her beloved Peter. Still, as Viola studied the backs of Britta, Anna and Jade-Marie, she imagined their potential, seeing it as something shimmering and actual, rising from the girls' shoulders. What might they do next with this great power they possessed? Oh, the scores they would settle! Oh, how the guilty would suffer at their hands!

Outside, as they all stood by that deep hole in the ground, shoes caked in soil, Father Daniel's voice battling the sharp coastal winds to explain that '*Man that is born of woman hath but a short time to live, and is full of misery*', Viola thought only of their power, of what it could achieve; she zeroed in on this, so as not to recall the last time she had witnessed this sombre ritual, how on that occasion the bodies of her father and brother had been lowered into the ground.

She did not have the strength to attend the wake at the gamekeeper's lodge; neither could she go straight back to the farmstead. The quiet there would likely unwrap the sorrow Viola kept so neatly packaged within herself; its exposure would only wound her mother further. Instead, the girl made for the emptiness of the harbour, to sit on the edge of the stone jetty that doglegged out to sea. She rested her back against the giant metal cross and let her legs hang over the edge, the wild sea licking hungrily at her heels. Then, she allowed herself to sob.

'What the hell are you doing?' A man burst out of a side door of the Customs House, interrupting her moment of

237

solitude. 'Get up, would you!' he yelled, jogging towards her, pulling on a great, flapping oilskin coat. 'Get up! You'll catch your death!'

Viola quickly stood, realising the man would drag her to her feet if she didn't obey. It was the Customs Officer, his expression twisted with horror.

'What on earth were you playing at?' he demanded.

Viola looked down to where she had sat, to where the sea snatched at the jetty like a tiger swiping its paw through the bars of a cage. These were the same waves that claimed a child every seven years. This was no place to hide and cry. She was playing at being stupid, was the answer to the Customs Officer's question, but it would be too pathetic to own up to that. Instead, she reached for the lifebuoy of Mary Ahearn's counsel.

'Hello,' she said to the Customs Officer, calming the chattering of her teeth and the hiccupping of her diaphragm, adopting the bright but quavering voice of a job interviewee, 'I'm Viola Kendrick, it's very nice to meet you.'

The Customs Officer was disarmed by this unexpected formality.

'You're a bloody idiot, is what you are,' he replied, but his earlier passion had been assuaged. He strode off towards the whitewashed stone and warm light of his office, calling back to her as an invitation: 'You'd better bring yourself inside, then, Viola Kendrick, get yourself dry.'

She followed him through the side door into a wide room with windows on all sides. The view took in the entire spread of the sea, as if the building were the bridge of a ship. Various pieces of radio and radar equipment buzzed and blipped, and added to this was the thunder of a small electric kettle.

The man went out to the waiting area beyond another door, where Viola knew, from her first moments on the island, there was a counter with tide times and a shipping schedule, a white, flaking wall and an uncomfortable bench. She hadn't needed to give him her name, it was right there, written in his ledger the day they arrived. He was the one who had driven them to the farmstead, and delivered Mr Crane to their door when the headmaster had tried to enrol her in the school. He knew who she was. Yet, there was the sense that all those tasks had been carried out by the Customs Officer in his official capacity, and this encounter was something different, so he was different too.

'I'm Saul Cooper,' he told her, returning with a blue, fusty blanket, holding it out and examining it on both sides before draping it over her shoulders. 'I should have said.'

He pulled up a chair by an electric radiator and guided her to sit.

Saul Cooper. More dots joined up for Viola – the Customs Officer and the male subject of Michael's spying mission were the same person. Somehow in Viola's mind the two had become disconnected. She looked about her with a keener eye, took in the orderliness of Saul's desk: documents stacked in wire trays. In the corner of the room, there was a low camp bed made up with white sheets and a rough, grey blanket, and beside it, a stand with a sketchbook and pencil. At the sink, shaving equipment and a toothbrush.

'You live here?' she said, unable to hide the pity in her voice. This man had seemed impressive that first day on the island, indomitable, with his barked questions and superior silences. Now, he was reduced – nothing but a grown man playing house, building himself a den.

He turned and regarded the bed, seeing perhaps how she saw it.

'I only sleep here when things get busy,' he told her. He set his eyes on the mugs, dropping in teabags and pouring on water.

Viola looked out the window, to the yawning, churning sea that surrounded them, wondering when 'busy' ever came to be.

'So, you were thinking of following Bethany Reid, were you, cherub?' he said gently, handing her a mug, the term of affection blindsiding Viola. *Poppet* was what her mother used to call her, before, when she spoke easier; her dad had called her *Vee-vee*.

'Thinking of showing fate a thing or two, were you?' Saul went on.

'Fate's fate,' said Viola, a quick, mechanical response, a pull-back from her grief. She blew across the surface of the tea.

'I need to be having a word with your mother, do I?'

He kept his tone light, and so did she.

'Probably. She thinks she can run away from it – fate.'

Saul pulled a face, confused: 'I mean, do I need to be telling Dr Bishy about you?'

Viola's attention was snatched from the steaming tea. 'Oh, no!' she protested. 'Don't do that!'

She watched him take this in, her censure of the man. Saul's face fell, became serious.

'I mean, I'm not, like, depressed or anything,' she countered, desperate to soften what she'd said, not to have her words reported back to Dr Bishy himself. 'I just wanted to sit there for a bit. I'm very happy right now. Things are going really well.' She meant it, strangely. 'I just needed to have a bit of a cry after the funeral, you know.'

Saul nodded. He looked to the door that led to the front desk – the route towards the chapel and the gamekeeper's lodge where everyone would be eating sandwiches now. Viola waited for him to speak again, the moment stretching out uncomfortably. She blew across her tea once more, so she might gulp it down faster and be gone.

'I, er...' He coughed, started again. 'I hope Leah Cedars is bearing up okay.'

He did not look at her.

Viola's senses were snagged by the name, by the quality of his voice when he used it. More dots joined up. The younger woman crying at the front of the chapel was Peter Cedars' daughter, who was, of course, the same woman who had come to the farmstead with him that time when he'd warned Viola about the snare. More importantly, this was the same woman Michael was spying on. This was Miss Cedars, the lovely Miss Cedars, who the Eldest Girls talked of sometimes, disparagingly so because of the way she fawned over Mr Hailey, the male teacher who was giving them practical demonstrations of the ways of the mainland.

Leah Cedars had managed to exist as several separate women in Viola's mind, but now, like that science trick with the coloured filters, circles of red, green and blue slid on top of one another to become a single white light.

They're definitely doing it – that's what Michael had said. Leah Cedars and Saul Cooper are definitely doing it.

'So, she's...' Viola did not know how to phrase it. Leah Cedars was being consoled by a different man at the funeral, in a way that suggested *they* were definitely doing it. Had

Michael got things wrong? Viola found herself falling easily into the guise of childish innocence. 'So, Leah Cedars, she's your girlfriend, right?'

Saul's eyes were on her. 'What did you say?'

'I said...' Viola faltered. The man looked pale, vulnerable. 'I said, she's your girlfriend.'

Viola expected him to deny it, to shift their conversation back to the funeral or her stupid act on the harbour's edge, but instead there was a palpable shift in him – a lifting of the chest.

'How do you know that?' he asked. He was trying out a certain swagger, a boyish smile playing at the corners of his mouth. It was touching, almost sad.

Viola took a breath to speak.

I saw you chasing the woman once or twice, heard her telling you to go away, so I sent a boy to spy on you, by accident really, as a distraction for him, and he came to the conclusion that you two are definitely doing it, which is odd because it seems to me she's definitely doing it with that man at the funeral today.

Viola couldn't say that. She knew how it felt to be hopeful, and how it felt to be lonely, to be crushed. She liked Saul. She wanted him to be happy, and that was likely within her powers, now that she knew how strong they were. It could be as simple as driving a nail into the softness of a heart.

'I know she's your girlfriend,' was what Viola said to Saul, 'because Leah told me herself.'

THE BOOK OF LEAH

I needed a back-up, a witness, perhaps even a lucky charm. The voice of two women equals the voice of one man – that is what I had been brought up to believe. It couldn't be the girls themselves, nor their mothers; they were too close, too vested. It amused me, I suppose, to speak for our island in the company of a *coycrock* redhead.

It was exactly as it had been the last time I visited the Reunyon Farmstead: she was ready with her defences. As soon as my feet crunched the gravel, she came thundering down the steps of the porch, spilling out a plea for vindication. Nothing to do with livestock this time, or the behaviour of her dog; she wanted to justify something she'd said.

'I felt under pressure and I didn't know what to say and I felt sorry for him and –'

'Felt sorry for who?' I cut in.

Her mouth clamped shut. She realised that she had done it again – spoken too soon. We looked one another up and down.

I appeared sallow and tired, I'm sure. I'd spent the past week living at the lodge, guiding my mother through her grief with very little space to navigate my own. She moved beyond shock and began excavating her anger – her husband's promised retirement years had been stolen. He was off, as she put it, 'lamping foxes for the rest of eternity'. This image – completely of her own creation – enraged my mother, yet it soothed me. To think that he was still out there, working the land, and at some point, when he was hungry, he would head on home for his tea.

I had decamped to the lodge with nothing but the black funeral clothes I stood up in. I'd sent Ben away; he seemed so surplus to what was going on, having never known my father. My mother was an enigma even to me. I wanted no witnesses as I failed, over and over, to find the right way to soften her pain. While staying there, I wore her clothes, along with some leftover items from my teenage ward-robe – a bobbled sweater, some wide-legged trousers with a forgiving, elasticated waist. On one occasion, I pulled a red checked shirt of Dad's from the clean laundry pile to wear.

'Take it off!' my mother snapped. 'Do you think I could even bear it?'

Moments before she had admonished me for not talking about Dad enough, for not keeping a sense of him alive. I knew then that it was time for me to go home. Her anger had cooled into an indiscriminate petulance about everything I did. I bundled the red checked shirt into my bag when she wasn't looking, and I was wearing it – symbolically, perhaps – as I stood before Viola Kendrick in the yard of that rundown farmstead. The sleeves were rolled up, the tails tucked into one of my neat teaching skirts. On top, I'd unbuttoned my heavy winter coat and loosened my scarf. January was merciless with its temperatures, as always, yet I'd broken into a sweat from trekking up the hill.

Viola wore an oversized checked shirt too, a blue one, the coincidence feeling like a sign – a good omen. The rest of her was less appealing. Her jeans were muddy at the knee and her hair was a heap of curls, an orange candy-floss haze. I considered asking her to change, to bind her hair into a long, fat plait of the kind I'd seen her wear in chapel.

'Viola, isn't it?' I said.

She nodded.

'And you know who I am?'

She gave a nod to that too.

'Well, I hear you've been hanging out at the stones with the Eldest Girls,' I began.

This came out more accusatory than I had intended and Viola was ready with her next defence.

'Don't worry,' I leapt in. 'I'm not here to tell you off.'

She glanced furtively back at the house; her mother was there, an outline at the window.

'What are you here for then?' she asked quietly, rubbing at her arms, jigging in her trainered feet to beat back the cold.

'Support,' I said.

She had been unsure about coming with me; I'd expected that. I didn't need to wonder what the Eldest Girls had told her. They despised me for stealing away their beloved Mr Hailey, and by rights, they could consider me in league with Mr Crane.

I had thought in the days since my father's death of the times they had asked me questions in class, seemingly innocent things – tangents, I'd assumed, to draw us away from the tedium of GCSE exam practice. *How come you wanted to teach here after being a pupil, didn't it put you off? Is*

Mr Crane as strict with you as he is with us? I thought how easily I'd brushed theses enquiries aside. No wonder the girls had taken their fear and confusion to a stranger, to Ben.

Just as my father said, we, the island, had let them down.

I told Viola what I planned to do. I asked her to trust me.

She asked if she could bring her dog.

'People think of that animal as a familiar, you know,' I warned, 'they don't like it.'

But it was a deal-breaker. If Viola was to be my support, the dog was to be hers.

Our walk was illuminated by a perfect half-slice of moon, no need yet for the torches that we all, without a second thought, carried in every coat pocket. The dog gave us pause to stare out across the water, making us halt every few yards so it could squat low in the grass verge.

'What is it doing?' I asked.

'Peeing,' Viola replied cautiously, as if there might be a trick to my question.

'But can't it just go all at once, so we don't have to keep stopping?'

She shrugged, suggesting there probably was a way to correct the animal, if only she had the desire to do it.

During our stuttering progress towards the harbour, I summarised my case, what I intended to say. I asked her if she was happy to back me up.

She puckered her lips in thought, then said, 'It's beautiful here really, isn't it?', which felt like an agreement, an understanding of what I was trying to do. Beside us, the waves were picked out silver by the particular glow of the moon, and I sensed that Viola was seeing this for the very first time, that she had been looking out across that ocean all these months and seeing no splendour, only distance.

'Yes,' I replied, 'it is beautiful here, despite everything.'

We passed the smokehouse, breathing in the salty, ashy taint that it left on the air, heading onto the cobbles, well lit ahead of us. On nights when the Counting House was to be occupied, they switched on the line of lanterns, strung across building fronts and from poles around the harbour mouth. Tonight, those lights winked at us, they waved.

'I really am sorry about your dad,' Viola said, a rush of words, as if it was important to state this before we stepped into the ring.

I'd heard the phrase so many times in the past few weeks – *I'm so very sorry for your loss* – and still had no idea how to answer. *Thank you. Are you? I know. Yes, me too.* All responses seemed cursory, pointless; the 'sorry' in the first place did me no good.

'Where's your dad?' I asked her.

'Dead too,' she replied, and I almost laughed when 'sorry' made its way to my tongue like a reflex.

I blocked it, asked instead: 'And you don't have any brothers or sisters?'

She sniffed, licked her lips and looked out beyond the boats that nestled against one another within the harbour walls.

'No,' she said. 'You?'

I followed her gaze, onwards, to the straight black line between water and sky.

'No,' I said. 'Same.'

We were being watched. The figure of Saul Cooper was picked out by lantern light against the front wall of the Customs House as we neared our destination. He was smoking, though he had given up years ago and become notorious for his sermonising.

'They'll be using the insides of your lungs to resurface the path to chapel,' he'd yell to the boatmen who kept up the habit, saying it in good humour, but meaning it, and the boatmen would mutter to one another about how there were none so holy as the recently converted. Saul's abstinence had led to his excessive consumption of fisher-men's mints, a sweet always sliding across the front of his teeth. The hot, peppery flavour of them had passed from his tongue to mine on All Hallows' Eve. An intrusive thought came – what would it taste like to kiss him now, his mouth sullied by tobacco? I chased that thought away.

Viola stalled at the sight of Saul, peeling his back from the building, stubbing out his cigarette with a toe.

'Keep walking,' I instructed, and Viola did, making for the stocks where she would tie up her dog. She stooped low to fasten a double knot, petting and calming the animal before she was willing to stand again. Then, in an action incongru-ous with her earlier hesitation, she gave Saul a tentative wave. This was all the invitation he needed. He jogged towards us, the length of his oilskin coat flapping like the wings of a bat.

He nodded and greeted the girl – 'Viola' – then turned to me, smiling oddly. 'Miss Cedars,' he said pointedly. His unctuous smarm had returned and perhaps it was a bless-ing; soft, attentive Saul, the one who called out, 'Leah! Leah!' in a plaintive voice, was so much harder to handle.

I stared him down. He was not to say anything comprom-ising in front of this girl, one whose word had a direct route back to the students of St Rita's.

'Where are you two ladies off to?' he asked.

'Viola and I are attending this evening's Council meeting,' I said. I put my arm around the girl and felt her, quite rightly, flinch at this gesture, at my drawing up of sides.

'Oh, are you!' He began to laugh.

'I am,' I said, stone cold. 'Just like you.'

I could feel Viola's eyes travelling from Saul to me, and back again. I wanted to pull from her mind, like a length of magician's scarves, all the conclusions she was leaping to. I let my arm drop from her shoulders.

'I don't go anymore,' he said airily. 'Neither does Bob Signal, nor the Reverend.'

'What?' This was news to me – and I supposed to most people on the island as well. 'But you're on the Council, so... Why not?'

His affected lightness dissolved. He sighed heavily and looked at his feet. 'Oh, I dunno, it became... Let's just say, there didn't seem to be much point.'

'"Not much point"?' I repeated. I was aghast. '"Not much point"!' My father's words were there, ready to direct him. *Remove the beam from your eye, Saul!* But the beam wasn't there, I could see that; it was long gone. He knew decay had set in, but had chosen the path of least resistance; he had decided to look away.

'Well, I will be attending.' I despised myself for the childish pride in my voice, diminishing what I was about to do. 'I shall be sitting in my father's place.'

'You know they won't let you do that. His place will be open to Paul only and –'

'Do you see Paul anywhere?' I glanced at Viola, to see if she had been alerted to my earlier lie about not having a brother.

Saul raised his palms in surrender. 'Come on, Leah, you know it won't be me making that decision.'

I bristled at his use of my first name.

'Then why are you not *making* it your decision?' I demanded. 'Why are you not banging on the door of the Big House, you and Robert Signal and Father Daniel, and forming your own Council?' He hung his head again. 'The Earl is the leader of this island, not that lot in there. You should be returning him to power, overthrowing this rot.'

'Look, Leah,' he said, weary of speech, 'don't you think that we –'

I didn't want to hear it – his pessimism, his excuses – I had urgent business.

'The reason you're not doing anything,' I told him, my parting shot, 'is because you're a coward. Your stepping back makes you nothing short of a collaborator.'

I strode away, towards the Counting House, feeling Viola vacillate behind me, before deciding to follow, matching me in step. Ahead of us, in the yellow light of the windows, two silhouetted tableaux were playing out. In the meeting room on the left, four men were taking their seats, ready to mete out justice for the consequences of a punctured heart. In the scullery on the right, a trio of women clustered, chatting and gesticulating, fussing around a tea urn.

We entered the lobby with its tired marble floor, a floor that had always made me wonder what Lark had been like when the stone was first laid, shiny and new, a hundred or more years ago.

'Turn left,' I told the girl, feeling her instinctively edge towards the right. 'Turn left.'

In the meeting room, in front of the raised stage with its red velvet curtains and carved and painted Union Jack above its proscenium arch, were two foldaway tables, pushed together on the parquet floor and spread with a white table-cloth. Jacob Crane sat at the head of this table, jacket slung across the back of his chair, his top buttons loosened. To his left, was Abe Powell, our lanky harbour master, in his battered and ubiquitous Fair Isle jumper, and at his side Jed Springer from the Anchor, still in his bartender's waistcoat. On Mr Crane's right, Dr Bishy wore his customary navy three-piece suit, unbuttoned to allow for the distension of his belly. There were five seats empty – one for Saul, one for the Reverend, one for Robert Signal, one for our Earl, one for my father.

Jacob Crane raised his hand as Viola and I entered, a sign that we were to stop where we were. The gesture was one I recognised and had been trained to obey. Should I be called to his office at school and cross the threshold a moment too early, he would hold me in place in the doorway while he finished reading the last few lines of a document. It occurred to me only then that there never were any last lines that needed reading; the hand was a tactic, a way to exert his authority from the very start.

Viola and I halted in the doorway as Jacob Crane ran through the apologies, his voice perfunctory, ticking things off on a lined notepad as he spoke.

'Brothers who send their absences this evening – Earl Catherbridge, Father Daniel, Robert Signal, Saul Cooper.'

'No, I'm here.'

I was to regret my challenge of Saul on the cobbles. There he was, taking the empty chair beside Dr Bishy, not bothering to remove his large, wild coat. If I achieved success that night, Saul would want to claim a piece of it. I would owe him.

Dr Bishy reared back from his new neighbour, as if to get a view of a rare and peculiar creature. Jed Springer shook his head, amused; Abe Powell kept his gaze steady, shark-like.

Jacob Crane's smile was stiff and he closed his eyes briefly for emphasis as he greeted Saul. 'Thank you for gracing us with your presence, Mr Cooper.' He turned to me. 'Do you have an urgent message, Miss Cedars? Will that explain this interruption of the Council in session?'

This was it, this was my cue.

'I'm here to arbitrate on the case of my father's death,' I told him.

Silence.

'I assume,' I went on, 'that it will be happening this evening?'

I looked to Abe, Jed and the doctor in turn, each of them immediately fascinated by the white nothingness of the tablecloth.

Mr Crane's smile grew more rigid. 'Though you think it should concern you, Miss Cedars –' he spoke kindly, slowly, the way he addressed the younger children of St Rita's '– and I understand how you might have come to this conclusion in the midst of your sadness, for which we all here are very sorry –' there were muttered condolences '– this matter does *not* concern you. So, you may leave.'

Viola twitched to go. I snatched a handful of her coat.

'I was present at the last,' I went on. 'Dr Bishy here was not.'

The doctor spluttered righteously into speech, one finger spearing the air. 'That was no oversight on my part, I assure you, I –'

'No,' I interrupted, 'I didn't say that it was. My father was dying, nothing could be done. But I was the one who received his final word on how his death should be recorded and Viola here –' I regathered my grip on her coat. The girl stood up straighter at the mention of her name, '– she was involved in the game with the heart.'

'Game!' Jed Springer slapped a palm against the table-cloth, making both Viola and me jump. He laughed, quite genuinely. 'Game!' None of the other men joined in and his amusement puttered out.

Saul stared at me open-mouthed.

'"Game" is the wrong word,' I agreed. 'They did it in all seriousness.' Viola gave a great gasp. 'But only as a keep-safe,' I went on. 'That is what they have been used for in our island's darker history – hearts with nails – as talismans to ward off evil spirits.'

I could feel Mr Crane readying his sword to fight me, so I raised mine – higher.

'My father was looking after Miss Kendrick here, while her mother was... is...' I didn't know how to phrase it.

'Unwell,' Viola put in.

'Yes, unwell. My father had been ensuring this girl was safe and cared for and she is very grateful for this. She would never have wished to bring him any harm.'

Viola nodded her head in agreement. Mr Crane tried to speak; I left him no gap.

'With his dying words, my father asked that Viola Kendrick and the Eldest Girls –' I held eye contact with our headmaster as I gave their names, ceremoniously. This was what did it, I believe, sealed my fate, speaking of them as he was wont to do, as single charms, not one collective spell,

253

'– Jade-Marie Ahearn, Anna Duchamp, Britta Sayers...' He glared back, unblinking. I could barely breathe but knew I must go on. 'My father said that they are not to be blamed for his death and that they are not to be punished but instead given shelter. Protection is something they tried to find for themselves with that goat's heart.'

Dr Bishy folded his arms, chins vibrating with the shaking of his head.

'The coincidence of his death was precisely that.' My voice grew louder now. I was outside of my body, watching myself speak. I had let go of Viola's coat and was observing my own hands before me, making passionate gestures. 'He had been sick for some time, we know now in hindsight. He had lost weight, he had been under a large amount of stress and had been experiencing extreme fatigue, which made him fall asleep at work. I can bring witnesses who –'

'Enough, Miss Cedars, enough!' roared Mr Crane. 'I have allowed you to speak for too long already. Should we need you as a witness, then we shall call you. Now you may leave.'

'I haven't finished,' I replied.

'Believe me –' he beat out the words '– when I tell you that you have.'

I looked to Saul, desperate for him to speak, terrified that he would.

'I will be taking up my father's hereditary seat on the Council,' I went on. I would say it all, everything I had planned.

'Seats pass to sons,' said Mr Crane as casually as he had read out the absences. He was flicking though his lined pad now, bored of me. 'Women do not sit.'

I felt Viola reach for my coat, as I had grabbed for hers, but she was too late to stop me. I walked towards the table and pulled back the seat beside Jed Springer, planting myself down. Our landlord issued another of his amused barks. This was how he dealt with Council meetings – Saul and the others kept away, Abe Powell was present in body but vacant of mind, and Jed Springer treated it merely as entertainment on a stage. His decision to stand back and laugh was better than the alternative – the kind of horror that was playing across Saul's face. Viola took a nervous step towards the door, as if she might run for help.

'Get up,' said my headmaster.

'I shall take the minutes,' I said, 'that's a woman's job, isn't it?' I showed them my teeth; it was supposed to be a smile. I pulled the phone from my pocket.

Ben had told me that this was the best of his devices for doing what I needed to do, though he also told me that it was lost. We turned over cushions and pulled out drawers in our search, Ben explaining that there was a democratic attitude to possessions at the Billet House – 'Borderline communist,' he said. Everything belonged to everyone. It occurred to me as we searched that he was pretending to have mislaid it because he didn't want me to take it – those mainlanders and their attachments to their phones. When I spied it, slid onto the very top of their understocked bookshelf, it felt as if it had been put there deliberately – hidden. Ben was not as pleased as I'd imagined he would be, reunited once again with an expensive phone that had been missing for weeks. Still, he charged it up, he demonstrated how to use the function I required and he handed it over.

I placed the phone in front of me on the white tablecloth. The men of the Council leaned back in their seats, while Saul leaned in, Viola too, slack-jawed.

I did a sweep of their anxious faces.

'Don't worry, gentlemen,' I said. 'I shan't be bringing forward a proposal for a phone mast.'

No one smiled.

'I'm going to record this,' I told them, pressing the buttons as Ben had showed me, hands shaking, betraying my desire to appear confident, in control. 'It'll make things much easier to type up later.' I cleared my throat and stumbled on. 'My first proposal as a newly appointed member of this Council is that, with the parents' agreement, the Eldest Girls shall be put in my charge for a time, to set them back on a godly path.'

I looked at Viola as I spoke, gauging her reaction, an indication of how the Eldest Girls would receive the news.

'Get up, Miss Cedars.' Mr Crane's voice came like a rumble of incoming thunder. 'Do not threaten your distinguished post at the school by continuing with this display.'

I did not get up.

'I admire you, Mr Crane,' I said, 'for juggling the headmastership of the school, your Council duties and your numerous chapel commitments alongside your teaching of the girls.' This script that I had written for myself, had I ever truly believed I would have the audacity to voice it? And was it really me saying these words? It felt as though the message was coming through me. This was the channelling of a spirit. 'But it is time that the Eldest Girls returned to the bosom of Lark's womenfolk.'

I felt power in the word *womenfolk*. In their mouths, it was used to diminish us; in mine, it was an amplification.

I could push it no further in that meeting room, though, the idea of our collective strength, our potential. To win, I needed to bring them back onside, make them see the reason in my argument, make this the Brothers' decision all along.

'I am a good and godly woman, am I not?' They were silent. 'Make your nods loud for the recording, please, gentlemen.'

'Aye,' said Saul Cooper, the only man present to know this wasn't true.

'Aye,' said Jed, an agreement delivered in a tone that suggested his vote meant nothing.

'I am a pure-born Larkian and much-loved daughter of this Council, am I not?'

'Aye, Miss Cedars,' said Mr Crane, his voice low, pointing me to the paradox – my being a much-loved daughter made this crime of speaking up all the more grave.

'And as someone who holds a distinguished post at the school, and as a woman, I am best qualified to tell these girls of womanly ways and how they might return to them. Do I hear any objections?'

There was only silence in the room.

Outside on the cobbles, Viola's dog keened loudly for the return of her mistress and I felt a sudden, painful connection with the animal. I too wanted to howl, bring everyone running.

'Then the motion is carried,' I said, as calmly as I was able. 'Is there any other business?'

The daughter said that the reward of sin is death. She said this about her own father.

His body was but six weeks in the ground and already she sought to condemn him, calling his demise a correction by the Lord. No other hand was involved in the too-early passing of Peter Cedars, according to this one-time beloved daughter of the Council, the man merely submitted to God's mercy for his wicked acts.

'*Hearken unto thy father that begat thee!*' was the scripture wielded in response around the island's tea urns.

'*Honour they father and thy mother, that thy days may be prolonged in the land which the Lord thy God giveth thee!*' said those who really wanted to show off.

The curate with the spiky hair, if ever she bumped up against this talk, would come back with: '*If we say that we have no sin, we deceive ourselves, and the truth is not in us.*'

She said this within the chapel walls, and she repeated it at the Anchor at the weekend, one eyebrow raised – an eyebrow that suggested, as heathens do, that the bible can be interpreted to prove just about anything.

She was challenged, of course, asked outright, 'Are you contradicting the word of the Council?'

To which the curate responded with a question in return. 'Is that what it sounds like to you?'

It felt dangerous, this way of speaking, the kind of behaviour that risked the full bell, book and candle – or a suspension at the very least. For that is what had happened to the now-not-so-lovely Miss Cedars.

'It's not a suspension!' spat Susannah Cedars at the Provisions Store when she overheard Eleanor Springer filling in everyone on her daughter's absence from school. 'It is extended compassionate leave because the girl's father has just died!'

Susannah Cedars, whose short hair was looking distinctly wild after missing the last two monthly hair salons, dropped her full basket of produce to the floor with a crash, bringing the store to a hush. She took in their stares, understanding that this was her own personal excommunication.

'You vultures!' she muttered as she walked away, abandoning her basket, smashed eggs and all. 'You enjoy your taste of flesh!'

This outburst only served to strengthen the Council's judgement: Leah Cedars was afflicted with a serious illness of the mind. As is the mother, so is her daughter. Turning up at the Counting House half-crazed, believing she had a right to speak as a member of the Council, appointing herself a conduit of God's word, dragging with her a bewildered hostage in the shape of the red-haired *coycrock* girl… it was all very, very sad. The woman was no longer up to her job.

On the Monday evening, after the announcement that Miss Cedars' class would be led by Mrs Leven until a suitable replacement could be found, the disgraced teacher had been seen thumping on Miriam Calder's front door, almost wrenching the dolphin door knocker from its plate. The daughter's hair was as wild as the mother's, and she was dressed in a strange combination of an oversized man's shirt and too-short trousers.

'I was there!' she was heard ranting at Miriam on her doorstep. 'Why would you believe him and not me? I have it all recorded!'

She demanded that her version of the meeting's minutes be published in the next *Lark Chronicle*.

'Mr Crane supplies me with the minutes,' Miriam replied firmly, as Miss Cedars pulled from her pocket a smooth rectangular something that she started flicking and tapping and cursing at, before thrusting it towards Miriam's ear. ('I truly thought she would strike me across the face with it,' Miriam told everyone, after the fact.)

This exchange was brought to an end by Frank Calder, coming to the door with his walrus moustache and his wooden crutch for the wonky hip that kept him from working and going to chapel and any other number of commitments on the island, though it did not prevent him from frequenting the Anchor. He nodded for his wife to step aside and, letting his crutch fall against the porch wall, he took Miss Cedars by the arm and wrestled her away, back down the cobbled slope towards the harbour.

'Remove the beam from your eye, Miriam!' Leah Cedars hollered in her wake, as everyone on the southern elevation opened their windows and doors to observe the evening's entertainment.

What people spoke of later was the eerie parallel between Leah Cedars' removal from the Calder doorstep and Jade-Marie Ahearn's ejection from chapel that first worship in September. No one spoke of the fishy miracle that had allowed Frank Calder, all of a sudden, to walk some distance unaided, grappling with a person much younger and fitter than he.

The next day, Lark woke to discover that someone had expressed their disapproval of Leah Cedars' behaviour by throwing a can of red paint against the front of her harbour cottage. No one was condoning such an act; it was a terrible shame that the white-rendered face of that lovely little cottage had been spoilt, especially as it was likely to be given to someone new, now that Peter Cedars was dead and his daughter had acted in a way that made her, with all due respect, unmarriageable. (Had anyone seen the handsome *coycrock* teacher at her side amid all this drama? No, they had not.) But if a can of paint was what it took to stop Miss Cedars from shrieking nonsense on people's doorsteps, perhaps it had been a necessary evil.

She was seen sounding off just one last time on the cobbles, in her pyjamas, as the sun rose and the red paint dried. Saul Cooper was at the sharp end of her tongue this time. He held her by the wrists as she came at him, demanding, 'You must have seen who did it! Don't give me that, you *know!*'

Then she disappeared. To the gamekeeper's lodge it was presumed, where her mother lived. For now.

As for the Eldest Girls, their curfew still stood, their futures uncertain. Further enquiries were needed – further 'examinations' – according to the published minutes of the Council meeting that had been called to discuss Peter Cedars' death and the issue of the mutilated heart (those decisions being reached after a hysterical Leah Cedars had been expelled from the Counting House).

Though the sword hung from a thread above their heads, it was widely reported that the girls had broken their curfew and returned to the stones, sneaking out at the dead of night.

Mary Ahearn, who some tentatively referred to as the gamekeeper proper, though no announcement of her promotion had been made, was heard in the Anchor at the weekend, stating loudly that she locked her doors and windows when she went to bed and kept the keys beneath her pillow. Rhoda Sayers and Ingrid Duchamp had taken to doing the same, Mary confirmed, 'to ensure the girls' safety'.

'The only way our daughters would be escaping from their bedrooms at midnight is through the keyhole,' said Mary. Her tone was flat and hard to read, but it was familiar – similar to how Cat Walton had spoken in seeming defence of Leah Cedars. There was a sense that the listener was being played with.

Girls can't escape through keyholes, of course, everyone on Lark knew that, but witches could. Witches do.

The night before the Feast of the Transfiguration, the island following the Lutheran tradition and celebrating this in February, Cat Walton hosted a meeting at the chapel. The attendees were as follows: the mothers of the Eldest Girls, Margaritte Carruthers, Ruth French, Benjamin Hailey. No invitation was extended to Diana Crane or Elizabeth Bishy, to Eleanor Springer or Hope Ainsley, yet Reuben Springer, of all the hopeless cases, was seen scuffing up towards St Rita's that night.

'We were planning the upcoming Easter Celebrations,' explained the curate in the Anchor after the event, pre-empting the expected objections. 'We thought we should give other members of the community the opportunity to participate.' Adding: 'By that, I mean give the usual volunteers a well-earned break.' For safety, she tagged on: 'So they may wholly concentrate on their devotional fasts during Lent without the burden of extra responsibilities.'

At the service for the Feast of the Transfiguration, Father Daniel read from the *Book of Matthew*, telling how Jesus took Peter, James and John up into the mountains, his face shining. There, a voice from above had told the men that Jesus was indeed the Lord's beloved son.

'*And Jesus came and touched them, and said, Arise, and be not afraid,*' said Father Daniel, lifting his eyes from the book, receiving earnest nods from the congregation in return.

The Eldest Girls were then ushered to the front, joined by the red-haired *coycrock* girl who had teased her fiery mane into a long, neat plait, and, like the others, wore a white chapel-best dress, clearly borrowed as it was too long.

All creatures of our God and king, they chimed, displaying their perfect harmonies once more, this time not hidden within the crowd. *Lift up your voice and with us sing*.

Mary Ahearn started the round of applause at the diminishing of their last beautiful note. Clapping was unusual in chapel, was considered *de trop*, so not everyone joined in, but those who did made enough sound for the rest. The girls, who were now closest to the altar, were first to receive the Sacrament of the Eucharist. Everyone saw the *coycrock* girl give a nod, red braid riding up and down her spine, before she made a throne of her hands and received the body of Christ with an *Amen*. They saw each of the Eldest Girls step forward after her and gently bow, opening their mouths and offering their tongues.

'Amen.'

'Amen.'

'Amen.'

All four drank from the cup.

As the rest of the congregation queued down the aisle, waiting their turn, as the girls stepped humbly away, Martha Signal dipped close to Elizabeth Bishy and said, 'Well, their bodies show no sign of rejecting the host.' Her voice contained none of her customary deference to the doctor's wife; perhaps it even exhibited a note of triumph.

This display of godliness, however, did not prevent the Eldest Girls from attending their Council-prescribed 'examinations'. They were escorted, in turn, from St Rita's to the clinic abutting the Bishy house on the southern elevation, a simple brick-built extension with a two-bed medical ward and a compact, carpeted consultation room that overlooked Elizabeth Bishy's magnificent garden.

Andy Cater, as representative of the Council, was sent to the Reunyon Farmstead to demand that the Kendrick girl also be brought forward for examination, but he returned shamefaced and empty-handed. The girl hadn't been there, he said; the mother had threatened him with a pitchfork was another version of the story that did the rounds.

Sister Agnes was asked, last minute, to chaperone the Eldest Girls to the Bishy surgery – an error in communication meant the mothers had not been aware of the appointment times, falling as they did during morning lessons. Sister Agnes elected not to accompany the girls into the consultation room itself – their privacy was to be respected – instead she watched them make their way to the far side of the clinic, then retired to Elizabeth Bishy's immaculate front room for a hand, or four, of gin rummy until each girl returned from her time spent under the doctor's care.

These examinations were to be of a psychological nature, with the girls' best interests at heart, but would certainly be rigorous. The learned doctor needed to ensure, through careful probing, that their fascination with sorcery was just that – a passing fascination – and not an outlying symptom of something more serious. Their reactions on leaving his clinic – Anna, mute and dead in the eye; Britta, biting her lip till it bled; and Jade-Marie, weeping and shaking – demonstrated the deep shame they felt for meddling with that goat's heart, an emotion the doctor should be applauded for successfully extracting.

Elizabeth Bishy relayed this outcome to the women of Lark as she sat, damp-haired, beneath the scissoring fingers of Hope Ainsley. The collected nodded their approval and went back to their reading of the *Lark Chronicle* and the various ageing editions of mainland magazines.

Except for Martha Signal.

'Are you sure he didn't check them in other ways?' she asked. She got up and idly scooped a few fingersful of grey hair from the floor. These were cuttings from Mr Crane's time in the chair, swept to one side now the man had gone. The men's session at the salon was completed first, Mr Crane the last customer that day. Of the women's session, Elizabeth Bishy always took the first slot.

Hope's scissors stopped. 'Checked them how?' she asked.

'You know,' said Martha. She cupped the grey hair clippings in one hand and rubbed them between the thumb and forefinger of the other. 'Extra nipples, bloody moles, strange warts, that kind of thing.'

'Why on earth,' said Elizabeth Bishy, her voice high, constricted, affronted, 'would he want to do that?'

Martha Signal had winced a little at her choice of verb – to *want to*. 'Because that would show that they have felt the devil's touch, wouldn't it?'

No one seemed to know how to reply. Eyes skittered from the powerful Mrs Bishy, reduced somehow by the limp wetness of her hair, to the short, dark wife of the island's accountant, who had recently developed a new and bolder way of speaking.

Martha persisted. 'And they hide things in there, don't they? That's what they say.'

'What who says?' Elizabeth Bishy's voice broke. She fumbled her words. 'Hide what in what?'

Martha's palm closed around the hair cuttings.

'Men say it, mostly,' she replied obliquely, 'I would imagine.'

'Men say what!' demanded Mrs Bishy, twisting in the hairdresser's chair. 'You come back here and tell me what you mean!'

But Martha had already put on her coat, dropped the cuttings into the pocket and exited the room.

Viola stands in the front room, disorientated.

The layout is identical to Leah Cedars' cottage next door, but the floorplan is flipped – a mirror image – and where Leah's place was a temple to a life half-lived, this home explodes with things: paintings, candlesticks, small statues of frogs and insects and fish.

In the recess by the fireplace, there is a floor-to-ceiling bookshelf with texts on crystal healing, past lives and the power of runes, the sorts of books Viola had searched for when looking for a gift for the girls, and now cannot believe are able to exist on the island like this, in so many volumes. In the centre of the room there is a green-baize foldaway table, lit by a fluttering tealight. A tuft of grey hair lies beside the candle, alongside a spread of cards that contain images of fire and sticks and queens. The card on the very edge of the table depicts a heralding angel. It reads: *Judgement*.

The old woman, cloaked in a pink dressing gown of pitted chenille, had grabbed Viola by the shoulder in the ginnel and steered her forcibly into a backyard, ordering her to tie up Dot outside, before bundling Viola into the kitchen.

Now, they are in the living room and Viola wonders if she should sit, if that will get the matter sorted faster so she can be on her way. She looks down at the sofa with its crocheted cushions, its appliquéd cushions, its sequined cushions, and camouflaged within them all, until that moment, cats – three of them, sleeping. This is why Dot had to be left in the yard.

'You keep cats!' With all that she has seen in the room, this is what astonishes Viola the most.

'No,' corrects the old woman, 'the cats keep me.' She shoves up the sleeves of her threadbare dressing gown to signal an end to their small talk. On the woman's bony wrist there is a fresh India-ink tattoo, crusted and red – a symbol, two triangles joined at their points.

'Dagaz,' she says, following Viola's gaze, fingering the scab, 'the symbol for community.' Then she makes a righteous fist, shakes it. 'This,' she says, 'has been a long time coming.'

'What has?' asks Viola.

'Everything has its time to die,' the old woman continues, 'and that time is now.'

It dawns on Viola slowly.

'You mean… you know?' she says. 'You know what's going on?'

The woman nods and Viola looks nervously down at the table again, at that angel with its trumpet – *Judgement*.

'Did you see it in the cards?' she asks, a little scared of the answer.

'Yes, I saw it.' The woman shrugs. Then she grins, not so proud. 'Also the walls are thin between these two cottages. I could hear you and Leah next door. So, tell me, where are the girls? We need to work together now.'

Viola allows herself to feel a prick of joy. This is help, this is a friend, and by the evidence in the room, not someone who would want to condemn the girls out of hand.

'They're going to school as if nothing has happened.' Viola speaks rapidly. 'And I'm going to the Big House because I think, I think …'

'You will find judgement there,' the woman finishes. 'That's your instinct.'

'Yes!'

It is like electricity coursing through a wire. It *is* time for this to happen, the old woman is right.

'But wait,' says Viola. The current is cut abruptly, the circuit broken. 'What did you mean – that this has been a long time coming?'

The woman steadies herself, one hand against the green baize, and looks away.

'Do you mean people have always known what is going on? Like, really known?' Still the woman does not look at Viola. 'People knew and they didn't do anything?'

'There have been attempts. The girls will have told you.'

'Yes, but …'

'I can't speak for the others.' The woman gives a heavy sigh. 'The girls' mothers certainly have no real idea of the true extent, or else blood would have been spilled long before last night.'

The mention of blood snaps Viola back to the urgency of the moment; she needs to go. Maybe this woman is no real friend, no compatriot in the fight. She is likely the same as everyone on Lark – her eyes have been averted for too long, never willing to be sure.

Viola turns for the kitchen, the way out.

'You have to be compassionate to those who looked away.' The woman follows her, imploring her to listen. 'The truth is slippery; it's difficult to get hold of. And if you do, what then? You can't escape it here. You have to shape it, make it palatable. Or else, how do you go on living? Some people can't, just ask that poor girl who –'

'Bethany Reid!' Viola whips back around, the girl's name bursting from her lips – a hard sweet released from the throat by a slap on the back. 'She killed herself because of what was happening to her and you all looked away!'

The old woman's voice is riven with remorse. 'She left nothing, no evidence, nothing we could use.'

Viola shakes her head. It is not good enough.

'But now we have three voices,' says the woman.

'Four,' says Viola fiercely.

'And Bethany is here too.' The old woman stretches out her fingers and plays the invisible strings of the air. 'I believe that. I think she came back as a fox. The men lost at sea, they are now deer and –'

Viola backs away, frightened by this talk. 'No,' she says.

The woman lets her arms float down and steps closer, peers at her.

'Did you lose someone?' she asks, trying to place a hand on Viola's shoulder.

She flinches from this touch. 'People don't come back from the dead.'

'You understand the pain then.' The woman speaks gently, sympathetically. 'You know it too well.'

'People don't come back,' Viola repeats. She had let herself think that they do, was haunted in the aftermath by that scene from their namesakes' play – Sebastian arriving in Illyria, returned from the dead, not in his watery tomb at all but able to hug his long-lost sister. The fiction tormented her. 'They just die,' Viola blurts, 'they just end. They don't even go to heaven because why would we want them up there, looking down on us, seeing what we're doing now and how we're getting it all totally and completely...' She chokes, unable to go on.

The woman gets her hand to Viola's shoulder this time and her touch is like a kind of magic. Viola's vision swims. She looks down, roots herself, sees her legs in pyjamas, her two feet in their boots, the kitchen tiles beneath. She sees that she exists, she is here, and that is enough. She looks up.

The woman smiles, tells her: 'I will do better this time, I promise. I have you beside me.'

Her words make Viola think of the ancient stones, that cryptic message left as an arrangement of rocks, and she sees the old woman and herself as some kind of continuation of that, a chain of events.

'I have to go,' says Viola, and from behind them, as if cued, comes the sound of the yard gate being opened.

Saul Cooper's voice calls: 'Margaritte! Margaritte! You in?'

'You need to leave this way!' The woman steers Viola back through the front room towards the door facing the harbour.

'But what about Dot?'

'I promise to look after her,' she says, 'you have to trust me.'

Viola nods, there is no choice, but also she thinks she can – trust.

She wrenches open the door and bursts free, hearing Saul Cooper arrive with his demands, 'Where is she? What's going on?'

The old woman's reply is swift and high. She plays a version of herself that others have come to expect.

'I turned the Eldest Girls into cats, Saul, that's what's going on. See, there they are, on the sofa.'

Viola makes faster progress without Dot tugging in her wake, but she knows the journey will be harder from here, now that she is alone. If only she can keep hold of that feeling she had with the woman's hand on her shoulder, the ground solid beneath her feet. Viola must remember that she is all of those who have come before her and all of those who will follow. A wave is building. She and the girls need only ride it.

Viola heads down the narrow passage behind the smoke-house where the gutters hold onto their odious puddles, before making northwards, along the fencing of the harbour loading bay, sprinting into the tarmacked yard, almost colliding with Abe Powell as he fills a wheelbarrow with logs. He stands, unfeasibly tall, his jumper loose on his bones, and he watches her as she hops backwards, then swerves around him. He wears the same dead stare as he did at the Council meeting, and she expects a challenge. He will ask her what she's doing there, what she's running from – something. But he doesn't. He lets her go without a word. She climbs the fence and spills onto the green estate land, sending a gathering of scavenging ravens cawing for the sky.

Ahead of her is a thicket of sycamore, hazel and pine, and Viola runs towards it, through it, knees high, to avoid the tangle of bramble and nettle. The copse gives way to a brick path, trees branching over on both sides, creating a tunnel of radiant green.

She pauses, orientates herself. This is undiscovered territory; she has never used this route before. She should make a wish – that's what you're supposed to do when you step onto new land. They had done it when disembarking from the ship, her mother closing her eyes and grasping Viola's hand, instructing her to send a request skyward. She had wished to go home, and it strikes Viola now that she wouldn't make that wish again. Deep down in her dark heart, she acknowledges that there will never be any going back.

She takes the path to the right where it slopes upwards and must therefore lead to the Big House. The incline gets steadily steeper, the pine trees deliver a lemony sharpness to the lungs. Viola rounds the corner.

She stops dead.

There is a well to one side of the path and someone is leaning over it, black hair falling forward, sobs echoing into the hollowness below. It is a scene from a fairy tale.

Viola knew that she would have to be the one to do it – make payment for the fetching of the heart.

'Do bad things happen on the mainland too?'

That was one of the first questions the Eldest Girls had put to her, the very afternoon she had emerged from her spying place and stepped into the stone circle. She hadn't understood what she was being asked, not really. She had struck forward blindly, replied, 'Bad things happen everywhere', her only concern being to sound cool, insightful.

Then she had spoilt it all by bursting into tears. Not because of the pressure to say the right thing or her fear that they would reject her – though those feelings played their part – but because she had inadvertently spoken the truth, one she had wanted to say aloud for a very long time. *Bad things happen everywhere, Mum. Accept that you can't stop them. Let's try and live our lives. Jump in with both feet. Move on.*

'My dad and brother were killed last year.' The story had poured from her in a great unstoppable surge. 'They were coming home from a football match together and there was a man at the tube station and he was sick in the head and he'd taken drugs – he was raving, saying mad stuff – and he had a carving knife and Seb just in the wrong place at the wrong time or had the wrong face or whatever and the man went for him and Dad tried to step in and it only got worse and both of them ended up … It was random. It was just … random.'

She'd not talked to anyone about it before – not even her friends back home, the ones brave enough to come to the house. Maybe it was because they seemed a little too curious, in love with the idea of such horror. Viola didn't believe that the Eldest Girls were more likely to understand, not at all. She knew they wouldn't even try to, and this, in itself, was the relief.

'My mum took me out of school because she started to believe that it was dangerous for me to be anywhere but home and then she decided that where we lived was dangerous too, so we came here, halfway across the Atlantic, because the radio said that Lark was very safe.'

The girls had just listened, observed. They didn't take her awful story and mould it into something recognisable, familiar enough for them to sympathise. Instead they pulled her into an embrace, a small and wonderful enclosed world built by the warmth of their bodies, and it was only when Viola was encircled like this, that the feeling struck – that she had spoken too much and not listened enough in return. She asked them, 'What bad things have happened to you?'

They reported it with peculiar detachment, which made their confessions all the more shocking. It was as if they were reciting memorised phrases; they used their school assembly voices.

'So,' said Britta, 'with your mainland view of things –'

'As a girl,' Jade-Marie cut in.

'– does that sound right to you?'

Viola could barely speak. 'It sounds… impossible,' she managed.

'Are you doubting us?' said Anna. 'Are you saying we're lying?'

'No!' said Viola. 'No! I'm saying it's impossible that this has been allowed to go on.'

For that reason alone, Viola knew that she would have to be the one to do it, to make payment for the heart.

She was stunned that evening in December when they had been caught unawares in the glare of the flash, their naked bodies captured, digitised, stored. She was appalled, of course she was, but at the same time she knew it meant less to her. To the Eldest Girls it was yet another violation, a scar upon a scar. To Viola it was a fresh attack, a new battle, and she had the confidence of the beginner.

'You like what you see, do you?' she'd called out to their trespasser, goading him.

He did not reply. He kept the phone held up, reframing and refocusing, so Viola had walked towards him, swiping a white nightdress from the ground to cover herself as she went.

Jade-Marie begged her to come back.

Britta's voice came like a bullet across the breech. 'You shouldn't be here,' she warned him. 'Men aren't allowed. It brings on a terrible fury.' The sea joined in with her – a Greek chorus. It boomed against the caves in the cliffs below, loud enough to shake the bones in their chests.

When Viola reached him, was able to look him in the eye, she saw that he was handsome. She could imagine the girls at her old school getting excited about someone like this, discussing his every feature in whispers on the bus – his eyes, his lips, his everything.

Viola spoke directly, with a confidence she didn't know she owned. 'Are you looking for some close-up action?' she asked.

He shrugged, smirked, then stepped forward as if he might claim his winnings right there and then.

'Hey!' She stepped back, putting up her palms.

The situation slowly turned, Viola reframed it – she must give herself this credit. Hadn't they, only moments before he arrived, expressed their wish to push things further? She had outlined an idea of how they could do this – what they would need. Was it really such a coincidence that he had turned up then, as they lifted their hands to the sky, making a promise to do whatever was required of them?

His being there, Viola decided, was not a problem; it was a gift.

'We need you to do something first,' she told him.

He slid the phone into the back pocket of his jeans, freeing his hands for the qualifying task, thinking it could be done there and then.

'We need you to fetch us a heart.'

He snorted, thinking this a joke.

'A real one,' she clarified, 'an animal one, from a cow or a sheep.'

He was the one to suggest it: 'Or a goat?'

They'd shook on it, made a deal. He would give them what they wanted, and they would give him what he wanted in return.

Viola knew that she would have to be the one to make the payment. The others were already sure they were going to hell for what they got up to at the stones.

'The Lord helps those who help themselves,' Viola told them as reassurance. 'It says so in the bible.'

'That's not from the bible.' Jade-Marie had shaken her head and pulled a face.

'It sounds like it should be, but it isn't,' said Anna, always ready with a footnote. 'There's generally more scripture to support the idea that the Lord helps the helpless, actually.'

'Well, that's also you, isn't it?' Viola suggested.

'Make your mind up, will you, *coycrock*!' This was Britta – the word *coycrock* a term of affection in her mouth.

In their lower moments, the girls would go so far as to ask themselves if they deserved it – if, in some way, what was happening to them was punishment for a sin. Viola would never stand for this line of talk.

'So, in that case, it's my fault that my dad and brother were killed?'

'Maybe,' said Anna dispassionately.

'No!' exclaimed Jade-Marie. 'No one is saying that!' She clutched Viola to her, mothering her with a stroke of the head.

'Then, what sin is it,' Viola asked, 'the one you think you're being punished for?'

Britta immediately had the answer. 'The sin of being a girl.'

From there, Viola suggested the harmonies. It was something active, positive, loud. It would demonstrate their holiness to the island and, more importantly from the girls' point of view, God would hear them.

Viola had an ear for music. In the school and church choirs, she'd sung solos, boarding minibuses to perform at events across the country, returning with a hoarse voice, mostly from hollering along to the *Now* compilations on the journey back. She missed it.

When the mothers seized upon the girls' singing display, thrusting them to the front of chapel, to show how good, how heavenly, their daughters were in the aftermath of Peter Cedars' death, Viola had to ask, 'So, your mums, they know?'

This brought about desperate exclamations of *no* and *you must never say anything* and *I couldn't bear it if my mum thought of me like that* and *they think this is just about spells.*

Not a soul on the island knew what was going on except them, they said. Viola countered this, forced them to concede that some people might; that they could be too scared or too toadying to do anything but look away. This was when Miss Cedars' name would bob to the surface – the main villain. *Oh, she definitely knows*, they'd stress, *it's not like we haven't tried to tell her enough times*. They mocked her with unkind impressions, especially of the way she clung to Mr Hailey. *She's brainwashing him*, they'd say, *making him believe it's all okay.*

Viola couldn't help but think that telling the truth would be the simplest way to end it all. We *wouldn't be believed*, was their response, *even with our mums onside, it would be buried all over again, we would be punished even more.* Viola tried to imagine herself in the same situation – her mother would be the very last person she'd go to, and after her, who was left?

Then, in a way, Viola *was* in their situation. She had offered her body to a pervert in the woods in return for his slaughtering an animal that she was too squeamish to slaughter herself. She saw how easy it was to lose sight of the line – the one that said, on this side is the victim and on this one, the perpetrator. She saw how hard it was to see yourself as blameless.

Viola would have to be the one to do it, or else she would join that list of potential eye-averters and collaborators – the people who just did nothing. She would be as bad as Miss Cedars. In some twisted fashion, it had also occurred to Viola, that if she did do it, she would better understand the girls' pain, and that would bring them closer together.

The finding of the heart, the girls' curfew, the death of the gamekeeper – all of this gave Viola a hiatus in which to prepare.

She visited Saul Cooper in his back office at the Customs House. She had a plan.

He would make her a cup of tea, and then, while he was in the middle of a talk on the various capabilities of his radio equipment, a subject in which Viola had expressed an interest as a pretext for her visit, she would throw herself at him. As practice. So she wasn't completely unprepared for what she was about to do at the stones. So that her first time was with someone kind.

This is how it would go: she'd would move from the chair to the camp bed and pat the space beside her, ask to see what was in his sketchbook and then... What would she do? She would close her eyes and kiss him, focus on his positive qualities, imagine he was physically someone else, younger, substitute his weasely face for that of a celebrity, if Viola could remember what any of them looked like without a working phone or TV. She could trust him, she thought, to be gentle.

'Mr Cooper,' she said, interrupting his lecture on Marine VHF, how it bounced its signal from mast to mast to gain distance across the ocean.

'Saul,' he corrected, which was good, a move towards familiarity.

She looked up at him, standing at the counter in front of that great sea-filled window, his fingers resting on the buttons of one of the communications devices, eager to carry on with his lecture – and Viola lost all courage.

He really was kind and didn't deserve to be used. He deserved to be happy, so she found herself blurting out, 'I think you'd make a good dad.' The saying of it made her squirm; how swiftly her thoughts had travelled from one idea to another, how easily she could embarrass herself.

He gave a quick splutter of laughter. 'Oh, yeah, what makes you say that?'

'Well, Leah said it, actually.'

Viola was stunned by how easily these fabrications came, one lie after another. Why was she doing this? Because we don't like Leah Cedars hanging around with Mr Hailey, she told herself. Viola could be the one to put an end to that. Saul deserved better than Leah, but what the heart wants, the heart wants. Viola was a cherub, Saul had said so himself. Viola could play Cupid.

'That's where Leah's mind is at right now,' Viola continued, feeling a certain light-headedness to be talking this way, so far from the truth. 'She's all about settling down and having babies, and of course she wants to do that with someone from the island. And, well, after what you did for her at the Council meeting the other night…'

The man beamed, literally beamed, light from the window glancing off his skin – a child awarded a gold star. Viola waited for guilt to stab – it didn't. No one was being hurt, after all. Having Leah would make Saul happy. Having Mr Hailey free from Leah's grasp would please the Eldest Girls.

Saul's expression changed then, a shift to something more meditative.

'I've been thinking about how you like to wander about the island with your dog,' he said carefully, measuring out his words, 'and I've been thinking about how Leah likes you and how you're also friends with those girls.'

Viola put down her tea, sloshing it onto the desk. Was he about to point out how incompatible these friendships were? Was he going to catch her in her lie? Dot started to lick at the tea that dripped from desk to floor.

'So, I was wondering if I could give you this.' He plucked a black radio from a charging station on the window ledge and offered it to Viola. She turned it over in her hands, twisting at one of the dials.

'Don't,' he said, 'leave it on channel eight. You'll reach me on that one.'

Then he got down on his knees to unplug the charging station, wrapping the cable through the prongs of the plug and handing this piece of kit to Viola too.

'What's this for?' she asked.

'I wondered if you could keep an eye on…'

'The girls?' Viola put in.

'Yeah, yeah, that's right. Just like Leah said, but…' He drove his hands into the pockets of his black trousers, took them out again, twitched at the epaulettes of his shirt, then at the end of his tie. 'But also an eye on Leah, if you see her.' Viola nodded slowly – this was the crux of it. 'Report back, you know. Tell me anything that seems... I don't know, worrying.' He couldn't look Viola in the eye.

'Spy on her?' she clarified. Before adding, meanly, 'Spy on your girlfriend?'

'No, no, no, no, that's not... It's not like I have to... That's not what I'm...' He pinched at the whiskery region of his mouth. 'You're a sensible one, a smart one, I reckon, despite your death wish around the water, and those girls that Leah thinks need protecting, well... I can see her trying to talk to them, you know, go up to those stones once their curfew's up. Without telling me. And after everything she said at that meeting and everything that's happened in between...'

Viola didn't really know what had happened in between. She had not seen Michael or the girls for some time now; she had been living on an island within this island. Viola had drawn some conclusions from the alarming splash of red paint across the front of Leah Cedars' cottage. *Punishment for her sins*, was the phrase that came distastefully to mind. The men of the Council had been correct on one point – Leah Cedars didn't know what she was talking about in that meeting room. She could not have meant what she said about taking the girls under her wing, or was at least being disingenuous. The Eldest Girls had made it clear that woman was not on their side.

'What it is, you see,' Saul stumbled on, 'is that, I think Leah – and you, naturally – you both need protecting.'

Viola nodded stiffly and looked warily at the radio in her lap. More protection, more safety.

Saul took a steadying breath, came to the point. 'Those girls have proved themselves to be, not witches but capable of... willing to... I mean, we can't be sure what they'll do next.'

An urge for violence rose within Viola, a desire to throw the radio back at him, let it strike him across the temple, bring blood. Maybe the man wasn't kind, after all.

She would have done it too, hurled that radio at him, if a memory of Seb hadn't come, bright and immediate as a message from the past – they are on the PlayStation, Seb coaching her through a new game, telling her to collect everything she finds as she goes – wood, medicine, an axe, a radio... 'What will I ever use it for?' Viola is asking. 'Who knows!' Seb says, wide-eyed before the screen, his tongue working at one corner of his mouth. 'Whatever the game throws at you next.'

So, she let Saul teach her how to press the button and speak into the thing, and told him thank you, pocketing the radio as she left.

When she finally caught up with Michael, some days later at the shell arch, they spent their initial moments together in silence, picking at the render, trying to free a periwinkle or a dog whelk. He was still sulking about the way she had spoken to him at Peter Cedars' funeral, but Viola wanted him to apologise first, for suggesting that she was some kind of murderer. It was Viola who broke the stand-off, desperate as she was for the latest on the lovely Miss Cedars. Michael's eyes gleamed as he imparted this drama to new ears.

'Suspended!' he announced with dark joy, explaining how Mr Crane had told the pupils at the end of chapel one morning that Miss Cedars had decided to take an 'extended break'. After that, the teacher was seen ranting in the streets on at least two occasions before disappearing: 'To her mum's probably. They're both as mad as each other.'

'Who threw the paint at her house?' Viola asked.

'Reckon she did it herself,' said Michael. 'She's completely dotty now.'

He looked down at the dog. 'No offence to the Dotty here present,' he said, and Viola fumed inwardly at his willingness to say sorry to an animal and not to her.

They fell back into their shell-picking silence and Viola knew she must act soon, else her confidence would slip away.

'You know how you said the Eldest Girls were looking for boys to have sex with at the Sisters' Stones?'

She was off; it would be done.

'Yeah?' He tried for a casual response – he failed.

'Well, it could be you, and if that's the case then you'll need to get in some practice, so you don't make a complete idiot of yourself.'

The boy gulped. Viola could see his mind leaping frantically from one thought to the next.

'Practice?' he said. 'How?'

'I'll do it.' She too tried for a casual response – she succeeded. 'I don't mind.'

Then, before she could question the sense of what she was doing, she launched herself forward and kissed him. They worked their mouths against one another for a while. His lips were dry, uncoordinated, the movement both forceful and boring. Viola opened her mouth and felt him resist this new development. She pulled away.

'You're supposed to use your tongue,' she said.

'O-okay,' the boy stammered, and as they leant in to resume their kiss, Viola probed his mouth in demonstration. He clumsily replicated.

'Now,' she said, 'put your hand up my jumper' – an offer he didn't need to be given twice.

This was as far as Viola had ever gone, but despite Michael's vast stores of encyclopaedic knowledge, she figured she was still the expert; she knew what was supposed to come next. She made herself do it – reach down and clutch at the front of his school trousers, feeling for the bulge that was supposed to be there, and was.

It was like a jolt of a thousand volts to the boy. He leapt to his feet. The leather satchel that was still slung across his body snagged him at the neck, and he readjusted it primly, pulling it forwards to mask his crotch.

'What are you doing?' he yelped.

'I thought… You said you wanted to… I thought we were going to… have sex?'

He blustered and scoffed. He was embarrassed, she could tell.

'Well, that's as may be,' he said, playing the adult, 'but that's not how it happens. You were doing it all wrong.'

'Sorry,' she found herself saying reflexively, immediately doubting herself.

'No, that wasn't right at all,' he went on, growing in assurance.

She straightened her jumper and the bra beneath it, humiliated. 'Why wasn't it?' she dared to ask. 'Why wasn't it right?'

'You are supposed to be more ladylike,' he said, speaking with utmost confidence now. 'Sex is something a man does to a woman, not the other way around.'

◉ THE BOOK OF LEAH

It was a blessing in disguise. The end of something is always the beginning of something else. They had gifted me time to focus, to renew my belief in the lectures I delivered to departing friends – *Lark is not the problem, because we are Lark. We are its future!*

This was my opportunity to make it so.

I had to accept that teaching was no way for me to shape the young, just as Saul Cooper, Robert Signal and Father Daniel had discovered that a seat on the Council was no way for them to steer the island. We were relying on old systems, creaking at the joints, manipulated and used. It was time to build something new, if we were ever to be rid of the rot, to be free from our very bad apples.

To my enemies, I was a delusional woman who shouted in the street, a woman too scared to stay in her own cottage because of a splash of red paint. I could be easily dismissed, and they would never see me coming.

My mother and I began to pack. We knew someone would come soon to tell us that our tenure at the game-keeper's lodge was up. We didn't want to give them the satisfaction of seeing us taken by surprise. By the time that Council dogsbody arrived, grubby fingers on some piece of spurious paperwork, everything of ours would be in boxes, ready to go.

'But where will we go?' my mother asked, as we wrapped artichoke-shaped candle-holders and bubbled-glass vases. I lifted down my framed teacher training certificate from the living-room wall, revealing a rectangle of light-starved wallpaper. I tried not to think about whether I would use this qualification again. I hushed the echo of Paul in my head asking, *Will you actually be a real teacher?*

'Do you mean, where do we go for now,' I said, 'or for good?'

'Both.' She had plucked from the mantelpiece the post-card Paul sent on his arrival on the mainland. It came on the August ship, in the last post of 2017. It was a photo-graph of two cliff faces and the sea between. Jaunty white script across the front declared, *And so the adventure begins.* On the back, he'd written a phone number starting 0208. London. From isolation, he'd thrown himself into a city of millions.

'Well, if we need to,' I told her, 'you can come and live in the harbour cottage with me, and then –'

She leapt in. 'And then we'll catch the April ship?' She was holding the postcard in both hands, pressing it against her chest.

I was shocked.

'Don't look at me like that, Leah,' she said. 'I have no one now. All those women, they don't care about me, they weren't true friends, and I will not give them the satisfaction of shrivelling up into some reclusive old hag like Margaritte Carruthers.'

I could have replied, *But you have me, Mum.* I should have defended Margaritte. I might have pointed out that

Paul clearly cared less than the women of Lark; he'd sent no further mail after that postcard, no news, no fixed address. He still didn't know that his own father had died. My mother had gone to the Customs House to use the international phone, standing out in the bluster at the cusp of the dogleg jetty, so as to be in clear sight of a satellite, weeping as she punched in the digits on the back of his postcard. Yet again she was greeted by an automated voice saying, *Sorry, the number you have dialled has not been recognised, please hang up and try again.*

'It's the same with my Tom,' Hope Ainsley had told my mother at the funeral, 'too busy on the mainland now to speak to his old mum' – as if this self-pity would console her.

I didn't remind my mother of any of this. There were more than two months ahead of us before the ships started running again, plenty of time to change her mind. I put down the jug I was wrapping, the one with the kingfisher handle that she liked to fill with daffodils in our brief spring, and I hugged her, told her everything was going to be all right, that there would be a place for us on Lark, a better place. I said it because she was crying, and I said it because I wanted to believe that it was true.

On February 14th, as my mother and I sat opposite one another at the kitchen island drinking tea, there came a knock. We looked up from our books and exchanged nods. My mother stood, brushed herself down and patted at her hair. Susannah Cedars was adamant that she would look presentable, nay, majestic, when our eviction came. We would be observed walking away down that hill, bags in hand, lackeys carrying our possessions in our wake. We'd been careful to box and seal as much as we could, so the detail of our lives would not be on display, picked over.

That lamp will have cost her a pretty penny in shipping.
A frying pan so big! No wonder he had a heart attack.

I expected the Cater brothers to be standing there as messengers, or perhaps we would suffer the ignominy of Luke Signal informing us that the lodge was now his and that us ladies were to show good grace and step aside. Mary Ahearn had, of course, capably taken over the management of the land after the funeral; she had, in some ways, taken over years ago, picking up the slack as my father's health deteriorated. Yet we still did not know if she would officially be named his successor. After my suspension from school, and her daughter's disgrace, the idea of Lark appointing its first-ever female gamekeeper seemed ever more absurd. The elder Signal boy was growing daily in confidence and wore a curl to his lip that suggested he knew something that we didn't.

When I opened the door, there was no one there – no Luke, no Mark or Andy Cater.

In the porch lay an object, the shape of it making me recoil at first. I picked it up. It wasn't completely smooth, the chiselled scoring of its creation was still visible, nor was it entirely even in shape, though symmetry had probably been the intention. I liked it precisely because of this unfinished and irregular quality. It was a St Valentine's Day gift. A carved wooden heart.

When word reached Ben of what had happened at the Council meeting, he had visited me at my cottage in the way that he had used to – by tapping on the back door at midnight. We'd kissed in the kitchen, begun to tear at each

292

other's clothes right there. I felt like a prisoner with access to their lover for just one night; I had to drink my fill.

Lying upstairs in the mess of one another, he said to me: 'I need to keep my job.' He pulled me closer, those narrow eyes of his darting left and right, herding me into his gaze. 'I have nothing here if I lose that. You at least have this roof over your head, you have your mother, her place, friends ...'

'History,' I added, in agreement, but yet again I was hearing a person I loved reel off an inventory of all the things they had with no mention of me. Did it go without saying that my name was on their list, or was I of no value at all?

'I think you need to stay there too,' I said. 'We need someone good on the inside. You could stay close to Ruth.'

He nodded. 'So, if anyone asks ...'

'You can tell them we're over,' I said.

He had grinned at this. 'You're dumped, Leah Cedars,' he told me, then he'd pushed his mouth onto mine, pulled his body on top of me again.

I wanted to give him a gift in return for the heart, leave something on his doorstep. This was the ritual of teenage crushes, something I'd missed out on. I felt a juvenile thrill at the idea of what I might do. I waited until my mother was asleep before pulling on the bobbled sweater and the wide-legged trousers, then heading out into the night.

Back at the harbour cottage, I felt like a trespasser in my own home, the steep, dark stairs creaking beneath my tread, the bedroom as smooth and still as a stage set. I pulled open the top drawer of my dresser and retrieved the phone, placing it on the windowsill and plugging it in. I watched it glow to life and beyond, through the window, I saw shadows shift along the harbour wall. I moved closer to the glass. Cats? Foxes? No. People.

I jerked backwards, flipping the phone face down to mask its light; I didn't want to be seen. Red paint had done me no harm, but what would come next? A brick, fire, men themselves?

I took a breath and peered out again. The figures were moving away from the harbour, towards the smokehouse. Not men – three girls, one of them with blonde hair, picked out by the shine of the waning moon. The Eldest Girls were breaking their curfew, walking swiftly towards the track that led up past the East Bay. That route would take them towards the farmstead, to Viola, or else through Cable's Wood and on to the stones. I felt a vicarious sense of triumph that they were not doing as they were told, but also I was fearful for them. Didn't they realise they could fall from a cliff edge in the disorienting dark, or be caught as prey?

As the phone gained its charge, I brushed my hair and put on some lipstick, smudging some of the dark cherry redness onto my cheeks.

There was a way to take a picture of yourself, to flip the lens. This was a 'thing' on the mainland, Ben had told me – a phrase he used all the time. One of us in the staff room would mention a seemingly common happening on the island, remark on someone's behaviour or describe a particular type of food we'd eaten, and Ben would chip in with, 'Is that a thing, then?'

Back home, he said, the kids at school – girls mostly – took endless photos of themselves, pouting, posing, deleting, retaking, filtering, embellishing, turning themselves into

alien beings. Then they posted these images online, beginning the desperate wait for approval. Ben had commented
more than once on how astounding it was, how strange, to
be in a school – to be in a place – where everyone wasn't
staring downwards all the time at a device in their hands.
People looked up when they walked about on Lark, they
considered one another.

'Perhaps too much,' I'd replied.

To which he'd countered, 'Better than doing it anonymously or via an online profile that is curated and contrived.'

I assured him that it was still a 'thing' to be curated and
contrived on Lark, just with no help whatsoever from a
mobile phone.

I took off all my clothes and contemplated my naked
body in the mirror of the wardrobe, the pale, soft flow of
me. Did my body make sense, join up? Was it sufficient,
plenty? The only pictures of me as an adult were the ones
on the wall of the school corridor, in work skirt and blouse,
the pupils the main focus. I didn't know if I was beautiful:
I'd never considered the question before, not properly. I'd
never had to. I knew that the blackness of my hair made
me special, a pure catch, and that had always been enough.
Until it wasn't.

Standing in front of that mirror at midnight, like the evil
queen in the story, it was suddenly very important for me to
know: was I the fairest of them all? Would Ben still want me
if we had met on the mainland with its bounty of women?
The idea that I was desirable made me feel exhilarated; the
idea that I was not, was a precipice looming at my feet. Was
this the 'thing' I was to grasp about photographing yourself, the intoxicating cocktail of vanity and shame?

I detached the phone from its charger, lay on the bed, flipped the lens and took the pictures.

The Billet House lay beyond the stables and the dog kennels. I took the brick path through the estate, torch in one hand, the phone in the other. Every so often I would accidentally nudge the home button, casting a ghostly blue light across the scene as I made Ben's lock screen blink into life. It was a photo of him sandwiched between his mother and sister, all three of them open-mouthed, laughing.

Doubt crept up on me slowly as I headed north. *Are you sure he wants to see you like that?* Doubt slipped its arm across my shoulders and leant in to ask the burning question: *Are you sure you can trust him with those photos?*

I'd read articles from the mainland, accompanied by studio shots of frowning women, stories of how naked pictures taken on phones, intended for just one pair of eyes, had spread like a virus. Would my pictures find their way into that fabled stash of dirty magazines and videotapes that were rumoured to pass from man to man on the island? Would Saul Cooper get his hands on them, giving him even more of a hold over me?

I stopped on the path and typed in Ben's passcode, unlocking the phone. I searched the bright squares for the one that would allow me to look at my pictures again, to reassess. A tessellation of me swooped onto the screen, thumbnails of my face, my body – all those different versions of Leah.

Then above me, more naked images. Not of me.

Dread flared hot in my throat, my limbs slackened. *Mainland girls, from before*, I thought. Then, desperately,

Please let them be mainland girls, please let them be mainland girls...

But also I could hear Ben telling me how he really needed to keep his job. I could see three faces scowling at me across the school canteen, and a phone being slid onto the dusty top of a bookcase in the Billet House. Just out of reach, beneath a bed, lay a pair of bloodied horns.

I clicked on the images, blurry, gritty, some obscured by a finger or a smudge of green, the flash blanching their bare skin as they shielded themselves – not posing, not pouting. Then the frame was trained on one girl alone, progressing closer and closer to the lens with each swipe of my thumb, a white nightdress being brought up to cover her body, higher, higher, her breasts now obscured.

Viola.

Viola and the Eldest Girls.

I asked for nothing in return when I dropped that phone into the depths of the well. The deal was that you surrendered something you held dear in return for knowledge, and I had not fulfilled my side of the bargain. A phone was worthless on Lark with no signal to serve it. The conversation I'd recorded was of no interest to anyone. The versions of me it held were stupid and gullible.

The phone landed with a distant crack against the piles of gold and the bones of all those forsaken wives.

I knew what I had to do next. Ask once again for forgiveness.

I cut across the openness of estate land, the moon guiding me, then onwards under the cover of Cable's Wood, where I came upon a deer and her young, startling them to their feet, meeting the dark blaze of the mother's eye before she was swallowed by the trees.

The wood thinned. The moon took charge again and I practised my words for when I arrived. *Forgive me, forgive me, for I did not know what I was doing.* I could hear their voices above the boom and shudder of the waves clashing with the north cliffs below.

I could hear the timbre of a man.

My instinct was to run back to the lodge, to my mother, but I could no longer be that version of myself – the one who looked away. I ran towards those voices, towards my final disappointment, my shins slicing through the ferns, until I caught sight of the Eldest Girls, huddling at the base of the hollow central stone.

Viola was separate from them, shaking, half-naked, standing just outside the boundary that was not to be crossed by men. A figure was stripping her of her clothes – a figure wearing the spiralling horns of a goat.

FRIDAY THE 13TH – APRIL 2018

Leah Cedars is always in Viola's way. She has a skill for it, these untimely appearances. She stands now in the middle of the brick path, her face ugly with tears. She is the troll on the bridge. *You shall not pass.*

'How could you?' Leah wails as she makes her way downhill, as she comes for Viola. 'How could you do this to me?'

Viola exhales in disgust. This is not the first time she has heard Leah shriek these words. It is the woman's most nauseating feature, her ability to make everything about her.

Viola backs away, calculating a new course to the Big House. She can't be wasting time arguing with a hysterical Leah Cedars.

'It was nothing to do with you,' Viola says, looking left and right, evaluating her exits. 'You should have stayed out of it. It wasn't your battle.'

'And what made it yours?' Leah Cedars' voice gathers its spikes. 'You're not from here. This isn't your problem to solve. You're nothing but a *coycrock*, an unlucky one – that piece of superstition proved true, didn't it? Just look at you, just look at what you've done!'

'I've done what all of you should have done a long time ago.' Viola feels sure in this statement, but Leah Cedars is shaking her head.

'I've been to the stones. I've seen with my own eyes. I've seen ...' Leah doubles over, sobbing. 'You killed him!' She manages between shuddering breaths. 'You killed him!'

It seems hypocritical to Viola, this expression of horror, this melodrama. She has heard Leah threaten violence, murder too – and convincingly so. Viola closes the gap between them. Why should she be the one to retreat? The uphill path is the quickest way to the Big House. Leah Cedars will just have to get out of her way.

'That's right,' Viola says, walking decisively towards the sometime teacher. 'Blame everything on me, on the Eldest Girls. Tell us we brought it all on ourselves.'

'That's not what I'm saying,' Leah snaps. The need to be right sobers her. 'You know that's not what I'm saying. I did everything I could to help you.'

'No, you didn't,' says Viola, brushing past.

Leah Cedars is selfish; Viola was never sucked in to believing otherwise. All Leah cared about was her public image and revenge for the way she'd been treated. All she wanted was Benjamin Hailey, no matter what he'd done.

'Why lie to me?' Leah snatches Viola's arm, looking her up and down: the muddy boots, the pyjama trousers, the torn nylon of her mother's coat.

'I told you there was a body,' says Viola. She allows herself to be smug. Leah the proud deceiver has been deceived in return. 'That's all. You just filled in the rest.'

'But you said it would look bad for me.'

'And it does.'

Leah tightens her grip. 'How?'

'You had it in for him. He betrayed you, everyone knows that.'

'What are you talking about?' Leah shakes her head. 'What on earth are you talking about?'

Viola pulls hard, trying to free her arm, and without warning Leah lets go, making Viola fly and stumble, almost fall.

'You're fucking mad,' Viola hisses.

'And you've sold your soul to the devil,' says Leah calmly, in return.

Viola wants to be cool as she walks away, but Leah's insult stings – *you've sold your soul to the devil* – it is a nettle leaf against the skin.

She could turn and defend herself, explain why he had to die, why what she and the girls did is a good thing, but Leah Cedars has already decided who Viola is. So she borrows a trick from the old woman – she plays the part that's expected of her, she revels in it.

'A curse on you, Leah Cedars,' she calls over her shoulder. 'A curse on you – and your wretched baby!'

Viola had fallen a little in love with the idea – sacrificing herself for the sake of the Eldest Girls.

She would be a martyr like St Rita, pierced in the forehead to understand the suffering of the Saviour. Or like St Jade, enduring bites from venomous snakes to stamp out evil on Lark.

Viola ceremoniously removed all her clothing above the waist – St Catherine the inspiration for this. The tapestry on the wall of their church back home showed the martyr barechested and proud, as she was led towards the breaking wheel.

'You girls keep on calling out for your Oak King, your Horned God...' This was how he announced his arrival, strutting into view, his head adorned with the horns of a goat. 'Well, he heard you. Here he is!'

'Men aren't allowed any further,' Viola told him. 'It brings on a terrible fury.' And she stepped beyond the brink of the circle.

As he came forward, the Eldest Girls retreated to relative safety by the hollow centre stone. Viola let her arms hang at her sides. She held her chin high. The cold was anaesthetising, but she still felt the aggression of his kiss, the teeth behind it, the way he grabbed at her breasts forcefully, more deliberately than Michael. She was doing so well, hiding her shock, masking her fear, then abruptly, where his cloying warmth had been, there was bitter winter air once again. He'd been wrenched away.

She would not be St Viola after all.

'How could you! How could you do this to me!' Leah was screaming, dragging him backwards, throwing him to the grass, the horns tumbling ignobly away. Leah drew back her fist and he raised his arms to his face, his knees to his belly, protecting himself from the imminent blow.

Then Leah's arm dropped. She fell quiet. He relaxed his armour. He peered up at her.

'Oh,' she said

He was swearing now, getting up, brushing himself down, asking her what the fuck she thought she was doing.

'It's you,' she said, and she laughed, a strangled sound that disintegrated into a strange wail of pain. 'But that's not your coat,' she said, 'you even smell like ...' They all stared at her, wondering what words, what noise, might come from her mouth next. 'Does your mother know you're here?' Leah asked. 'Does Mary?'

'The fuck they do,' he replied, zipping the blue parka, flipping up the hood.

Anna came forward to throw a coat around a shivering Viola.

No one spoke.

Viola was reduced now, half-naked in the freezing air.

He was palpably on-guard, disturbed by the arrival of this deranged woman.

Leah Cedars was unsteady after the directness of her initial attack, but she found the strength to take charge, falling back into a classroom role, her voice sharp as a skewer.

'Are you hassling these girls, Luke?'

Luke Signal shook his head, not in response, but in disregard. He retrieved his gun from the grass by Viola's feet, and the girls twitched at the way it clacked in his grip. Had he brought it for cover, to explain his business out in the wood at night, or as insurance that he would get his payment as agreed? More vitally, would he use it now?

'Fuck this,' said the boy, the man, eyeing them each in turn before gobbing in the grass. 'I'll be coming for those keys to the lodge soon, yeah, Miss Cedars,' he said, a final, malevolent rejoinder. Then he disappeared into the gloom.

They regrouped at the base of the centre stone, where candles were lit in jam jars and they huddled for warmth. Leah Cedars leapt immediately to the subject of blame. Under no circumstances were the girls to believe that they were at fault for what had happened there tonight.

Viola felt patronised by this lecture. Not their fault? She had engineered the whole thing! She might not be to blame, but she deserved the credit. Saul Cooper was now in her confidence and she would have had leverage with Luke Signal too if Leah Cedars hadn't come blundering in.

'The older generation are to blame,' Leah went on. 'The attitude of those men bleeds down into the young of the island. We grow up to think of ourselves as inevitable victims, while the boys are told they are conquerors, entitled to take whatever they want.'

Viola sighed, waiting for Leah to get to the point, or for the girls to eject the woman from their circle, whichever came first, but the others seemed to have forgotten how much they despised Leah Cedars. They were nodding along.

The teacher trained her gaze on Viola, her head on one side, to all appearances kindly, compassionate. 'You know, you really shouldn't have put yourself in that situation. You should never let yourself be abused in return for, well, anything.'

Viola couldn't hold in her anger any longer. 'Let myself be abused?' she spat back. 'Let myself be abused!'

'Okay, okay,' said the teacher. 'That sounded wrong. That's not what I'm saying. You know that's not what I'm saying.'

What was she saying? Viola looked to the Eldest Girls. Why were they not jumping in to defend Viola, to argue with the woman? Why did they continue to nod so obsequiously?

'We have to start saying no,' Leah said. 'We have to fight back.'

She spoke as if they were weak, as if they had been coming to the Sisters' Stones all this time just to hide, as if they weren't already on the frontline, battered and muddied, striving for victory.

'You have no idea,' Viola snapped. 'No idea at all what's going on.'

The Eldest Girls looked shocked at this outburst, and Viola was readying herself to let loose some fury on them too when Leah said: 'I do.'

'Huh?' said Britta.

Leah looked down at her hands, at the weaving of her fingers. 'I do know what's going on,' she said, such weight to her words. 'I do know and I did, I mean... Oh, this is so hard, I'm so sorry.' The girls' eyes were heavy with sorrow.

Their breath came in anxious hitches. 'I mean, I think I always knew. I could see what was going on, but I couldn't *let* myself see. I know this makes no sense, but you have to understand – it never happened to me, my father made sure of that, and I just couldn't bear for it to be true, because I love this island so much. I just decided that it wasn't true, that it was… I don't know… impossible! And I made up all those excuses for myself, for why my friends were running away to the mainland, I built up this fortress of denial, but then my brother left because of it, and my father died, and I just couldn't…' Leah broke down. 'I'm so sorry,' she cried, 'I'm just so, so sorry.' The Eldest Girls gave vent to their tears then, the four of them falling into one another, hugging desperately.

Viola stood separate, observing this – the outsider again, the *coycrock*.

'You told me you had no brothers or sisters,' she said, something to break them apart, anything to discredit Leah. 'You lied to me.'

Leah Cedars looked up from their embrace to smile dopily at Viola, as if this was apology enough. High on her confession, the teacher continued in earnest – Luke Signal should be brought to justice, she told the girls. They should stand up in chapel and speak the truth of what he'd done, get the congregation behind them. Then, they could start talking about everything else.

The girls dipped their chins; they backed away.

'No,' said Anna firmly. 'No one will believe us. They'll think like you did, that it's all impossible.'

'I'll back you up,' said Leah, 'I'll be a witness.'

The girls flickered glances at one another.

307

Viola said aloud what they were scared to. 'And who will listen to you? Everyone on the island thinks you're insane.'

The teacher sniffed proudly and turned to Viola, squaring her shoulders: 'So, what would you suggest?'

That you fuck off and leave us alone.

'We have our own means,' she told Leah. 'Our own methods.'

Leah held Viola's gaze, as if checking the temperature of their exchange. There was silence, into which the teacher gave a great, withering sigh, before saying: 'And the photos?'

The girls' heads lifted, guilty, as one – Viola's too. Leah Cedars had seen the images?

'What photos?' said Jade-Marie too quickly.

Leah inhaled a steadying breath. 'The ones Ben... Mr Hailey... took of you.'

She was biting back fresh tears, pushing down a feeling too awful to expose – but she had exposed herself. Viola could see it then, piercingly obvious – the real reason Leah Cedars had come to the stones that night. She had expected that horned god to be Benjamin Hailey. That was why her temper had run to fire one minute, then was immediately doused. She wasn't here out of any love for the girls, she was here for herself, for Mr Hailey.

Viola grinned.

This was where her Eldest Girls would step in. They liked the new teacher from the mainland; they adored him. He had made their time at school so much more interesting, more tolerable, they said. He was funny, he was cool, but most importantly, he was theirs. They would not stand for Leah Cedars accusing him of something so terrible as taking naked photographs of them. Viola waited for them to put Leah straight, to defend their dearest teacher. *Oh, no, not Mr Hailey! How could you believe for a moment it had been him!*

But they didn't say that.

Jade-Marie spoke falteringly. 'Oh, he took those photos for a... a... a project we're doing together.'

There was quiet. A tealight puttered out, casting its spiral of smoke into the cold air. Jade-Marie cringed almost imperceptibly, but Viola caught it; she had spoken out of turn. A look passed between the girls. There was a secret here, one that Viola was not party to. The idea that they would hold something back from her, something this huge, struck Viola like a punch.

'No!' said Leah forcefully. 'That just isn't right.'

On this, at least, were Viola and Leah in agreement?

'You have to speak out about Ben,' Leah went on. 'This is our way to open it all up. The island will believe you if you accuse him, because that man is an outsider.'

◉ The Book of Leah

We lived amongst our boxes, our dread growing larger, becoming an extra brooding tenant in that lodge.

'Why don't we just go?' said my mother, one afternoon, as she searched for something long ago packed and now needed. 'I can't stand this any more.'

'Or we could move Mary Ahearn in?' was my reply. 'Appoint her ourselves.'

The idea felt delicious; the notion that we would actually do it buoyed us for days.

We invited Mary to the house to share our plan, opening one of the bottles of wine we hadn't felt like drinking at Christmas. Mary looked immediately out of place – a muscular, green boulder perched on a tall stool at the island of my mother's shiny, white kitchen. This sight alone made our suggestion seem ridiculous.

'I don't know,' was Mary's response as she swilled wine around her glass. 'Jade-Marie and her friends are getting a lot of grief at school. Wouldn't this make things even worse with Crane?'

We nodded sympathetically, we sipped. No one spoke for a while. My thoughts were loud – *What kind of grief,*

Mary? What kind? Do you know? I mean, do you really *know?* They became too loud: I had to speak.

'What kind of grief?' I made it sound casual, innocent, and therefore easier, I imagined, for Mary to reply – but I had put her on the spot.

She looked up guiltily. 'Well, the stuff with, you know, the heart and with... Peter. The idea that the girls are going up to the stones to do... magic.'

'Nonsense!' shot back my mother.

It was a comradely outburst, not an honest one. I had heard her gossip with the other women, before my father's death, about how those girls were up to no good. She patted the top of Mary's hand on the counter and I allowed myself to wonder for the first time how much my mother really knew. My instinct was that she was unaware of it all, blissfully so, but I was also astute enough to realise that this was the kindest conclusion to come to, for her and for me.

'You know it was Luke,' Mary went on. She eyed us cautiously, still unsure if she could speak freely.

My father had been her ally certainly, giving her work after Neil Ahearn drowned, but the fact remained that he had sat on the Council, alongside Crane and, until his recent retreat, Luke Signal's father, Robert. My mother and I were, in Mary's eyes, still under the Council's wing.

'He killed a goat,' Mary said. Perhaps our earlier renegade proposal gave her the reassurance to continue. 'Luke killed it and then took its heart to the stones. It was some sort of punishment, you see. He thought the girls, my Jade-Marie –' her voice teetered; she took a breath to pull it back '– he thought they were fair game, out there beyond

311

the woods on their own, if you get my drift, and didn't like being turned down.' She gulped her wine like it was beer, or maybe medicine. 'I keep an eye. I've had to. At work, the boy's got lazy. He's a hotshot with that rifle, let me tell you, but is he managing to kill any foxes? Is he heck!'

We were quiet again.

'So, there's no way he should get the job,' said my mother, stating the obvious conclusion to Mary's account, 'let alone the lodge.' Then she added: 'To think of all the dinners I've given him', as if this were the real betrayal.

'Crane knows it's him,' Mary put in. 'We took the heart to him as proof – Rhoda, Ingrid and me – proof that our girls were being harassed. We know they're acting a bit all over the place right now but is it any wonder? You've heard Crane's solution to it all, though – lock 'em up!' She finished her wine with an aggressive swig. 'Why should we lock up our girls and not that little bastard?'

She set down the glass gently and straightened her jumper – a small, decorous action to demonstrate that her anger was not for us.

'And who was it, do you think,' I asked, adding that touch of innocence to my voice, 'who told Luke the girls were fair game?'

My mother turned slowly to scowl at me. 'Leah Cedars, you do ask the strangest questions!'

She was right; it was a strange question. I wanted them to see that it was and wonder why I'd asked it. Hadn't Luke's behaviour changed all of a sudden and only recently, about the same time a handsome new stranger stepped on our soil? The two of them moving into the Billet House, the elder perhaps encouraging the younger to give free rein to that dark something lying there, ready within him, cultivated during his childhood growing up on an island like this.

'Oh, they say all sorts of crude stuff at the Anchor, the men,' was Mary's too-easy response. 'It gets back to me,' she said, 'I don't miss nothing.'

The three of us around that kitchen island were our own worst enemies – scared to tell each other what we really knew and honestly felt, how in our quietest moments we suspected the most terrible things, impossible things. How would we ever gain strength in numbers if we continued to depend on the comfort of our doubts?

My mother tried to top up Mary's glass but Mary placed her hand across it. She wanted to get home for Jade-Marie. We should just leave things as they were, was Mary's parting decision, bide our time, see who the Council appointed as gamekeeper. As if that was going to be any surprise. I didn't want to let her go. The girls had rejected my call to action and now Mary was too. I would not be herded back into that pen with the perpetrators, the collaborators and the ones who stood by.

'We could go to the Big House,' I said, taking a keen grip of Mary's arm as she made for the door, 'get the Earl to appoint you.'

Mary shook her head, laughed the idea away.

'Wake the Earl?' she said. 'Oh, no, I'm not sure we've quite got to that yet.'

The day after her visit we found the first fox.

It was outside the back door, its throat torn, probably by a badly set snare. The second carcass, the following day, had a shotgun wound to the stomach at close range, as if it had been dead already and fired at for good measure, for

313

amusement. This made me wonder if our conversation with Mary had been overheard somehow, if her words about Luke's laziness with the foxes had got back to him.

I also wondered – the mood on the island being what it was – if Mary had staged the whole exchange as some kind of bait for us, if she was in league with the boy.

There was no third fox. The next day, there was Viola. She stood on our doorstep, as red of pelt as those earlier offerings, but very much alive.

'Mr Hailey wants to see you at the stones,' she said, delivering the message flatly, as if forced to, her hands thrust into the pockets of a long padded coat several sizes too large. Her dog was sniffing frantically at the ground, the fox scent likely still potent to its sensitive nose.

'When?' I asked.

'Tonight,' she replied, 'after school. Sunset.'

Then she was gone.

I could pretend that I mistrusted the motives of the girl, that I took my time deciding if it was judicious to meet a man like Ben in a place as remote as the stones. I could pretend that the lure had not worked instantly, troublingly, rendering me useless for the rest of the day, counting the hours until the sun began its descent, but I was done with pretence; of course I would go.

He was standing at the very edge of the high north cliff when I arrived, craning for a better view of the dramatics of the sea. The winds were calm enough that day to allow it; any other time he'd have been swiftly buffeted to his death.

'There's a terrible fury going on down there, regardless of whether I walk into the middle of those stones,' he said with

314

a smile, in place of a greeting. He pulled down the hood of his heavy blue parka and leant in for a kiss.

I leant away.

'Who told you that,' I said, my voice dry, official, 'about the fury? The Eldest Girls?'

He considered me with amused confusion; my tone, my rejection of his kiss, they were merely a riddle to be solved.

'Those girls are...' he searched our surroundings for the right words '... full of stories!'

I knew that line, he wasn't the first to deliver it: girls make things up; they tell fibs, are prone to embellishments and fantasies; they don't know their own minds.

'I threw your phone down the well,' I told him.

'Shit!' he said. He looked genuinely distressed, as if it truly had been gold or the body of a forsaken wife. 'What, by accident, or –'

'On purpose,' I said.

'But... why would you –'

'Because I found naked pictures of the girls on it.'

Below us, rocks bowled and seethed as the sea recoiled.

He nodded slowly, sighed.

'The girls already told you?' I said.

'Yes.' Another sigh. 'But you do know that was Luke, don't you?'

'If the girls are to be believed,' I said blandly.

'Come on, I told you what they're like at the Billet House. Luke's the worst, always taking bits of my clothing – like this coat. He helps himself to my deodorant and aftershave. When you bring home any food, you have to...'

'Did the girls help you come up with a story about the goat horns too?'

315

I folded my arms against the cold.

'Excuse me?' he said, all equanimity wiped away in an instant, replaced by an expression I'd never seen on his face before, something hard-edged, volatile. 'What is this? Why have you dragged me up here? So you can give me some kind of dressing-down in the freezing fucking cold? I'm not one of your pupils, you know. You're not at the front of class anymore, Miss Cedars.' He spat out the sibilance of my name, disgusted with it.

This was what I had been digging for all this time, been sure I would unearth – the real Ben, the surly, poisonous individual hiding beneath that charming, affable façade. Did I think I would feel victorious when I found it? I was only frightened, too scared to shout back at him: *It was* you *who dragged* me *up here!* I took a step back, another accusation in itself.

'Oh, for fuck's sake! You're afraid of me now? Who do you think I am?' He threw his hands to the sky. He began to pace. 'This island!' he said, raking his fingers through his hair. 'This fucking island, it's so…'

I edged backwards again. I wanted to go, but he wasn't done. He flew at me and I cried out, cowering as he put his face intimidatingly close. His words were brittle. 'Luke Signal left the horns on my bed one night as a joke, okay? Left a great bloody stain on my pillow, thank you very much. I don't know what happened to them after that – am I supposed to? Were the girls wearing them in these naked pictures *I've never seen*? I don't know. I don't fucking know!' He was yelling now, had hold of me by the shoulders. 'You know that phone was lost for weeks and weeks. You know that! You know! Because *you* found it. You did! I won't apologise for something I haven't done, Leah, I won't do that, because I am not the problem here. I am not the problem!'

There was a sudden strike, a loud crack in the air, and Ben was gone.

For the briefest instant I suspected a lightning bolt, a divine response, or that the wind had delivered him to the hungry sea below. No.

He was at my feet, in the grass, jaw cranked wide in shock, his hand filled with spit and blood. Beside me stood Saul Cooper, in shirt sleeves despite the cold, breathing fast, opening and closing his just-used fist. The radio on his belt let out a phlegmy cough.

I couldn't piece the moment together. I spun around, expecting an audience of some kind.

'What are you... What... ?'

Saul moved to place an arm across my shoulders; I jerked away.

'I heard that you were...' His voice petered out, eyes examined me all over, searching for injury. Kind Saul was back, gentle Saul. 'I thought you were in some kind of trouble, Leah, and...'

Ben got to his feet, squeezing his eyes shut and flaring them, reclaiming his sight. He worked his head left and right, then thrust himself chest-first in Saul's direction.

'What the fuck, pal?' he said, the last word an insult.

'You need to leave,' Saul said in his Customs Officer voice. He held up his palms to show that he was the calm one.

'Oh, I need to leave, do I? I need to leave, eh?' Ben butted his forehead against Saul's, held it there, tensing his bloodied jaw, pushing the man backwards, closer and closer to the overhang.

'Stop it, Ben!' I cried. 'Stop it, both of you!'

The prospect of that fall was horrifying. I grabbed Ben's hand and pulled him backwards, away from the brink, the touch sobering him.

'Oh, I'll leave all right,' he said, shaking free of my grip, leaning into Saul once more, no contact this time, just the threat of it. 'When's the next ship home?'

'Friday the thirteenth of April,' Saul replied.

Ben barked out a laugh. 'Unlucky for some!' He turned away to brush himself down. The front of his coat was spattered with blood. 'But not for me.' He gave me the merest of glances, a brutal stab of the eyes, as he strode past, back towards the woods.

I felt Saul move closer.

'Wait!' I called, following Ben. 'You're leaving? Is that what you came here to tell me?'

He stopped. 'I came here because you asked me to, Leah.' His anger was gone, sloughed away, beneath it something raw, bruised. 'I didn't expect a bloody ambush with –' he gestured to Saul '– lover boy here.'

I winced at the description.

Ben turned back towards the wood.

'Wait!'

I ran to catch up with him, snatching hold of his hand. He kept on walking as if I wasn't there, but he didn't pull away. He let me keep pace. He hated me; he wanted me.

Saul chased behind us, calling, 'Leah! Leah!', telling me to be careful, warning me that Ben was a madman.

'Don't leave,' I said urgently, close to Ben's ear. 'I couldn't bear it if you left.'

This was how I felt. This was the truth.

318

'I have to.' He kept his eyes forward as we were swallowed by the darkness of the wood. 'This place...' He shook his head. 'It's so fucking messed up.'

'I know!' I said. 'I know it is, but you're the only good thing in it. You and... You and... this...' I took the flat of his hand and placed it against my abdomen. He turned in the mud of the path to look me in the eyes. I nodded.

'Oh, god,' he said. 'Oh, shit.'

This wasn't upset, nor delight, certainly fear.

'But didn't you... Weren't you...'

I shook my head, not understanding.

'Oh, shit,' he said again. 'Shit!' But sounding lighter now, astonished.

Something complicit passed between us – *oh, look what we have done!*

We turned to the interloper in our private moment.

Saul Cooper had stopped, frozen, a few paces behind us, his eyes cast low, horrified by the sight of Ben's hand resting against me. Ben sent him a stare that told him he wasn't welcome. I was cruel.

'Go away, Saul,' I said. 'Go away. This has nothing to do with you.'

He looked at me beseechingly, desperately, and I couldn't bear it.

'Just fuck off, Saul!' I said. That word had never left my mouth before; I'd saved it to wound Saul Cooper. 'Just fuck off and leave us alone.'

Ben pulled me in to his chest and I watched Saul stagger backwards, looking about him dizzily, as if others might be witnessing his humiliation. The radio at his belt coughed, making excuses on his behalf. He didn't take the path back to the stones but blundered into the thick of the trees instead. I should have called after him, made sure he was all right, but I was selfish.

'I can't bring up a child here,' I told Ben as we stood there alone in the dark. 'When you leave on the thirteenth, will you take me with you?'

The headteacher was locked out of his own school, the most senior pupils carrying wooden batons to enforce the revolt. This happened every mid-Lent Monday.

The weapons this year were in the hands of Britta Sayers, Anna Duchamp and Jade-Marie Ahearn. They beat them against the doorframes to keep a rhythm to the chant.

Out you go, and stay you out,
We're claiming back the day,
Say yes to fun, and in you'll come,
Oh, master – whaddya say?

Every classroom window with a view onto the playground was colonised by faces, little noses pressed against the glass. The children's fierce and uncompromising headmaster occupied the centre circle of the netball court, arms folded, foot tapping, about to get a taste of his own medicine. The younger ones squealed and giggled, watching this act of revenge unfold – a revenge that fell within the bounds of safety, the headmaster being in on the joke.

The sound of the Eldest Girls thumping their batons was thrilling in its barbarity. *Boom boom boom boom* – they counted the student body into another round of the chant.

Out you go, and stay you out,
We're claiming back the day.
Say yes to fun, and in you'll come,
Oh, master – whaddya say?

It was customary for Mr Crane to hold his ground for three renditions of the chant, then, loudly, playfully, he would agree to close the school. At this, everyone would spill from the building towards the chapel, so the festivities could begin. Mr Crane was well rehearsed after thirteen years in the post; he roared out his given line with Santa Claus good cheer: 'Oh, all right then, let's take the day off!'

But – *boom boom boom boom* – the Eldest Girls counted the pupils in for another round of the rhyme.

Then another.

Then another.

By the seventh turn, the girls were chanting alone and no one was smiling, Mr Crane especially. The little children were confused and growing anxious.

'What's going on? Why aren't we letting him back in?' asked a tearful Second Year infant.

Their teacher, Barbara Stanney, exchanged worried glances with her assistant, Faith Moran, before hurrying to the main doors, where Ruth French and Benjamin Hailey were already trying to prise batons from the unrelenting clutches of Anna and Jade-Marie.

Britta, meanwhile, orchestrated an end to it all, flipping the lock of the double doors that led onto the playground, before kicking those doors wide open. She held her baton aloft for one brief, triumphant moment, then released her grip, letting it drop from this great height with a clatter, an action that only the handsome *coycrock* teacher seemed to find amusing.

Anna and Jade-Marie relinquished their batons in similar fashion – a high hold, a noisy drop – and before anyone could ask what on earth they were playing at, the girls called out to the younger years, who ran cheering from their classrooms, the tiniest ones grabbing the hands of senior pupils as they went. This small but buoyant gang poured out across the playground, flowing around their headmaster, still stranded there in the centre circle, not giving him a backward glance, as they made their way to chapel carried along in joyous song.

'Look at them,' Ruth French was heard to mutter, not disparagingly, 'the Pied Pipers of St Rita's.'

For the clipping of the church some adults were required, otherwise there would not be a long enough loop of arms to reach all the way around the chapel's exterior. The teachers who had, by now, caught up with their excitable charges, joined in, along with the three holy sisters – Agnes, Sarah and Clare – and some mothers of children from the younger years. The circle in place, Father Daniel began the hymn, one they knew the verses of without the aid of their books – 'All Things Bright and Beautiful' – and above them the bug-eyed gargoyles, with their horns and wings and fangs, stuck out their tongues in approval.

The singing done, the clipping could commence, and they advanced towards the grey stone walls in their circle, elbows drawn in, hands held high, before retreating, arms at full stretch. Advance, retreat, advance, retreat. The younger children *oooh*-ed and *aah*-ed in time with the motion.

Then it was time for the play.

When the weather was fine, as it was that day (by Lark standards this meant when the rain was not heavy and no storm was lashing), the play was held outdoors at the harbour. Rufus Huxley had set aside his school-caretaking tasks for the morning to construct the makeshift stage – a series of pallets screwed together, a pole frame on top, from which hung red silky curtains, fishing-net weights in the hems so they did not dance with the wind.

The committee of unusual suspects, who had been meeting at chapel in the preceding weeks to plan the Easter celebrations, these mid-Lent festivities included, set up a refreshment stall at the front of the Provisions Store, offering hot tea and coffee in mugs, orange squash for the children and a batch of freshly baked hot cross buns.

It was manned in rotation by Cat Walton and Ruth French, Martha Signal and Reuben Springer, Mary Ahearn and Ingrid Duchamp, while Rhoda Sayers ran back and forth, refreshing the sugar pot and the squash jugs. At one point, Margaritte Carruthers stood serving and custom slowed, word trickling across the cobbles that she had spiked the drinks with truth tinctures and love potions, or even a hallucinogenic dose of belladonna. Still, the usual women of the committee, Diana Crane and Elizabeth Bishy, Eleanor Springer and Miriam Calder, stood in line for their drinks and a sticky bun, only so they could say, with absolute authority, that the quality of the buffet was definitely not as good as last year.

'Once the sun is past the yardarm,' Eleanor Springer reassured her clan, 'Jed will open up the Anchor.' Then she bit into one of Martha Signal's hot cross buns and pretended not to like it.

Dellie Leven was expected to take to the stage to introduce the annual production of *A Midsummer Night's Dream*, having taught the girls for much of the year, until Leah Cedars' departure required her to pick up the slack of the Fourth and Fifth Year seniors. But it was the handsome *coycrock* teacher who leapt up onto the pallets, announcing that he was to be the day's Dionysus, leading them all in a celebration of theatre, merrymaking and ritual madness.

Raising his voice above the chatter on the harbourside, he urged everyone to settle onto the benches that Huxley had arranged before the stage in crescents. The view from these seats took in not only the performance, but the expanse of a sea neither moody nor calm – a critic reserving its judgement perhaps, until the final curtain fell.

Parents with younger ones lined the front rows to ensure the best view. Before they sat, they removed the leaflets placed along the benches at regular intervals, held down by pebbles with holes in the middle, whittled by the action of the sea.

This was a new addition to proceedings – a programme.

Some cooed their appreciation of the A5 sheet headed *THE PLAYERS*. On the front was the novelty of a new photograph, sharply focused, taken no doubt with one of the *coycrock* teacher's fancy mainland devices. It was a group image of the Eldest Girls, the three of them leaning against the mossy wall of the graveyard, the low glow of a sunset warming their faces, the sea grey and soupy behind them. On the back of the pamphlet were individual headshots of each girl, also new and seriously posed. Beneath these were typed strange little biographies – *Jade-Marie Ahearn first got a taste for the stage playing 'third sheep from the left' in the celebrated St Rita's Nativity play when she was just three and a half years old. Since then, she has gone on to become Lark's most talked about alto-contralto, turning down endless offers to appear at the Albert Hall.*

Others deemed these programmes unnecessary, wasteful even, especially when the wind snatched a few, sending them swooping out to sea.

The usual suspects – the headmaster, the doctor and their respective wives; Jed and Eleanor Springer, Miriam and Frank Calder, etc. – commandeered the benches on the right. Sister Agnes led her holy comrades, Sister Sarah and Sister Clare, to sit on this side too, though towards the back so that their starched white wimples would not obstruct anyone's sightlines.

The 'unusual suspects' – Rhoda and Ingrid, Martha and Ruth, etc. – took the left benches, forcing the middle-grounders to choose sides. Dellie Leven, Hope Ainsley and Sarah Devoner all opted for the relative safety of the right, immediately questioning their decision – if the angling of their necks was anything to go by – when Father Daniel took his seat on the left next to the flowing white hair and flowery skirts of Margaritte Carruthers.

Abe Powell did not sit, refusing Reuben Springer's encouraging pat of the bench space beside him, choosing to stand instead, cradling a lukewarm cup of tea. The *coycrock* girl was seen arriving stony-faced with her dog, unwilling to insert herself in the throng. She was avoiding the doctor, everyone knew, was overdue a medical examination, and that was likely why she took a seat, off to one side, on top of the stocks. Only the younger Signal boy, Michael, made a move on her, leaping up from his spot beside his mother,

Martha, to sit on that splintery top board too, the girl edging away, creating an appropriate gap between them.

Saul Cooper observed all this from the Customs House, leaning against the white render of the building, smoking a cigarette. In the last moments before curtain-up, as the Cedars women arrived – Susannah and Leah, perching at the very end of one of the empty back rows on the left – Saul strode over decisively and took his seat on the right, next to Diana Crane.

'Ladies and gentlemen of Lark!' Benjamin Hailey was confident in his ringmaster's voice. Though, dressed as he was, in a pair of shiny, pointed shoes, slim-fitting trousers and a pink shirt – of all colours! – the gathered agreed he had more the appearance of a clown. 'I know you are used to seeing a story of fairies and mechanicals and love in the woods at these celebrations every year, but as our lovely Eldest Girls will also be the Eldest Girls in 2019, I'm afraid you'll have to wait until then to see them put on that particular show. This year we have been working on, well, a pet project of ours, something a little bit different …'

There was an uneasy rumble along the benches, turning to yelps when, on the snatching back of the red curtains, the play began with a literal bang – a blast of fire and a puff of coloured smoke – the science teacher's obvious influence. The residual haze cleared to reveal Jade-Marie in a white ruffled shirt, brown hair scraped back, a moustache drawn on, sitting at a desk of conical flasks, concoctions and books. She spoke in a language not unlike Shakespeare, her English laced with Latin.

'*The reward of sin is death. That's hard,*' she began nervously. '*If we say we have no sin, we deceive ourselves, and there's no truth in us.*'

Murmurs of agreement came back from the benches – this phrase was familiar, coming as it did from the *First Epistle General of John*.

Jade-Marie was granted the confidence to be bolder.

'*Why then belike we must sin, and so consequently die.*' She looked out across the faces below her, as if expecting an answer. There was silence, except for one infant asking noisily of her mother why the girl had pen on her lip.

'*These metaphysics of magicians, and necromantic books are heavenly!*' Jade-Marie was strutting in a masculine fashion across the pallet stage, hands on hips. '*Lines, circles, signs, letters and characters,*' she continued. '*Ay, these are those that Faustus most desires.*'

Dellie Leven was heard to mutter, 'Oh, dear Lord!' before crossing herself.

Heads turned, as surreptitiously as they could, towards the headmaster. Would he call a halt, now that the initial godliness of the play, like those paper programmes, had disappeared on the wind? He did not. He stared forward.

Anna and Britta arrived on stage then in white night-dresses as the good and evil angels. The mood of the crowd softened; this would be a morality play after all. And it was, in essence. One man sells his soul to the Devil and takes the consequences – there was an admirably pious message in that. But there was also something to be drawn from the way the three girls dressed while playing the gossiping scholars – in blouses that tied at the throat, the current trend among the women who surrounded the tea urn after Sunday service. When Faustus and the Devil (a deep-voiced Britta, resplendent in a headdress of coiled goat horns) taunted the religious men at the Vatican office, the set bore a resemblance, through its particular arrangement of props, to a certain office closer to home, at the school of St Rita's.

For a scene in Act Four where Faustus conjures up the ghosts of Alexander and his paramour, Anna and Britta arrived on stage in dripping wet robes. This was supposed to signify their journey back across the River Styx, but they more closely resembled a drowned fisherman and a sodden little girl, than they did figures from Ancient Greece.

Should anyone have dared to point out these parallels, though, they would only have incriminated themselves, become complicit in the accusations. The allusions were there, but also they were not.

What transpired on the stage was absolutely a morality play, one that spoke to the deep, shared understanding of a community. The audience listened as one, that was how it felt – as one mind, one collective subconscious, both good and bad, if a clear line can ever be drawn between the two.

When the girls delivered their epilogue – '*Cut is the branch that might have grown full straight...*' – many of that audience found themselves crying, surprised by their emotions, unable to explain coherently what their tears were in aid of.

The curtains closed to a hush; the slip and slop of the sea in the harbour the only sound. The red-haired *coycrock* girl left immediately, head down, scuffing away past the smokehouse, as the Eldest Girls' mothers broke the contemplative tension, standing to clap and cheer, allowing the others around them to do the same, to have their release.

They applauded on the left, and they applauded in the middle.

They even applauded on the right – but how could they not?

Friday the 13th – April 2018

The brick path ends and there it is, rising up before her – an ornate gothic tower of dark stone, its windows mullioned, dead-eyed. Viola takes the mossy, flint-lined steps two at a time and arrives on a terrace where stout cannons nose out of a parapet. The place is not forbidding as such, just eerily familiar, like the setting of a long-forgotten dream. Then she remembers – she has seen the Big House before, in the black-and-white photos on the wall of the Customs House. Here is the place in full colour, though mostly it is shades of grey.

She runs headlong at the huge, braced wooden door, chopping at the latch with the edge of one palm. There is no time for the pleasantries of knocking; the pale sun is beginning to mount the treetops in her wake, making it ten o'clock, half-past perhaps, Viola can't be sure. She has never been able to understand the adult fascination with wearing a watch – the time is always right there, on your phone. Now she gets it.

Viola throws open the door into the stillness of a hallway, silent but for the rasping of her own breath. It is window-less, all darkness, and she falls momentarily blind as the door clunks back on its latch behind her. Her eyes grow accustomed, and into view comes the face of a tall and decorative clock, a mechanical sun ready to take the place of a cloudy, painted moon. There is no tick, no movement; both hands rest at twelve. Ahead of her are bookshelves, rows of untouched encyclopaedias, the alphabet portioned out in gold foil on their spines.

To her right, a stairway.

She grabs the post, its finial carved into the shape of a pomegranate, and launches herself at the steps. Above her comes the *tsk-tsk-tsk* of feet striking stone – someone alerted to her presence.

'Hello?' calls a female voice.

They meet on the half-landing, almost bump chests. The woman is short and sturdy, mother-aged, black-haired. She wears a striped linen dress, covered over with an apron.

'Can I help?' she enquires tightly, not meaning it at all.

'Where is the Earl?' Viola demands, out of breath.

'Who needs to know?'

'Me!'

Viola ducks left, tries to slip past, but the woman is quick. In this half-landing of the stairway, she makes herself wide.

'Eh-eh-eh-eh!' she admonishes, as if Viola is a small child or a dog. 'Where do you think you're going?'

Up! Viola thinks. *I'm going up!*

She will prove that a red-haired girl doesn't mean bad luck, show everyone that the good angel speaks louder at her shoulder than the bad. Everything will come together as she has promised. There may be no detective inspectors on that incoming ship, but there will be a ship, a shaft of light in the gloom, and it will herald the arrival of reason.

'The Eldest Girls!' Viola says, spluttering it, making the woman jerk in her chin. Viola has coherent sentences prepared for the Earl but nothing for his indignant gate-keeper. 'The Eldest Girls,' Viola repeats, 'it's the Eldest Girls and I'll... I'll...'

I'll huff and I'll puff, says a voice in her head, because the time for gentle negotiation has gone.

'I'll burn this place to the fucking ground if I have to,' Viola cries, her voice singing off the bare stone walls. 'I will smoke the old bastard out if you will not let me past!'

Viola was truly sorry.

She went to tell him so, fearful that she would find the Customs House deserted, a later search of Cable's Wood revealing Saul's body, swinging from a tree. He had saved her from the death-lick of the sea on the day of the game-keeper's funeral and this was how she repaid him: with humiliation. Viola had witnessed it all. Though it hadn't really been her fault; it was that woman, yet again, stymie-ing Viola's plans.

She lifted the hinged front desk and let herself into the back office. The place was ominously deserted, the first part of Viola's premonition coming true. A small, oscillating fan turned its eye this way then that on the edge of the coun-ter that ran beneath the sea-filled window. It wasn't warm outside but the sun that shone into the office became trapped, magnified. Saul's sketchbook lay open on the counter by one of the radio consoles, its pages riffling upwards at the atten-tion of the fan, dropping down again as it rotated away.

Viola peered at the drawing-in-progress, a striped pencil resting in the fold of the book – proof at least that Saul was recently alive. It was a sketch of a gathering of herring gulls, a trio of them squabbling on the harbour railings, one directing its mean gaze to the viewer, one wide-beaked, mid-squawk, and another lifting into the air, splaying its improbably huge webbed feet. The drawing was good; Saul was good.

She flipped to the start of the book to see more and found sketches of Lark's buildings – Customs House, Counting House, Provisions Store, Anchor – with Lowry-like figures populating the cobbles, then another of the harbourside from a different angle, taking in the masts of the boats, the chimneys of the smokehouse and the sun setting behind the hills. After that came portraits, Saul practising his mastery of hands by drawing the boatmen at work on the nets. Then followed a head-and-shoulders sketch of Leah Cedars, looking down pensively, black hair falling across a shaded cheek. In the corner of the page he'd drawn her full-length, striding, carrying an armful of folders.

Viola turned the page, snorting at what she saw next. It was a naked sketch – a cartoon fantasy version of Leah Cedars, hazy and curvy, with too much breast and thigh and hair, the eyes disproportionately large. Another naked drawing followed, altogether different. Here, the style was naturalistic and Leah was flawed, her breasts not inflated, her stomach not so perfectly flat. She was posed as if straddling the viewer, her hands between her legs, head tossed back, eyes closed. Open-mouthed, she was at the peak of pleasure.

Viola dropped the book; she didn't like this image. She knew that Leah Cedars was having sex with both Mr Hailey and Saul Cooper, if Michael Signal was to be believed, but it suited Viola to think of Leah as stiff, ungiving, because if she really was the woman shown in that drawing, then it meant that she was powerful.

Viola headed back out again, across the cobbles, following the sound of familiar laughter drifting from the Anchor. The day had hit noon and the shutters and windows of the pub were cast wide to chase out the stale smells of the night before.

She walked a curve towards the building so as not to be seen approaching, positioning herself at an angle by the window to lock in. Saul was there, on a stool at the bar, tipping back the last amber splash of a pint. Jed Springer removed the empty glass and replaced it with a full one. Viola wasn't sure what was most shocking: the sight of Saul Cooper passing time with the waistcoated landlord, one of the brothers of the Council who had conspired against his beloved Leah, or that he was at least two drinks up at lunchtime, the Customs House sitting unmanned.

'Bad Angel is about fucking right,' Viola heard Saul say.

Jed Springer chuckled. 'Too fucking right, and if...' The landlord paused to look over his left shoulder, then his right, a little comedy routine – he wasn't really worried about being overheard. He leant in close for the next bit. 'If the mother is anything to go by, she's got a tight Swedish pussy too, very nice, thank you very much.'

Jed made an okay sign with fingers and thumb, nodding enthusiastically. They both sniggered, the truth not import-ant – schoolboys at the back of the bus. The men's bathroom door swung open at the rear of the bar and Luke Signal sauntered out, still buttoning his fly.

'Who's got a tight pussy?' he called across the room. 'That you, Saul?'

More laughter. Saul gulped away the first few inches of his new drink. The mirth settled, the conversation stalled. Luke's dark gaze wandered towards the harbour beyond the window and Viola snatched herself out of sight, pressing against the open shutters – not fast enough. There was a low, muffled exchange within and a smattering of derisive grunts. Viola peeled off and cut a slant across the cobbles, making for the stocks.

'Hey!' Saul's voice halted her.

He didn't run to catch her up. He took his time.

'Where's that dog of yours?' he said, coming to stand beside her, too close. There was a sway to his body.

'At home,' Viola said, not looking him in the eye.

Then, quieter, he asked: 'And my radio?'

Viola chewed at her lip.

'What radio?' She grinned, trying to be playful, reminding him that they were friends, conspirators.

'Ah, don't give me that, *coycrock*,' he slurred. 'The radio you used to play that stupid fucking trick on me. Hand it over.'

Her face fell, as if slapped.

'What's the matter?' he sneered. 'Don't you like being spoken to like you're a piece of shit? Fucking sucks, doesn't it? Hand it over.'

He held out his hand.

'I'm gonna tell Leah you were drinking with Jed and Luke,' she hit back. She heard how she sounded – like a child, spiteful, hurt. She wasn't his 'cherub' anymore.

'You tell her what the fuck you like, *coycrock*.' He gave an arrogant sniff. 'Make up whatever shit you want. You're good at that.'

'She lied to me too!'

'That right?'

'You two are supposed to be together! I gave you a chance to fight for that. You could have been the hero that night,

338

shoved him off the edge of the cliff, that… that…' at a loss for words, she stole from Saul '… that piece of shit.'

He had to smile then, just a little. 'Yeah, well…' He sighed and turned to go back to the Anchor.

'That's it, is it?' she said. 'You're just giving up?'

'I'm going to finish my drink.'

'Why?'

'Because I'm thirsty, and because… what is it you say, or your mum told you? … you can't run away from your fate.'

'Fate's fate,' Viola muttered reluctantly.

'Fate's fate,' he parroted.

Something passed between them then – a sadness. Viola shook it off.

'But why drink with *them*?' she implored.

He rolled his tongue across his teeth, looked out to sea.

'Because I have to live here,' he said. 'And so do you. Which is why you hang out with that bunch of devil-worshippers, I'm guessing.'

'You know they're not. You know!'

Luke Signal emerged from the Anchor then and Viola watched him, over Saul's shoulder, pint in hand, settling himself against the doorframe to observe their conversation. He nodded a greeting to her and she shivered, involuntarily.

'We're not so different, you and me, kiddo,' said Saul, placing a heavy hand on Viola's shoulder. 'We've both lost the ones we love to Benjamin fucking Hailey.'

Her eyes were still on Luke, the two of them silently re-negotiating their debt, so this summing-up of Saul's almost flew past her ear. Almost.

'What do you mean?' Her attention returned to him, the childish voice back. 'I haven't lost anyone.'

'No?' Saul removed his hand, shrugged. 'Whatever you say, *coycrock.*'

Then he walked away, back to his new friends, his old friends, his brothers, and Viola kicked at the stocks – hard – made the boards clatter in their frame.

He was right; she knew it.

In the run up to the mid-Lent play, the girls had not shown up at the stones. In the days after too, no sign. Viola threw back her covers every night at 11.30 p.m., put on her mother's coat and sneaked out of the farmstead, skirting along the edges of the hallway to avoid the nosiest of the floorboards, stepping over the piles of brittle, incoming leaves. It wasn't that she risked waking her mother who slept like the dead – an analogy Deborah Kendrick used commonly before the incident, and once inadvertently afterwards, leading to the most terrible silence. Viola's tiptoeing was for Dot's sake, dreaming by the stove behind the closed kitchen door. If disturbed, she would be too eager to come along.

The girls had given Viola their excuses.

'We have to go and work on our project with Mr Hailey,' Jade-Marie had said the last time Viola had seen them. They had exchanged complicit smiles, Anna sensuously winding a piece of blonde hair around a finger.

Viola refused to ask what the project was, or to suggest she should join them; she wouldn't lower herself. She understood the games girls played, had observed and participated in far more than any of these three amateurs had. They were pushing her to ask the questions only to have the satisfaction of turning her down.

Oh, we couldn't possibly say.

Oh, I doubt Mr Hailey could agree to anyone else joining in.

Once she had seen this play of theirs – the 'project' – she knew there would be consequences. Not that Viola was apportioning any blame to the girls – she wasn't Leah fucking Cedars. The play had done what it set out to do: prick the island's conscience. Souls had been sold to the devil, it said, and not the obvious ones, not the souls of those who tattooed their wrists and congregated at the Neolithic circle. But that play had been a hand grenade, and Viola was appalled at Mr Hailey for pulling the pin. She was even more furious that the Eldest Girls had trusted his guidance on this, without consulting her.

They were meeting at the stones earlier.

Viola worked it out when she arrived one midnight to find the detritus of a ritual recently discarded. She started coming earlier too, retreating to her old position, crouching low in the ferns to watch. The girls stretched their arms to the sky more desperately than before. They called out to the goddesses of nature, time, the sea, the earth, to Bethany Reid, to the lost fishermen, to their guiding saints, Rita, Brigid, Anne – mother of Mary – and to St Jade. To everyone, anyone.

Like before, Viola chose her moment to step forward.

'I could have told you so,' she said coolly, as she entered the circle of stones.

The girls' arms drooped, swallowed by the folds of their voluminous nightdresses.

'You were punished, I suppose,' she went on.

They looked at their feet.

'Why did you listen to that piece of shit?' Viola watched the insult ripple through them. 'In the end, he's just a man. In the end they're all like that, they let you down.'

She choked on these too-grown-up words, the emotion catching her unexpectedly. She was talking about Saul, she thought, but it was her dad she meant, and Seb. Their dying felt like a deliberate desertion, the worst betrayal ever.

Britta turned to the other two, that unspoken language passing between them, and they rejoined their hands, reforming their circle of just three, whispering one of their old incantations.

Clean we are, pure we be
Our minds fall open and we can see
Take the dark, turn it to light
Wash this away before the night.

They went back to the start, murmuring the verse again, faster, faster, Viola watching, thinking, *I've lost them, I've lost the ones I love to Benjamin fucking Hailey.*

But she would not be like Saul. She would not give up. She could still be the hero.

'Speak to me!' Viola begged.

The chanting stopped, the circle broke. They lined up to face her.

The coldness of their gaze was so unbearably painful.

'You've been causing trouble,' said Britta.

'What?' Viola didn't understand.

'You've been meddling in Mr Hailey's business,' said Jade-Marie.

Anna nodded, the final verdict. 'And he told us that we are never to trust you again.'

They stand outside the bedroom and wait, impatiently. They will kick down the door if they must.

It has been done before and can be done again, explains the woman on the stairs whose name is Hannah Pass. She has done it herself, without any help from the gardeners, without even a change of her neat buckled shoes. She directs Viola's attention to the scars in the wood, says the door will never be the same again, which is a shame because much of the interiors are original ... different handles but, you know?

'Sorry,' Hannah added, 'I talk too much when I'm anxious.'

She calls out with matronly authority, mouth close to the jamb, 'Lord Catherbridge! I am asking you very nicely to please open up!' She turns to Viola then, speaking quietly, 'Did you actually bring matches?'

Viola looks at her, confused.

'To burn the place down...'

'Oh!' Viola shakes her head. 'No.'

Hannah tuts, disappointed, and speaks again to the door.

'Lord Catherbridge! I'm going to give you a count of three and then we'll break it down like before, do you understand?'

There is a harrumph from within, not a human one, the sound of bedding being moved perhaps, a towel dropping or the pushing over of a pile of clothes.

'One!' calls Hannah and, in her head, Viola instinctively adds the requisite *-elephant*.

Viola had not needed to threaten a fire; mentioning the Eldest Girls was enough.

'Calm down,' was Hannah's response to Viola's demands on the stairs. She spoke with the kind of sternness that made you feel safe. 'No one is going to be burning down anything. Well, not yet.' She had taken hold of Viola by the upper arms, a settling gesture. 'I am a member of the St Rita's "Easter Committee",' she'd said then.

'Two!' Hannah bellows, and there is, perhaps, the shuffling of feet on boards.

'Easter Committee' was obviously supposed to mean something – Hannah had emphasised the words, given a pop of the eyes – but Viola didn't understand the reference.

'The unusual suspects, they call us,' Hannah went on. 'A left-bencher?'

Still, Viola could only blink.

'I have a daughter, for Pete's sake!' She'd thrown her arms wide. 'She's in the Fourth Year seniors! Just two years from being sixteen!'

Viola knew then that the woman was on her side.

'Three!' All is silence behind that bedroom door.

'Time's up!' calls Hannah, and turns sideways, putting a shoulder to the wood, encouraging Viola to take the same stance, and she does, though after her run across the island she seriously doubts that she has the strength left to break down a door.

'Put the weight on the back foot,' Hannah coaches, 'and then after three we'll –'

There is a loud scrape – a bolt being drawn back. Hannah and Viola relax their combat poses. The brass handle rotates. In the dark gap appears a reedy man, grey-haired and surprisingly bright-eyed, but the skin beneath those eyes slides down his face like candle wax.

Viola feels the disappointment viscerally, in her gut.

This is the Earl?

This the man who might save them, seize back authority, overrule the Council, expose its abuse of power and stand up for those at the mercy of impossible causes? He is nothing but a feeble old man in a dressing gown. Viola had expected to wake a sleeping giant, one capable of biting chunks from cliffs and pushing islands out to sea.

Hannah speaks to the man cheerfully, efficiently, as if the pantomime outside the door had never taken place, or as if it was entirely normal.

'Ah, Lord Catherbridge!' she trills.

'What is it?' he bumbles, those bright eyes making a swift assessment of Viola.

'There's something *very* important that you need to do.' Hannah's tone drops low, becomes urgent, her faith in Viola's plan seemingly still strong, so Viola gathers herself, summons all residual hope.

'You're needed on the Council, sir,' says Hannah, setting it all in motion. 'It's a matter of life or death.'

MARCH 2018

It was true that she had meddled in Mr Hailey's business, but she had done it for them.

Faced with that firing line at the stones – their three reproachful faces – Viola held back her desire to wail *After everything I've done for you!* She knew that shouldn't matter, and it didn't. She had never expected gratitude, any kind of payment. But their acceptance, their friendship – she'd considered that hers, immutable.

Britta tossed a dark gaze to Anna, then Jade-Marie, getting their nods of permission to go on. 'Mr Hailey's getting us out of here,' she said.

Viola's throat tightened. 'What?'

'The project isn't the play.' Britta spoke from beneath the fall of her hair. There was a sense of apology to this explanation, but also condescension. Did Viola *really* believe they were relying absolutely on spells and chants and the reassurances of a red-haired *coycrock*? A play was not enough to solve everything. 'Mr Hailey is preparing a document about us.'

'A dossier,' Jade-Marie put in, pleased with the word, one clearly gifted by Benjamin Hailey. 'We've given him statements, had our photos taken. He's going to hand it in to the authorities on the mainland.' She was perversely excited about this.

'*We're* going to take it.' Anna jumped in with the clarification. 'Mr Hailey's going to take us with him.'

'On... On the April ship?' Viola stammered.

Britta shook her head. 'The August ship. He's going to finish one whole school year so as not to...' She paused, searching it seemed for another of the man's expressions. 'So as not to arouse suspicion.'

'What... Mr Hailey's really a policeman?' Viola was a girl in a rabbit hole, a child tumbling down a well. 'So... he's... he's working undercover or...'

'No, he's just a teacher,' said Jade-Marie. 'Just a man.' Quickly adding, 'But he does care about us.'

'You're going to leave your mums behind, your dads?' said Viola. She turned to Anna. 'Your little brother?' The true cry within her was: *What about me? What about me?* 'What about the girls here who are about to turn sixteen?'

'That's all been sorted.' Jade-Marie beamed with evangelical fervour. 'We'll send for them once we get there, once we've got it all settled.'

'But that makes no sense,' said Viola. She wasn't angry anymore, nor confused, because this was clearly madness; it wasn't real.

'You don't understand,' Anna cut in with her voice of all reasonableness. 'Everything's been worked out, it's –'

'No!' Viola yelled, 'No!'

There came that hum again, that singing of the earth, the sensation of it vibrating through them – an undiscovered chord. All four girls stood and listened as the tremor receded.

Then Viola asked calmly, 'What's the difference between speaking out over there and speaking out here?' Jade-Marie inhaled, her response ready, but Viola wouldn't hear it. 'You think things will be different if you cross a huge stretch of sea? Well, believe me, they won't be.' Viola knew this. They knew this. 'You're worried about the payback if you tell, just think what will happen to the people you leave behind if you speak out somewhere else. How will they suffer for you doing this? Will there be more losses?'

Britta folded her arms. 'Now you're just being dramatic.'

'Am I?' Viola told them a story then, one that they had told her. 'Ten men head out in the middle of the night on a fishing boat meant for five ... That's even stranger when you consider that most of the men on board are not fishermen.'

'Shh!' Jade-Marie covered her ears and closed her eyes, unable to bear it.

Viola continued, 'In the weeks before they leave, these men talk about revolt, even murder, but no, they decide to do things the right way, get proper justice. Others had gone over to the mainland and been ignored, but no one could ignore the voices of ten men who had crossed an unforgiving ocean to reveal the truth, could they?'

'Okay,' said Britta, 'you can stop now.'

Viola refused; she would make them see. 'They didn't even tell their wives about their mercy mission, for the women's own safety. Just left them to their doubts. Left them forever it turned out. Because that boat never reached the mainland and it never came back. The storms got them. Or... what if that boat was scuppered on purpose?'

'The inscription on the cross at the harbour says it was an accident,' whispered Jade-Marie, tears falling.

'Yeah,' said Viola, 'but you don't believe that, do you?'

Their silence was answer enough.

'It's all we have, Viola,' Anna said – a gentle lament. 'It's all there is. We can't rely on nails in hearts, we need something more... something...' She tailed off; she hung her head.

'The heart worked!' Viola cried out. Her faith in this was still strong. Peter Cedars had died because of them! If they could only harness this power, control it... But the girls were looking at their feet, not willing to agree. So, Viola spoke cruelly, only to be kind. 'Mr Hailey isn't going to take you with him on the August ship.'

Britta sighed. 'He said you would do this.'

'I bet he did,' said Viola. She laughed; that got their attention.

'Go on,' said Jade-Marie.

'He can't take you with him on the August ship because he's leaving on the April one! Friday the thirteenth. He's got Leah Cedars pregnant and they don't want to have the baby here.' Viola watched their faces fall, drain of colour. 'They're probably worried about what will happen if it turns out to be a girl.'

Britta's jaw was working, building up to a refusal. Viola got in first. 'I heard them, Britta! Saul Cooper did too. Out here in the woods. Ask Mr Hailey yourself. Ask Miss Cedars. Though I'm not sure they'd tell you the truth.'

The girls looked at one another, eyes widening. The sea swilled and churned somewhere beneath them. The wind chased furrows through the long grass at their feet.

'Shit!' This was Anna. 'Fuck! Shit! Fuck! Shit! Fuck!' She alternated the only bad words she knew, looking for a release and getting none, angry tears drenching her face. 'Oh, god!' she cried. 'Oh, god! Bethany Reid had the right idea!' She directed this viciously at the others. 'That's the only way out of this fucking place!' Then she turned, in a great swirl of white nightdress, and stamped away, out of the circle.

It was Jade-Marie who realised it first, that Anna wasn't heading back through the woods; she was making towards the cliff edge.

'Anna, no!'

They sprinted after her, yelling for her to stop, telling her she didn't mean it, but her stride was certain, fast.

Jade-Marie snatched hold of her friend, trying to halt her with the restraint of a hug, but Anna broke free, she carried on; she howled: 'I'm doing this for all of you!'

'It won't do us any good to have you gone!' Britta pleaded, moving with her, the wind clipping her words as they drew nearer to where the edge was, or where it might be; the gloom made it impossible to see. Each step could be their last.

The sea crashed louder, closer, it warned them; they were on the brink. The group staggered to a halt. Anna's teeth were chattering. Britta and Jade-Marie clung to a hand each, the wind making sails of their nightdresses.

'This will get their attention,' Anna said. Her eyes were already dead, her voice a flat line. 'It will bring the mainland authorities here, like when Bethany killed herself, but I've got you to tell them it was no accident. You can tell them why I did it.' She began to mutter a prayer in the same voice they had used for their spells. 'O *Almighty God, King of all Kings and governor of all things, whose power no creature is able to resist ...*' These were her last rites.

Viola stood behind them, breathless, watching their swaying outline, three girls as one body, lurching towards the tow of the black sea beyond, heels driven into mud, inches from the edge. She knew she should step forward, help wrench the girl back, but she was gripped by something – the truth of what Anna had said.

'But why does it have to be you?'

At Viola's voice, Anna's supplications petered out, the words dropping like shingle from the ledge. Her head turned, her pull slackened. Jade-Marie seized the moment, enveloping her shivering friend, if only for one last embrace.

'*Greater love has no one than this, that someone lay down his life for his friends,*' incanted Anna.

'Yes, there should be a sacrifice,' said Viola. 'But why should that sacrifice be you?'

Viola stepped towards them, the circle forming without her asking. They breathed as one: earth, fire, air and water; north, south, east, west; black, blonde, brown, red. Their heads touched, and a strange light, at once imagined yet real, formed itself between them, glowing brighter, gathering into an enthralling shape.

'It's not a sacrifice,' said Jade-Marie, 'unless you offer up something that matters.'

'Yes,' said Viola. Then she corrected that note, ever so slightly, making the harmony ring true. 'But why,' she asked, 'must it matter to us?'

◉ The Book of Leah

We are Lark. The island is its people. We are its future.

You can believe but not practise.

You can find out how to be a better person, a different person, one the island deserves.

You can put one foot in the water, hold one foot on land and feel the difference, but you will never really know until you wade in, cross over.

You can make a bed, you can lie in it and accept the consequences.

'I'm moving back to the harbour cottage,' I told my mother over breakfast. 'So I can prepare to leave on the April ship.'

She paused in the sipping of her tea, that was all.

'I'm going because –'

'I know why you're going,' she cut in.

I nodded, wondering if she really did. This was how we got to be the community that we were, how we arrived in this miserable position, because we were never willing to listen. We always assumed, always believed we knew the answer before we'd heard it, before we'd even asked for it.

'So,' I went on, 'do you want to come with me?'

'To the harbour cottage,' she replied plainly, spreading marmalade on her toast, 'or to the mainland?'

I'd thought she would leap from her stool, immediately pack a bag; that she might have one already filled, the mainland in mind. How often had she baited Dad with the seditious idea of a holiday, a cruise, the possibility of visiting Paul…

'I think we should go to the well,' she said 'take something of Dad's to trade for the "absolute truth". He can help me to decide what to do.'

I chanced a smile; she was obviously joking. Her voice was as playful as the one she used on the little children at chapel – the one she'd no doubt used on me while I was growing up – a furnishing of the trivial and the fantastic with a business-like seriousness.

'Now, what did your father hold dearer than anything else?' she asked, chewing toast, casting her eyes around the room, which was empty of everything apart from our day-to-day essentials. Still we waited for the eviction that would inevitably come.

It crept up on me, slowly; she was speaking in earnest

'You, Mum,' I told her. 'Dad held you dearer than anything else.'

She looked at me levelly, shook her head.

'No,' she said. 'It was you. Always you.'

Of course, I thought, *I am Leah, a mistress of betrayal right from the start.* A child created in love that stole all the love for herself.

'Do you want to throw *me* down the well, then?' I laughed nervously.

'Sometimes,' she replied, with a straight face. 'But I'd rather you caught that ship.'

We walked down the brick path, through the tunnel of sycamore and birch. The showers of March had made everything sprout lushly, and April was offering us a small taste of sun, penetrating the leaves, the ground dancing with soft snatches of light. I tried to seal a picture of it in my mind – the smell, the feeling. I plucked a nascent sycamore key from the floor and put the hard lime-coloured unreadiness of it in my pocket.

My mother, a long cardigan wrapped around her, talked about Martha Signal, how she had pulled my mother aside on the cobbles to say that she knew her elder son was straying, misbehaving. She was ashamed of him, she said, but also, she felt guilty – she and her husband had not done enough to counter the influence of others, and they would have to work harder to make sure Michael, their younger, was protected. 'Don't think me bad,' Martha had said, 'when I tell you that I still love Luke though, very, very much.' I thought of the boy, the man, sprawled on his back after I'd thrown him to the ground, anger twisting his face, the blood-hot sense of relief that had drenched me when I realised he wasn't Ben.

'I'm a selfish person,' I blurted out. 'I'm acting selfishly.'

'Yes, you are,' agreed my mother, 'this is a conversation about me! Me and Martha Signal. She's invited me to be part of the "Easter Committee", you know.'

'But Easter's gone,' I said.

'Ah,' she replied, 'if only it were that simple. If only it came and went, never to return.'

We peered over the well's edge – to the gold and the bones that lay out of sight, to the mobile phone that had, in its way, been traded for some truth.

'We can ask the well a specific question, can we?' I said. 'Dad never told me that.'

'Oh, I don't know the rules, Leah. No one does. We're all making it up as we go along.' She looked at me suddenly. 'You're not pregnant, are you?'

'No!' I said, startled.

She nodded slowly. Her heavy-lidded eyes – a mirror of my own – did a brief check of my face and belly for a lie.

'Okay,' she said. 'Okay.'

She held the picture over the deep darkness below – that studio portrait of the four of us taken by a cousin of a cousin of someone who'd visited the island way back when, with their roll of marbled backdrop, their white umbrella and a lamp on a stand

'Don't you want to keep it for the memories?' I'd asked her at the house when she'd selected it for her sacrifice, working the hinges of the frame to set it free.

'Got all my memories up here,' she'd replied, tapping the side of her head. 'And also I have Paul's copy somewhere in one of these boxes. He never took it with him to the mainland. Just don't tell the well that, in case it dilutes the amount of truth we get in return.'

She let the picture slip from her fingers and the paper swayed left and right, following the path of least resistance, our faces, our smiles, falling out of focus, then disappearing.

We stayed peering over the well, as if the reward of knowledge would fly right back up in physical form, something we could grasp a hold of.

'Why are you being like this?' I asked my mother.

'Like what?'

'Different,' I replied. *Not upset* is what I wanted to say but instead I said, 'Happy.'

'I'm taking a leaf out of your book, Leah. I'm choosing to be that way.'

She drove fists into her cardigan pockets and rested her hip against the well. I found my body echoing hers, so I adjusted my stance, slightly, to be the same but different.

'Is that what I'm doing?' I asked. 'Choosing to be happy? Because right now it feels like I'm running away.'

'Or running towards.'

I shrugged. 'Has the well given you your answer yet?'

She put her fingers to her temples and closed her eyes, mouth ajar as if receiving the host.

'I'm not going,' she said, blinking her eyes open again. 'But I knew that before I threw the photo in.'

'Then why did you –'

'It was always best to make your father feel like he had some say in a decision, even though he didn't.' She said it conspiratorially, leaning close, as if the whole trip to the well had been a game for my benefit, as maybe it had.

Then she burst into tears.

'At the end of the day,' she said, as we held one another under the chlorophyll glow of the trees, 'I'm too scared to go. The future is for the young.'

On the last Saturday, Ben and I drank at the Anchor with Ruth French and Cat Walton – the outrageous act of two people who were secretly about to leave. Ruth and Cat were unaware of our plan; Ben wanted the school to think that he was following through on his contract for the whole year. He didn't want any knowing glances from Ruth across the staff room 'rousing suspicions' – the suspicions of Miriam Calder and Mr Crane, I assumed, but also those of the Eldest Girls.

'They'll feel betrayed by my going,' he said.

'Why?' I asked, and when he couldn't formulate a response, I didn't push him, because I knew I was betraying them too.

The cliques in the bar that Saturday night were more defined than ever. The Calders drank with the Cranes and the Bishys. Dellie Leven and Faith Moran and their boatmen husbands held an uneasy middle-ground. Eyes flickered to me – the madwoman. They were all poised, fielders manning their bases, waiting for a freak shot. I shaped my smile carefully for each group of people. This I would not miss: the constant need to locate myself, and manage the way the island saw me.

Saul Cooper appeared, late into the evening, taking a stool at the bar, sitting hooked over his drink, never giving us his face, speaking only to Jed. I looked to Ben and saw how his jaw tightened, controlling the testosterone fizz of a score unsettled.

Mary Ahearn also came in late, insisting that I bump a glass against hers in a way that made me suspect my mother had told her what was going on, despite her pledges to keep my departure a secret.

'I hope you've got some gin in that juice,' Mary said with a wink, sucking up the foam of her bitter. I had, just the one shot, for courage.

When we left around 10 p.m., as I hugged Cat and Ruth a little too tightly in our goodbyes, Viola was on the cobbles with her dog, sitting on top of the stocks, her back to us, looking out towards the boats bobbing and clinking in the harbour. She had the air of someone who was waiting. I had only ever seen her in that oversized maroon coat with its

358

mud splatters, dirty jeans underneath. That night she wore a striking furry coat – leopard print. Her hair was not its usual orange halo but shone oily in the glimmer of the half-moon and the string-lights, the curls defined.

She turned at the sound of us on the cobbles, one knee jutting out sideways, revealing heavy boots of the kind Britta Sayers preferred, too big on her feet, and also the hem of a skirt, short and black. Her lips were blood red; she looked like a child who'd been left alone with her mother's make-up.

'Viola!' I called.

'Leave her,' said Ben, making a grab for my hand.

They had been talking in the Anchor, the men and their wives, I'd heard them, about what should be done with the *coycrock* girl. Her mother was a lost cause, but the girl could be saved if she was taken under the Council's wing. I knew she shouldn't be out there, dressed like that.

'Viola!' I called again, and she stood then, pulling the leopard coat tighter around her, making off towards the smokehouse, hunched over, as if this might render her invisible.

'Let her go,' said Ben. 'Don't invite more trouble.'

That was how he saw it – the girl making us meet that night at the stones. Not as something fortuitous and necessary.

'But she was our Cupid,' I said, as Ben walked me to my door, 'in the end.'

'Then how do you explain Saul Cooper turning up?' he asked. 'And this?' The skin on his chin had split nastily, an inch-long laceration that had needed stitches from Dr Bishy, Ben telling the man that he'd tripped during an

359

early-morning run, and no, he wasn't prepared to have the sewing-up done at the Counting House as a public event.

'It was a coincidence,' I'd said, the only explaining I ever wanted to do when it came to Saul Cooper.

Ben and I parted without even a kiss. We knew that we were being watched from the windows of the Anchor. I fumbled for my keys at the front door – since the paint attack, I never left the cottage unlocked – and that was when I saw Luke Signal lope out of the darkness on the path from the East Bay. I saw him look across to the stocks, pause, unsure, then lope away again, back in the direction he'd come from.

Tuesday evening, I sat at the green baize of Margaritte's table one last time. She dealt out my cards, focusing for the longest time on the Star – a picture of a naked woman pouring one vessel of water into a pond and another onto the earth, an eight-pointed guiding light above her, a tree of life within reach. Margaritte wanted me to understand how auspicious this card was; it signalled broader horizons, the courage to seize opportunities, wonderful revelations, the chance of finding a true home.

She flipped smoothly into scripture: '*And I saw a new heaven and a new earth: for the first heaven and the first earth were passed away; and there was no more sea.*'

'*And God shall wipe away all tears from their eyes,*' I replied, '*and there shall be no more death, neither sorrow, nor crying, neither shall there be any more pain: for the former things are passed away.*'

We were quiet for a moment.

Then: 'No one ever comes back,' she said. I was used to this now, Margaritte knowing things before she'd been told.

'They all cross over with promises to bring help and are never seen again.'

'I'm not promising that,' I told her. 'I'm not proud. I'm only saving myself and...'

'Your future children?' she finished, a rescue from the embarrassment of a confession. I am a witch, and also a whore; my crimes are clearly two-fold.

I looked down at the mirroring of our splayed hands on the table – my fingers white, the nails short and neat, yet to be troubled with any real work; Margaritte's thin but heavy-knuckled, the tracks of veins leading to nails that had grown thick and pearly.

She turned over one hand to reveal the angriness of a new India-ink tattoo on her wrist.

'You?' I said. 'It was you?'

She nodded.

'They've needed my counsel these last few months.'

She unbuttoned the top of her blouse, pulling it and her silky slip aside to reveal older symbols across her upper chest, some faded to almost nothing.

'The fishermen have them too, hidden under their shirts, for protection at sea,' she said. 'But you need them on the land too, I find.'

Thursday, I packed.

Margaritte had found me a suitcase, a rare object on the island. When I asked where it had come from, this hard, cream clamshell with its paisley lining and mildewed pockets, she had shrugged as if she could not remember, told me that the universe had heard my need and delivered.

I had very little and would take only essentials. My mother was going to move into the cottage soon, whether it was Luke who claimed the lodge or someone else. I didn't want the place to feel empty, stripped of all life.

The wooden heart I lifted from the window latch and fingered the rough grooves of its carving for a moment, appreciating again the effort, thinking how I had never thanked Ben for making it, this surprising skill of his. Then I returned it to the window. I had the real thing joining me on my journey to the mainland, a real love. I needed no keepsake, no charm.

Intention to travel was to be registered the day before; I left it to the last moment. Even then, there would be almost a whole day for the news to drop like a stone in a pool, sending its ripples to the edges.

Saul was out on the dogleg jetty when I crossed the cobbles, binoculars held to his face, braced against the safety of the railings that abutted the Customs House. I fought the sea breeze, holding down my lifting coat, pulling back the hair that whipped against my face, and went to stand beside him.

'What can you see?' I asked.

He dropped the binoculars to glance at me, returning to them quickly.

'An egret, I think, a white one, on the rocks out there. They come this time of year to breed.'

'Really,' I said flatly; he'd used that word deliberately it felt – *breed*.

'Take a look.' He handed me the binoculars, nudging them gently so I could pick out the small outcrop a few hundred metres from our shore, something white on top, extending its long neck.

'Beautiful,' I said. 'You like birds?'

'I like nearly all of the visitors to our island.' This time he *was* scoring a point; I chose to concede it.

'The seals came back this year too,' I said, the lives of wild creatures being so much easier to discuss than our own.

'Oh, no, they haven't been back here for years,' Saul said with a shake of his head.

I didn't understand. I'd heard one of the boatmen that week say that he had seen them. Had he lied? Seen things? Convinced himself of something out of blind hope?

'The seals have some sense at least,' said Saul, and he grasped my hand suddenly, making me flinch. I looked him in the eye, found myself gripping his hand in return.

'Could it not be mine?' he said. 'The baby?'

The craving in his voice was unbearable. I gulped and gulped, willing myself to respond with something gentle, but instead I croaked out an accusation: 'You drink with Jed Springer now?'

He let go. He stepped away, contemplating me for a moment, taking in the long view.

'Right,' he said, his tone brisk. 'Let's get you registered for this ship, then, shall we, the lovely Miss Cedars!'

He pulled opened the side door of the Customs House and we entered that way. I saw his back office for the first time – the radio equipment there, the vast horizon of ocean in the window. I saw the camp bed, the toothbrush, a sketchbook. I saw the chisel and the whittling knife, beside a half-worked piece of oak.

What was it, I wondered, with our island and our misplaced hearts? One riven with nails, harms the wrong man; another is carved with love by the wrong man in the first place.

I said nothing.

At the front desk, I filled out my particulars on a form and watched Saul copy this across into a ledger, using a fountain pen.

'This one is for island records,' he said. 'I'll enter all the necessaries on the Border Agency computer.'

I let him record my profession as 'teacher', no discussion as to whether this was still true. My training certificate was rolled up in my suitcase. Soon I would know what it was worth.

'Visiting Paul, are you?' Saul said as he wrote, an official voice, cheerfulness a duty. 'To tell him about your father? Your mother never did get through on the satellite phone, did she?'

I wasn't sure how to respond. Were we playing a scene? Pretending everything was fine, that I was only going for a short while and returning the following month. Was he pretending that Ben's name wasn't already there in the ledger above mine?

I looked down at the watermarked page.

Friday 13 April, 2018
Outgoing passengers.
Passenger No. 1 – Leah Cedars

Ben's name wasn't there. But he knew that he had to register. I'd told him. I'd told him!

'Do we have until midnight?' I said.

Saul glanced up, a little too expectantly. 'For what?'

'To register to travel.'

He checked the clock on the wall above the desk as it twitched a minute after six.

'Ah, you're well within the time limit,' he said, returning to his calligraphy. 'You don't need to worry, Leah. You don't need to worry at all.'

There was barely a moon.

It was the perfect night for sleeping on your troubles, not for rising up, challenging them. But still, all across the island, in the twilight, in the evening, in the black and dark night, they were about and misbehaving – as *Proverbs* tells us women are wont to do. They were being loud and stubborn, not abiding in their houses, slipping through the keyholes.

They were in the streets, lying in wait at every corner.

At nightfall, Leah Cedars was seen at the Billet House. She walked straight in, forgoing the politeness of a knock, and there was the glimpse of a scene – figures illuminated, two men close, then jumping apart. The door snapped shut on its hinges.

All that remained were voices.

'He's not here,' said the one who sounded like the land-lord's brother. 'It's only us.'

'Try the Anchor,' said the other in a low monotone – this was surely Abe Powell.

'How can I?' she replied. 'It's a weekday.'

Feet shuffled awkwardly on the boards within.

'Crane and Bishy are going up to the farmstead,' came Abe Powell's voice, tentative. 'To speak to the girl while the mother sleeps. Does your handsome teacher help them?'

'No,' said Leah Cedars quickly, firmly. 'No.'

'Then maybe,' came Jed's suggestion, 'he'll be out looking for the Eldest Girls. He's always got some business with them.'

'Thank you, gentlemen,' were Leah's prickly last words. 'I'm sorry to have disturbed you in *your* business.'

The younger Signal boy caught Leah as she was leaving; or she caught him, depending on where you believe the power lies.

He wanted to know what she was doing there. He called her 'Miss'.

'I might ask the same thing of you,' Leah Cedars replied, squinting at her watch. 'What are you doing here at this time of night?'

'I'm looking for my brother?' the boy said – a question or a suggestion, rather than a clear statement.

Leah nodded; she sighed, told him: 'I'm not "Miss" to you anymore. I'm no longer your teacher.' And it was this fact perhaps that allowed her to be selfish, to leave the boy to his skulking, in the darkness, at that late hour.

She did try the Anchor, though she'd said she could not. She was seen, her face distorted by the condensation and the bottle-end glass, squinting in, not finding what she was looking for. She took the path up to St Rita's too, stepping inside the emptiness of the chapel. She was seen rattling the chains that bound the gates of the school.

On her return to the cobbles, she stood for the longest time in a dim corner by the harbour, one hand on the door of the Customs House, deciding. Within those walls, an officer was carving himself another heart, a smaller one, as if for a child, sitting in front of a window that was no longer sea-filled, but black. This was the trick of the moon on nights like these; it convinced you that the sea was no longer there.

Onto the cobbled stage stepped the *coycrock* girl. She was attired as she had been every night that week, her lips redder than her hair, wearing a coat that would have made a marvellous lure for the training of hunting dogs, if cut into many pieces.

Perhaps that's why the boy with the gun was with her; he wanted the coat off her back.

'The knickers off her pussy, more like!' was what was said in the Anchor, laughter echoing out onto the harbourside. At the bar, there were congratulatory slaps on the back at a wisecrack well made, and a call for another round of drinks.

'Oh, quit with the sour face, Eleanor,' barked the waist-coated landlord to his unsmiling wife. 'You've got to be able to stand a joke if you're going to be serving here on the weekdays.'

Then came a roar. The *coycrock*-turned-harlot was darting for cover.

'I see you! I see you!' thundered Leah Cedars, out on the cobbles, rounding in on her prey. 'If you lay so much as one finger on that girl, Luke Signal, I will slit you from throat to belly like you did that goat, like you did those foxes that you left on our doorstep, as God as my witness.'

God was her witness, and not the only one.

She spat in his face, said some, who watched from their windows.

Then she was gone, the boy too.

In the alley beyond the smokehouse there was a flash of vanishing fur as the headmaster and the doctor stumbled out of the pub, towards the harbourside, pink of cheek, torches swaying. They stopped, they conferred, they continued on – off in the direction of Cable's Wood.

They were not the only ones.

The island would get its production of *A Midsummer Night's Dream* after all, with so many bodies moving through the gloom, answering the irrefusable call of the trees and of the stones. They all needed their wits about them on a night like that, when you couldn't see your hand in front of your own face, let alone a trail of petals on the path. Every one of them had supped on a potion of their choosing – alcohol, disappointment, power, lust – as disorienting as a dose of belladonna in a mid-Lent teacup.

Intoxicated like this, changed, they entered the gloaming, destined to lose hope, to return home frustrated, not willing to talk of what happened, deciding instead to consider it no better than a dream.

Except for one.

One of them would answer the song when it came, lifting up from the north cliff to reorient those who drifted through the night; to gird the loins of those who must act; to cleanse the soul of the sinners before they sinned.

'*Come, Thou Long Expected Jesus*', the hymn rang out, '*Born to set Thy people free.*'

Come, said the girls, come one man to stand for all the rest, one loss that can be accounted for, explained away at the gates of heaven when it is time to beg admittance.

It cannot be true that the pure souls are drawn skywards to paradise by the moon, and the wicked ones fall in a fit on the ground to be transformed into beasts – the line cannot be drawn as simply as that, because how then would you explain the fishermen who became deer and the girls who became foxes?

There must be exclusions, exemption clauses, extenuating circumstances – a means to justify doing bad for good reasons, when your judgement day comes.

Or maybe it is easier to believe that no one watches over us anyway. That when we die, we just end. Perhaps that's kinder to both the hunter and the hunted.

So, come, say the girls' voices, lifted in song. Come one man to set all the women free. Bring forth a fellow who did not listen when *Proverbs* told him to *keep thee from the strange woman*. Bring forward the man who thinks himself exempt. Deliver to us a betrayer, a turncoat, a traitor, a man of violence, either of the hand or the mouth. Come a man that would have fallen and writhed upon the ground and become a snake anyway. Come a man like that.

The branches shift, the ferns whistle at the touch of the wind. Below, the sea rolls in anticipation.

The girls stand ready, naked as virgins; their weapons are themselves.

Their horned god steps forward, into the circle – into their house – a path he does not realise leads directly to hell. A mist settles on the earth, in league with the paltry moon, so they see only his silhouette, the shape of his coat, the coils spiralling from his head, no details of the face. This anonymity makes it easier.

He is an outline. He is a rough idea. He is no one.

The three-part harmony is joined by a fourth voice to deliver a song familiar from chapel. Oh, it is so very hard for girls to dance with a devil clinging to their backs; they must first shake him off.

The horned god is told to move closer, to take his pick, have a taste of their bodies, their weapons.

Though the real weapon, the wooden baton, is concealed behind one back.

As lips meet lips, wood meets skull with a swinging crack, a method learnt at school, beating against the doorframes.

Out you go, and stay you out,
We're claiming back the day.

A scream goes up and the other roamers pause among the pines, if only to blame it on the foxes – always the foxes – before beginning their journeys home, discontented.

The beast thrashes on the ground, it tries to crawl away, and they fumble in the darkness, hold it by the ankles. Still the beast gargles and will not stop.

Will it ever stop?

They ask for the spirit of St Jade to come now, to give them the courage to go on, to finish what they have started – and she does.

It makes no difference which girl finds the strength at the last. As one man will stand for all the others, one girl will stand for all those present at the stones that night, for all those who came before and all those who will come after.

She moves, this girl, not barefooted, but sturdy-booted, into the ferns, feeling out the shape of him with her toe, searching for his throat – the Adam's apple. Then she raises her heel and she brings it down, hard.

A final stamp. The snake is dead.

✝ EASTERTIDE: FRIDAY THE 13TH – APRIL 2018

In the morning, everything is clear, sparklingly so.

It may as well be December 25th, a different kind of Christmas, because the red-haired *coycrock* girl cannot sleep, cannot wait.

In her room at the old Reunyon Farmstead, she sits upright in creased and grubby bedclothes, pulling aside the faded green curtains one more time to check.

At the first inching of the sun, she tells herself, she can get up, but for now the fingernail moon still rules, glowing gently through the mist.

So, she changes the rules – why not? She put them there in the first place. Let the day turn at her pace. If she leaves now, the sun will have reached the horizon by the time she gets there, and maybe no rules will be broken after all.

She swings her feet onto the boards, steps over last night's discarded clothes – the short, black skirt, the leopard-print coat, the lace-up boots all covered in dirt – and she finds socks and a jumper. She is too impatient to change out of her pyjamas or to clean her teeth.

She will not stand in front of the bathroom mirror and see her lips stained red from the night before.

She goes downstairs, pulls tight the drawstring fastenings at the top of two rucksacks that sit in the hall – one for her, one for her mother, just in case – then she runs back upstairs, to fetch the radio from its charging stand at the end of her bed, forgotten in her anticipation.

This is just a small error, not a portent. It is nothing to do with the date.

Her mother had come to fear Friday the 13th, to fear all omens – single magpies, a crack in a mirror, speaking proudly of something before it is done. But Viola believes the date is fortuitous. The number thirteen is made up of a one and a three which, when added together, become four – something real, something stable.

Earth, fire, air, water. North, south, east, west. Black, blonde, brown, red.

In a world that gives you many reasons to be frightened, every hour of every day, the thirteenth is a mere bagatelle – and Viola believes her mother is starting to realise this. She is beginning to resurface.

From her hiding place in the kitchen pantry, just weeks ago, Viola observed Deborah Kendrick march that young man, the doctor's messenger, out of their kitchen, the spikes of a pitchfork trained at his chest, and Viola knows that if last night the headmaster and the doctor came calling, she will have done something equally brave and disobedient.

As is the mother, so is her daughter.

Though sometimes the daughter gets there first.

Viola grasped it early on: fears grow tall and prosper when you run and hide from them, and no matter where you go, they find you. Instead she has walked towards the things that scare her on Lark, talked to them, seduced them, sung to them, stolen from them, loved them, deceived them. She is still frightened, still capable of being harmed, but how much lighter she feels this morning, despite the violence of the night, how full of positivity she is, knowing that in the face of her fears, she has been daring.

The same horse that delivered death to town carries on its back a new hope.

Viola lifts Dot's bright red lead from the hook by the kitchen door and snaps it onto the dog's collar. She pulls on the maroon coat and drops the radio into her pocket.

When the incident happened, she was told to sit down to receive the awful news – her father and brother were dead. Viola did not allow death to creep up on her this time, tap her on the shoulder and make her jump; it did not find her hiding in the obvious place. Viola commanded death; she bent it to her will. She and the Eldest Girls harnessed their power within the protection of the Sisters' Stones, and they brought about their own terrible and necessary fury.

Maybe someone does watch over us, after all, Viola thinks, as she steps out of the front door, closing it quietly behind her, ready to be the dog walker, the first voice in the story. Maybe everything we think and do is seen and judged. Maybe someone is keeping accurate scores. Perhaps the umpire is wise and fair.

The idea buoys her into the day and down the splintered wooden steps of the veranda, Dot gambolling at her heels, and for the first time in a long time, Viola feels that almost forgotten weightlessness of just being a child.

JUDGEMENT.

She is too late to save the hair on their heads.

Viola runs, and behind her Hannah runs too, pushing the Earl, still in his dressing gown, jaw juddering as the wheelchair does battle with the cobbles.

The harbourside is chaos.

Teachers seesaw left and right, arms outstretched, desperately corralling their runaway pupils, battling the mothers who want possession of them too. Boatmen drop their nets and cluster – edgy, on guard – while the Provisions Store women gather at the shopfront, aproned and afraid.

Except for Britta Sayers' mother.

She is at the window of the Counting House, beating at the glass, screaming, 'You bastards! You bastards!'

The Eldest Girls are in there.

Viola sprints for the grand blue door, which does not yield, her hands smacking painfully against the wood. She joins in with the thumping; kicking at the panels, demanding to be let in, getting no answer. She skitters left, to the window where Britta's mother wails, desperate for a view inside, but the velvet drapes are pulled tight. She skitters right, and sees Council women and their hangers-on huddling in the kitchen. At the sight of Viola, they promptly, viciously, drop the blind.

'What's going on?' Viola hollers, scattering her question into the crowd that builds behind her. 'What's going on?' she begs.

They shake their heads; they cannot say, or will not.

'Crane and Bishy dragged them down the hill by their hair!' Britta's mother is on her knees now beneath the window, her sobs as violent as coughs. 'Find Mary! Get Ingrid!' she demands, though the mustering of people only stare. 'Somebody! Please!' she yells.

A clunk comes – a lock being turned. The crowd murmurs anxiously as the Counting House door swings open to reveal... Diana Crane, chin high, lady of the manor. She thrusts forward the hairdresser, who trips on the sill, a vanity case in one hand; in the other – a head.

A head!

The harbourside cries out in dismay, but Diana Crane can only tut and sigh. She reaches for the hairdresser's wrist, thrusting it into the air, shaking it roughly. Not a head – just a handful of brown curls, long ropes of black and amongst them the shorter blonde strands of Anna Duchamp's under-ear bob.

'What are you doing to them?' screams Britta's mother. 'What have you done!' The sobs submerge her; they drag her down.

Diana Crane is visibly appalled by the woman, as if her hysterics are more repulsive than what is going on inside.

'Stripping them of their ornaments,' Diana says, her voice heavy with entitlement, spooning out blame, 'taking away their filth. Something we should have done a long time ago.'

The hairdresser scurries away across the cobbles, sheepish, and as she flees, she lets her bounty drop, the hair tumbling with the wind, making people skip and yelp as it snags against their feet.

'Shave me too!' cries Viola, propelling herself forward, snatching at clumps of her own red tangles, trying to yank them ceremonially free.

'Step back!' orders Diana Crane.

Viola does not; she puffs up her chest.

'Viola!' calls Hannah, the crowd slowly parting to allow the wheelchair through. Hannah works one-handed, her other arm wrapped around a tearful girl in St Rita's uniform – her daughter, the resemblance clear. 'Tell them that the Earl is here to sit on the Council. Tell them!'

Viola turns back to see Saul Cooper emerge from the Counting House, moving Diana Crane aside with more urgency than respect.

'Go!' he instructs Viola, pointing in the direction of the farmstead. 'Go home. Don't get yourself involved.'

This is a kindness, but it is too meagre, too late.

'How could you!' Viola launches herself at him, kicking, scratching, biting. Gasps go up from the now not insubstantial crowd as the drama escalates. 'You were supposed to call the mainland!' She spits; she claws. 'Not them!'

'Someone has died, Viola!' he shouts in his own defence, peeling her grip from his clothes and his skin. 'How was I supposed to say nothing? They killed someone!'

A deep *oh* reverberates across the harbourside – confirmation: the rumours are true – and Britta's mother sinks lower, her face pressed against the stone. Someone dares to crouch down and soothe her – Anna's mother, Ingrid, newly arrived.

'Fetch Abe Powell to sit in Council,' Saul urges Viola. 'Father Daniel too. That's how you can best help those girls.'

'Abe Powell won't speak for them,' she cries, 'and nor will you! You think they're devil-worshippers!' She tries for another swipe, but Saul holds her fists fast.

'Fetch Abe Powell! Fetch Father Daniel!' he calls over her head, instructing the crowd. 'They're needed at Council!'

A jostling of bodies follows, the elected ones dispersing on their hunt for the men. Viola is forced backwards then as the Earl is pushed through, Hannah lifting the wheels of the chair over the threshold, Saul Cooper taking command of the handles as she is told to step away. The Earl twists his head, keeping his bright eyes fixed on Hannah – a reluctant child on his first day of school.

He is not enough. It is not enough. Viola can see how the day will slide inexorably towards disaster. This death will not bring the authorities to Lark. Jacob Crane will show no mercy.

So, she leaps.

Viola is not strong but she is small; Diana Crane is not so quick and wide as Hannah on the stairs. The girl slips through, feeling Diana fruitlessly grasp at the sleeve of her coat. She pushes past Saul, past the Earl, and bursts into the men's meeting room.

She is in.

There is no Council set-up, no white tablecloth. The space is curtained, dim. Three men, jackets off, sleeves rolled up, huddle as if readying themselves for combat: Jed Springer, Dr Tobiah Bishy, Jacob Crane. Up on the stage, between the red drapes, below the carving of the Union Jack – the Eldest Girls.

Their dead eyes come alive at the sight of Viola but they do not move. They sit on chairs, hands clutched in laps.

They are shivering, barefoot, in white smocks not dissimilar to the nightdresses they wear at the stones.

The sight of their scalps – brutalised, visible, raw – the remnants of their hair swirling at their feet, is too much. *What next?* screams Viola's mind. *What comes next?* And she knows she must answer this question herself, or else the Council will.

'These girls are innocent!' Denial is her first instinct. Viola's voice bounces off the high, white ceiling as hands seize her, pulling her back. Deception comes next. 'Leah Cedars did it!' she yells. 'You all heard her in the harbour last night, threatening to kill. She did it! She did it!'

'Leah had nothing to do with it!' Saul speaks loudly. His is one of the pairs of hands that restrains Viola; Diana Crane is the other. The Earl sits abandoned by the doorway.

'Don't listen to him!' Viola exclaims. 'He probably helped her do it!'

The three men of the Council watch this protest as if beholding a strange and gratuitous invention.

'You stop this!' Saul demands, pushing his face close to Viola's.

'Leah Cedars did it!' she hollers.

Saul shakes her fiercely. 'You stop this! You stop this!'

There is a skirmish in the lobby; all attention is drawn to the door. If Viola needed any further proof that she is powerful, it arrives; she has evoked a presence with the mere mention of a name. Leah Cedars blunders in, disoriented, as if she'd expected to pass through that meeting-room doorway and find herself somewhere else.

Saul drops Viola's arm. Like a magnet, he is drawn to Leah, desperate to usher her from this place, but the bottleneck of people in the lobby behind her will not let this happen.

The human tide is at the door.

They shove one another forward, and the school receptionist, the doctor's wife and the librarian can no longer hold them back. This meeting will be public, come what may.

Viola wrenches her other arm free and careens into the middle of the room, barging past the three men of the Council who do not know which way to move: towards Viola, towards Leah, towards the advancing people who now line the walls and fill the corners. The Eldest Girls pierce Viola with insistent stares, imploring her to shush, but she will not. She feels a thrill, a new impetus, at the increase in her audience. There is nothing left to lose. If she is to die, then let it be like this, in defiance.

'Saul helped her do it,' Viola bellows, 'because he is fucking her!'

She hits the *F* hard, raising a hiss of disapproval from the women present. Viola laughs, the sound bubbling up unbidden. In the midst of all this, still a swear word is outrageous?

'I knew nothing of the body until this morning.' Leah Cedars' voice comes loud but robotic, as if speaking is a new skill for her. 'The girl came to my house to tell me that the Eldest Girls had...' she swallows hard '... killed Mr Hailey.'

A wild note of alarm peals through the gallery.

The handsome coycrock *teacher! Dead?*

'No!' objects Viola from the middle of the room. 'She lies!'

The men of the Council move towards Leah; Saul inserts himself between them and his beloved, the stand-off lasting but a moment as more spectators surge in, bumping everyone from their positions. Three women are pulled through the massing crowd and take their places at the front – Mary Ahearn, Rhoda Sayers, Ingrid Duchamp.

They cry out at the sight of their daughters, their butchered scalps. The Eldest Girls cannot keep their terrified silence any longer; they keen plaintively in response. The distance between them and their mothers is a devastation.

'Stay back!' warns Jacob Crane. 'You leave those girls to their shame. Don't make matters worse.'

His words work instantly. The women go rigid; they swallow their whimpers. Viola feels it too, rushing through her veins like a drug – the compulsion to obey. With Jacob Crane present, can anyone else ever take charge?

Leah Cedars is willing to try.

'I counselled those girls to turn away from the dark arts,' she says, a mollifying tone to quench the flames of the dragon.

'Judas!' Viola puts in.

'Hush, Viola,' Britta manages, from the stage above her.

'I have counselled them to confess,' continues Leah, turning to the women of the gallery, the mothers. 'I told them they must talk of the … *darker arts* that have acted upon them, the real things that have warped their minds.'

She is met by blank gazes; she is speaking in riddles.

Viola seethes with irritation; her fists clench. Leah Cedars is doing no good.

'Leah Cedars is the one with the warped mind!' Viola taunts, reclaiming the attention of the room – but it is short-lived. The packed lobby groans once more, it heaves, delivering another body into the space.

Benjamin Hailey.

Horrified cries of 'Mary, Mother of God!' break out at the sight of the teacher: windswept, breathless, very much alive.

A laptop cradled to his chest, he takes up position beside Leah and something passes between them, tenderness perhaps, an overwhelming feeling. Leah Cedars snaps her head away, unable to bear it.

'See!' Leah says, using his appearance to her advantage. 'The *coycrock* girl lies.'

'I never said it was him,' Viola spits back. 'You assumed! You assumed!'

Benjamin Hailey looks from Leah to Viola, lost.

'You're a liar, Viola Kendrick!' Leah Cedars' voice cracks with emotion.

'And you … you …' Viola gropes for a comeback, her eyes landing on Saul, the way he is looking so pitifully at the object of his affection. Of course, thinks Viola, of course, why shouldn't it be true? 'And you,' she accuses Leah, 'are pregnant with Saul Cooper's baby!'

A fresh exclamation from the spectators. Saul lurches for Viola, intent on silencing her, but she darts away from him, runs to the furthest corner of the room, pulling the radio from her pocket, holding it aloft as bait.

'He gave me this and told me to spy on Leah,' she continues, almost gleeful, almost enjoying herself. Saul lurches for her again and Viola dances from his grip. She catches her breath and carries on: 'Leah Cedars told Benjamin Hailey that it was *his* baby, so that he'd take her with him on the April ship.'

Saul gives up the chase and spins on his heels, meeting the gaze of the Council men who watch this petty scene with growing anger and impatience.

'This is a complete lie,' he says, palms flattening the electric atmosphere.

Leah Cedars takes hold of Benjamin Hailey's arm, an appeal for him to look at her, but his attention is fixed on Saul, regarding him with an almost tangible air of violence.

'It's not true,' Saul persists in his official tone – a quavering version of it. 'The stranger... I mean, Mr Hailey... isn't even registered for travel today.' He says it as if this piece of trivial bureaucracy is the real crux of the allegations.

Viola pokes at the embers; she throws on petrol. 'No, Mr Hailey's actually leaving on the August ship, because he's promised to take the Eldest Girls with him.'

The tremulous chorus from the mothers soars again, a shrill jigsaw of 'What!?' and 'Why?' and 'What's going on?' Mary Ahearn seizes Benjamin Hailey's shoulder, demanding he turn around and look her in the eye.

'Stop this!'

Jacob Crane's voice is like a sledgehammer against glass.

'A boy has been murdered,' he says, pacing the room, reclaiming it. 'Lured to his death. And these girls here have admitted to it.'

All eyes return to the shaven captives, up on the stage, quivering in their seats.

'No!' wails Ingrid Duchamp, and Anna can't help but respond, an involuntary sound like an animal trapped.

Jacob Crane continues: 'They have confessed to the sin of murder, and also to the sin of witchcraft.' Dr Bishy and Jed Springer fold their arms and nod. 'They carried out these acts in the service of the Devil.'

Murder, witchcraft, the Devil.

The hands of the onlookers fly to their faces, to their breasts, in shock. Any sympathy for the wretched girls immediately fades.

'Under duress!' objects Mary Ahearn. 'They confessed after you brought them here and tortured them!'

The headmaster rounds on the woman. 'We brought them here to separate the diseased sheep from the lambs, to be done with their sorcery of silence.'

'To strip them of their ornaments,' Diana Crane puts in, receiving a sharp glance from her husband – this is not her time to speak.

'*Regard not them that have familiar spirits*,' Jacob Crane intones, turning with frightening swiftness to point a finger at Viola. She chokes on her surprise and retreats until her back presses against the raised stage. He moves steadily towards her, mouth wet with spittle. '*Neither seek after wizards, to be defiled by them: I am the Lord your God!*' This is not the man who stands up in chapel and reads; this is a monster who believes himself divine.

He turns from Viola, as swiftly as he had attacked, impaling the gallery with his gaze, a finger trained on the girls.

'A brother is dead at the hands of these sisters, these women who have reawakened the island's shameful history of superstition and necromancy, women who have danced naked and fornicated with the Devil …'

'No, no, no!' Ingrid's cries burst free again.

'Mama!' calls Anna, sending all three girls into shuddering sobs. Viola reaches up across the raised platform of the stage, as if she might be able to grab hold of an ankle, touch them.

'The bible is very clear.' Jacob Crane's voice rises in intensity – the coming of a terrible storm. 'And we on the Council always defer to His word, which is this…' He takes a pause, he pronounces their sentence. '*Thou shalt not suffer a witch to live.*'

The mothers howl, the gallery gasps, the Eldest Girls scramble from their seats and bundle together as one at the back of the stage. Viola uses the last of her physical strength to haul herself up onto the platform, pushing up through her arms, dragging her belly across the wood. She throws herself at the girls' trembling bodies, murmuring a desperate, 'I'm sorry, I'm sorry, I'm sorry, I'm sorry, I'm sorry…' as Mary Ahearn breaks loose from the throng, teeth clenched, and launches herself at Jacob Crane.

'No!' yells Rhoda, fearful of recompense, but Jed Springer has hold of Mary before she can reach the headmaster's throat.

'I gave you due warning, Mary Ahearn,' Jacob Crane roars above the hubbub. 'And I made your duty clear – any person allowing a child to slip from the path of righteousness may as well have a millstone hanged about their neck and be drowned in the depth of the sea. You failed in your task of raising your daughter and now she faces the consequences of your actions!'

'So drown me then!' cries Mary Ahearn. 'Drown me like you drowned my husband!'

As the words leave her mouth, the blood leaves her body, the muscles go too, the bones – she becomes limp. The room is submerged in silence. Viola lifts her head from the embrace of the other girls and feels the vibrations of this seismic shift – the power of something said aloud that has been long buried or dismissed.

What next? asks Viola's mind, but no longer as a scream. *What comes next?*

'You killed my Neil,' mutters Mary, as much a discovery to herself as a means to bring down this monster. 'You killed him… you scuppered their boat!'

Jacob Crane shakes his head firmly. The wives and the hangers-on of the Council take their cue to caw objections, but the gathered have stepped back, a hung jury, uneasy in their wavering.

The proceedings judder, they stall.

'And it shall be, when he shall be guilty in one of these things, that he shall confess that he hath sinned in that thing.' Benjamin Hailey speaks up – the outsider. He reads the scripture from his laptop, his face illuminated. *'And he shall bring his trespass offering unto the Lord for his sin which he hath sinned, a female from the flock, a lamb or a kid of the goats, for a sin offering; and the priest shall make an atonement for him concerning his sin.'*

No one responds, not even Jacob Crane.

Leah Cedars turns and appraises the man beside her as if he were a stranger once more – a stranger all along. He has never been a religious man.

The Eldest Girls lift their heads and wait.

The *coycrock* teacher looks about him, to the anxious spectators, gauging his reception. He goes back to the screen, brings up fresh words. The apple of his throat rises and falls. He begins.

'"On September the first, 2017",' he reads, '"on the first day of term, Mr Crane called me to his office early, before school started, so that he might speak with me alone."'

Viola feels the bodies of the Eldest Girls react, suddenly alert. She searches their expressions.

'The dossier,' whispers Jade-Marie.

They hold their breath as one.

Benjamin Hailey continues: '"Picking up his bible, Mr Crane said that, now I had turned sixteen, I had been chosen to lead the other girls by example and learn the errors committed by Eve so that I did not copy them and multiply the sorrows of everyone living on Lark. We were to act this out, he said, in his office there and then, so the understanding would be in me and I would never forget."'

The headmaster lunges forward, swiping bear-like at the teacher's laptop, but Benjamin Hailey turns away in time, saving the screen.

'"I was told to kneel",' Mr Hailey continues, '"and Mr Crane explained how Eve had been beguiled by the serpent and then he unzipped the fly of his trousers and took out his – "'

'No!'

The swipe is successful this time, the laptop clatters to the wooden floor – but at the hand of Diana Crane.

'I will not have it,' the woman cries, her husband frozen at her side. She is charged with rage, it crackles from every inch of her.

Mr Hailey dives to the floor, the laptop still breathing, and the gallery cluster around him to see the screen, to shield him from further interruption.

'"February the twentieth, 2018. Dr Bishy took me into his surgery and I was told to undress. When I asked him why, he said that he suspected that the mark of the devil might be found on my body and said that I was to remove everything, even my underwear, because bad spirits were known to hide within the cavities of a woman's body and he would need to go inside me and expel them so that – "'

'Enough!'

A heel breaks through the crowd, striking the lid of the laptop, stamping it shut.

'Enough of this... this... pornography!' hisses Elizabeth Bishy, the doctor's wife, looming over the scene. 'What kind of pervert encourages young girls to tell stories like that? Why on earth would you do such a disgusting thing?'

She reaches down, snatching at one of the laptop's sleek but dented edges. Mr Hailey moves quickly, slamming his two fists onto the lid, pressing the machine hard against the floor. Diana Crane elbows through to join in the fight.

'Because they are true!' comes a shout, arresting this brawl.

Heads turn to the door where Leah Cedars stands hand-in-hand with the bewildered Earl. Abe Powell is at her shoulder, Reuben Springer clutching his arm. Leah looks to Abe for reassurance, the physical protection to continue – he nods.

'Because these stories are true,' she says firmly. She looks to the Eldest Girls on the stage who have risen to their feet, then to their mothers who look ashen, stunned. 'My friends left the island because of this abuse. My brother left so he would not be coerced by these men.'

'Lies!' screams Diana Crane.

Leah nods at Jacob Crane and Dr Bishy, at the statues they have become. 'My father sat on the Council with these men in order to keep me safe. Abe Powell sits so he will not be punished for who he chooses to love. Robert Signal and the Reverend refuse to sit at all because these men, who claim they speak for God, only bend His scripture to their will.' She turns to the gathering of people encircling the new teacher, the laptop now held tight against his chest. 'You know this!' she implores them. 'You know!'

'And we're supposed to listen to you, are we?' snarls Diana Crane. 'A daughter who condemned her own father?'

'I condemn your husbands,' Leah snaps back.

Sarah Devoner and Miriam Calder fix Leah with indignant stares. Diana Crane laughs showily, and turns to address the audience.

'We're to believe the words of this woman above the word of our Council?' The gallery avoids her gaze; they look at their feet. 'A woman who plays with the Devil's cards, who rants in the street, who spits in the faces of our men?' They shake their heads slowly – children chastised. 'She is nothing but a bitter spinster with a vendetta against those who have what she wants. To believe her is to believe the ramblings of a madwoman.'

Leah tightens her jaw, keeps her head high, but mutinous tears fall down her cheeks.

Diana Crane brushes herself down and cuts a purposeful path across the room to stand beside her husband once more – marking this victory.

'Then believe me instead.'

Britta Sayers sways at the edge of the stage.

'We killed a boy,' she says. 'We did it to bring the authorities to the island. Bethany Reid killed herself because the same thing was happening to her, but we killed a boy.'

Jade-Marie steps forward and fumbles for her friend's hand, gripping it. 'We thought if we could lure Luke Signal to the stones and... kill him,' she says, 'then people would at last pay attention to what was going on.'

'He took pictures of us, you see,' Anna speaks. 'Pictures he shouldn't have taken. That's why we chose him. And because he tried to make Viola have sex with him, and because… because…'

She trails away and Viola understands why. None of it sounds just; it all sounds impossible. How can the telling of the final score ever convey the emotion of the game?

'We had to kill someone, just someone,' Viola says, coming forward to complete the line-up. 'Believe me.'

'See!' blusters Dr Bishy. 'See!'

'Guilty!' Mr Crane attests.

The gallery can only nod, but the verdict feels uncertain, weak.

There is silence, then:

'Also believe me!'

Hannah Pass stands on the opposite side of the Earl to Leah, inhaling deeply as the whole room swings its attention to her. Viola provides the encouraging nod Hannah needs to continue.

'I have always suspected that the Countess left the island, and her husband –' Hannah takes the hand of the man beside her in his wheelchair '– to save their eldest daughter from the attentions of the doctor.'

'No!' says Elizabeth Bishy. 'Don't listen to that woman.'

'I will be heard,' says Hannah. Viola and the Eldest Girls band closer together on the edge of the stage, the very edge. 'The Earl remained in his position here but he lost in his struggle to turn the island, to steer it into clearer waters, and he has become ill as a result.' Hannah swallows hard. 'I have a fourteen-year-old daughter,' she says, 'and every day I think: I must leave. I must leave, because I can't keep her safe.'

There is no time to react – another voice rises up.

'Believe me.' It is the hairdresser, Hope Ainsley, who had earlier cowered in the Counting House doorway. Abe and Reuben move aside so she can enter the room. 'My Tom and his Bernadette did not leave the island to marry. They left because Bernadette couldn't stay in this place after what that man had done to her.'

Hope raises a trembling finger to single out the head-master. The man's breath comes in great heaves now, his wife blanching at his side. The hairdresser looks to the stage, to the Eldest Girls, her eyes red, and she croaks out a *sorry*. 'I was too scared,' she says, 'to know what to do.'

'Believe me.'

Another voice. A middle-aged woman steps forward from the gallery to say how she could never understand, though she always had suspicions, why her sister took her nieces away from the island. 'I have sons,' she says. 'Was I just lucky?'

'Believe me.'

Another voice, a young woman's, words steeped in regret, recounting how a former classmate had tried to confess what had happened to her in the headmaster's office one morning. 'It never happened to me, so I thought she must be making it up.'

And more voices.

'Believe me...'

'Believe me...'

'Believe me...'

'Believe me...'

'Believe me...'

† Eastertide: Friday the 13th – April 2018

This is the sound of a community waking slowly from a dream, not willing to call it a dream anymore. This is a piece of pure knowledge gifted from a deep well. This is a story in reverse – an island pushing away its capricious giants.

The velvet drapes are thrown open, casting a headmaster and a doctor in a fresh new light. The landlord hands over his licence, shamefaced, with muttered excuses for his allegiances – 'You said they were willing, Jake. You said it was always mutual.' Wives back away into the corners of the room. Three girls are lifted gently from a stage into the desperate arms of their mothers.

They ride the wave of these accusations and revelations; it carries them from the room. The collective act of confessing, of listening, has buoyed them – for now. Soon they will come crashing back to the shore – they must. The body of a boy lies silent and alone at the edge of the woods, and justice on his behalf has yet to be served.

The *coycrock* girl returns a stolen brooch to the palm of her enemy and is told that she must keep it.

'It's supposed to ward off witches but thank goodness it does not work!'

The radio is not accepted back either.

'Hang onto it,' says the Customs Officer.

'But what will I ever use it for?' she asks him.

'Who knows?' he replies. 'Whatever fate throws at you next.'

So, the girl heads towards daylight, a trial still to face, her pockets full.

Outside on the cobbles, Father Daniel leads the community in songs of sorrow and mourning. Margaritte Carruthers stands alongside him, arms raised to the sky, her blouse unbuttoned enough for them all to see the upper markings on her chest. The curate with the spiky hair moves about the crowd with a wooden voting box and slips of paper, assuring everyone who offers up testimony that they may remain anonymous, if they wish.

The Customs Officer and the handsome *coycrock* teacher steer the headmaster and the doctor out through the lobby into the unforgiving day. The sight of the red dog lead on the wrist of the housekeeper's daughter sends the red-haired *coycrock* bursting across the threshold, to be reunited with her animal familiar, to rub her face into the damp roughness of its fur.

A horn blares, deep and resonant, and heads turn to see a distant grey vessel on the horizon. The April ship.

Margaritte Carruthers takes this as her cue to raise the dead, to honour them – the fishermen drowned, the spirit of Bethany Reid, the boy whose body lies in an open grave of bramble and fern.

The crowd jostles the headmaster and the doctor in the direction of the stocks. The girl's dog barks in her arms, offering condemnation of its own.

'Shoot that damn' dog, Luke! Take a shot!' slurs the headmaster venomously into the blustery air.

It is an order that makes the *coycrock* girl clutch her companion even tighter, the name wrenching the attention of the three girls still locked in the embraces of their mothers.

Luke. The sacrifice. The body in the woods.

The headmaster must be delirious, they imagine, or else forgetful, using that name.

'Let the dead rise up!' croons Margaritte, head thrown back, eyes closed in rapture. 'Let them see us reborn as this divine child, a new vision of God within us!'

And the dead seemingly do as they are told, because there he is – the boy with the gun, Luke Signal, flesh and blood, alive. He lopes towards them from the direction of the smokehouse.

I boarded the April ship.

I could see no other choice, no place for me on Lark. I stood awkwardly between its past and its future. In that meeting room, I had said what I needed to, but only as a means of opening a door that others might walk through. If I could summon up the arrogance to think that I held such importance, I might say that I'd performed the task that I had been put on the island – on this earth – to do. It was done, and now I was done.

He arrived on the cobbles a different man – Luke Signal. His lope that day was born of deep sorrow and guilt, all his customary swagger wiped away.

His little brother was dead when it was supposed to have been him.

Michael had been curious of late – Luke told this to anyone who would listen, clutching at them, gathering them around him, needing them to bear witness. His stream of justification, of confession, was punctuated by guttural sobs. His little brother wanted to know about kissing and touching, he said, what goes where and who does what. Luke had thought it funny, easier, to send the boy off for a practical demonstration rather than explain it to him himself. There was a promise waiting at the Sisters' Stones – four girls, naked, willing – a red-lipped Viola had said it would be so.

Luke described in tender detail, if only to injure himself, how he had swapped boots with his brother and lifted onto Michael's broadening shoulders the oily weight of his oversized wax jacket. On the boy's vulnerable head he had positioned a pair of spiralling goat horns. All will be fine, was Luke's assurance to Michael, at the last. In the pitch black, Luke had told him, those girls won't know the difference.

And they hadn't.

When they stood on the stage that morning in the Counting House and confessed to the gallery what their intention had been – to kill Luke – they believed that's what they had done. There was no missing coda to their story to be offered once the women's testimony was over – *we meant to kill Luke but...* They were sure that the body of the elder Signal boy lay there, still and bloodied, in the mud beyond the stones; they had reconciled themselves to that sin – that specific sin. The taking of this boy's life was different from the taking of another's – it was less. The sacrifice of Luke was a fair exchange for a greater good.

The girls had been under the spell of odious men certainly, so much so that they had adopted their behaviours, their means. They had put their trust in force and the inflicting of damage. They believed they could control a person's fate.

When the elder Signal boy arrived on the harbourside, the girls might have thought him a true ghost, or else he was the brief apparition of relief. Had they managed to bring about long-needed justice *and* escape a black mark against their own names? *Hallelujah! He is risen!*

This relief could only have been fleeting. They understood the violence they had exacted, how irreversible it was, even if they hadn't – as Saul had, as I had, in the unforgiving light of day – gone to the trouble of looking beyond the boots and the jacket, pulling aside the ferns and seeing that skull, that throat, looking into the open eyes of the boy who lay beneath.

Michael: inquisitive, eager, my best student, cruelly sacrificed for the sins of those who went before him.

Martha Signal did not share Luke's need for self-punishment. She and her husband had been occupied that morning in the lifting of the broken body of their younger son from the place where he'd been beaten to death before delivering him back to his bedroom – forever his childhood bedroom – as a temporary resting place. Soon, they would face the unbearable task of lowering him into the ground. This was punishment enough; too much, in fact. Martha wished to mete out some punishment of her own.

She swooped across the cobbles like a harpy, her son's avenging angel, and was not for a moment softened by the sight of the four girls on their knees, weeping at the revelation of what they had really done. Martha had defected from her friends in support of these girls; she had helped to found the Easter Committee with the girls' interests at its heart – and this was how she was repaid? They'd meant to rob her of a child however the night had turned out. Martha wanted a scalp.

She seized one of them, any one of them. If a boy was to stand for the wrongs of all men, this girl could pay for the crimes of her sex too. Viola still had hair, shining vividly in the lunchtime sun, and Martha took a fistful, dragging the girl towards the harbour's edge.

There were screams and protestations, a desperate battle at the waterside to restrain a woman hell-bent on drowning a novice witch, a murderous girl. Gasping her threats, Martha promised to hold Viola's head beneath the surface for the terrible thing she had done. Ben and Saul left their guard of Crane and Bishy in the stocks to wrestle with Martha, in defence of a red-haired *coycrock*.

I stood back.

Over and over in my mind I replayed the moment I had caught Michael in the shadows of the Billet House. *What are you doing here, Miss?* I wished to rewind the hours, send him home to his mother. I prayed that I would be able to forgive myself, in time, but I knew I would never forgive the girls. Maybe one of those four did have to die. *And mine eyes shall not pity; but life shall go for life, eye for eye, tooth for tooth...*

When I thought of all the damage she had wrought, Viola seemed, like Luke, to be the best candidate for sacrifice, and in saying that, in expressing my desire to see her suffer, I understood that I was demonstrating how contagious evil can be. It passes from mind to mind, from hand to hand, dressed in the guise of justice, until we cannot distinguish the face of the enemy from our own.

It was the mother who saved her daughter, or at least bought her a temporary reprieve. Deborah Kendrick had been drawn to the harbourside, perhaps by the sound of chaos carried on the wind, or by the hymns sung to soothe. Perhaps she had been brought there by that unspoken something that allows a parent to know when their child is in danger. She wrapped her arms around Martha Signal, an aggressive embrace that pulled the woman off balance, backwards, away from the water, forcing her to release the girl.

The *coycrock* mother rocked Martha when she began to howl at the failure of her vengeance, at the futility of it, joining her in a lament for which there can never be any solace: 'It isn't fair, it isn't fair, it isn't fair...'

As this drama played out, the April ship growing more defined on its journey from the horizon towards us, I kept my distance. I did not try to intervene or have my say. It was as if there was a great body of water between me and that painful scene, not a stretch of cobbled ground. I cared about what was happening, the people involved, of course I did – I wept as I watched, thinking of all that we had lost and the inevitable suffering still to come – but I understood very clearly that it was no longer my place to find an answer.

I did not live there anymore. I was done.

As the girls were hurried away for their own safety, as Martha was consoled and as Luke's guilt continued to pour forth, the crowds remained, the hymns began again with renewed fervour. I returned to the harbour cottage to put the last of my things in the suitcase. I looked about each room, saw the mess that Viola had made of the carpet, the bed, sensing her fingertips on everything, but I refused to let it touch me. I considered instead what I would miss most. Nothing physical: the chime of boat rigging in the evening breeze, the familiar ashy scent of the smokehouse, the sun setting on the west coast, the lustre that the moon paints across our sometimes unforgiving waves. I unhooked the carved heart from the window latch and dropped it into the pocket of my coat.

The incoming stevedores unloaded their cargo as I walked across the cobbles for the last time, found my mother in the crowd and hugged her goodbye. The supplies we had longed for all winter piled up on the quayside, the Lark boatmen neglecting their side of the task, continuing instead in their songs of consolation and regret, and in the discussions about the proper apportioning of justice.

In the front office of the Customs House, as I took a seat on the hard wooden bench opposite the black-and-white images of the Big House, my feet on the boards where I had once lain with Saul, sacks of post for individual islanders were thrown down and sat ignored. Inside those parcels – clothes, toys, books, cosmetics, so many small shards of mainland life to splinter the Larkian way. Any other year there would have been a queue out of the door in anticipation of these offerings, but that day Saul worked in quiet conference with the ship's purser at the main counter, logging all that came in and the little that would go out, including me.

In the back office with its vista of sea the mainland crew laughed and drank tea, and at one point the captain came through the doorway to enquire about the gathering of people on the harbourside. *What were the hymns in aid of? Was there a reason two men were secured by their feet in the stocks?*

'Island tradition,' said Saul, without looking up from his paperwork, not missing a beat. 'It's the Feast of St Rita,' he lied. 'She's the patron saint of impossible causes.'

The captain returned to the teapot, and I suppose he thought that Saul and I could not hear him when he recounted this information to his crew, adding quietly that we were the strangest of the strange, us people from Lark, not like the mainlanders at all.

I had convinced myself that I knew the ocean – the sound it made as it licked the walls of the harbour at night, how close you could get to the tidemark on the East Bay and remain safe, the agreement that every seven years we owed it a sacrifice. But the feeling of the sea when you are out there upon it is entirely different from how it feels to stand at the edge of the land and look across, wondering.

Holding tight to the railing of the deck, the wind came in crisp, suffocating blasts, the broil of the grey waters causing a constant looming roll. The rules were different on the water; the ship was trespassing. There were no safe places at sea, and I was beginning to understand that that was the case on land too. Lark had been the entirety of my fathomed world but the further we drifted across the North Atlantic, the smaller the place became, its details falling away, questions rising. The last twenty-seven years seemed improbable.

One of the first things I did, once settled on the mainland, was to get a tattoo. I had been looking for a church, but tattoo parlours were startlingly easier to find and Margaritte had always taught me to listen when the universe is speaking.

There was a parlour just five minutes' walk from the house where I rented a room. I passed it on my way to the small high-street supermarket where products – cereals, rice, tea – were offered in endless flavours and brands, but all in tiny quantities designed to last just a week, not months. It was peculiar to hand over cash in return for these goods, my biscuit tin fund supporting me until I garnered the strength to work out how to extract money from my bank account. Stranger still was having my groceries run through the till by a woman who knew nothing about me, and sought no blessings from the blackness of my hair. I saw her eyes flicker upwards, though, when she thought I wasn't looking, no doubt assuming that such an unusual colour must have come from a bottle.

To find a church, I had to walk several miles. The first one I came upon had the flintstone grandeur and spire of a religious building, but inside it was set out with tables where people drank wine and ate steak. Further afield was the Church of Our Lady, whose services felt similar to those at home and so became a small comfort to me in this unfathomable, new world. I sat in the back pew, greeted the smiles that came my way and shook hands when it was time to pass peace amongst us, but I stayed seated for the Eucharist, unsure if the baptism of my previous life held good there.

My teaching qualification, I had decided without any investigation, was worthless, nothing but a piece of decorated paper.

The night before Pentecost, as I ate dinner alone in the small shared kitchen, a strong breeze blew the window from its prop, making it bang against the outside wall. *And suddenly there came a sound from heaven as of a rushing mighty wind, and it filled all the house where they were sitting.* I should have been fasting that evening, so rightly deserved no such sign, but still I took it as one – a guiding spirit. I wore a bright red scarf on Sunday, sat three rows from the front and offered my tongue for the host.

In the choosing of a tattoo, I was more forthright. I leafed through books of designs as I drank tea made by a young woman with the kind of white-blonde hair that certainly came from a bottle. There was a bright stone in her nose and inkings climbed her neck, richer in detail and more vibrant in colour than the ones that marked Margaritte's silvery skin.

I considered angels and eagles, lions and bulls, and the woman with the white hair suggested a mandala.

'I could combine the elements of all those animals,' she said. 'They're like your four selves. In the square structure of a mandala it will work really well.'

Before she could begin her work, I had to sign a form. *Yes, you may cause me this pain, I agree.* Then came a tick-box questionnaire about my medical history. I said 'no' to everything, including the question, *Are you or could you be pregnant?*

I am sure that I had carried a child. Three months passed without any bleeding by the time I confided in anyone besides Ben. Margaritte told me to lie back on her cushioned sofa while she held above my belly a gold ring on a length of silk, to determine the baby's sex.

The ring stayed still and I sensed this wasn't right.

'It's inconclusive,' said Margaritte, her voice a dull camouflage for the thing she did not wish to say. The following day I woke in agony, my pyjamas soaked with blood. I staggered to the bathroom and sat, crying, clots sliding down the white slope of the porcelain.

I couldn't take this to Dr Bishy, so I returned to Margaritte, and she nodded like she already knew, as if she had dealt with this circumstance time and time again. She gave me a tincture to drink to help the passage of the bleeding, and because I could not get the sheets clean, I took them up to the incinerator behind the Big House where my father and I had disposed of that slaughtered goat.

'There is no baby,' I told Ben, when we were together on the ship.

He had boarded too, Saul willing to make a late entry in the ledger, Ben's swift departure the most important thing, for all.

We avoided each other until the last night of our journey. So much had been expressed on that final morning on the island, it seemed possible that I would never speak my thoughts or feelings to another person again. Yet there was still a last loose thread connecting me to my old life; I needed to cut it away.

We ate together in the small canteen with its plastic tables and nailed-down seats, its choice of one dish and its views of an ocean slowly being consumed by the darkness. It was a last supper.

Out there, on the sea, everything took on a different shade – people too. The man sitting opposite me was not the same person who had made my body come alive in the moonlight, and made the words of 'I think of thee!' pierce me like delicious thorns. Only the last line of that poem remained true, though it rang sharp now, different.

I do not think of thee – I am too near thee.

'You tricked me,' he said, and I was ready with my denial – *There had been a baby! Without it, I would never have entertained the thought of boarding a boat!* But I was willing to concede that this was deception of a different kind; it was one of the lies I was telling myself.

And also, there had been Saul.

'Yes,' I replied. 'I did deceive you.' *I am Leah, it was what I was named to do.* 'But I wonder,' I told him, 'if that doesn't make us even.'

Margaritte's cards were accurate; he was my Knight of Cups, my charming fraud. His friendship with the Eldest Girls, his protection of them, was heartfelt certainly. But where did that leave me in his affections? I wasn't told the truth of his relationship with them in case I was in league with Crane, complicit, delivering hysterical girls who sang too loudly in chapel straight into his grubby hands. To not trust me, I could understand. To want to have sex with me anyway – it was incomprehensible.

'What were you running away from?' I asked. 'In the first place, I mean. What did you go to Lark to escape?'

He pretended not to understand.

'A girl?' I offered.

He shrugged.

'Yourself?' I said – not really a question.

He changed the subject. He asked me what I was going to do when I reached the mainland – did I need his help to find a job? I shook my head and told him I was going to track down my brother. It was the truth, but I still haven't managed it. I live within Paul's telephone area code and though this covers hundreds of square miles, one of my fellow lodgers told me, apropos of a separate matter, that it's surprising how often you bump into friends and acquaintances in a city of several million. Maybe Paul will find me if it's meant to be, if he is ready to be found.

'So, were you really going to take the Eldest Girls away on the August ship?' I asked Ben.

He took his time to answer, playing with the remnants of a chicken curry, ploughing furrows in the yellow-stained rice. 'I was going to take their stories,' he said, as if this equated to a 'yes'.

'They trusted you,' I told him.

'And they were right to.' He believed that. 'I still have the laptop. I still have their stories.'

'Yeah? And what are you going to do with them?'

We held one another's gaze. This was all that united us now, our knowledge, the great burden of carrying it.

Or else, we could let it go, look away.

The last night on board, I dreamt, in the sickeningly vivid way the ship's motion provoked, that I had watched Ben throw his laptop over the side of the ship, the Eldest Girls' first-person accounts irrevocably gone. The dream stays with me and I can convince myself that it really happened, though I am likely mingling my conjured-up image of that dented computer falling to the waves with the real memory of a phone being swallowed by the blackness of a well.

I suspect Ben deleted their words and I too should put a match to this book or throw it into the murk of the Thames. What stops me is that the bible lacks a chapter from Leah's point of view, a woman's point of view. Ruth's book, Esther's – they're not enough. After looking away for far too long, it is hard now to accept that it is the right thing to do.

The island will be reborn under the guidance of admirable women, like Mary Ahearn, Margaritte Carruthers, Hannah Pass, my mother. They have the responsibility of taking the events of that night, the consequences of them, and shaping them into a story everyone can live with – and live by. The truth of a situation is always whittled away by history; a person's virtues and good intentions, the great change they brought about, can be neatly separated from their killing of an innocent young boy. I see a distant future where Viola and the Eldest Girls are considered saints.

For me though, Friday the 13th April is when I remember St Michael, a boy who led an army against Satan, unwittingly.

I must believe that the island will come to good, that it will evolve into a place where sympathetic magic is allowed to flourish, where a man will not pay court to the powerful to keep his daughter, his livelihood or his secrets safe, where the word of the Lord is wielded only in the name of love not rule. Only then will those who ran away consider coming back.

As the April ship set off on its return leg, as I stood at the bow to watch Lark be lost to the horizon, I saw the doctor and the headmaster released from the stocks and led along the dogleg jetty to its very limit beneath the shining cross. I stayed to watch the millstones be tied about their necks, and then I stepped down, beneath deck.

I looked away.

ACKNOWLEDGEMENTS

Thank you to the wise and witchy women who shared their knowledge, especially Lissa Berry, and to the warm and welcoming churches who let me loiter on the back pew.

This book began as a conversation on Twitter between an editor and a writer who didn't really know each other – thank you, Alison Hennessey, for replying, and for your endless rigour ever since. 'Rigour', to be clear, being one of my favourite words.

Thank you to Louise Lamont, as always, but in this case, for the dead body.

Early work on this book was supported by a grant from The Authors' Foundation via the Society of Authors to which I would urge other writers with works-in-progress to apply.

Verse 4 of 'I Danced in the Morning (Lord of the Dance)' by Sydney Carter (1915–2004), ©1963 Stainer & Bell Ltd, 23 Gruneisen Road, London N3 1DZ, England, www.stainer.co.uk, is used by permission. All rights reserved.

Extract from *The World of the Witches* by Julio Caro Baroja, translated by O.N.V. Glendinning (Chicago: University of Chicago Press, 1964 and London: the Orion Publishing Group, 1964) is used with the kind permission of the publishers.

NOTE ON THE AUTHOR

Julie Mayhew is an actress turned writer. She is the author of four previous novels, including the award-winning *The Big Lie*, and writes drama for radio and the stage. With support from the BAFTA Crew development scheme, she has started writing and directing for the screen.

@JulieMayhew

NOTE ON THE TYPE

The text of this book is set in Linotype Sabon, a typeface named after the type founder, Jacques Sabon. It was designed by Jan Tschichold and jointly developed by Linotype, Monotype and Stempel in response to a need for a typeface to be available in identical form for mechanical hot metal composition and hand composition using foundry type.

Tschichold based his design for Sabon roman on a font engraved by Garamond, and Sabon italic on a font by Granjon. It was first used in 1966 and has proved an enduring modern classic.